The Master raised himself on one elbow and looked at the naked woman standing in front of the mirror. He smiled. In life, Mara Fleming had been a troublesome wench but her sumptuous body now provided a delicious earthly vessel for his beloved Queen, Sedet.

As his greedy eyes played over the ample curves of the swelling breasts that had once been Mara's, Sedet turned towards him and he caught the flash of her violet eyes.

'It is a satisfactory body, Master, but do you not find a certain vulgarity in it?'

By way of answer, the Master pulled her down onto the black silk sheets and crushed his hard body against her opulent flesh . . .

# Empire of Lust

## Valentina Cilescu

**Delta**

First published in 1994
by HEADLINE BOOK PUBLISHING

A HEADLINE DELTA paperback

10 9 8 7 6 5 4 3 2

ISBN 0 7472 4191 0

Typeset by CBS, Felixstowe, Suffolk

Printed and bound in Great Britain by
Mackays of Chatham plc, Chatham, Kent

HEADLINE BOOK PUBLISHING
A division of the Hodder Headline Group
338 Euston Road
London NW1 3BH
www.headline.co.uk
www.hodderheadline.com

# Empire of
# Lust

# Introduction
# The Story So Far

The master is a vampire sorcerer who feeds on the sexual energies of his victims.

Imprisoned within a flawless block of crystal by Allied sorcerers at the end of World War II, the Master's only chance of escape was to find a new body to house his evil spirit. At last he succeeded in tricking the white witch Mara Fleming into luring her lover, cynical journalist Andreas Hunt, to his doom.

The Master lives again. Now liberated from its crystal prison, the Master's spirit has taken possession of Hunt's body, banishing Andreas's spirit to the crystal where it languishes, helpless but hungry for vengeance. The Master has also robbed Mara Fleming of her body, claiming it for the spirit of his long-lost Queen, the Egyptian priestess Sedet. What the Master does not realise is that Mara's indomitable spirit has now entered and possessed the body of his favourite vampire slave, Anastasia Dubois. Trapped within this unfamiliar but alluring body, Mara plots to use her magical gifts to defeat the Master's evil ascendancy.

From his base at Winterbourne Hall, an exclusive house of pleasure deep in the English countryside, the Master now plots the defeat of his enemies and the triumph of his evil empire of lust. The next item on his agenda is to further his political ambitions and enter Parliament, aided by a cunning subliminal propaganda campaign and the sensual lures of power, corruption and sex.

One by one, influential politicians and media figures will

be targeted for 'initiation' into the Master's realm of the undead. Time is running out for Mara and Andreas, for the spectre of sensual, immortal evil is already stalking the corridors of Westminster . . .

# Prologue

In one of Winterbourne's many exotic bedrooms, a naked young woman was sitting in front of a dressing table, her auburn hair falling in long, wavy tendrils over the creamy whiteness of her bare flesh. Somewhere in the distance a clock was chiming the half-hour, but the girl was silent, contemplative.

Mara gazed into the mirror. The emerald green eyes still took her by surprise, even now, when she forgot for an instant the change which had overtaken her. The green eyes, the mane of auburn hair, the svelte yet succulent body . . . these all belonged to Anastasia Dubois, the vampire-woman who had long been the Master's favoured whore.

But the spirit behind the green eyes was clear and bright. The unmistakable, indomitable spirit of Mara Fleming.

Telling herself that there was no time to sit and think, she put on her make-up swiftly and brushed her hair. It had taken time and courage to adapt to this new body, this new life – this macabre world of the undead where all around her worshipped the evil Master, and she must do so too or pay the terrible price of discovery.

Mara shivered, suddenly feeling the danger acutely. She could not afford to drop her guard, not for a moment. If the Master realised that Mara Fleming lived on within the body of his whore, he would surely destroy her, as swiftly as he would swat a fly.

She stood up, intending to get dressed. In an hour's time she must attend upon the Master and his Queen in the great hall. The Master had told her that he had work for her to do. The thought of what that work might be terrified her, fear clutching at her stomach like a skeletal hand. But one thing was for sure: there could be no thought of defiance.

As she stood in front of the mirror, she ran questing fingers over the rosebud points of her firm breasts, over the smoothness of belly and thighs. Little shivers of pleasure ran through her and her lips parted in a silent sigh. Since she had entered the body of Anastasia Dubois, sex had taken on a whole new meaning. Without sex, she could not survive. Sex gave her more than pleasure: it gave her the excitement of a growing power within her, sharpening and amplifying the psychic skills that she had known since childhood.

Hungry for love, she lay down on the bed, sinking gratefully into the softness of the feather mattress. Over the weeks and months since her return from Egypt, Mara had coupled with many of the Master's acolytes on this bed. And yet, although her flesh was hungry for sex and her pleasure came again and again, always there was an emptiness, a sense of loss. She was missing Andreas more than she could ever have imagined.

She stroked and pinched her nipples, and felt a warm tide of cunt-juice flood out of her as she let her right hand slide down the belly to the auburn triangle of her pubis.

Hunger. Sex. Need, need, need.

It felt strange to be pleasuring this body that had belonged to another woman; strange to be running her fingertips over the pulsating stalk of this unfamiliar clitoris. But the pleasure was familiar, reassuring. It was the same pleasure she had always felt whenever her lover Andreas Hunt had run his tongue between her plump love-lips, awakening her again and again to the most delicious lust.

Yes, the same pleasure – but greater somehow. A more all-encompassing ecstasy. An orgasm of the soul?

She rubbed her clitoris harder and faster, delighting in the way this new body responded to her touch exactly as the old one had. And she imagined that it was not her hand, but

Andreas's, between her thighs, stimulating her in the old, familiar way.

Fuck me, Andreas. Fuck me hard. I want to come again and again.

Her cunt was running with juice now; she scooped up a little and ran it over the head of her clitoris, delighting in the slipperiness as her finger slid over and over the heart of her sex.

She really could feel Andreas's spirit all around her, like the warmth of his body, pressed up against her as their loins fused and they began to fuck – a long, luxurious coupling that would leave both of them drained yet euphoric.

She missed her lover with the sickening intensity of physical pain. Knowing that she was so close to reaching him sometimes comforted her, but more often than not its legacy was despair. Still, there had been odd moments of direct contact – fleeting moments too brief to satisfy, too intense ever to forget. On some sudden impulse she would look into the eyes of one of those around her – Ibrahim, perhaps – or Gonzales – and would be startled to see Andreas looking back at her. Once or twice he had found the strength to speak, and as his hand touched her she had felt the electric shock as their souls united – one brief split-second of ecstasy and pain before he slipped away and she was left alone once more.

But she was not alone, she knew that now. Andreas was watching her, waiting for her. Sometimes she could hear him calling out to her, and she had replied, wondering if he could hear her. Wondering if in his mind he could touch and caress her, as she had caressed and fucked him in her dreams.

As she fingered her clitty into vibrant, throbbing life and felt her orgasm overtake her with the intensity of an earthquake, Mara dreamed of Andreas; and knew that she could never rest until she had released her lover from his cruel, unending torment.

# 1: The Ring

Donal O'Keefe pushed his way slowly through the crowd and began to wish he had chosen another day to come to the market. He should have known it would be bedlam. On this warm, sunny Easter Monday, Greenwich was packed to bursting with browsers, bric-à-brac enthusiasts and trendsetting students, all hoping for the bargain of a lifetime.

The aroma from a crêpe stall reached his nostrils and jolted his memory. He glanced at his watch and groaned as he felt himself carried along by the jostling throng. Half eleven, and he was meeting Caít at twelve. She'd never forgive him if he didn't get her a birthday present, not this time.

The girl in the crocheted top and black palazzo pants had a wonderful backside. Donal watched, mesmerised, as she wriggled her way through the narrow gap between the stalls. As she squeezed past him, he felt the tautness of her firm young flesh pressing against his crotch, the fleeting touch of her hand on his groin as she brushed past him with a smile and an apology.

Instinctively, like a lost dog, he followed her through the crowd; transfixed by the mass of long blonde hair that tossed and gleamed on her smooth brown shoulders.

You could see bare flesh through that crocheted top. She was wearing nothing underneath – not a stitch. Didn't she feel the cold? For an instant he had glimpsed her nipples, pink and succulent beneath the flimsy filigree, and he had longed to touch them. To taste them . . .

If he could just catch up with her, find some excuse to

press himself up against her again . . . surely it wouldn't be difficult, not in this heaving crowd. It was funny really. He didn't normally behave in this crazy way, running after total strangers with his tongue hanging out. Caít would have been quite amused to see him lunging after this tall, slim girl with the mobile backside and the long, long legs. But he dismissed the thought from his mind: he didn't want to think about Caít and her sensible high-necked blouses.

All Donal wanted at this minute was to touch the girl, to feel her perfect body pressing up close against his. His cock was twitching into painful rigidity, he needed that girl's firm, sweet flesh to soothe the ache of his desire. If he could only talk to her, touch her . . . maybe some mad impulse would overtake her and she would let him reach up under the hem of her crocheted top, to cup her pert young breasts in his greedy hands. Or take her soft pink nipple into his eager mouth . . .

Fantasy boiled and bubbled in his brain, tormenting him with impossible images of the young girl's nakedness. Desperate to reach her, Donal shoulder-charged the man in front of him and pushed past, ignoring the curses and the ominous clinking as he bumped into a trestle-table full of antique china.

There she was! Talking to a pale thin woman who ran a jewellery stall, over by the steps to the car park. The woman was nodding and running bone-thin shaky fingers through her ragged black hair, streaked with grey. He hurried towards her, not caring how many toes he trod on or grannies he knocked over as he hustled his way past the stalls.

As he burst through the crowd into the empty space before the steps, the girl broke off talking to the woman and turned to face him. She was beautiful: porcelain skin and large, glittering eyes that seemed to see into the heart of him.

She smiled and he took a step towards her. His legs felt wobbly and at that moment a small child ran full pelt into him, making him stagger and put out a hand to steady himself.

When he looked up again, the girl was gone. He glanced

around him in all directions, but there was no sign of her. Only the thin stallholder remained, holding a chipped mug of coffee in her shaking hand. The dull pain of loss was in his belly, his cock still throbbing with thwarted lust.

'That girl – the blonde one. Where did she go?'

The thin woman shook her head.

'Dunno what you're talking about, love.'

'Her name – do you know what she's called? I need to find her.'

'Told you, darlin' – no idea what you're on about.' She paused, scrutinising Donal's pained expression. 'Lookin' for somethin', are you? Present for your girl?' She clutched the edge of the table, racked by sudden spasms of coughing. Her eyes seemed hollow and dead.

The woman's words jolted Donal back to reality and he suddenly thought of Caít. Caít, who would be sitting alone in the Bar du Musée, looking at her watch and wondering what the hell had happened to him. Yet again. He couldn't let her down, not on her birthday.

He glanced around the variety of second-hand jewellery on the grubby cloth. Utter tat, most of it. Brooches with no pins and stones missing out of them; heavy costume rings with vulgar lumps of coloured glass. Caít would hate this stuff.

Then he caught sight of the ring. An elegant crystal band which, as it caught the noonday sunlight, seemed to burn with an inner white fire. The thin woman saw him looking at it, picked it up and handed it to him.

'Special piece, that. Very old. Eastern, I shouldn't wonder. Never seen nothin' quite like it.'

He slipped it on and found it fitted snugly. It would be a little big for Caít's ring finger, but if she didn't want to put it on her middle finger it was pretty enough for her to wear on a chain round her neck.

'How much?'

'Twenty-five.'

Donal gave a sharp intake of breath.

'Fifteen.'

The stallholder gave a dry chuckle.

'I'd be bankruptin' myself if I let you 'ave it for fifteen quid, darlin'. Cost me more than that.'

Donal looked at the crystal ring, wistfully turning it over and over in the palm of his hand. Caít would love it, he was sure she would. But twenty-five quid . . .

'Tell you what, love, I'll knock a couple of quid off the price, seein' as you like it so much. How's twenty-two suit you?'

'I . . . let's say twenty.' It wasn't that he was driving a hard bargain – he'd only got forty quid in his pocket and he still had lunch to pay for.

'Well . . . I like your face, darlin'. Twenty it is.' She pressed her skull-like face close to his and he could smell her breath, foetid and strong as a corpse's. 'That ring's made for you, do you know that? I knew it, soon as I saw you.'

He handed over two ten-pound notes and slipped the ring into his back pocket. I've got to get away from this death's-head creature, he thought as her claw-fingers clutched at his hand and he pulled away. The ashen-faced spectre was the most complete contrast he could imagine to the sleek, tanned figure of the girl he had so fleetingly touched, so yearningly desired. How his cock still ached for her . . .

As he turned to go, the stallholder called after him. ''Ope she likes it, darlin'. Does my heart good to see two young lovebirds 'appy, so it does.'

He hurried away from the market and headed for the Bar du Musée, refusing to turn around and look at the woman. She'd had the strangest effect on him. Even in the warm spring sunshine, he felt chilly and slightly sick. And as he passed the fast-food stalls with their pungent aromas of fried onions and garlic, he just couldn't get rid of that woman's unmistakable smell: the powerful stench of death.

The Master raised himself on one elbow and looked at the naked woman standing in front of the mirror. He smiled. In life, Mara Fleming had been a troublesome wench, but her body had provided an entirely fitting earthly vessel for his beloved Sedet. And there was a fine irony in the events he had engineered: once cleansed of their puny mortal souls, the ephemeral human bodies of the lovers Andreas and Mara had attained a certain immortality as the earthly hosts of the Master and his Queen.

Yes, this was a body fit for a queen. And, soon, his queen would rule over a far more worthy domain. Already the game was afoot.

As his greedy eyes played over the ample curves of the swelling breasts that had once been Mara's, Sedet turned towards him and he caught the flash of her violet eyes.

'It is a satisfactory body, my Master, but do you not find a certain vulgarity in it?'

The Master slid off the bed and pulled her close to him, the stiffening flesh of his penis grinding against her taut, tanned belly.

'You are sweet succulent joy,' he murmured, kissing her throat and breasts. 'You are perfect beautiful sex and I want to fuck your tight wet cunt.'

He pushed her back onto the bed and she sank down onto the black silk sheets with the Master astride her. She reached out and began stroking the dancing, yearning limb of his prick.

'It is good . . . so good to feel you fucking me after so long in the shadow of fear. I had begun to believe you had abandoned me to the pain and the darkness.'

'Never,' cried the Master. 'I have sought you for four thousand years, my chosen one, and I would have sought you for four thousand more. You alone are worthy to sit beside me, to share the glory of my power.' He slid his hand down her belly and pushed apart her slender brown thighs, pressing his fingers up between the plump love-lips that oozed with spent cunt-juice and sperm.

He began rubbing her clitoris with deliberate strokes that made her close her eyes and begin to breathe in shallow, staccato gasps.

'In my realm there shall be no more pain for us, only pleasure. Joy and sex and power. The elect shall rejoice and worship us, and others shall suffer for your pleasure, my Queen.' He grasped her breast and pinched the nipple hard so that she groaned with delight.

'It pleases me to hear you talk so,' she breathed. 'Your strength flows into me, awakes the fiery demons of lust within me. But there is yet a strange pain of fear within my breast. A fear I cannot explain, though its seed burns within me.'

'Banish doubt from your mind,' commanded the Master. 'Here at Winterbourne you are the undisputed Queen, feared and adored by all. You have power over the life and death of all who stray into your path. And soon, very soon, you shall have a realm worthy of you, for you shall sit beside me as Empress in my empire of lust.'

'There are hostile presences in this house,' insisted Sedet, gently masturbating the Master as she ran her sharp nails down the flesh of his taut belly. 'Shadows just beyond the realm of sight. There are those in our ranks whom I cannot quite trust, even among the elect. Ibrahim and the Dubois girl . . .'

The Master silenced her with a kiss, masturbating her more brutally now, so that she lost the power of speech and could only moan in an incomprehensible language of desire.

'Foolish imaginings all,' he told her, his free hand slipping underneath her buttocks and toying with her puckered arsehole. 'Do not waste your sexual energies on such petty fears. Since my trusted servant Heimdal took over the running of Winterbourne, all cause for fear has been banished. I swear to you, Sedet, there are none here who are disloyal. None but the faithful shall approach my beloved Queen. And as for the rest . . .' He pinched her clitoris and she gave a sharp cry of pain. 'The rest shall die.'

Parting her thighs with his strong hands, he thrust his cock into the hot, wet depths of her. Her cunt was tight as an angel's, with all the fire of the demons in her glorious rounded backside. Such delicious pleasure! And pleasure that would

12

never end. As he rode her, he planned what he would do: first he would fuck her, then she would work on him with her wicked mouth, and finally he would flip her over onto her belly and enjoy the delights of her wonderful arse. And then . . . perhaps then, they would begin all over again. They could fuck and fuck and fuck for ever and never tire, their life-energies growing and mingling with each new coupling.

Immortality was a wonderful thing. He felt sure that universal power would be equally stimulating.

Mara knelt before Heimdal and took his huge throbbing prick between her glossy red lips. The bearded blond giant murmured with pleasure as her tongue curled about the jade ring which passed through the swollen flesh, a stone serpent with its tail in its mouth.

Her breath was coming in short shallow gasps as she began sucking him off, cradling his large and heavy balls in her slender white hands. On the mantelpiece, a white marble clock ticked off the seconds, echoing the thunderous pounding of her heart. Thus far, she had been lucky. The Queen had had some small suspicion of her in the beginning but the Master had refused to listen to her doubts and it seemed that, little by little, he had banished them from her mind.

No-one, apparently, had noticed the subtle changes in the Master's favoured handmaiden. Not one of them had realised that the soul inhabiting this sleek, firm-fleshed body was no longer that of Anastasia Dubois, that Anastasia's perfect, luscious body now played host to the soul of the white witch Mara Fleming.

But Joachim Heimdal was a very different matter. He had known Mara for years, since before he had ever dreamed of Winterbourne. And Heimdal had formidable psychic powers, which Mara herself had helped to nurture and harness. Now here she was in his private apartments at Winterbourne, playing the handmaiden to his every base desire. It was fortunate indeed that her own powers were so superior to his that she had been able to block out any attempt at a psychic mind-probe. She had read his mind. He suspected nothing. And yet, as she ran her tongue over his prick, moistening the massive shaft, she felt fear mingling with the excitement in her belly. She must be careful. More careful than she had ever been in her life.

His bear's-paw hands were on her shoulders, gripping her so hard that the fingernails left deep red indentations on her naked, creamy-white flesh.

'Suck me, suck me harder, you glorious little whore,' growled Heimdal, his blond head thrown back and his blue eyes closed as he savoured the delicious sensations Mara was bestowing upon him. 'You were never this good before, Anastasia. Winterbourne has been teaching you some useful lessons.'

She began sucking at the cock-ring, using her tongue to turn it round and round in his glans. But he began thrusting with his hips, forcing his shaft down her throat so brutally that he half-choked her.

Mara was ready for him and swallowed him with relish. Scared of discovery though she was, she was excited too. Ever since that fateful day in the Valley of the Tombs of Kings, when her spirit had slipped silently into the body of Anastasia Dubois, Mara had awoken to a whole new world of sexual pleasure. Sex had always been her major preoccupation in life: now, it was her life, her food, her drink. With each new coupling, each wonderful new fuck, her body grew stronger and more sensually aware. Untainted by the evil of her undead Master, her bright spirit nevertheless enjoyed all the benefits that her new, immortal body bestowed upon her.

And yet, she had not forgotten who she really was, or her mission – to overthrow the Master's embryonic empire of evil and rescue her lover Andreas Hunt from the torment of his captivity. She was working slowly, cautiously, taking the time to worm her way into the trust of the Master and those around him. Her powers were strengthening with every day that passed, soon to be magnified to an undreamed-of extent by the transformation of her life-force. And Andreas was growing in strength also, his spirit reaching out to her and sharing the consciousness of her quest. Together, perhaps, they would be a match even for the Master . . .

She ran sharp fingernails over the velvety sac which contained Heimdal's balls and felt his flesh tense with pleasure. Her cunt was moist and hot, running with the juice of her burning desire. She wanted him – wanted him in her cunt, thrusting and ramming home, distending her soft flesh and filling her up with his foaming spunk. But she would be patient. She had all the time in the world . . .

He slid almost out of her mouth and she caught the tip of his prick between her lips, teasing the glistening purple head with the points of her teeth. She knew how much Heimdal enjoyed the spice of pain and, sure enough, she felt him writhe and shudder as his shaft grew suddenly harder still. In a few seconds, he would shoot off into her mouth, and she would drink his come as though it were sweet nectar, her soul feeding on the life-giving energies of their coupling.

And then . . . then, she would be ready for more.

As she felt his bollocks tense and pour their tribute into her mouth, she let one hand fall down to her breast and began teasing the nipple. The brief contact was enough to bring her to her own orgasm and she shuddered with pleasure as her cunt tensed in a series of long, luxurious spasms.

Heimdal withdrew from Mara's mouth and smiled down at her. His bright blue eyes were glittering with lust and he ran greedy hands over the generous swell of her breasts, pinching and smoothing the firm white flesh.

Mara returned his gaze and got to her feet slowly, covering his muscular, naked body with kisses as she rose slowly to his cock, his belly, his chest . . . Finally she pulled his face down to hers and kissed him passionately, her naked body crushed against his. His heart was thumping as hard as hers, racing with need for her. Her tongue forced its way between his lips and the base of her belly ground insistently against his still-erect prick.

'Fuck me, Lord Heimdal,' she groaned. 'Give it to me now.'

He kissed her neck, and she shivered as she felt his lips brush the tiny faded scars on her pale throat – the stigmata of all the Master's disciples. What must it have been like for poor Anastasia to feel the savage bite, the life-blood draining from her as she filled with a dark, demonic sexual energy that both consumed and sustained her? And now Mara was inhabiting her body.

'You're a hot little harlot, Dubois,' growled Heimdal, pulling her closer to him and running greedy fingers down the ripe curve of her backside. 'The Master did well in initiating you to our ranks. You will indeed be useful to the cause.'

He put his arms around her waist and lifted her up, with no more difficulty than if she had been a tiny child. Fastening her long white limbs around his hips, he felt for the warm sanctuary of her cunt and pushed her down in a single stabbing movement, impaling her on the upraised spike of his penis.

Mara threw back her head and groaned as they fucked together. And as Heimdal's cock rammed into the very depths of her, she felt the tide of pleasure rising in her belly and thought once again of Andreas Hunt . . .

'You have done well, LeMaître. Dare I say, better than I had expected?'

The Foreign Secretary flipped open the lid of a carved wooden box, and pushed it across the desk.

'Cigar?'

The Master shook his head and took a sip from the sherry glass. Lord Easingwold was no fool. He would have to proceed with caution if the Foreign Secretary was to become a willing follower.

'I am glad that you are pleased with my work. I am told I have a certain . . . persuasive ability.'

Easingwold laughed and drained his glass.

'To have persuaded the Egyptian government to abandon its claim to the Aswan collection after a forty-year dispute . . . Let us simply say that Her Majesty's Government is very much in your debt, LeMaître. You have enjoyed a more than creditable tenure as our Ambassador to Egypt. Now, though, I believe it is time for another challenge. Washington DC, perhaps . . .?'

LeMaître smiled. It was all going according to plan.

'You do me great honour, Lord Easingwold. But I feel my talents lie elsewhere.'

The Foreign Secretary looked at him quizzically.

'Meaning?'

'Call it a whim, but I think I should like to be the next Ambassador to India.'

Lord Easingwold shook his head.

'I'm afraid that's not possible, LeMaître. Surely you have heard? I appointed a new ambassador only last week. A Dr Pendleton − distinguished scholar, used to be Master of Hinckley College, Cambridge. He leaves for New Delhi in a few days.'

The Master leaned over the desk, his eyes narrow and glittering. His smile was thin-lipped and determined.

'I think you will find our Mr Pendleton is no longer in any position to take up the post,' he said quietly. 'I believe he had a car accident last night − most unfortunate.'

Lord Easingwold stared at him, suddenly uneasy.

'So there is a vacancy which needs to be filled,' continued the Master, casually toying with his cufflinks. 'And as I am fluent in all the languages of the Indian sub-continent . . .'

'Quite.' The Foreign Secretary swallowed hard.

'Of course, I am prepared to show my gratitude.'

'I don't think I understand . . .'

The Master turned round and nodded to his associate, Cheviot, who was standing behind his chair.

'Bring her in.'

Cheviot walked over to the door and opened it. Easingwold just sat and stared, open-mouthed as a goldfish, as a tall dark-haired young woman with violet eyes and an ample bosom strode silently into his office. She was wearing a short tight skirt that moulded the supple curves of her firm buttocks and

17

a diaphanous blouse with a plunge neck that concealed nothing of the bare, swelling breasts beneath. She pouted and ran her pink tongue over her glossy scarlet lips.

The Master turned to Lord Easingwold with a smile.

'I don't believe you have met my associate, the Lady Sedet. She has been so looking forward to meeting you. I'm sure you'll enjoy being entertained in her own special way . . .'

Andreas Hunt was jolted out of sleep by the sound of Mara's voice, calling to him from far away. Had he really heard her, or was it just another trick of his disordered brain? Damn this crystal prison which kept him from her, freeing him only for the briefest moments, giving him the most tantalising glimpses of liberty. And damn the weakness of his spirit, which had not yet found a way to break free of this endless captivity.

No sound now. Just the thoughts in his mind, tumbling over and over each other in their desperation to get out.

He strove to hold onto reality. What time of year was it now? What time of day? The last time his spirit had floated free it had been early spring, with the blossom like a pink and white cloud and the thin yellow sun filtering through the trees like watered-down lemonade. His consciousness had entered the body of the servant Gonzales and watched in an agony of lust as Mara fucked with Heimdal on the stone steps leading to the Master's summer-house.

Afterwards, he had touched her shoulder as she walked past him, brushed the hard juicy buds of her nipples with his borrowed hand as she looked into his eyes and whispered: 'One day soon, Andreas. One day we shall both be free . . .'

There were tears glistening in the corners of her eyes. He remembered that now.

Oh shit, he was getting maudlin. And now was definitely not the time to start discovering he'd got a latent poetic streak. The only poem he'd ever felt any affinity with was the one about Eskimo Nell.

'Andreas, Andreas. Can you hear me? Answer me, Andreas . . .'

He heard her calling to him more clearly now. And he answered her. But the psychic link was not a good one today. She kept on calling out his name as though she could not hear him.

He had to tell her, had to explain this strange phenomenon that he didn't understand himself. One minute it had been there – he had felt its presence like a dead weight on the lid of the sarcophagus, almost squeezing the life out of him. If you could call it life. And when he had floated free of his body, he had looked down on it and seen it lying there, a tiny brilliant thing amid the dust. As he had looked down at it, losing himself in the bright crystal facets, he had become aware of a dark, all-too-familiar presence. A presence that chilled in its evil and – like Andreas himself – hovered between life and death.

Delgado? But Delgado was dead – and it served him right. He'd never been anything but trouble for Andreas Hunt and Mara Fleming. Apparently the fool had got himself fried by a bolt of lightning whilst having it off with some tart on a tigerskin rug. Andreas had heard Gonzales talking about it to that blond berk who thought he was a Viking – Heimdal, that was it. *Lord* Heimdal, he'd taken to calling himself. Well, if having a ring stuck through your dick made you a member of the nobility, Andreas was happy to remain plain Joe Public. What was it with these Germanic types and dick-piercing? From what he'd heard, they didn't call it the Prince Albert for nothing . . .

Anyway, there he'd been, looking down on the crystal ring and wondering what it had to do with Delgado – and the next minute, it was gone. He didn't understand why, but he was sure it was significant. It might even provide that all-important key to unlock him from his crystal prison.

'Andreas, Andreas . . .'

He called out to her now, with all his strength.

'The ring, Mara. You've got to find the crystal ring. I don't understand why, but it might just be the lucky break we're looking for . . .'

\* \* \*

'So you like it then? You really do?'

Donal snuggled up on the sofa next to Caít. Her flesh felt warm and exciting, even through the thick layers of woolly jumper she insisted in wrapping herself in. Why did she dress like a frump? She had such a wonderful body under all that camouflage. Firm breasts and an arse to die for. He planted a kiss on her cheek and to his surprise and pleasure she did not flinch away. On the contrary, she turned to him and returned his gesture with a full, open-mouthed kiss on the lips. He gave a murmur of delight as their lips met, hot and yielding.

'Yes, I really do. It's the nicest thing you've ever bought me.' She grinned. 'In fact, I think it's the only thing you've ever bought me.'

Donal was indignant.

'I bought you flowers once. Violets. Back in Galway.'

'I paid for them, remember? You forgot your wallet.' She paused. 'Spent the money on that bloody guitar of yours, more like.'

Donal sighed.

'Don't be like that, Caít. You knew I was a struggling rock musician when you met me. I never said it would be easy.'

'Yeah – but I didn't think we'd still be struggling after all this time.'

'Now don't be mad at me, Caít darlin'. Things'll come right for us, you'll see. Come here and give us another kiss . . .'

He nudged a little closer and slipped his hand surreptitiously underneath the hem of her jumper. To his amazement, she didn't snap at him or push him away. On the contrary, his touch on her naked flesh seemed to relax her, making her uncurl like the petals of a flower too long in the dark. She gave a little moan of pleasure as he pulled the jumper up, exposing the twin mounds of her breasts.

It had been a long time, but Donal O'Keefe had not forgotten how to undo a woman's bra with one hand. He certainly wasn't going to let a chance like this pass him by. In one swift movement, he freed the catch and the elastic sprang away, baring Caít's smooth, sleek back.

There was an excitement in his belly – an excitement that reminded him of when he'd first courted Caít, back in Ireland. He remembered those nights down at the dance hall, when he'd slipped away from the band to meet her in the darkness of the changing room; when they'd only just begun the slow, tentative exploration of each other's bodies. There had been other women since then, of course: since their marriage, Caít's diminishing interest in sex had ensured that. But deep down it was still Caít that he wanted, Caít who made him hot like no other woman . . .

He eased the bra cups away from her breasts, and let out a sigh of lustful approval. It seemed an eternity since he'd had a chance to play with her breasts and now, suddenly and without warning, Caít was having a change of heart. He was going to make the most of it while it lasted. The ring had been a bloody good buy – well worth the twenty quid he'd forked out for it. If a simple birthday present could make her this randy, he'd be buying her more presents in future.

'Oh Donal, kiss my breasts,' whispered Caít. 'I'm so hot for you.'

He could hardly believe his ears, but his cock was hard and throbbing and the taste of her hardening pink nipple on his tongue made him wild with lust for her. He wondered if he should take her into the bedroom, where there was more room to fuck, but he didn't want to spoil the mood. As he sucked at her nipple, he slid his hand underneath the hem of her skirt and ran greedy fingers over her smooth bare flesh.

As his fingers climbed her thigh to the secret triangle at the base of her belly, Caít gave a groan of pleasure and slid down until she was lying almost flat on the sofa, with Donal half on top of her. Her thighs relaxed and he burrowed his fingers deeper into the moist pleasure-garden, twisting her dark pubic curls around his fingertips and delighting in the fragrant wetness of her cunt. Caít had never been like this – not even on the night when she had given him her virginity on the floor of Farmer O'Hagan's barn.

'I want you, Caít,' groaned Donal, her juices slippery and inviting on his fingertips. 'Please, please . . .'

'Fuck me. Fuck me now,' she gasped. Her voice was different – filled with a hoarse urgency from which all modesty was banished. 'I've got to feel you inside me . . . your cock in my cunt. I'm so, so wet for you.'

Unzipping himself in a frenzy of hunger, Donal pulled out his cock. It was ramrod-stiff and throbbing with an almost painful intensity of desire, yearning for release. Pulling up Caít's skirt, he ripped down her sensible white panties and prepared to force apart her thighs. But he did not have to persuade her – her thighs spread wide to welcome him, the moist pink heart of her cunt dripping with sweet honey-dew.

He thrust into her in a single stroke and she gave a long shrill cry as her cunt stretched to accommodate his thick shaft.

She felt like silk around his prick as he thrust in and out of her – at first slowly, then faster and faster in a rising crescendo of passion. Caít's hands were clutching at his back, her carefully manicured fingernails raking the flesh like a tigress's claws. She was almost screaming with desire now and Donal could feel her cunt muscles beginning to tense in the first spasms of orgasm.

'I'm coming, I'm coming!' she cried and her cunt tightened around Donal's shaft.

Desire overwhelmed him as with a final thrust, he felt his spunk jet out of him, leaving him gasping on her naked belly.

Afterwards he put his arm around her and played absentmindedly with her breasts, exhausted but half-hoping that she would get hot and order him to fuck her again.

The television was still blaring away in the corner, talking heads droning on at each other about the budget deficit. He picked up the remote control and pointed it at the screen, channel hopping through the films and the costume dramas until he hit the late news. He was about to switch off but Caít stopped him.

'No. I want to watch.'

A tall man was shaking hands with the Indian Prime Minister, wreathed in smiles and flower garlands. There was a beautiful young woman on his arm, tall and curvaceous with a mane of long dark hair and violet eyes.

'It's only the new Ambassador to India. What's up – you fancy him or something? Ouch!'

He suddenly became aware of a sharp pain and looked down. Caít's fingernails were digging into the flesh as she gripped his arm. But she wasn't even looking at him. She was just staring, wide-eyed as a startled rabbit, at the television screen. A low hiss was escaping from her clenched teeth, like the sound an angry cat makes when it is threatened. Then she let go of his arm and started playing with the crystal ring, twisting and turning it round the base of her finger as though it was burning her skin.

'What's the matter, Caít? For pity's sake, what's got into you?'

The pictures moved slowly across the screen. The tall man and his luscious companion got into a long dark limousine and turned to wave at the cameras as they drove off through the streets of Delhi.

Without warning, Caít sprang into sudden and violent life. Grabbing a heavy paperweight from the table beside her, she lifted her arm and for a moment Donal thought she was going to hit him with it. But instead she aimed it at the television set, hurling it through the screen.

With a crash and a shower of blue sparks, the television fell silent. Content now, Caít turned to Donal and kissed his astonished face, running playful fingers down the open front of his shirt.

'I'm in the mood for love,' she breathed. 'Why don't you fuck me again?'

# 2: The Ambassador

Mara Fleming climbed the steps from Regent's Park underground station and smoothed down the skirt of her smart suit. Anastasia's dress sense was taking some getting used to but it was vital that she should play the part to perfection. If anyone should suspect the truth . . .

She was glad that the Master had decided not to take her to India with him. This time, at least, Sedet's pathological jealousy had worked in her favour. But of course, there was still Heimdal to contend with – and Geoffrey Potter – not to mention her newfound responsibilities.

Before he left to take up his new post, the Master had appointed her his sexual emissary. As the most alluring and skilful of his 'hostesses', Mara was to spend her time recruiting important guests for Winterbourne's very special nights of pleasure. The Master had supplied her with a list of those she was to lure to Winterbourne – MPs, businessmen, media figures and the great and the not-so-good from all walks of life. Once enticed to one of Winterbourne's orgies, they would be initiated into the Master's evil empire of the undead. All Mara had to do was use her sexual powers of persuasion. As for Mara, choice didn't come into it. If she did not carry out her duties to the letter, the Master's vengeance would be swift and terrible.

She crossed the road from the tube station and headed towards the offices of NewScene, an up-and-coming publishing house which specialised in philosophy and political thought. There was an unpleasant feeling of nausea in her stomach, the butterfly-fluttering of a child about to make her stage debut in the school play. Did she look good enough? Would she succeed in ensnaring her victim? And what was she doing here anyway? She sighed, knowing that she was as much a victim as the man whose fate she had been sent to seal.

Mara caught sight of herself in a window as she walked past. She had to admit she looked pretty hot: the suit might be smart but the skirt was oh-so-short and the fabric of the blouse was a diaphanous white muslin that left nothing to the imagination. The lacy black bra underneath had been an inspired choice; through it, her large pink nipples were clearly visible each time her emerald green jacket fell open. The tight green skirt moulded perfectly to her skin, showing off her rounded hips and taut belly.

She walked on, past the old church and towards the park. She had to admit to herself that she felt good, in spite of the nerves. Each day that she evaded discovery she felt stronger, more capable; and her psychic powers boiled and bubbled within her as they had never done before – as though this body in which her spirit was imprisoned was also a gateway to the summit of knowledge . . . and pleasure. Sex had been more fun than every lately, too. She had a desperate hunger for it; a thirst that could never be quenched, no matter how often she fucked. She wished that Andreas could be with her to share it.

Here it was: NewScene Publishing Ltd. She hesitated on the pathway outside the elegant Regency terrace, her hand on the gilded finial of the wrought-iron gate. It wasn't too late. There was still time to run, to break away . . .

But in her heart, she knew there could be no escape. The Master had found her once and he would find her again.

With trembling fingers, she reached out and rang the doorbell. The entryphone crackled into life.

'Yes?'

'Miss Dubois, from the Winterbourne Trust,' stammered Mara. 'I have an appointment with Mr Chesterton.'

26

'Come in. I'm unlocking the door now.'

A buzzer sounded and Mara pushed open the door. The entrance hall was richly decorated and the receptionist ushered her into an opulent waiting room filled with antique furniture. Evidently the recession hadn't done NewScene Publishing much harm.

She waited, adjusting her hair in the mirror opposite. It seemed strange to be looking into a mirror and seeing another woman's face. Would she ever get used to the sight of the Master's Queen wearing her body like some costly fur? As she gazed into the mirror only the light in her eyes reminded her of her true identity.

'If you'd like to come in, Mr Chesterton is ready for you now.'

Mara followed the receptionist through a heavy panelled door into a large office, elegantly decorated in Regency stripes. Behind a huge mahogany desk sat a middle-aged man with greying blond hair.

'Miss Dubois, sir,' said the receptionist and left, closing the door quietly behind her.

Chesterton leant back in his chair and pressed the tips of his fingers together, like a church steeple.

'Do sit down. What can I do for you, Miss Dubois?'

Mara sat and crossed her legs, making sure that the tight green skirt rode up as high as possible on her sleek thighs, revealing an alluring glimpse of stocking-top and blue silk gusset. Was that a glint of interest she saw in his dark brown eyes? Or was his air of studied indifference genuine? She began her prepared speech.

'As you know, I'm from the Winterbourne Trust. We are a charitable organisation, dedicated to the advancement of excellence. Our founder, Anthony LeMaître . . .'

'Ah yes, LeMaître.' Chesterton leant his elbows on the desk, his chin resting in his cupped hand. 'Quite the high-flyer, isn't he? Strange that none of us had even heard of him until he got that job in Egypt. I'll bet there's a murky past to be uncovered there.' He grinned, and Mara disliked him instantly, physically attractive though he was. 'Still – as long as he doesn't get found out, eh? Why is a pretty girl like you involved with a colourful character like LeMaître?'

'I . . . we worked together on a project in Egypt,' replied Mara, not entirely untruthfully. 'And Mr LeMaître feels that you might be interested in supporting our latest charitable cause.'

She got up and walked round to the other side of the desk. Chesterton looked up at her in surprise as she ran her fingers through his hair, then smoothed the palm of her hand down over his shoulders, his back, his belly.

'We're having a little fund-raising event next week, at Winterbourne Hall,' breathed Mara, bending to plant a kiss on the nape of his neck. She smiled as she felt him shiver with pleasure at her touch. 'A very exclusive affair. I'm sure you'd enjoy yourself . . .'

She began unfastening the buttons of his shirt and he relaxed under her hands, surrendering entirely to the force of her will. She could feel him vibrating with sexual excitement, thrilling to the gentle caresses she was bestowing on him.

The power of mystic sight overwhelmed her and she saw into Chesterton's mind, recoiling at the dark depravity of what she found there. She'd read the interviews he'd given in the Sunday supplements and now she could see that all his talk of reputation and moral integrity was a sham. Chesterton was an amoral sensualist for whom success was the ultimate aphrodisiac. There seemed to be not a grain of goodness left in him to corrupt. He would make a perfect disciple for the Master.

'Well . . . I don't know if I should,' murmured Chesterton, reaching out and fondling Mara's backside playfully. 'Don't want to get caught in the wrong company, do I? NewScene has such a spotless reputation to maintain, you know.'

'It'll be very discreet,' purred Mara, disliking Chesterton so much that she didn't care what happened to him. 'And besides – I'm very persuasive.'

Mara finished unbuttoning Chesterton's shirt and peeled

it open, baring a tanned, firm belly which she kissed passionately before sliding down to her knees in front of him. His hand played with her long hair as she unzipped him and felt for his cock.

It was large and firm, just as she knew it would be. Chesterton was in fine shape for a man of his years. She pulled out his penis and testicles, and began running her tongue over the velvety sac, delighting in the sense of power as he began moaning quietly. His hands gripped her shoulders tightly and, as she ran her tongue over the tip of his engorged glans, he forced her head forwards in a sudden movement, making her take the whole of his thick shaft into her mouth.

Unpleasant, self-seeking and corrupt he might be, but as soon as she tasted his salty-sweet pre-cum on her greedy tongue, Mara felt the fires of lust surging and crackling through her body.

*Got to fuck, got to fuck.*

The need for sex overwhelmed her, and she sucked at Chesterton's stiffening cock with an almost divine fervour. Her hands cradled his balls, gently stroking and squeezing them into tense delicious expectancy. And with each second that passed she felt stronger, more alive, more excited.

'Give it to me. Suck harder, harder . . .'

Chesterton moaned softly as she took him to the brink of pleasure and held him there, a hostage to his own lust. His whole body was trembling and she was trembling with him, a little trickle of sweat running down into the deep valley between her breasts.

Suddenly she released him from her mouth and he groaned with protest, desperate for her to continue and bring him the release he craved. He looked at her with wild eyes, crazed with frustrated desire, as she got to her feet in front of him and then walked away, towards the door.

'Where are you going?'

Turning the key deftly in the lock, Mara turned back to face Chesterton and smiled. He was gazing at her, open-mouthed, his cock arching stiffly upwards from his lap.

Dazed, he gasped: 'Please, please . . .'

She was by his side in a moment, stroking and rubbing his penis until he almost wept with need for her. Then, still facing him, she sat astride her, taking his cock into her like a rapier into its scabbard. The exquisite pleasure of the moment took even Mara by surprise. The cunt felt so incredibly sensitive that she could hardly bear the intensity of each new thrust.

As she fucked him, the room began to spin around her and she held on very tightly to him, levering herself up and down on his erect prick. The mists of her mind cleared as her psychic sight sharpened and she thought she heard a voice from far away calling out to her.

'Mara, Mara!'

She knew it was Andreas, but his voice was faint, hard to distinguish. There were pictures too – the bricked-up cellar where the sarcophagus lay; swirling dust; the distorted image of Andreas's face; his mouth opening and closing in silent pain.

And something else. Something about a ring.

She fucked Chesterton with enthusiasm, riding the mounting crescendo of lust. She could feel his cock twitching inside her, hardening even more than before, getting ready to spurt its load into her. She didn't want him to come before she did.

Wriggling her fingers between their bellies, she began rubbing the throbbing bud of her clitoris. Strange, so strange to be rubbing another woman's clitty with another woman's fingers. Strange to be feeling another woman's pleasure . . .

'The ring, Mara. Find the ring.'

With a little sigh of delight, she abandoned herself to the delicious spasms of orgasm. And the tensing of her cunt muscles was sufficient to bring Chesterton to a crashing, shattering climax.

As he clasped her to him, panting hoarsely in her ear, she whispered to him seductively.

'You will come to Winterbourne, won't you? You can't imagine how grateful I'd be . . .'

\* \* \*

It was a hot afternoon in New Delhi. Sedet moaned and writhed on the bed as the Master wriggled the tip of his tongue into her arse. His hand was under her belly, manipulating her clitoris with a demonic skill.

'Harder, harder now,' commanded the Queen. 'I want to come again before you put your cock inside me.'

Sunlight filtered through the window of the British Embassy, turning the entwined bodies to molten gold and casting long, mysterious shadows on the floor. On the rich coloured carpet lay the naked brown body of an Indian girl, the blood still damp and sticky on her slender throat. She lay very silent, very still. She had served her purpose.

On the other side of the bedroom sat Takimoto, face contorted with lust as he gazed longingly on the spectacle of the Master pleasuring his Queen. He had desired that lithe succulent body for so long and now she was opening up the treasures of her cunt and arse, surely to torment him. His cock grew hard as iron as he watched the Master bring her to a second juddering orgasm, then draw her up onto hands and knees and thrust his prick into the very depths of her. Outside, in the streets of New Delhi, gaudy lorries and bicycle rickshaws sped by in a cacophony of vibrant life, their drivers blissfully unaware of what the Master held in store for them.

'You may give me your report now, Takimoto,' instructed the Master, sliding his prick slowly in and out of Sedet's silken cunt. The slow, steady rhythm pleased him, drawing out the pleasure and making his whole body vibrate with a powerful undercurrent of excitement. 'How is the Logos project progressing?'

The Logos project was at the very heart of the Master's plans for power. For months now, Takimoto and his colleagues in Tokyo had been working on equipment which would enable subliminal messages to be broadcast on television sets, cinema screens and computer terminals. And now it was to be tested here in India . . .

'The Logos system is almost ready,' replied Takimoto, unzipping his pants and taking out his cock. The Master had not invited him to participate but he would risk the consequences of displeasure. He could bear it no longer – his sex-hungry body was desperate for release. As he masturbated his shaft, he continued: 'The initial indications are extremely favourable. I myself have persuaded many women to fuck with me by means of the Logos system. But our experiments to date have been only on a small scale. What is needed now is an extensive field trial.'

'Patience. You shall have what you desire. Next month, I think, when we have settled in. A plan has already formed in my mind – it remains only to finalise the details.'

The Master turned and looked at him over his shoulder, a cynical half-smile playing about his lips. He gave a hard thrust into Sedet's cunt, and she growled with sudden pleasure, clawing at the bedspread with her long red talons.

'I see abstinence does not suit you, Takimoto.'

Takimoto swallowed hard, caught in the act like a guilty schoolboy wanking under the blankets in the dormitory.

'N-no, Master. The beauty of your fucking . . . I could not contain myself . . .'

The Master laughed, cupping Sedet's full, firm breasts in his eager hands and squeezing them hard.

'Even the immortals must have their sustenance. And who would not be crazed with lust at the sight of my beautiful Queen?'

The Master was riding her faster now, his balls slapping up against the golden globes of her backside. As his spirit met and mingled with the spirit of his Queen, they cried out together and his cock-juice spurted into her belly.

He withdrew from her and lay back on the bed.

'Pleasure me, my Queen. Pleasure me with your mouth.'

Sedet knelt over him, her full breasts pendulous and golden as ripe fruit. Takimoto looked on with aching lust, longing to touch and yet knowing that she was beyond his wildest aspirations. He might be one of the elect, one of the immortals, but he was left in no doubt as to his ultimate unimportance.

Eyes closed, the Master murmured with pleasure as Sedet ran her tongue over his thighs and belly, teasing him back to erect wakefulness.

'Our faithful servant Takimoto needs a fuck,' he remarked. 'Do you think we should help him?'

Sedet sniggered, running the moist point of her tongue up the Master's shaft. She turned to look at Takimoto.

'One day, perhaps, I shall accord you the supreme pleasure of tonguing out my arse. One day, when you have proved your worth and stand beside us in our new empire. But for now,' she smiled and licked the Master's testicles, 'for now, you must seek your pleasure and your sustenance elsewhere.'

The Master laughed.

'You have served us excellently thus far, Takimoto. I chose well in bringing you to Winterbourne. And for your reward . . . I have provided for your pleasure. Those who serve me faithfully, I shall not abandon. In my kingdom, beyond the empty realm of death, there is only the most supreme pleasure.'

He clapped his hands and the door of the bedroom opened, revealing a turbaned houseboy.

'Bring in the girl,' commanded the Master. 'I think you will find her to your liking, Takimoto.'

The Japanese businessman gasped as the girl was dragged in, gagged and bound hand and foot. Even behind the heavy beaded veils, he could see that she was a real beauty. His cock ached for her at once. He could scarcely believe the Master's generosity. Already, he was imagining the sound that the whip would make as it bit into her naked body, the sound of her piteous cries as he rammed into her, tearing through her virgin hymen. His mouth watered in anticipation.

'She is truly mine, Master?'

'Yours to do with exactly as you wish. In herself she is of little importance – I had her kidnapped from one of the poorer districts – but I have divined that she has a sensual nature and may make a useful whore for Winterbourne . . . if you can teach her some pretty tricks with her cunt and arse . . .'

Takimoto needed no second bidding. The girl was on her knees before him and already he was pushing his cock between her lips, his hands exploring the soft feminine curves of her young body.

As she tasted Takimoto's prick on her tongue, the girl's eyes closed in ecstasy and she began sucking at him like a practised whore.

'I told you she had potential,' muttered the Master as Sedet fellated him in turn, squeezing his balls gently with her slender golden fingers.

Once more in the body of the black servant Ibrahim, Andreas stood in the Great Hall at Winterbourne. Strength ebbed and flowed in him like a fickle tide as the bodies surged about him, a sea of naked flesh writhing and twisting on the marble floor.

On the other side of the room stood Heimdal, master of ceremonies par excellence, his blond head thrown back in silent laughter as an African slave-girl took his massive prick into her capacious mouth. She was a skilful little whore, brought to Winterbourne only a week ago from a North African bordello where she had sucked cocks for a few pennies and offered up the treasures of her silky black arse for the price of a plate of couscous. The Master himself had initiated her, refreshing himself for his trip to India with the sweetness of her young flesh.

Now she was fellating Heimdal with such artless skill that he was shaking with wild laughter, his voice rising above the cries of the faithful like the roar of a lion.

Andreas stood rooted to the spot, still too dizzy and disorientated to function properly. A girl was clawing at his ankles, calling out the name that was and was not his.

'Ibrahim, Ibrahim!'

He looked down at her with eyes that could not quite frame her pretty red-lipped face, drinking in her naked body, the smooth skin sparkling with little beads of sweat. There was a trickle of something red and sticky running from the corner of her mouth to the moist channel between her heavy breasts. She was trying to claw her way up his naked leg now, towards the loin cloth which so inadequately veiled his prick. He could feel it uncoiling like a waking serpent. It filled him with a strange seductive warmth and he wanted to yield to it, but his link with the body was an imperfect one, fragile as a spider's web. He tried to move but his arms and legs felt heavy, sluggish.

'Fuck me, Ibrahim . . .'

Someone pulled her back down to the ground and stuck his cock up her arse – it was a middle-aged man with a thin cruel slash of a mouth. His face struck a chord in Andreas's memory. Images of another time, another life. Where had he . . .? Who . . .?

Sir Anthony fucking Cheviot. That was who the bastard was. It all seemed so long ago that they'd crossed swords in Cheviot's Whitby constituency, but even now the sight of the odious MP made Andreas feel sick with rage. He swallowed and blinked. Cheviot's face swam in and out of focus, as Andreas sought to control the raw energy which flowed through him. He felt a surge of annoyance. Bloody hell, this was so stupid, so frustrating! He was beginning to feel like a faulty light-bulb, flickering on and off with unpredictable frequency – and always at the most inconvenient moments. He had sworn to get himself and Mara out of this unseemly mess and now was not the time to lose control.

And suddenly there she was: Mara – his Mara. Not as he had once seen her, with her long dark hair and violet eyes, but as soon as he set eyes on her he knew it was she, and not Anastasia Dubois, walking into the Great Hall. She cast a brief glance in his direction but her eyes did not linger. Had she seen him? Had she understood? That moment on the steps of the Hall, when she had touched his hand and he had spoken to her . . . Then, he had been so sure that she knew. But now . . .

He had experimented with contacting her telepathically

many times since then. Sometimes he had managed to get through but it wasn't easy. Let's face it, he was no expert . . . One minute he would be suffocating in the black heart of the crystal and the next he would find himself in God-knows-whose body – for a second, a few moments only – and then the link would be dissolved. If it didn't stop soon, he was in danger of forgetting who he was.

Andreas Hunt, that's who he was. Ace investigative reporter on the *Daily Comet*. Trilby-wearing super-snooper and multi-purpose pain in the arse. Andreas Hunt – psychic? Hell, this stuff didn't come naturally. A year ago, he'd have called it a load of crap.

Now, it was his only lifeline.

His cock ached for Mara. It didn't matter that she was inside some other woman's body. It was Mara he saw when she moved. Mara's breasts bobbing free inside the tiny diaphanous blouse. Mara's lips parting in soundless pleasure as the South American made her bend forwards over the back of a gilded chair and pulled up her skirt, thrusting into her with the reckless hunger of a starving man.

Andreas felt jealousy rise in his gorge like a tide of vomit. His head was swimming, the doorway of his consciousness opening and closing as he struggled to focus on Mara. His woman. The woman he yearned to fuck. He imagined how it would feel to be inside her once again, to slid his hard cock into the yielding wetness of her cunt, to cup her full firm breasts in his hands as he thrust in and out of her.

He could almost feel it. He *could* feel it – the wonderful, indescribable warmth of Mara's cunt, clenching and unclenching around his hard-on like the mouth of some lewd sea-creature.

The thick black penis was twitching beneath his loin-cloth. The girl was clawing at him again, trying to get his attention, but he couldn't give a damn about her. All he could do was stand and stare at Mara. To his amazement he could feel each thrust of the South American's hips, feel the pleasure growing and burning on him. Oh God, he was going to come . . .

As he came, spurting thick creamy spunk into the white cotton loin-cloth, Mara turned her face towards him and looked him straight in the eye. Her lips did not move but, as his consciousness flickered and died, he heard her words distinctly.

'Don't fight it, Andreas. Sex will bring you power. Sex will bring us together.'

'Is all ready?'

'It is as you instructed me, Master.'

'You may proceed.'

The screens flickered into life and the Master sat back in his seat. They did not have much time. Takimoto had done well to procure the use of this television studio but it was essential that their little experiment was finalised before anyone started asking too many awkward questions. Tonight, the people of New Delhi would all be watching their television screens, expecting to see the winning ticket drawn in a million-rupee charity lottery. The ticket would indeed be drawn but that was not all they were going to see.

Takimoto ran the VTR and a slow smile spread across the Master's face. The images were too fleeting for the eye to register consciously but, subliminally, they were dynamite.

First, footage of a smiling female presenter, talking about the lottery. Nothing controversial there.

## RIOT

More images from the studio – the presenter standing beside a huge painted cauldron, filled with lottery tickets.

## RIOT. FUCK.

Back to the pretty presenter – still smiling, still desirable in her gold-trimmed sari. The Master felt his cock stirring as he looked at her, the hard points of her tits pressing against the thin sari blouse. He cast a sidelong glance at Sedet and ran his hand up her thigh, feeling under her skirt for her glorious, slippery cunt. Sedet's hand slipped silently onto his lap, unzipping his flies and taking out his cock. Her hand was silky-smooth and so, so cool.

He wondered how the Indian presenter's skin would feel against his and idly imagined the pleasure of reddening that perfect creamy-beige flesh with a cat-o'-nine-tails . . . or maybe a bullwhip. Yes, that was the perfect answer. He would have her tied up and stripped naked, so that he could enjoy the perfect spectacle of her virgin terror before he wielded the whip on that soft, soft flesh.

Sedet's hand was masturbating him, skilfully, knowingly. She knew what was in his mind and she was smiling at the prettiness of it. His thoughts were also hers.

*And afterwards*, she seemed to be telling him, *afterwards I shall torment that pretty flesh whilst you fuck her. But which of us shall have the sweet, succulent delight of tasting her blood . . .?*

Sedet was coming. The Master could feel her cunt tensing as he ran his hand backwards and forwards along her crack. Her mind opened to him like a flower and he saw them as they had been so long ago, fucking on the banks of the warm, slow-moving Nile as the Egyptian sun baked down upon their naked flesh. The warm slipperiness of Sedet's juices stimulated his own desire and he felt pleasure rising within him.

Now the screen was filled with flickering images of naked bodies fucking; there were no distinguishable individuals, only a tangled mass of writhing flesh, cocks and cunts and firm, quivering breasts. The words filling the screen for a split-second, whispered silently and seductively to the subconscious mind:

FUCK AND TASTE THE DELIGHTS OF PLEASURE

The Indian presenter was reaching into the gilded cauldron to take out the winning lottery ticket. But on the next frame, flickering past so fast that the naked eye could not consciously perceive it, was the image of a whore sucking LeMaître's cock, and the words:

RIOT. TASTE PLEASURE, BUT OBEY.
LEMAITRE IS YOUR ONLY MASTER.

The Master gave a little shudder of pleasure as Sedet manipulated him to an agreeably warm climax. As the spunk was about to jet out of him, she threw herself to her knees and took the abundant, pearly liquid into her mouth. Stray droplets spattered his trousers and Sedet licked them away with obvious relish.

'You are certain that our little experiment will prove successful?' said the Master leaning back in his chair and zipping his still-hard cock into his designer pants. 'I have yet to be convinced that such a campaign will prove effective. Remember, Takimoto: there are to be no mistakes this time.'

Igushi Takimoto gave a small, subservient bow.

'I can assure you that all is as you instructed, Master, Mistress.' He paused. 'Will you permit me to furnish you with a small further demonstration?'

Sedet looked impatient but the Master nodded.

'You had better not be wasting my time, Takimoto.'

Takimoto reached for a switch on the console and flicked on another monitor. The screen lit up, revealing a room in which were seated neat ranks of beautiful men and women, all shaven-headed and dressed in saffron robes. They were sitting in sober silence, hands folded and eyes downcast.

'Explain this charade,' demanded Sedet coldly, running impatient fingers through the long mane of dark hair.

Takimoto smiled and bowed unctuously.

'Mistress, these are the most devout, most religious young men and women in this holy city. Each is passionately devoted to the cult of the god Krishna and each is sworn to lifelong celibacy. They have been invited to come here in order to view a documentary about the life of their guru. Naturally, the documentary has been . . . subtly enhanced.' He turned back to the Master. 'Will you allow me . . .?'

'You may proceed.'

The Master and Sedet followed Takimoto out of the studio, down a long corridor to a door marked 'Suite 9. Private.'

As Takimoto opened the door and entered the room, there was no reaction from the assembled men and women. They continued to look down at their folded hands, like discarded puppets in a box. Sedet glanced at them contemptuously.

'I can see little purpose . . .'

But, as the Master followed them into the room, a sudden and dramatic transformation took place. The men and women raised their heads and began staring at him with a fierce and alarming intensity. There was a fire of adulation in their pleading eyes. A low keening sound escaped from their parted lips.

All at once they were falling over each other in their desperation to reach the Master, ripping off their own and each other's clothes in a mad contest to expose their naked, henna-patterned flesh.

'Master, Master!' they screamed, falling at his feet and tearing at his clothes with clawlike hands. 'Take me! Fuck me, fuck me now!'

As Sedet looked on with contemptuous amusement, the Master unzipped his flies and took out his stiffening dick. He turned to Takimoto with a half-smile.

'You have done well, my servant. And now,' he looked at the weeping, lust-crazed girls begging him to fill up their luscious virgin cunts. 'I feel a need upon me. Come, my Queen. Now it is time for us to slake our thirst.'

# 3: Obsessions

The man in the leather jacket and battered cords pulled up his collar in a vain attempt to keep the rain from trickling down the back of his neck. As he lurked like a burglar in the shrubbery, fat wet droplets bounced off the leaves, drenching him. Dry with sunny spells, indeed.

Max Trevidian had been keeping watch on the house for three days now and he still had nothing worth reporting. He'd seen a few comings and goings, a few black limos with darkened windows and hordes of underlings – gardeners, servants, that sort of thing. He'd nearly been spotted once or twice and he'd had to be careful to avoid the dogs. He'd not had a sniff of anyone important, though. Up to now, it was all as clear as mud.

He took out the dictaphone and clicked it on. Maybe if he voiced his thoughts they'd eventually resolve themselves. He spoke quietly into the microphone.

'Winterbourne Hall. That was the last entry in Chesterton's diary. He went to his club and told friends he was going 'somewhere special' for the evening but that he'd be back at his desk on the Monday morning. Since then . . .'

The sound of a door slamming made him look up and he caught sight of a striking red-haired woman walking down the front steps of Winterbourne Hall.

The Dubois woman! He was sure of it – he'd seen photos of her. This was his first real break.

As he watched, the flame-haired woman climbed into the front seat of a red BMW, next to a tallish blond boy. They drove off down the long winding driveway.

Caít picked up the scalpel and – carefully and clinically – began slicing up the pile of newspapers in front of her. She worked swiftly and silently but her breathing was fast and shallow and her eyes held an almost fanatical gleam.

Every foreign news page had at least one picture or snippet of news about the charismatic new Ambassador to India. It was said he was building up a real rapport with the locals, setting himself up as the big peacemaker.

Caít gathered up the cuttings and began pasting them into the scrapbook, carefully yet feverishly. She knew her fascination was fast becoming an obsession – she was as baffled as Donal about the television incident – but there was a burning compulsion within her. She had to fill her life with images and words about this man that she found so repulsive yet so compelling.

As she dotted the page with glue and pressed down the cuttings, the crystal ring on her right hand seemed to glow with a hidden fire. Caít did not notice, she was entirely absorbed in her collection.

She spotted a picture she had missed – a photograph of LeMaître addressing a group of village elders, somewhere in a poverty-stricken corner of South India. It was little more than a dusty hamlet but you could see the audience were transfixed by him. Every one of them was looking at him, following his every word as he spoke to them, his lips forming into that familiar half-smile . . .

In a sudden burst of anger, she stabbed at the page, meaning to slice out the picture but catching the side of her finger with the razor-sharp blade. Wincing, she pulled her hand away and a drop of dark red blood dripped from her cut fingertip onto the face of the Master.

As the drop of blood hit the newspaper photograph and soaked into the newsprint, a terrible feeling of foreboding overwhelmed her. She started trembling, unable to explain the feelings that were surrounding her, hemming her in.

She felt angry, trapped, afraid . . .

What were these images inside her head? Whose were these glittering eyes that seemed to bore into her soul, baring every evil thought she had ever had? How could a simple picture of Anthony LeMaître fill her with such terror – and such rage?

The drop of blood crept swiftly across the newspaper cutting, the porous paper drinking it in greedily. Could one small drop of blood really cover so much paper? The picture was half-obliterated but the eyes still seemed to dominate the grey landscape. Was she imagining it, or could she really feel a sudden surge of energy that compelled her, against her will, to meet that cold unforgiving gaze?

And the angry voice inside her was still whispering, hissing, cajoling: *Hate. Despise. Resist. Destroy . . .*

Changes were happening inside her, and she didn't understand them. Couldn't understand the blind hatred that was twisting her insides, nor the growing, swelling, irresistible need, deep in her belly.

There was no time to dwell on thoughts or fears. At that moment Caít was jolted back to reality by the sound of a key turning in the lock.

'I'm back, sweetheart! What's for dinner?'

Hurriedly, Caít wound a handkerchief round her finger then bundled up the scrapbook and cuttings and thrust them into the bottom drawer of the sideboard, just managing to push it shut before Donal walked into the room. He was wearing a ludicrous knitted hat and a stupid grin, and she knew instantly that it had gone well.

'Good gig, was it?'

She put her arms round him and kissed him tenderly, drinking in the warmth from his body, the fire that burned into her from his hardening crotch.

He returned her kiss, laying his guitar case down on the sofa so that he could put both arms round her and slide his hand down onto her smooth backside. She was looking good. These last couple of weeks she'd really smartened herself up.

Tight leather skirt, silk blouse. Suddenly he realised how much he fancied her.

'Not bad at all, darlin'.' He thrust his hand into the back pocket of his jeans and pulled out a wad of notes. 'Two hundred each for the night – and a repeat booking for next week. The Lounge Lizards are really on their way up, you make my words.' He unfastened the top button of her blouse and pressed his lips to the moist crease between her breasts, tasting the delicious aroma of her sweat. 'Fancy helping me celebrate? Forget the cooking. There's a late-night French restaurant I know up town. We could go out for a meal and maybe later . . .' He let his hand skim the surface of her breast, lightly teasing the sensitive crest of her nipple.

He had half expected the usual brush-off, but certainly not Caít's enthusiastic response.

'Let's go to bed. Right now.'

She pulled his face down to hers and crushed her mouth on his, thrusting her tongue between his lips with such fervour that she left him gasping for breath. His cock was hard and throbbing now, pressed close against his belly, and the hunger within her was wild and terrible. She wrenched up the hem of his shirt and began raking her fingernails over his bare back, making him wince with surprised discomfort.

'Steady on, Caít – you're hurting!'

He eased away from her, and for the first time he noticed the reddened handkerchief, still wound round Caít's cut hand.

'Mother o' God, what you been doin' to yourself?'

'Oh, it's nothing. I just . . . cut myself when I was chopping up some vegetables. It's just a scratch really.'

'You poor girl . . .'

Caít ignored Donal's solicitous words, and turned her attentions to the buckle of his trouser-belt, cursing softly as her fumbling fingers failed to undo it. He obliged her, loosening first the belt buckle and then the buttons of his 501s. Underneath, he was wearing tight black pants that moulded the heavy outline of his swollen cock. She ran her hands over

44

his bulging balls, weighing their sap-filled bounty, and a sudden, joyous thrill ran through her.

She stepped away from him and began to pull off her clothes. He watched her, transfixed. This was not – could not be – the same Caít who used to refuse to get undressed unless all the lights were out. It couldn't be the same Caít who had condoned his flings with other women because sex 'wasn't her thing'.

No, not Caít. This was some other creature – some love-hungry sex siren stripping for him in his own living-room, not caring that the curtains were open and God-knows-who could see in as she peeled off her blouse and reached for the catch of her tiny lace bra.

In a single movement she had freed the catch, liberating the pert mounds of her creamy-white breasts. She slipped off the scrap of material and let it fall to the floor. But Donal wasn't looking at the bra, he was gazing open-mouthed at the twin rosebuds of her nipples, hard and succulent and aching to be kissed. But it was more than that . . .

Caít laughed at his confusion.

'Don't you like it? I had it done today, just to please you.'

She smiled as he stared at her, at once astounded and aroused by what he saw: a thick silver ring, its heaviness distending the soft flesh as it passed through her right nipple.

Caít? He just couldn't understand it . . .

Caít took away his doubts with a kiss, and then another. Her fingers worked deftly at his shaft, pumping him to a divine hardness that made him groan with the anticipation of pleasure.

'Let me fuck you. Let me take you to bed . . .' he begged.

'No,' replied Caít. 'I want you to take me right here.'

She led him over to the window. Even here, on the seventh floor, they weren't alone. Lights shone in the windows of the tower-block opposite. If anyone was taking the time or the trouble to watch, they would see everything – every curve of Caít's naked body, every thrust as Donal shafted her. Donal's heart was in his mouth. He wanted her – wanted her like mad.

His dick was sticky-wet and pulsating for the wet heat of her cunt. But to do it here, where anyone could see them . . .

'You're a crazy woman, Caít! What if . . .?'

But Caít wasn't listening to him. She was pulling up a chair until it was right in front of the picture-window, bending over it so that her firm white breasts hung over the wooden back like juicy pendulous fruits.

She turned to look at Donal over her shoulder.

'Take me, Donal. Take me now.'

Banishing all his reservations, Donal embraced her, pressing his body against hers and reaching for the delicious weight of her breasts. They felt so good in the hollow of his hands. He squeezed them tight, then pressed his cock between her thighs, its top searching for the entrance to her cunt.

'No, not there.' Caít smiled at him in a way he had never seen before. There was a hunger in her smile; an intensity that made him shiver for a moment, overtaken with a sudden cold. 'Not there, darling. I want you to fuck me in the arse . . .'

In the green room at QTV, Mara sipped at a glass of tepid champagne and toyed with the food on her plate. In her new body, she no longer had the physical need for food or drink. Sexual energy was her sustenance now. But the simple act of eating or drinking comforted her somehow and reminded her that she was not the vampire-creature Dubois but Mara Fleming, a mortal woman trapped in an immortal frame.

She half-listened to the conversations around her, though she was not really interested in what any of her companions had to say.

'Simply wonderful show tonight, Robbie. Absolutely fab.'

'Loved the interview you did with Gerry Pickford. That's the way to handle these bloody socialists – give 'em hell!'

'Did I do OK, Sir Robert? Do you really think so?'

The undisputed centre of attention in the green room tonight was Sir Robert Hackman, well-known TV personality and presenter-chairman of the current affairs show, *Westminster Tonight*. Tall and hawk-like, with a distinguished sweep of grey hair, Hackman was a self-proclaimed media bulldog – a terror to anyone who had a secret to hide. He could make or break a man's reputation in the space of a single interview, and he knew it. Smug and self-satisfied, arrogance oozed out of him as he preened himself and listened to the empty praise of his acolytes.

Mara watched him with interest, wondering just how many secrets of his own Sir Robert was hiding. According to Heimdal, it was an open secret that Hackman had 'specialised' sexual tastes. Just exactly how specialised, she would no doubt soon discover . . .

Someone was tugging at her arm. She turned and hid a grimace as she saw Geoffrey Potter. Ever since Geoffrey had become an overnight sensation with his bestselling political blockbusters, he had been a hot property on the interview circuit. Needless to say, it hadn't been too difficult for Heimdal to arrange for him to be one of the interviewees on *Westminster Tonight*.

He pulled her towards him, his lecherous hands taking the opportunity to roam all over her backside. She longed to push him away but dared not give him any reason to complain about her to the Master. It was almost impossible to believe that this was the same Geoffrey Potter who had once been so shy that he couldn't look at Mara's naked body without blushing.

Of course, that had been before Geoffrey met the Master. A lot had happened since then. The Master made things happen.

Geoffrey whispered in her ear as he pawed the smooth curve of her buttocks. She couldn't suppress a little shiver of anticipatory pleasure as she listened to his words.

'Time to move in, you gorgeous little slut. Don't worry – he knows all about you. He's hot for your sex already.'

Giving her a little pat on the backside, he grabbed her by the wrist and led her across the room to where Sir Robert was still basking in the warmth of adulation. Pushing his way through the crowd, he tapped Hackman on the shoulder and the great man wheeled round, initially irritated.

'What do you want? Can't you see . . .? Oh! How charming . . .'

'Allow me to present Miss Dubois to you, Sir Robert. One of our most senior researchers from the Winterbourne Trust . . .'

'Indeed.' Hackman looked her up and down with pure lust in his eyes – in fact, lust was probably the only pure thing in him, mused Mara.

For a moment Mara felt lost in the cold depths of Hackman's steely grey eyes. Her psychic sense told her that there was already much that was evil in this man, much more than the Master could pervert and corrupt to his own dark purposes. Suddenly she felt the terror of her captivity. She was the unwilling prisoner of the Master's black desires and ambitions, which forced her to actions she deplored in order to preserve her true identity.

She must not flinch. To show any sign of reluctance would be to alert Geoffrey and Heimdal to other subtle changes in her. With a tremendous effort of will, she forced herself to smile at Hackman.

'Delighted to meet you, Sir Robert. Geoffrey has told me so much about you.'

Hackman ran the point of his tongue over his lips, in a lizard-like and unpleasantly predatory gesture. He took hold of her hand and raised it to his mouth. She shivered as the cool moisture touched her skin, shivered with distaste but also with the anticipation of excitement. For, although her spirit reviled the man, her flesh was aching with the relentless hunger for sex.

'I don't suppose I could interest you in a few drinks back at my flat?' he said.

'Well, I . . .'

Hackman took Mara by the arm and drew her away, leaving the gaggle of disappointed admirers staring in his wake. Mara glanced behind her and noticed that Geoffrey's face was a mask of jealous lust. Later that night, she knew that he would exact a cruel penance from her for tormenting him so with her body. Many times she had tasted the fruits of Geoffrey's jealousy; baring her breasts to the cat-o'-nine tails until her flesh was a mass of criss-crossing welts, and Geoffrey fell to fucking her, his greedy tongue lapping up the blood from her wounded tits.

But, for now, there could be no thoughts of Geoffrey or of the night to come. For now, she must accept the task she had been set by the Master: to ensnare Sir Robert with her lascivious skill and lure him to Winterbourne – and his doom.

They walked in silence down a flight of stairs to the car park and got into the back of Sir Robert's chauffeur-driven Rover. All the way to Hampstead, he behaved like a perfect gentleman and Mara began to wonder if she hadn't made some sort of mistake after all.

'So you're interested in recruiting me for a charity fund-raising event, Miss Dubois?'

'That's the general idea, yes. But first we'd like you to come along to Winterbourne for one of our . . . introductory seminars.'

'I see.' The car was turning into the driveway of Sir Robert's home: a tall Victorian villa set among a copse of lime trees. 'I'm a very busy man, Miss Dubois. And a very choosy one. I don't ally myself to just any cause. But I'll admit your Mr LeMaître intrigues me. He has potential.' He turned to Mara and smiled. 'I could make him or break him: I haven't quite decided yet which it is to be.'

They went into the house and had drinks in the sitting room. Hackman didn't try anything on. Maybe he was too shy? But he didn't seem the type. She thought of making the first move but Hackman seemed to have anticipated her. He stood up.

'Would you like to see the rest of the house?'

'Yes . . . why not?'

Mara was surprised to be led, not upstairs to the bedrooms, but down a flight of stairs towards a cellar door. Anxiety knotted her stomach though she knew he could not harm her.

What could he do – kill her? The thought set waves of hollow laughter echoing in her head.

Hackman unlocked the cellar door and led her inside, clicking on the light switch.

'This is my very private collection, my dear. I hope you like it.'

Mara's gaze travelled round the cellar walls as she tried to fathom out what this was all about. The walls were lined with portraits of perhaps twenty-five or thirty men and women. Some she dimly recognised; others were complete strangers to her. And in the middle of the room was a bed, covered in black satin sheets. She turned to Hackman, baffled. But he wasn't looking at her. He was looking at his collection of portraits, walking from one to the next with a smile of satisfaction spreading across his hawk-like face.

'Brent Isaacson,' he muttered, stroking a gilded frame. The portrait was of a youthful, dark-haired man in a blue suit. 'Do you remember him?' Without waiting for Mara's reply, he went on. 'The CPI scandal. Ah yes, I destroyed him . . .'

He moved on to the next picture. Recognition suddenly hit Mara.

'Isn't that . . .?'

'That's right, Miss Dubois. It's Sir Jeremy Pendersley, the former Attorney-General. I destroyed him, too. Just one interview, that's all it took. But the nation needed to know, you can understand that, can't you? His filthy life had to be exposed for the public good. Consorting with common whores . . .' He smiled, a cruel, think-lipped leer that chilled Mara's blood. 'They all deserved it, every one of them. They all had it coming to them.'

Mara's head reeled. One by one, Hackman went through the portraits, telling of the lives he had wrecked, the dreams he had ended, the good reputations he had destroyed. Suddenly, Mara realised that Hackman was not just elated by what he was saying, he was excited, too. She couldn't help noticing the swelling bulge in the front of his suit pants. So, she thought to herself. So this is what turns you on . . .

She sat down on the edge of the bed and reached behind her and tugged down the zipper of her skintight black cocktail dress.

'It's so hot in here,' she sighed. 'I simply must cool off.'

Hackman turned to see Mara peeling her dress down over her shoulders, exposing two creamy-white breasts encased in a flimsy satin bra. He gave a little groan and his hand moved automatically to the front of his trousers, rubbing at the aching hardness which only Mara's silken cunt could assuage.

She wriggled out of the dress and let it fall to the cellar floor; then stretched out on the bed, coquettish and suddenly hungry for love.

'Come and undress me,' she breathed. 'Come and show me what you're made of. Let's see what secrets you have to hide, Sir Robert.'

'One moment.' Hackman flipped a switch on the wall and a whirring sound filled the cellar.

'What . . .?'

'Don't be alarmed, Miss Dubois. It's just a few little devices I've had installed to increase our pleasure. Don't you find the cameras excite you?'

She looked around her and saw the camera lenses glinting as they pointed at her, the videotape already spooling through the cassette; saw the dozen video screens as they slid silently out of alcoves in the walls and flickered into life. So this was Hackman's little perversion . . . Well, what the hell? She could live with that.

'Now come and undress me,' she repeated, holding out her arms to him. 'Strip me naked. I want you to strip me and fuck me. Hurry – I want you now.'

And in a strange way it was true. She did want him, needed his sex as a deep-sea diver needs oxygen. The hunger within her was growing, swelling. Hackman threw off his clothes and joined her on the bed, clawing at her bra and panties as the cameras ran and the lights caressed Mara's naked flesh.

As he ripped at her satin panties, Mara reached out and took hold of Hackman's dancing prick. Hot feverish desire was pulsating through it and the energy soaked into her, reviving and exciting her. She felt more alive than she had ever done.

She masturbated Hackman's cock, at first gently then with greater and greater energy as the excitement overtook her and her cunt began to overflow with sweet slippery moisture.

'Want you, want you,' groaned Hackman as he knelt over her and watched her milking him with her soft and skilful hands. 'Got to have you now, you little slut.'

His fingers felt for her pubis and pushed roughly between her cunt lips. She groaned as his fingertips met the throbbing flesh of her clitoris and parted her thighs wider and wider to take him inside her.

She turned her head as he drove the head of his cock into her and was surprised by the thrill that ran through her as she watched herself being fucked from a dozen different angles, on a dozen television screens.

'Harder,' she commanded him as he ground his pelvis against hers. 'Tonight, I'm going to fuck you dry . . .'

The Master climbed the steps from the huge sunken bath and accepted the silk bathrobe offered to him by the pretty youth with the velvety brown eyes. There was such innocence in those eyes, mused the Master, running his hands over the lad's perfect body. Enough innocence for him to enjoy the prospect of corrupting it – almost as much as he had enjoyed corrupting the soul of the Hindu girl whom he had tricked into sharing his bath that afternoon. The warm, rose-scented water was still tinged with the drifting redness of that delicious virgin's betrayed innocence . . .

Although the energies of coupling had strengthened and revived him, the Master hungered still. The youth's body was sweet, succulent and tempting. There was time. He had no further engagements in Delhi until the evening. It would be so easy, so swift, for his dark spirit to overwhelm this pretty lad's resistance. In a single thrust he could be inside that firm tight backside. Already he could feel its velvet rings closing around the iron-hard shaft of his cock . . .

'Master, Master!'

The Master turned in irritation, to see the houseboy Sanjay waiting for him in the door of the cool marble dressing-room.

'I told you I was not to be disturbed,' snapped the Master, knotting the belt of his bathrobe.

Sanjay fell to his knees, a picture of abject terror.

'Forgive me, Master, but it is the English journalist. She is here again and she will not go away.'

'You have told her I will not see her?'

'Yes, Master. Many times. But she will not listen to me. Still she refuses to leave the Embassy.'

'I see.'

Despite his annoyance, the Master was intrigued by this determined young woman's bloody-mindedness. Initially, he had thought of her as a petty annoyance – a minor impediment to be brushed away and ignored. But lately, Sedet had put other thoughts into his head. Might not the woman be of some small use to them? Could they not manipulate her in some way to enhance media coverage of the Master's many triumphs? He was beginning to glimpse the truth of Sedet's words. He came to a decision.

'Tell her that I will see her in my office, for ten minutes only, at four o'clock. If she is not there, she will not have a second opportunity. And Sanjay . . .'

'Yes, Master?'

The Master nodded in the direction of the sunken bath.

'Deal with the girl's body. I have no further use for her.'

Liz Exley sat in the Ambassador's office, hovering between nervousness and excitement. This, at last, was the opportunity she had been waiting for. The chance to get a story that would transform her from an anonymous hack reporter to a world-famous foreign correspondent on a cable-news channel. And maybe more . . .

She still didn't understand why LeMaître had suddenly

changed his mind and decided to see her. After avoiding her and her camera crew for weeks, he'd finally invited her to come and see him. From the information she'd gleaned about LeMaître, he wasn't the type to do anything without a reason – and that made her nervous.

But she wasn't going to let any man – not even a highly attractive man like Anthony LeMaître – intimidate her.

As though activated by her thoughts, the door opened, and in walked LeMaître, cool and suave and elegant in a well-cut grey suit, despite the heat of the day. He gave her a curt nod of greeting, then sat down opposite her, on the other side of his desk.

'You wished to see me.' It was a statement, not a question. 'I shall be interested to hear what you have to say. You have scarcely given me a moment's peace over the last few weeks.'

The Master looked the news reporter up and down with a critical eye. She was a striking woman, no doubt about that. Tall and slim, with cropped blonde hair framing strong features. A powerful athletic body, hard with muscle. Normally the Master did not favour this type of woman but Exley was exceptional. She brimmed with energy and intelligence, and his cock hungered for her.

She returned his gaze unwaveringly, refusing to be intimidated by this arrogant, if handsome, man who seemed so interested in the flimsy Indian cotton fabric of her summer blouse, so thin that dusky pink shadows betrayed the presence of her bare nipples beneath.

'I'm a reporter, Mr LeMaître. It's my job to be a thorn in people's sides. But it doesn't have to be this way.'

'Meaning?' The Master caught the waves of sexual energy pulsing out of the woman and tasted the intoxication of her desire. This woman was hot for him. Perhaps Sedet had been right after all . . .

Liz Exley leant forward over the desk, giving the Master ample opportunity to feast his eyes on her naked breasts, like small firm apples within the thin white blouse.

'We could work together,' she said. 'You're an interesting

character, Mr Ambassador. The folks back home want to know all about you. You could supply me with the stories they want to hear . . .'

'And in return?' The Master was amused by the woman's barefaced cheek. What could she possibly have to offer him?

'In return, I'd make sure they only get hold of the stories you want them to hear.'

Warning bells sounded in the Master's head. The woman was effectively trying to blackmail him! It was amusing really. The poor fool had no idea that her life – or death – rested in his hands. One touch, one kiss . . . and she could be dead. Gone forever, like so many other minor irritants, never to be thought of again. Why tolerate any danger around him – even the minuscule danger presented by this unwary reporter?

And yet . . . Liz Exley was beautiful, intelligent, and she was hot for him. Really hot. He could feel the sex vibrating through her, smell the heady fragrance of her cunt as she grew ever hotter and wetter for him.

She wanted to be fucked and the Master wanted to fuck her. He sure as hell didn't trust her but he was intrigued by her. He wanted to taste the sweet depths of her depravity, and discover how far she would go to assuage her thirst for power.

Yes. Not now, but soon they would fuck, and he would discover the extent of her hunger for the ultimate. She would perhaps prove useful to him in his quest.

If she disappointed him, he could always have her killed.

# 4: Logos

'Sex will bring you power, Andreas. Sex will being us together.'

Andreas Hunt lay helpless and alone in the darkness, and thought over the irony of Mara's words. It was all very well telling him that sex would free him from this living hell, but precisely how was he supposed to get any? The infamous chat-up lines that had got him thrown onto the street by countless irate fathers wouldn't be much help to him here and now.

In any case, where was here? When was now? And was this feeling, this lonely, imprisoned consciousness, still Andreas Hunt?

His thoughts went back to the golden days when Mara had first moved into his flat and they had fucked all day and all night. Her thighs were silken and bronzed around his hips as she knelt astride him, the hardened shaft of his cock sliding smoothly in and out of her cunt. He remembered the moonlight caressing her golden flesh as she rode him to the summit of pleasure, her head thrown back in ecstasy and her long dark hair tumbling in great waves over her full breasts.

Oh God, he missed her, wanted her.

A familiar feeling gripped him: a dizziness like standing on the deck of a ship in the darkness, riding into the eye of the storm. An insistence plucked at him and, with a soundless cry of fear, he felt his soul sucked out of the crystal, into the suddenness of brilliant light and sound.

The sensation was exquisite and for a few moments he lay there, afraid to open his eyes in case this was just another cruel dream, another desperate illusion refracted into his brain by the crystal cage.

His spirit had flesh, unfamiliar but warm and alive; and as he lay motionless amid the soft warmth, another's hands were upon him, stroking, kneading, soothing. He opened his mouth and a little cry of pleasure escaped. Warm moisture now; a slick wetness that cooled as it touched the eager skin, raising goose-pimples on his inner thighs.

'Relax, Andreas. It's me. Relax and let the pleasure overtake you. Let pleasure make you strong.'

Could it be? Could it?

Fighting the heaviness, he forced open his eyelids. As he gazed up through the curtain of auburn hair, into the brilliant green eyes, fear and confusion turned to recognition, to elation . . .

'Mara! Mara, where . . .?'

'Hush, save your strength . . . You're with me; that's all that matters right now. We don't have much time.'

She turned and lay on top of him, taking his penis into the warmth of her mouth. Instantly he felt an electricity enter him, a surge of strength and hunger. He needed her, needed her now. Needed to feed on the raw energy of her sensuality.

Mara lowered her cunt to his mouth and he almost wept at the familiar scent of her, the divine taste of the love-juice that trickled out of her onto his tongue.

Her voice, in his head, whispered to him of hope and freedom.

'Drink my sex, Andreas. Drink it deep. The power of our coupling will give you strength for what lies ahead . . .'

Max Trevidian drank down the vodka in a single draught and refilled the glass from an already half-empty bottle. He wasn't normally a drinking man but this looked like being another long night. He smoothed his hand over a tired, hollow-eyed face. Sooner or later, he was going to have to get some sleep.

The house was in more of a mess than usual, empty coffee cups littered everywhere among the books and papers. Ever since his Aunt Aurelia had died, Max had been the sole occupant of Felsham Manor and that was the way he liked it. Max Trevidian was strictly a loner – he lived alone, worked alone, and – more often than not – drank alone. At any rate, he'd been doing a lot of that lately. He no longer minded the long hours on his own. In his line of work, there was no room for incompetent sidekicks and well-meaning amateurs.

He played back a tape of one of LeMaître's recent telephone calls to the Foreign Office – intercepted quite by chance by a radio ham from a mobile phone. He – or rather his client – had paid a small fortune for that tape, but it offered little help: everything the Ambassador said was too enigmatic, too understated, too careful by half. He sensed something bad in the air, something that just might be the iceberg-tip of a massive conspiracy. But you couldn't operate on hunches, could you? Like Anthony LeMaître, Max Trevidian was a careful man.

Trevidian stared at the cork pinboard on the study wall, trying to derive some sort of inspiration from the jumble of cuttings. Nothing made sense. And one thing bothered him more than anything else. That photograph of LeMaître, shaking hands with the Indian Prime Minister. He knew that face. Hell, he'd even worked with the guy once. That was Andreas Hunt.

So what the hell was going on?

The Master and Sedet disembarked from the train at Vejnapur, a flurry of white-clad bureaucrats bowing and scraping in their wake. The Master was annoyed. This was not as he had planned it. He had private business to transact in Vejnapur. He turned to Takimoto with a wave of the hand.

'Get rid of them.'

Takimoto gave a little bow and relayed the Master's command to the officials via the interpreter. They looked a little crestfallen but a handful of rupees cushioned their disappointment.

The gleaming limousine looked very much out of place

amid the noise and dust of this grubby little corner of South India. But the Master was not interested in the scenery, or in the tedious little lives of the inhabitants of Vejnapur. With a glance at his watch, he slid into the back of the car, grateful for the anonymity of the tinted windows.

'How long until we reach the village?'

Takimoto consulted the map as the chauffeur steered the car out of the tiny goods-yard of the railway station.

'Twenty minutes, maybe twenty-five, Master.'

'Good. I have waited too long for this moment.'

They drove along parched roads that were little more than dirt tracks. Sedet looked at the peasants toiling in the fields and thought of her days in Egypt, when she had been the Master's High Priestess and they had begun their reign of sexual sorcery upon the banks of the Nile.

But the Master was not thinking about Egypt, nor even about his plans for political power. Today was personal – very personal. The Master never forgot a grudge, never neglected to pay back a debt of treachery. In all his years of captivity within the crystal prison, he had never acquired the contemptible habit of forgiveness.

'We are here, Master.'

The limousine swung into the centre of a village – a little larger and more prosperous than most of the villages around here. Fat oxen worked the land and pretty women with sloe-black eyes peered at the Master shyly from the doorways of their shacks.

He ignored them, waving them away with silent irritation. Takimoto would ensure that none of them ventured too close for comfort. There was only one person he had come to meet and he certainly did not require dozens of witnesses to their meeting.

A ramshackle hut stood at the end of a long, winding dirt track, cut off from the rest of the village by a high fence and surrounded by flower garlands. There would be no-one here to observe the historic meeting. Outside the hut, on a bed of nails, lay the fakir Gurandjit, guru of his village and a holy man of many summers. Indeed, it was said that Gurandjit's powers were so great that he had already lived for more than two hundred years.

There were many such stories in India – every village had its ancient holy man who claimed extraordinary mental or occult powers, and longevity beyond the dreams of mortal man. Only the Master knew that, in Gurandjit's case, the stories were true.

Naked save for a white loin-cloth, the fakir's emaciated brown body lay on the bed of nails, the wickedly sharp points hardly seeming even to kiss his flesh. His eyes were closed, as though in sleep or meditation.

'It has been many years since we met.' The Master looked down at the old man and felt all his hatred flooding back. They had met once before, half a century ago. Only this time, the tables were turned. It was Gurandjit who was to be the helpless victim. He did not have the assistance of his treacherous Allied friends to help him here . . .

The old man's eyelids snapped open.

'Who dares address the fakir Gurandjit?'

The Master's lip curled in a cruel sneer.

'You do not recognise me, old man? I found our last meeting rather a memorable one. Let me refresh your memory. There were five of us there: five sorcerers in the dark cellars beneath Winterbourne Hall. And a flawless block of crystal within a granite sarcophagus . . .'

'No . . . it cannot be . . .' The fakir's face grew white with recognition as he struggled to get to his feet. But the Master's powers were stronger now than they had been that night in 1945, when the Allied magicians had imprisoned their adversary in a crystal prison from which they had believed he would never escape.

'You betrayed me, Gurandjit,' hissed the Master. His anger was a tangible force now, pressing down on the fakir's chest with all the strength of his vengeance. 'Did you really believe that I would not one day return to settle our account?'

The fakir squirmed on the bed of nails, unable now either

to move or to breathe. He opened his mouth but no sound came out. His eyes were bulging out of their sockets as he fought for breath; and still the inexorable force was pressing down on his chest.

'Nothing to say for yourself?' A cynical smile twisted the Master's lips. 'Then die!'

Raising his hands above his head, he lowered them very gradually, his clenched fists cutting slowly through the air. As his hands moved downwards, the pressure on the fakir's body grew more intense. The nails were pressing hard on his flesh, their points first denting it then drawing little beads of dark red blood as they broke the surface.

As the Master's hands opened and sliced through the air in a sudden movement, the fakir let out the thin high cry of his death agony. His powers were helpless against the Master's invincible will, and the nails penetrated his flesh and bone, impaling him like a butterfly on a pin.

Without a backward glance, the Master turned and walked back towards the village, suddenly in a very good mood indeed. Perhaps he would indulge himself with a dark-eyed village virgin, piercing her cunt as efficiently as the nails had pierced the unwary flesh of the fakir Gurandjit.

Caít didn't usually visit this part of town, especially not on her own. She didn't know what had come over her. Normally she'd shun these dingy backstreets like the plague, shutting her eyes and ears to the sights and sounds of sleaze.

For this was the tacky, shameless end of town, the part that the sex industry had claimed as its own, where strip-joints rubbed shoulders with sex shops and massage parlours. It was a world that had always terrified and disgusted Caít, but now here she was, walking further and further into this underworld of sex, with a feeling of guilty pleasure hot and strong in her belly.

The ring felt warm and reassuring on her finger. Even since Donal had given it to her, she had been reluctant to take it off. It felt like a part of her now, an element of the living flesh. Without it, she'd feel lost and afraid. It was almost as if the ring was whispering words of encouragement to her as she walked along the cracked pavement.

All eyes were on her but she didn't care. Their appreciation excited her as never before. She had worn her shortest skirt, her tightest T-shirt, her tartiest stilettos; and still she wanted to be more completely the whore to their eyes. She longed to fill them with such uncontrollable lusts that they would want to push her up against the filthy wall and pull up her skirt, fucking her there in broad daylight. And no matter how she cried out to them to stop, they would go on fucking her because they would know the secret which already burned in her belly. She wanted them as much as they wanted her.

This was the shop. She's always avoided it in the past, averting her eyes when Donal had pointed out some of the more extravagant clothes in the window. Fetishwear! Even the sound of the word had made her feel sick.

And now here she was, standing outside the shop and looking into the window as calmly as if it were some ordinary dress shop. Leather, PVC, rubber . . . What would it feel like to be dressed up in leather and chains, to have the kiss of rubber on her soft white skin?

Breathless with excitement, she pushed open the door and stepped into the dimly lit interior.

To her relief, the shop seemed empty. She wandered around for a little while, picking up items and feeling them, running the fabric through her fingers. Black rubber. She felt sure she'd love to be fucked in a black latex bondage suit. Or a leather harness that criss-crossed over the breasts and between the buttocks. But would she ever dare buy anything?

'Can I help you?'

She turned round to see a tall thin girl dressed in a shiny black catsuit and red patent boots. She had spiky black hair and her lips were glossy red, matching the long talons of her fingernails.

'I . . . I'm not sure,' babbled Caít, suddenly ill at ease.

'I see. A beginner. Well, there's nothing to be ashamed of,

you know.' The woman walked over to the shop door and turned the sign around to read 'Closed'. 'There. Now we're all alone and cosy. Just you and me. My name's Kara. I'm here to help, you know. What is it – something a little special?'

Without waiting for a reply, she searched through the racks of clothes and pulled out a tight PVC dress, backless and cut low in the neck, with a long slash from thigh to hem.

'How about this? It would really suit you, with your figure.'

'Well, I don't know . . .'

But Caít was already staring at it with undisguised excitement, imagining its skintight embrace.

'Here, come with me and I'll help you try it on. It can be a little difficult to get into if you're not used to it.'

Caít followed Kara into a changing cubicle, suddenly aware of how attractive the young woman was, her svelte body lithe and desirable within its tight black sheath. She wondered what it would be like to run her fingers over those pert leather-clad breasts . . .

'Now, take your clothes off, sweetheart – yes that's right, *all* your clothes. This dress is just so unforgiving, I can't tell you!'

Kara's hands were on her back – cool, gentle fingertips lingering too long on the warm flesh as they sought the catch of Caít's bra. They released the hook and eye and the elastic sprang away. A cool, cool palm massaged Caít's bare back, then smoothed down to the waistband of her little cotton panties.

'Off with these too, I think,' breathed Kara as she gently tugged down the panties, revealing Caít's timorous backside, round and juicy and inviting. 'Don't be shy,' she murmured as she planted the first of many kisses on the creamy globes of Caít's buttocks, making her shiver with delicious guilty pleasure. 'Just relax.'

It was the strangest thing. Caít suddenly realised that she *wasn't* shy, or afraid, or embarrassed. Not in the least. She was hot, pulsating with the powerful, irresistible need for sex. The red dress was completely forgotten now, all she wanted was for Kara to go on making passionate love to her with those skilful, unforgettable fingers.

But Kara had other, more ambitious plans.

'Turn around,' she breathed. 'I want to kiss you.'

Caít obeyed like an automaton, programmed now only to respond to sex. Sex was all she wanted, needed, desired. She didn't care where it came from or what form it took.

Pressing her face against the glossy brown triangle of hairs between Caít's thighs, Kara wriggled her tongue between the plump love-lips with practised skill. The pleasure was unbelievable. Already her cunt was dripping with a flood of sweet slippery love-juice that begged to be lapped up by Kara's willing tongue. She had never known excitement like it. It was like the revelation of a whole new world of sensual pleasure. Never, never had Donal made her feel like this.

The pleasure was so intense that Caít gasped and flinched for a moment but Kara held her fast.

'Relax. Just relax and enjoy it. And afterwards, you can suck me off . . .'

New Delhi sweltered under an unforgiving sun, a brassy heat-haze floating over everything like a sickly yellow cloud.

The tatty cinema stood in a cluttered side street off Chandni Chowk, hemmed in by signs proclaiming 'Vijay Deluxe Suitings and Shirtings', 'Palika Bazaar' and 'Rama Pharmacy for Health, Vigour and Vitality'. Gaudy posters of matinee idol Shri Radhna and his latest leading ladies were plastered over the peeling exterior like mismatched patches on an old dhoti.

Even on this suffocatingly hot afternoon, the cinema was packed to the doors. Rich and poor, high and low caste alike had crowded in to view the first showing of *Divine Splendour of Krishna*, Shri Radhna's new feature film. The audience were packed in like sardines but there was no tension, only a happy holiday atmosphere.

It was strange how, after the first reel, the mood changed abruptly. Sultry heat turned to suffocating humidity, light-hearted banter to open irritation and, in the eyes of some, simple friendship began its transformation into lust . . .

Within the space of ten minutes, the first breath of tension had erupted into full-scale riot. The cinema manager looked on in helpless horror as men and women tore at each others' clothes, desperate to assuage this new hunger that had overwhelmed them so suddenly.

Up in the projectionist's booth, the Master roared with laughter as he watched his victims fuck like helpless puppets, their bodies shaken with spasms of desire they could no more control than stop breathing. In a few minutes' time, when he had had his fill of the spectacle, he would perhaps go down into the auditorium and quell the riot. But then again, perhaps he would let it take its natural course. It made such a pretty picture. It diverted him most agreeably to see that straightlaced high-caste virgin being so beautifully sodomised by the old man, whilst his companion thrust his cock into her tight little rosebud mouth.

He turned to his companion.

'So far you have done well, Takimoto. I think the Logos system is at last ready for its first real trial.'

He felt good, better and stronger than he had ever done. Nothing, but nothing, could stop him now. With a growl of satisfaction, he turned back to Sedet, still on her knees before him. Prising apart the smooth, golden globes of her arse-cheeks, the thrust his tool into her glorious bottom like a piston into a well-greased cylinder.

Tomorrow, he would ring Heimdal and tell him of the new plans. Instruct him that the faithful of Winterbourne must begin to prepare for power. The empire of lust was closer now than it had ever been.

'For fuck's sake, Geoffrey, not now!'

Heimdal's patience snapped as Geoffrey Potter pestered him for the umpteenth time that morning about the new Japanese girls Takimoto had brought over from Kyoto.

'But you said I could have them when you'd finished with them. My sexual energy levels are low – I'm tired of fucking the same stale old whores. If you won't let me have them, I'll go out and get myself a juicy little virgin with fat tits . . .'

Heimdal sighed and counted to ten.

'It's too dangerous. You can't go round just fucking whoever you like, can't you get that into your thick head? The Master has a spotless reputation to protect. Cross him and you'll know the meaning of the word pain.'

'Then why can't I have the Japanese girls? Just for one night?'

'I've already told you, you idiot. Cheviot and Montgomery are coming back from India on a flying visit soon. They have been working hard for our Master and will be tired. I have to have something fresh and new to offer their jaded palates.'

'So when . . .?'

'You may have the girls when they have finished with them. Now shut up and go away.'

Geoffrey left reluctantly, casting resentful glances at the temporary master of Winterbourne. Really, thought Heimdal, that boy is just too much trouble. He didn't like to question the Master's judgement, but why on earth had he bothered with Potter? True, he had had his uses in luring the stupid white witch Mara to her doom, but Potter was scarcely worthy of his position among the elect. He would have to have a word with the Master about discipline.

Heimdal was feeling jaded: he needed sex. More specifically, he needed the Dubois slut. But she was away on business – the Master's business; ensnaring herself an unwary bishop, no less. In the months since he had become master of ceremonies at Winterbourne, Heimdal had seen a new dimension to the Dubois girl. To begin with, he had thought of her as an empty-headed bimbo: a whore whose only use lay in the manipulation of her delectable body. But he had come to glimpse new depths within her; depths of sensuality that almost reminded him of . . . Mara.

But Mara was dead and he was glad. Whilst she'd been alive, she had been nothing but trouble to him, overshadowing his psychic powers. Now that she was gone, and the Master had done him the supreme honour of admitting him to the ranks of the undead, he had truly come into his own. And the Dubois girl had a proper respect for him. It was plain to see the adoration in her eyes as she sucked his cock or took him into her devilishly tight little cunt.

His penis throbbed as he remembered last night, when the slut had come to his bed with Joanna Königsberg. All night long they had fucked – and how he had stiffened with pleasure as he watched the Dubois whore licking out Joanna's pert little arsehole! How he had spurted his come all over those creamy buttocks!

And she had hardened him again in an instant, sucking him to the point of ecstasy, and toying with his jade cock-ring far more skilfully than Mara had ever done. She knew just how to drive him crazy with lust, nipping the sensitive flesh of his glans with her sharp little teeth before taking the whole length of his shaft down her capacious throat. Yes, she was a useful little slut. The Master had shown shrewd judgement in appointing her his sexual emissary.

In a few days' time, Winterbourne would once again host one of its famous orgies: secret gatherings to which only the beautiful, the powerful or the influential could hope for an invitation. Gatherings which would begin in pleasure and end in delicious death for so many . . .

Heimdal lay down on the bed and took out his cock, admiring its massive size in the huge ceiling mirror above him. He liked to pump his shaft whilst he watched; it gave him a huge hard-on and a real thrill when the pearly spunk spurted out of him. He liked it even better when one of Winterbourne's skilled whores was wanking him – or, better still, squeezing his dick between her big soft breasts.

As he stroked himself into huge yearning hardness, the door opened and in came Royston Birbridge IV, captain of industry and now one of the Master's most trusted henchmen. Heimdal turned his head towards the newcomer but did not stop wanking.

'What is it now? Can't I have a moment's peace without somebody wanting me for something?'

'Sorry to bother you,' replied Royston, 'but there is a message from the Master.'

Heimdal sat up, suddenly alert.

'Tell me. Quickly.'

'Logos is to take place the day after tomorrow, in New Delhi. Success is assured.'

A smile spread across Heimdal's face.

'Excellent. Was there anything else?'

'Only one thing more.'

Royston disappeared for a moment, talking to someone standing behind him.

'Hurry along, Mr Heimdal does not have all day.'

He reappeared a moment later.

'The Master has sent you a gift,' he explained. 'With his compliments. He hopes it will not disappoint you.'

He flung the girl into the room with such violence that she fell to her knees before Heimdal, her diaphanous sari parting to reveal perfect golden-brown skin, still marked here and there from the bite of Sedet's whiplash.

As Heimdal tore off her flimsy robe and feasted his eyes on her delicious, childlike nakedness, his cock grew so painfully stiff that he knew he would have to have her now – again and again. She was a real beauty: her skin a silky, creamy beige, and her breasts pert and juicy as sap-filled buds. She was looking up at him, wide-eyed and trembling, and the scent of her fear made him rampant with desire.

'On your knees, girl,' he commanded, picking up a supple birch rod and dealing her a stinging slap across the back and buttocks. 'And swiftly! It is time for you to honour me with your body.'

Mara felt deeply uncomfortable, unease stretching her nerves to breaking point as she scanned the rows of bookshelves. As a white witch, this was definitely not the sort of bookshop she would have chosen to frequent, but if she was to have a chance of outwitting the Master she must learn to fight fire with fire.

She ran her eye along the top shelf, skimming the dusty, leather-bound titles: *Ars Magica, The Necromancy of Abra-Melin, Black Magic Rites and Rituals* . . . Could any of these be of use to her? There had to be something here that could help her to free Andreas.

'Can I help you, miss?'

The dry, croaky voice made her start and when she turned round she found herself confronted by a thin, stooped man in a rusty black suit. He looked about a thousand years old and every bit as unsavoury as the literature he purveyed.

'Can I help you?' he repeated. 'Is there perhaps something . . . special you're looking for?'

Mara swallowed hard, fighting back the impulse to flee. It had taken her long enough to track down this backstreet shop and she wasn't going to run off like a frightened schoolgirl menaced by a tramp.

'Do you stock anything on . . .?' She couldn't say it.

The spectral figure shuffled closer, until his face was almost up against hers. She recoiled as she registered the leprous scales of his white skin, the trail of spittle hanging from his pendulous lower lip.

'Anything on what, my dear?' There was something obscene about that voice, about those watery blue eyes that lingered too long on the crests of her nipples, bobbing unfettered beneath her skintight T-shirt.

'On . . . on vampirism.'

It sounded so weird, comical even. The old man probably thought she was some bimbo horror-freak who liked to dress up in black and get screwed in graveyards. How could he even begin to comprehend the horrible truth?

But he wasn't laughing at her. He was pressing up against her, forcing her back against the bookshelves as he spewed his hot, sweet-sour breath into her face.

'Ah yes, vampirism. Darkest of all the black arts. A sweet sensual infection of the blood that kills and yet preserves.' He leered and pressed his cadaverous body against her breasts. 'Small wonder it should hold such appeal for a beautiful woman like you.'

Mara struggled to steer the conversation away from such dangerous waters.

'Have you anything? It's rather urgent, you see. I need the books today . . .'

He wasn't listening. Dumbstruck, she stood rooted to the spot as the bookseller calmly pulled up her T-shirt, exposing the perfect globes of her breasts. His hand felt hot and sweaty on her flesh and she wanted to wrestle free of him; but there was a horrible fascination in his touch as he weighed and kissed her breasts.

'So cool, so very smooth and cool,' he murmured, running his tongue appreciatively over the bare flesh. His gaze flickered upwards and for a moment she found herself gazing into the alarmingly steady gaze of those rheumy blue eyes. 'So cool . . . not quite like living flesh . . .'

For an instant Mara felt her blood freeze with terror. Could this man really have glimpsed the truth about her? Could he possibly have guessed . . .?

No, don't be silly; of course he couldn't. She was just imagining it.

'I have some special titles in the back room,' hissed the old man, pressing so close to her now that she could feel the outline of his hardening penis against her belly. 'If you come with me, I could show them to you.'

His bony fingers were hitching up her skirt little by little, pushing aside the gusset of her silk panties and insinuating themselves into the warm, wet cavern of her womanhood. He was repulsive and yet it was so hard to resist, so hard to turn away from the promise of sex and the new strength that it would bring.

*No. No. Mustn't let him fuck me. There's an evil within him and it's already spreading through me like cold black water. Rising, rising, trying to drown me . . .*

His fingers worked inside her, tormenting her into unwilling

71

pleasure, melting away her resistance like the heat from some dark sun.

A sound broke the spell, the quiet click of some small machine. Pushing the old man away, Mara looked around her. Nothing. And then, between the shelves, she saw him. A youngish, rather unremarkable man with wavy brown hair, half-hidden in the shadows, a hand-held tape recorder to his lips.

Their eyes met for a second and she saw the mixture of fear and lust in his gaze. He was staring at her bare breasts, the creased skirt pulled up high on her thighs, revealing creamy buttocks imperfectly veiled by coffee-coloured silk and lace. For that split-second moment, she looked at him and wondered . . .

But she must not stay. This was a bad place, a place of danger and fear. Swiftly adjusting her T-shirt and skirt, Mara wrenched open the door of the bookshop and escaped with a sigh of relief into the cool clear air of a late spring morning.

New Delhi was sweltering under a steel-blue sky. On the Boat Club lawns outside the government buildings, the mood of the crowd was turning increasingly mutinous. The Chief of Police sweated and cursed as he barked out emergency instructions to turbaned riot cops with batons and guns. One false move and what had started off as a peaceful protest meeting could turn into yet another bloodfest of sex and violence.

He couldn't understand it. There seemed no obvious reason for it – any of it. Over the last few days, there had been an alarming escalation of violent disorder in and around the city – a riot at a downtown cinema; rapes, murders and abductions at a series of mosques and Hindu temples; obscene and bloody orgies of sexual anarchy in the most public and sacred places. No-one could understand why it was happening here and now. And, without a cause, how were they going to find a solution?

Much to the annoyance of the Indian establishment, it

seemed that there was only one man in the whole of India with any ability to calm the violence. Indeed, it was increasingly being said that if it was not for the skilful intervention of the British Ambassador, LeMaître, the entire city would be in the chaotic grip of an indisciplined and lustful mob.

From her seat in the press box, Liz Exley looked down on the seething mass of discontent beneath her. What had looked like an unpromising freelance assignment in India was fast turning into the sort of lucky break that could turn her into a media star overnight. All this sex and violence might be hell for the Indian government, but it certainly wasn't doing her career any harm. And with a little extra help from Anthony LeMaître . . .

Not long to wait now, she would be seeing him tonight for dinner, and she flattered herself that no man could keep information a secret from her for long. She had seen the way he'd looked at her that afternoon at the Embassy, undressing her with those grey-green eyes of his, imagining what it would be like to have his hands on her tits and his dick up her arse. Well, Liz Exley was no fool, no poor little ingénue. She knew how to dress to please a man. Maybe to ensnare a man, too. And it sure as hell wouldn't be any hardship. She was looking forward to luring Mr So-clever LeMaître into her bed – and she didn't think he'd take too much persuading.

The crowd was moving slowly together now, a rippling mass of multicoloured flags and headscarves. They didn't seem to be paying any attention to the speaker or to the wall of video screens relaying his message across the lawns. What was it that they were chanting? Some weird, meaningless mantra that had them glassy-eyed and swaying together like flowers in the wind. The low moaning was tense, unnatural, unsettling. Liz leant forward in her seat, her heart beating faster as she watched the tension gather like black clouds before a storm. She'd seen this happen before. It couldn't be long now.

Suddenly a woman cried out; hands were tearing at her clothes, stripping her naked in the sunshine, and she was falling, falling. Bodies were tumbling over each other, and the air was full of the cries and scents of sex as men and women fell upon their fellows, their minds filled with only one thought: the desperate need to fuck.

On the makeshift stage, a woman was sitting astride a naked man, riding up and down on his cock, her mouth open in screams of laughter and lust. In front of her stepped a second man and in an instant his dick was stuffed firmly down her eager throat. On a dozen video screens the unholy trinity fucked for the glory of their unknown Master. It would make great TV news footage.

Excitement coursed through Liz's veins as she flicked on the microphone and began the commentary.

'This is Liz Exley, KBC News, reporting from New Delhi. Rioting broke out again this afternoon on the Boat Club lawns . . .'

If she stuck around long enough, maybe LeMaître would turn up right on cue to do his Seventh Cavalry routine. It was getting to be quite a habit, she'd noticed. That was something she'd have to ask him about once she'd got him between the sheets . . .

'Harder, harder!'

Mara raised the whip again and brought it snarling down upon her victim's back. He flinched in pain as the tip bit into his bruised and broken flesh but Mara knew that, for Stig Halvessohn, only the most acute pain would bring pleasure. Already his dick was swollen with desire, its purple head slippery with delicious sex-fluid that Mara longed to taste.

But this encounter was about Halvessohn's pleasure, not hers. Her task was use his perverse desires to lure him to Winterbourne. And use them she would, if only for her own self-preservation. How he'd panted for her when he saw her in the tight black leather basque, his tongue hanging out like some pathetic dewy-eyed mongrel. How he'd begged her to let him kiss her spike-heeled boots, crying out with pleasure when she had kicked him away and ground the point of her heel into the back on his hand.

She looked down at him as he squirmed at her feet and felt only the merest shred of pity for him. She had read the papers and knew he was the kind of guy who wasn't happy unless he'd evicted fourteen widows before breakfast. You couldn't feel pity for evil. The Master was welcome to this future disciple.

She whipped him harder, now investing in each blow the full weight of her own resentment and pain. Victory would come but victory was slow – and Andreas seemed so distant and unattainable.

No, she didn't feel pity for this creature, but what she did feel were the first stirrings of lust. As Halvessohn moaned and writhed under the torments of the lash, Mara slipped her fingers inside her knickers and began wanking herself to the rhythm of the sweet torture.

Her cunt was wet and her fingers slid easily across the erect bud of her clitoris, its hypersensitive head swelling out of its protective hood.

As she brought the whip down once more, she heard Halvessohn cry out and felt him shudder as his spunk jetted out of him in hot white spurts. Seconds later she too was quivering with pleasure, molten ecstasy dripping out of her and down the insides of the sleek white thighs.

She turned Halvessohn's prone body over with the tip of her boot and he stared up at her, glass-eyed in the aftermath of pleasure. He clutched weakly at her foot as she passed, but she pushed him aside, knowing how her cruelty excited him. The more excited he was, the more likely he would be to take up the Master's invitation. As she walked across the room to the door, his white, bloodless lips opened and closed feebly, 'Perhaps we shall meet again . . .?'

She turned back to him and spoke a single word. A command.

'Winterbourne.'

# 5: The Hunger

It had to be a dream. *Oh God, let it be a dream . . .*

Caít ran on, lungs aching as she gasped for air. The heat was terrible, infernal, and she longed to stop for a moment just to catch her breath; but the voice in her head told her that she must ran faster, ever faster, or she would never escape.

What was she running from? She could not quite recall but the fear was there within her and somewhere in the back of her mind she could still hear the footsteps close behind. Or was that just the thunderous pounding of her heart?

The tropical heat was suffocating and wet, moisture dripping onto her from every leaf she brushed against as she clawed her way through the dense vegetation. Was she imagining it or was the jungle closing in on her, striving to capture her in its deadly embrace?

Steam and sweat poured off her and she could smell the hot sweet spicy smell of her own cunt, intoxicating and overpowering. There was no escaping the need in her. And perhaps that was what she was really running away from – the need within her own belly.

The overwhelming need to fuck.

She stumbled on through the jungle, the sound of her pursuer's footsteps still echoing in her head. And she thought she heard the sound of mocking laughter close behind.

Her clitoris was pulsating in time to the rhythm of her heartbeat; faster now, faster and harder. She thought she would die if she could not fuck and release the terrible pain of tension that shook her body like a rag doll.

Breathless and weeping with exhaustion, she crashed through the vegetation and found herself at the edge of a wide, coursing river. The sound of her own breathing and the pounding of footsteps whirled round and round in her head as she gazed down at the foaming white waters.

Trapped, and not daring to turn back, Caít leapt into the river with a cry of anguish and ecstasy. And the waters closed over her as though she had never been . . .

Waking with a start, Caít rolled over and saw Donal asleep by her side. At one time, his constant sexual demands had disgusted her. Now she looked at him and felt a familiar hunger gnawing at her belly – a hunger which Donal O'Keefe was scarcely able to satisfy. How could just one insignificant man satisfy this need within her which was so powerful?

And yet the need was here and now; and, here and now, Donal was all she had.

She peeled away the duvet, exposing the golden tan of his muscular shoulders and back. He sighed in his sleep as she ran her eager tongue over his naked flesh, but did not wake. She would have to use some other means to rouse him.

Rolling him onto his back, she planted kisses on his shoulders, his chest, his belly. Growing bolder now, she fastened her lips on the tip of his cock. Semi-erect even in sleep, it responded instantly to her touch, and she smiled to herself as she began fellating him with insistent lips and tongue.

Where had she learned such skill? She couldn't begin to know. Donal was the only man she'd ever had. And she'd certainly never had any interest in oral sex – much to Donal's chagrin. But now . . . It was as though someone older, wiser, wickeder was inside her head, whispering new thoughts into her brain, showing her new and exciting things to do with her body. And Donal's . . .

He murmured and his eyelids flickered open, blinking in the half-light of the oncoming dawn.

'What . . .? Was I dreaming? For a minute, I thought . . .'

Then Donal saw Caít's red lips closing round his cock and

realised to his amazement that this was no dream. This
sensation was delicious – better than he'd ever had it, even
from the classy whore he'd sometimes paid when the band
were flush with money and randy with some paltry success.
Much more of this, he thought, and I'll be shooting my load
right down her pure little virgin throat. If I do that, she'll
never forgive me.

'Cait? What's come over you? I thought you hated . . .'

She took her lips from his cock, just for a fleeting moment,
and instantly he regretted his words.

'No, don't stop!'

She smiled.

'It's all right, Donal, I'm not going to. I'm going to take
your cock in my mouth and I'm going to suck you dry. And
when I've done that, you can kiss my cunt for me. And when
you've done that . . .'

'What?'

She laughed.

'We'll start all over again.'

The horses thundered down the final furlong in a flurry of
dusty earth and gaudy silks. Mara sat at a table in the
Members' Enclosure, not really interested in the races. She
sipped at her drink, trying not to appear too obvious as she
watched a group of Hooray Henries and their buck-toothed
girlfriends throwing champagne over each other.

In the centre of the group was the man she was interested
in. Nick Weatherall, MP, favoured son of the landed classes,
glamour boy of the Nationalist opposition, and utter dimwit.

He was good-looking, you couldn't deny that. Tall, dark-
haired, with deep blue eyes to die for and a drop-dead-
gorgeous bum. Good dress sense, too, and rumour had it he
was hung like a stallion. You didn't sleep with Nick Weatherall
if you wanted intelligent conversation, but if you wanted a
thorough shagging . . .

Everyone knew Weatherall had only won the Chester
South seat because his father had been MP before him, and

the farming community round here were somewhere to the right of Genghis Khan. You could put up a talking chimp and the punters would vote for it, just as long as it was wearing a blue rosette.

In himself, Weatherall was harmless enough scum – an unpleasant little git, certainly, but he didn't have the brains to think up anything dangerous. But as the obedient mouthpiece of whoever was pulling his strings, Weatherall could be an extremely useful weapon. Women, in particular, adored him and Weatherall was always happy to oblige if the party Whips wanted some troublesome bluestocking bringing to heel.

Better still, Weatherall was rich. Extremely rich. When his father died – and rumour had it that that might not be too far in the future – young Nick would inherit the entire Weatherall fortune which included not just several hundred thousand acres of prime English countryside but the merchant banking business, too. Already, Nick Weatherall had taken control of most of the other family businesses. Nobody knew for sure but it was rumoured that, between them, the Weatheralls were the richest men in Britain.

So whoever got to pull young Nick's strings was sure of a rich reward: money, connections, a voice at the heart of the British Parliament. Little surprise then that the Master was so determined to play puppetmaster.

Mara sat and watched Weatherall. He really is a prize prat, she thought. Just look at him, spraying the front of that girl's dress with champagne. And what is she doing? Pelting him with chocolate mousse. Mara sighed. It seemed such a waste. Weatherall was a hollow shell of a man: divine to look at, no doubt great to screw but with nothing between the ears. The man was slime, too. A total waste of a great body.

*If only it could be Andreas behind those deep blue eyes. Andreas's cynical smile on those perfectly formed lips.* Mara sighed and sank back into her chair, imagining what it would be like if Andreas turned up here at Chester Races and fucked her in the Members' Enclosure. That was the sort of joke Andreas would enjoy.

She ought to make a move. She was only too grimly aware that she had a job to do. A job for the Master. To seduce Weatherall's body and then seduce his mind – such as it was.

She got up and walked over to the rail, close to Weatherall and his cronies. He surely couldn't fail to notice her in the dramatic black-and-white suit, cut so low in the neck and so high in the thigh that she'd had to bribe the stewards to let her in.

Without even looking behind her, she could feel his eyes on her, following her to the rail and staring at the curve of her backside as she took out her binoculars and pretended to scan the track. His was a pathetically weak intellect and oh so easy for her psychic sense to penetrate. In any case, her senses were so heightened now that she could visualise him without even trying; his eyes round with lust and his mouth sagging open as his gaze travelled down from her glossy knot of auburn hair to the black-and-white skirt stretched alluringly across her buttocks as she bent forward. Was he wondering what colour knickers she was wearing under that short, short skirt? Of course he was. She grinned to herself as she wondered how he'd react when he realised she wasn't wearing any.

'I . . . er, excuse me, miss – I think you dropped this.'

It might not be very original but it worked every time. Mind you, Weatherall wasn't much of a challenge. Mara turned round and accepted the proffered handkerchief with a smile.

'Thank you, I didn't realise.'

Weatherall smiled and she saw him swallow. A practised womaniser and here she was, making him nervous! She wanted to giggle but instead returned his gaze steadily, smoothing imaginary creases out of her blouse with knowing fingers.

'Hi – my name's Weatherall – Nick Weatherall. Bet you fancy having a drink with me, eh?'

Mara felt more like telling him to go screw himself but smiled sweetly and accepted a hearty pat on the backside. He might be a blockhead but he certainly was one helluva good-looking guy, mused Mara, as she allowed herself to be led over to a secluded table and accepted a brimming glass of champagne. So he was hoping to get her drunk. He'd wait a long time.

Weatherall babbled on about his constituency and Mara noticed that his many hangers-on had all retreated to a discreet distance, no doubt familiar with their beloved leader's line in seduction. She smiled at all his prattle, then slid her hand across the table and laid it on top of his.

He was so astonished by the gesture that he stopped in mid-sentence and stared at her.

'I say . . . am I boring you? Can't have that, can we?'

Mara shook her head.

'Oh no, not at all. It's just that . . . well, I've been longing to meet you for such a long time, Mr Weatherall . . .'

'Call me Nick.'

'. . . and I wondered if maybe we could go somewhere quieter to get to know each other a bit better . . .'

She moistened her lips with the tip of her tongue and saw a little shiver of anticipation pass through Weatherall's body. His mind was like glass to her now. She saw a swirling mass of colours – the purple and red and gold of desire, patterns she had once seen in the mind of Andreas Hunt. She remembered the time in the library when she had fucked him on the hard wooden floor. Their minds had been one, that day. As his cock pumped in and out of her willing belly, she had been bathed in the colours of their coupling – a sumptuous richness that grew to a cascade of sparking light as they reached orgasm together.

And now Weatherall was hot for her. So hot, she could feel the desire pulsating to the rhythm of his heartbeat. It would be so simple just to kneel before him, here on the grass, and suck him off. And she thirsted so for the taste of his spunk on her tongue – the electrifying surge of passion as her own orgasm overtook her.

Without taking her eyes from Weatherall's, she slipped her hand between the pearl buttons of her blouse and stroked her nipple gently. She was already so aroused that it grew instantly hard at her touch, pressing against the sheer white fabric.

Weatherall gave a gasp as his eyes travelled downwards to Mara's hard insistent nipples, the dark circles of the areolae clearly visible through the thin blouse. There could be no misunderstanding.

Mara touched his hand again. Raising it to her lips and kissing it, she took each of his fingers in turn into the warm cavern of her mouth, and so exquisite was the sensation that Weatherall felt as though it was his cock her lips and tongue were teasing. Just the sight of her lips closing on his fingers was enough to make him come in his pants . . .

She released his hand and smiled.

'You understand? Somewhere a little . . . quieter. We don't want to be disturbed, do we?'

'N-no. Of course not. Just a mo, while I get the bill.'

Red-faced and sweating, Weatherall clicked his fingers and a waiter appeared from nowhere, no sign on his expressionless face to suggest that he had seen what had just happened. But Mara could see the twitching outline of his cock beneath those respectable black trousers and on a sudden impulse she reached out a hand and stroked his crotch as he passed. To her disappointment, he didn't drop the tray he was carrying but she felt him tremble as her fingers brushed the rock-hard shaft of his penis.

Weatherall took out his wallet and peeled off a handful of banknotes, tossing them onto the silver tray. The waiter raised an eyebrow at the pile of tens and twenties.

'Keep the change.'

Weatherall got to his feet.

'Shall we go? I think I know a place . . .'

At that moment, a figure appeared from the crowd: a tall, distinguished man with just a touch of grey at the temples. The family resemblance was obvious.

'Nick—'

'Father! I'm rather busy at the moment. We're just about to . . .'

'Yes, I can see that.' Weatherall senior looked Mara up and down with an appreciative eye. 'But I'm afraid you'll have to cancel your plans for now – I had a call from the Party Chairman five minutes ago, on the car phone. Seems there's some trouble he needs you to sort out. Must be bloody desperate if you're the best he's got, that's all I can say.'

Weatherall turned to Mara with an apologetic sigh.

'I really am so sorry. If you're going to be here later in the week, maybe we could . . . Look, here's my business card. Call me – I like a girl with a bit of spirit . . .'

A moment later he was gone, his long lean limbs striding away across the paddock to his father's black Bentley.

Feeling irritated and desperately frustrated, Mara drowned the last of the champagne in a single draught and wandered back to the rail to watch the horses come down the home straight. It was one of the major races of the day and other people also got up from their seats and came over to watch, pushing each other forward in their efforts to see what was going on.

One of the bodies pressed against her with greater insistence than the others. At first Mara thought the contact was accidental, but then she felt a hand on her backside, smoothing across the flesh, easing up the hem of her short skirt.

She could have wriggled free but why should she? Her whole body was crying out for the sexual contact that would restore and revive her. She was an addict now and she needed a fix. She pressed back gently against the hand and shivered with delight as it pulled up her skirt in a single, swift movement – then discovered the wicked secret of the naked buttocks beneath.

'Little slut,' a hoarse voice whispered in her ear. 'You're begging for it, aren't you? Well, I'm not one to disappoint a lady.'

Both of his hands were on her buttocks now and her body was singing with a physical hunger that made her want to cry out loud: *Fuck me, take me, do whatever you will* . . .

She clung onto the rail, the horses now thundering past in

a multicoloured blur. All she could see were the swirling patterns of desire – her own and the nameless lover who was even now parting her buttocks with his strong fingers, pressing a fingertip into her forbidden gate.

Two fingers in her arse, and she thought she would die for the need of him. *Give me more, more,* she begged in silent need. *I want you in my arse and my cunt and my mouth! I want you to spurt your seed all over me and make me drink it down until my belly overflows with your come . . .*

Seconds later, his cock was in her, sliding into her in a single rapier-thrust that left her gasping. He was strong and assertive and, as he grabbed hold of her hips and pulled her onto his prick, she settled easily into the rhythm of his fucking.

There were people all around her – behind and to the sides of her. She wondered which of them could see what was happening and how many more had guessed what was going on right next to them. In this tightly packed crowd, you could even feel your neighbours' breathing. Could they feel her fucking? Did it make them feel good to press up against her naked flanks as her unseen lover's cock thrust in and out of her, like a well-greased piston rod?

'I'm going to make you come, you sweet little whore,' breathed the man as he fucked her, his fingers still toiling deep inside her arse. 'Your cunt's good and wet, but I'm going to make it a lot wetter before I'm finished . . .'

She longed to cry out, to give voice to the pleasure that was washing over her like mighty ocean breakers on a beach. But she must keep silent. No-one must know the secret of this guilty, delicious, unforgettable fucking.

Her orgasm overtook her so suddenly that she could not suppress a little sigh. Sinking down onto the rail in the last paroxysms of pleasure, she heard a distant voice ask if she was all right. A moment later, she felt her lover's cock twitching as he shot his load deep inside her belly.

'You're a good fuck, little tart. Maybe we'll do it again sometime.'

As he withdrew from her and melted away into the crowd, she glanced back over her shoulder. The grey-flecked hair and Savile Row suit were unmistakable. Of course, she'd known all along that it was Nick Weatherall's father.

Well, the father had seemed well satisfied with their little interlude. Maybe next time she'd succeed in seducing the son.

Max Trevidian bit into a cheese sandwich and clicked off the television set, cutting off Liz Exley's breathless commentary in full flight. So it was happening again – more trouble in India. Another riot – this one so steamy it should have been X-rated. One minute, fifteen million people were watching a perfectly innocent lottery ticket being drawn, the next, they were spilling out into the streets, tearing off each other's clothes and fighting and fucking, fucking, fucking . . .

Why was it all happening? He didn't know. But he'd take money on Anthony LeMaître having something to do with it. If not, why was he invariably hovering about somewhere in the background, ready to step in and take all the credit for pouring oil on troubled waters? Trevidian scratched his head. It sure was weird – the Indians couldn't get enough of the guy. What was it they were calling him now? 'The Saviour of India', that was it. Instead of saying what a wonderful job he was making of calming down all these riots, maybe they ought to be asking themselves who was causing them – and why.

He hauled himself out of his chair and went across to the map he'd stuck on the back of the door. Already it was bristling with coloured panel pins. He ran through the list again: Chesterton, Henley, Hackman, Endsleigh, Halvessohn . . .

Who next? He picked up a yellow-headed pin and stuck it in the map, mouthing the name silently: Derek Manley.

Mara turned off the television set and smoothed back her long auburn hair. So many scandals, so many dangers; and all the Master's doing. The Master's powers were growing, and what was she doing? She was helping him!

What horrible twist of fate had brought her to this? Why . . .? And then she remembered why. Remembered that night, in the cellars of Winterbourne Hall, when the Master's soul had overpowered her will and guided the crystal dagger she held into the heart of Andreas Hunt.

Now she could never rest. Never give up until she had righted the wrong that she had done.

The books she had been reading did not contain the answers she was looking for. No simple ritual of exorcism would break the sorcery that held Andreas captive, or destroy the ancient evil that was the Master.

And his Queen. Mara looked into the mirror above her dressing table and thought of Sedet's sly smiling face; the violet eyes that had once shone with the light of truth, now clouded by the evil spirit that lurked behind them. Sedet was a danger to her and to Andreas, she knew that. Perhaps more of a danger than the Master himself, now so puffed up with his own self-importance that he had not even bothered to look into the mind of the Dubois slut who had lately grown so much more . . . versatile.

It was obvious that Sedet still did not trust her. Over the centuries of her captivity, the woman had developed occult powers which, whilst by far inferior to those of the Master, complemented them perfectly. He was intellectual, incisive, practical; she was intuitive, ingenious – and consummately cruel. Sedet's powers were great, but Mara's were greater. Thus far, she had not succeeded in seeing into Mara's soul, but Mara knew she would not rest until she had succeeded.

Mara had witnessed the depths of Sedet's cruelty and felt fear: real, tangible fear that gnawed at her belly like a captive rat. Sedet liked her victims to linger. She had them captured on the streets of London or Paris or Calcutta – it mattered not, so long as they were young and beautiful and afraid. Then they were taken to the Hall of Darkness, the torture chamber she had had built in one of the abandoned cellars, where she stripped and beat them and hung them like sides of meat from hooks on the walls and ceiling. All were young and strong. Those who showed most defiance suffered the most and gave Sedet the greatest satisfaction – filling her with the sexual energy which she believed would make her invincible. It could take a long, long time to break a man's spirit.

On one such night, Mara had been present when Sedet took her pleasure. Her victim had been a young man – a Norwegian boy Heimdal had found sleeping rough in a Soho street. He was blond and beautiful, with smooth golden skin sprinkled with flaxen hairs.

How Sedet had laughed at the boy's pain and at his thwarted desire as he hung helplessly from the wooden X-frame and was forced to watch his cruel mistress fucking on the hard stone floor.

The swarthy body of the servant Gonzales was covered with little beads of sweat as his backside moved up and down, meeting Sedet's rhythmic thrusts as her pelvis rose to take him deeper, deeper into her silken cunt. The boy was weeping with frustration – Madam LeCoeur's subtle aphrodisiacs had ensured that there would be no escape for him from the lust which shook his poor captive body.

Sedet was on her hands and knees now, full firm breasts pendulous and heavy, the swell of her golden backside as tempting as twin golden apples. She tossed her dark hair and laughed; and as her scarlet lips parted, the boy glimpsed her teeth, perfect white and oh-so-sharp.

She looked up at the boy, limbs stretched painfully on the frame. His head was caught in a metal harness that prevented him from looking away and he had not the strength of will to close his eyes. Mara felt his pain as though it were her own and yet she could do nothing to help him. He must endure the exquisite torture of Sedet's pleasure.

Sedet was well satisfied with her new toy. He would afford her much enjoyment before she allowed him to die. She turned to Gonzales with a lascivious smile.

'Bugger me,' she commanded him. 'I want this poor fool to see what he is missing.'

Gonzales obeyed with silent precision, doglike in his devotion to the beautiful, heartless Queen who used him as thoughtlessly as if he were some cheap sex-toy. But Gonzales did not care. Mara had seen into his soul and knew that the muscular Colombian was obsessed with his mistress's golden body. What did he care if she took her pleasure and then cast him aside without a thought? Her pleasure was his pleasure. Had she not initiated him into the legions of the undead? He would willingly have sacrificed his life for her – if he hadn't done so already.

He pulled apart Sedet's arse cheeks with a gentle reverence.

'No, you clod! Harder – I want to feel the pain . . . Ram your dick into me . . .'

Gonzales thrust into her and she shuddered with pleasure, her eyes closing for a moment as she savoured the feeling of Gonzales' massive penis stretching the delicate membrane of her arse. In Gonzales she had chosen her slave well: the poor fool was so stupid that he was utterly in her psychic control, but his body was perfect, virile, forever exciting. It gave the Master such pleasure to see Gonzales' huge cock distending her arse, whilst she sucked him off. And it was giving her such pleasure now to see the poor blond boy weeping with frustration, his dick swollen with desire as he watched his naked temptress taking her pleasure with another man.

The Queen came to a shuddering climax and Gonzales obediently pulled out his cock, wanking himself until the spunk rose in his balls and spurted out over her golden backside in thick pearly droplets.

Mara had been trying to switch off the scene but now she was brought back to reality by the sound of Sedet's voice, summoning her.

'Come here at once, slut!'

With the utmost reluctance, Mara approached the Queen and knelt down before her, head bowed.

'You deserve to suffer for such inattention,' snapped Sedet. 'But seeing as I am in such a good mood, I shall show you mercy. In fact, I think I shall allow you a little treat.' She gave a chilling smile. 'Lick the spunk off my backside, slut. Now.'

Mara longed to defy her, to spit on her then turn and walk away from this chamber of horrors – walk away for ever from Winterbourne, from the falsehood of this existence that was and was not life. But for Andreas's sake, she dared not risk paying the price of defiance.

'I obey, Mistress Sedet.'

She licked off the pearly droplets slowly and sensuously, as she knew Sedet liked her to do. The Queen delighted in humiliating her, but this was as nothing compared to the ordeals she would be forced to undergo if she failed to carry out her task to her mistress's satisfaction.

'You are a useless slut,' concluded Sedet, rolling onto her side on the cold tiled floor. 'But since you are here, I may as well derive what pleasure I can from you.' She snapped her fingers and nodded to Gonzales. 'Beat her. Then make her suck you off. If she does not please you, beat her again.'

Mara gasped as Gonzales pushed her up against the wall and the lash cut into the flesh. She must not cry out. For such indiscipline, there would be a high price to pay. She thrust her hand into her mouth and stifled her cries as Sedet turned back to her blond captive. Her lips were curved into a smile but her violet eyes held a cold dark emptiness that left no room for hope.

'Enjoy the show, sweet boy,' she breathed. 'Soon, I shall be taking my pleasure with you.'

Mara shivered as she remembered that dark night, only weeks ago, just before Sedet accompanied the Master to India. She did not doubt that, on their return, there would be more sweet flesh for Sedet to feed upon, more ordeals for her to endure. But, for now, she must try simply to survive and find some key to unlock the gateway of Andreas's astral prison.

She sat down on the bed and pulled on her stockings. Time to go down to the Master's private office, where Heimdal would be waiting for her. Why had he summoned her? Was it to punish her for her failure to secure Weatherall's attendance at Winterbourne? The much-vaunted 'fund-raising evening' was to take place in a few days' time; if Weatherall was not present, the Master would be sure to find out. And if the Master was displeased with her . . .

She got up and smoothed down her skirt, secure at least in the knowledge that she looked good. Heimdal might be angry but he'd always had a soft spot for her. She might be able to play upon his vanity, too. He was so very certain that he was irresistible – and perhaps that wasn't entirely untrue. Heimdal did have a good strong body and an enviably massive prick.

Walking quietly down the curving central staircase, Mara gave a nod of recognition to Charlotte and Olivia, two of Winterbourne's newest whores: luscious little English roses Madame LeCoeur had found in the sixth form of some terribly respectable convent school. A world-famous madame with years of experience in the brothel trade, Otalie LeCoeur certainly had an eye for sexual potential, mused Mara. Of course, few girls could resist her promises of a glittering career in 'modelling' and, once inside the doors of Winterbourne Hall, Heimdal made very sure that they would never want to leave . . .

Heimdal was relaxing in the Master's office, leaning back in the black leather armchair while a tiny oriental girl knelt between his legs, massaging sweet oils into his cock.

To Mara's surprise, he smiled at her affably as she knocked and entered.

'You're looking very tempting today, my darling little slut.'

'Do you wish me to pleasure you, Master Heimdal?'

'Why not?' He turned to the Chinese girl and waved her away. 'You may go now, Ling-Chu.' Seeing the look of obvious disappointment, he added. 'I shall perhaps fuck you later – in the conservatory. You may wait for me there this evening.'

The girl left and Mara took up her position on the floor in front of Heimdal. He roared with delighted laughter as she ran her tongue lightly up the underside of his shaft and began masturbating him gently.

'Your skills have developed well since your return to Winterbourne,' remarked Heimdal, running a massive bear's-paw of a hand over her auburn locks. 'It seems your trip to Egypt has augmented your sensual and psychic faculties. That is good, very good . . .'

Mara looked up at him questioningly, trying to banish any tell-tale nervousness from her voice. Could he have guessed? Could he possibly have glimpsed the truth?

'You wished to see me?'

Heimdal laughed and stroked her face, tracing the sensuous pout of her moist lips. She ran her tongue over his fingers and was rewarded by a low growl of pleasure.

'So, so eager, my little slut. You please me with your willing ways.'

'I . . . failed with Weatherall, Master Heimdal. I am sorry. I will try again . . .'

He waved aside her confession with a dismissive gesture.

'Weatherall can wait until another day. His money and political influence will be useful to us, I grant you, but you shall have plenty of opportunity to meet him again over the coming weeks. No, the Master wishes you to concentrate your efforts on other prey . . .'

Mara sucked Heimdal's cock with genuine pleasure, her lusts awakened by the relief of having turned away his anger. And she realised suddenly that she was hungry – hungry for sex. His cock tasted salty-sweet and slippery love-juice was oozing from its pierced tip. As she toyed with the jade cock-ring that passed through the glans, Heimdal continued.

'The Master has arranged a pretty little tableau, sweet slut, and you are to have the very great honour of being one of the main performers in it.'

'I don't understand.'

'Patience. Suck my cock and listen. Tonight, you are to have dinner with a very important guest, and will then go with him to the Club Venus, in Soho. Your escort will be a certain Jerry Singleton . . .'

Mara stared at him in amazement.

'You mean . . . *the* Jerry Singleton?'

'Yes, my dear whore. The Right Honourable Jerry Singleton MP, Chancellor of the Exchequer and Deputy Leader of the Republican Party.'

'What am I to do?'

'It is quite simple. You are to wine him, dine him, utterly corrupt him . . . and make sure that the newspaper photographers I have arranged to be there obtain some really compromising photographs. Now come here, you irresistible slut, I want to stick my cock up your divine little arse.'

# 6: The Immortals

Andreas stirred from his uneasy slumber, suddenly aware that Mara was having sex. He could hear her breathing – hoarse and quick – smell the sweat as it trickled down between her breasts, taste the sweet ooze from her delicious cunt.

And whoever it was she was fucking, she was thinking of him. He could hear the silent words forming in her mind: 'Fuck me, Andreas, fuck me, it's so, so good to fuck . . .'

He reached out to her, dreaming for a moment that he could feel her in his arms, their bodies moving together in perfect synchronicity. And suddenly it happened again – the strange, sickening sense of vertigo as an irresistible force pulled at him, dragging his helpless spirit into the dizzying eye of the hurricane.

No matter how often it happened, it was still stomach-churningly unpleasant – not that different from going down the death-slide at a theme park. He'd once had to do that six times in one day – the editor had sent him off to get 'intimate photos' of some disgraced member of the royal family and his latest fancy piece. Of course, the guy had spotted Andreas straight away – hardly surprising, seeing as he was bristling with telephoto lenses. And what had they decided to do? Spend all fucking day on the white-knuckle rides, that's what. Andreas had spent most of *his* day with his face in a paper bag. He'd got the photos, though. And what had happened? They got pushed off the front pages by the world's biggest cucumber and a story about a man with two willies. That's tabloid journalism for you.

Moments later, the swirling mist cleared and his spirit was floating free – bobbing like an untethered balloon. Where was he? What . . .?

The he saw her. Mara – his Mara – fucking that slimeball Heimdal, sitting on his lap and taking his big fat dick into her cunt. Jealousy bit him like a slap in the face, but it was as though Mara could sense him there in the room with her. Her face was turned towards him and she was smiling, silently pleading with him.

*Drink it in, Andreas. Drink in the energy.*

Suddenly he realised what she meant. All at once he stopped feeling jealous and let the pure power of sex flood into him. He felt like Frankenstein's monster as the raw energy fizzed and crackled around him. He wanted Mara – wanted to fuck her, wanted to feel what Heimdal could feel as he thrust into the depths of her, kneading and pinching at her naked breasts.

And, in the strangest way, he *could* feel. Not in any physical sense but in the dimension of his mind. He was becoming a part of what he could see, plugging into the energy. Mara was right – the power of sex was making him stronger, more aware, more alive . . .

Heimdal clutched Mara to him, forcing his prick deeper into her belly as he ejaculated with a groan of pleasure.

It was like a light switch being flicked off. The energy stopped flowing into him and Andreas felt suddenly helpless and alone once again. Mara was looking at him, her eyes full of warmth and sadness and desire and hope – could she see him? Had she at least truly sensed his presence there, reaching out to her?

Time to go. Time to let go.

As the scene faded and consciousness ebbed away from him, he surrendered once more to the dark. But the darkness held a new quality somehow. Something he could not define – the seed of dawn . . .? As the crystal prison closed in on him and he slept once more, his dreams were all of Mara.

Beneath the heavy granite lid of the sarcophagus, Andreas lay trapped within the crystal – pure flawless crystal; or was its mirror-smooth surface now marred by the first faint scar of a hairline crack . . .?

Mara and her companion were dancing on the floor of the Club Venus, holding each other close as they moved together to the sensual rhythms of the salsa beat.

Two women dancing together: one slender with long auburn hair, the other taller and more heavily built, with a cascade of dark brown curls; both clad in skintight black PVC. No-one turned a hair – why should they? At a discreet fetish club like Club Venus, there were no rules, no judgements.

The small group of men by the bar were wearing all the right gear but they looked uncomfortable.

'Do you think we've been had?'

'Looks that way. I've seen nothing here tonight that would make page seven, let alone the front page.'

'Load of fuckin' perverts – want shooting, if you ask me.'

'Mind you, I could go a bit of that.' The tall thin man took a swig of beer and indicated the two women dancing in the spotlight. 'The one with the dark hair's got great tits.'

It was a slow dance and the two women were kissing now; fondling each other, running their hands over each other's bodies. It was easy, so very easy, for Mara to stumble on her high heels and reach out to stop herself falling.

So easy to catch hold of that cascade of dark brown curls . . .

The wig slipped sideways and fell to the ground.

'My God! It's . . . it's . . . it can't be!'

His companion slipped off the bar stool and put a hand on his arm.

'Shut up, Kevin, and get your camera out. It's only the bleeding Chancellor of the Exchequer – in a frock!'

The Master sat on the verandah and sipped iced tea as he watched the Hindu holy-man having Tantric sex with two delicious little temple sluts beside the embassy swimming pool. Such admirable control these Asian mystics had of their sexual appetites, worthy almost of the immortals. Such a delightful ability to walk the tightrope between pleasure and pain. He glanced at Sedet and felt the waves of excitement rippling through her; he knew that she was imagining how it would feel to be the hand that inflicted such refinements of torture . . .

For now the holy man was passing a six-inch-long iron pin through the hard, brown nipple of the dark-skinned girl who straddled him, a bright gemstone sparkling in her navel. Such a pretty display. So well trained was the girl that she barely winced as the second pin pierced the head of her clitoris. Such party tricks would be much sought-after at Winterbourne . . .

His attention turned from this agreeable sexual entertainment to the pile of newspapers on the table beside him. They were no less agreeable. In fact, matters were turning out in a most satisfactory manner, despite Sedet's obsession with danger and conspiracy. He valued his Queen's intuition, of course, but deplored her tendency to rely on the vaguest of sensations. Take her dislike of the Dubois girl, for instance: clearly a feeling borne out of pure resentment. Dubois had never been anything other than entirely loyal and in recent weeks she had proved more useful than even he could ever have hoped. Heimdal spoke highly of her and now there was this amusing scandal with the Chancellor of the Exchequer. Best of all, Anastasia Dubois was a great fuck.

He scanned the headlines, certain now that his plans for political power would not fail. Already he was a household name, a world-famous peacemaker – the 'saviour of India'. And the news from England was better still. He had an initiate in the Shadow Cabinet now – Derek Manley, the Shadow Home Secretary with a blameless reputation and an unfortunate weakness for pretty blondes. Manley had been a pushover. Best of all, there had been plenty of sex scandals to rock the Republican establishment to its very core – and now the corruption had spread to the heart of the Government itself. Jerry Singleton had been careless, very careless . . . The Master picked up one of the photographs, and scrutinised it.

Who was that auburn-haired slut in the tight PVC dress, dancing so close to Singleton on the spotlit dancefloor? Yes, the Dubois girl was far too useful to be dispensed with. He would simply have to bring Sedet round to his way of thinking.

Takimoto came out onto the verandah, his inscrutable expression concealing a heart of exultant lust. The Master would be pleased with him.

'It is done, Master. He is dead.'

'Excellent. You may sit here beside me and tell me all the details.'

For several weeks, the Master had been waiting to hear of the tragic – and entirely unexpected – death of Gareth Hughes, Republican MP for the London borough of Caxton-upon-Thames. It would be a tremendous shock to everyone – with the exception of the Master – when Hughes was discovered dead in his luxury riverside penthouse, electrocuted in his bath with a cheap prostitute.

'You will stand for the seat, of course?' Sedet stretched out her lean tanned limbs and stroked the bronzed body of the temple slut as she twisted the iron spike through her nipple.

'That is the plan, mistress Sedet,' agreed Takimoto. 'Arrangements have been made.'

'Indeed I shall.' The Master folded up the newspaper and put it down on the table. 'And of course, I shall win.'

'But . . . you will stand for the Republicans?' Sedet looked disgusted.

The Master laughed.

'My God, no. For the Nationalists.'

Mara got out of the car and threw the keys onto the seat. She was glad she'd managed to persuade Geoffrey to let her borrow the BMW convertible; she was sick to death of having to put up with him on every journey she made. Over the last few months, he had grown almost pathologically jealous and fucking him had become a chore. There was a crazy, wanton cruelty in him that revolted her. It was almost impossible now to imagine him as the young innocent boy whose virginity she had taken one night, long ago, in a woodland caravan park.

Here, high on the cliffs above the Atlantic, Mara felt closer to the peace that she had lost. Here, where the gulls wheeled in the turbulent blue sky and the sea crashed grey and defiant on the rocks below, she felt in tune with the forces of Nature which had always been her guides.

She walked along the clifftop, enjoying the feeling of the wind in her hair. There it was, in the distance: Cym y Mawr, the stone circle where so long ago, in another body, another life, she had been initiated into her coven as a white witch.

As she got nearer to the standing stones, she could feel the energy vibrating within them, recognising the life force within her and welcoming her in.

Stepping into the circle, she felt a wave of relief wash over her. At Winterbourne, where she must act the undead whore, Mara felt trapped and afraid, her psychic powers forced into the service of an evil power she both feared and despised. But here, within the womb-like security of Cym y Mawr, she could get back in touch with who she really was. She was not the vampire-creature whose body she was forced to inhabit.

She was not Anastasia Dubois. She was the white witch Mara Fleming.

Sitting down on the grass, she took a small wooden box out of her bag. Inside was the ivory dildo that had been used in her initiation, so very long ago. Only by using it again, here, in this sacred place, could she hope to recapture the true essence of her being.

She lay down on the warm grass, and gazed up at the blue cloudless sky as she drew up her knees and began stroking the yearning flesh of her belly and thighs.

She was excited; her clitty already pulsating with the anticipation of sweet, blissful release. She had waited so long and surrendered herself to the pleasure of the Master and his evil companions. Now, at least for a few hours, she was free.

Unbuttoning her blouse, she bared her breasts to the summer sun, the breeze that played across the clifftop whipping and caressing her flesh as she lay among the standing stones. Her nipples were hard, yearning, eager for her touch as she pinched and stroked them into ever-greater hardness. Little by little, a familiar warmth spread through her belly and her cunt grew moist and hot with excitement.

Sliding her hand down from her breasts, she let her fingers trace the firm, taut flesh of her belly; and the flesh that was awakening to her familiar touch was the flesh of Mara Fleming, once again warm and vibrant beneath her fingertips.

*Got to fuck. Got to fuck.*

The sun was warm and comforting on her bare thighs and she sighed with pleasure as she felt between her cunt lips and her fingers were instantly bathed in the most abundant cascade of honey-sweet love-juice. Her clitoris was as hard as the ivory dildo she pressed gently against the entrance to her vagina, stretching the delicate flesh as the carved surface slid easily, silently home.

With eager fingers she slid the little hood of flesh backwards and forwards over her throbbing clitoris, while with the other hand, she slid the dildo in and out of her cunt. The sensations were delicious, irresistible: all the sensations of innocent pleasure that she had enjoyed before that day when the Master had robbed her of her true identity. She gasped with joy as she reached out for that innocent pleasure and embraced it, knowing for certain at last that it was not lost, that Mara Fleming had not been tainted with the evil that surrounded her.

As joy washed over her, she felt her whole being transformed, transfigured in a golden light that seared and warmed and caressed like a cool flame. She was floating free in the golden light, her soul spinning and swirling in an ocean of ecstasy the only sounds the faraway cries of the gulls and the soft secret murmur of her own breathing.

Pleasure, pleasure, pleasure. Growing and swelling like a spring tide within her. With each thrust of the ivory dildo into her cunt, awakening the powers of goodness that she had suppressed for too, too long. Opening up the gateways of her mind, and welcoming in a second presence. A presence that at first she was afraid to recognise. A faraway whispering, deep inside her soul.

*Come to me, Mara. Don't be afraid. Don't fight it.*

Andreas?

*I'm strong now, Mara. Feel the energy within me. Let my strength bring you to me.*

Andreas! As she pressed the carved dildo into her once more, she felt a surge of electricity thrill through her, making her clitoris throb with the approach of the most immense orgasm she had ever experienced. Her cunt was dripping wet with moisture and she had to will to fight the overwhelming sensations. She abandoned herself utterly to the pleasure and, with a cry, fell spinning into the glittering vortex of her soul's ecstasy.

*You're here, Mara. Here with me at last.*

She opened her eyes, suddenly disorientated and afraid. Where was the golden light of the clifftop, the clear blue sky that had arched above her, only moments before? All was darkness, silence, the scent of death and decay. She was lying on a cold stone floor, covered in dust; the only light the glimmer from a sodium-yellow lamp that hung from the damp cracked wall. She stood up and took the lamp from its hook, using it to peer into the darkest corners around her.

Fear gripped at her stomach. She had been here before. But how could this be? One moment she had been lying on the grass on the headland; the next, she was in the dark and terrifying depths of the bricked-up cellars at Winterbourne. She knew those rusty-red smears on the floor, that massive granite shape that loomed up in front of her, black and menacing. It was here that she had spilt the life-blood of Andreas Hunt. Here that she had seen the horror within the sarcophagus: the cast-off body of the Master, trapped within its crystal prison. She backed away, suddenly filled with panic.

*Don't be afraid, Mara. Come close. Closer now.*

The voice was soundless, one soul speaking to another without words. But she knew it instantly as the voice of her dead lover. Was Andreas truly here? Or was this another of the Master's cruel tricks?

On trembling feet, she approached the sarcophagus.

*It's me, Mara. Touch the lid of the sarcophagus. You have the power within your fingertips.*

'No, I can't!' Mara gasped out loud, terrified to touch the sinister black stone that seemed to reek of death and evil. 'It's a trick . . .'

*It's me inside, Mara. Waiting for you. Touch the lid of the sarcophagus. Before the strength goes out of me again.*

Filled with fear, she stretched out tremulous fingers towards the smooth granite lid. As her fingertips touched the smooth surface, it began to glow and vibrate. She tried to pull away but could not. It was as though she was becoming part of the granite, melting and transforming with it.

As she looked on, the granite seemed to dissolve and become transparent.

*Look down, Mara. Look into the crystal.*

I can't . . .

She knew what she would see. The body within the crystal, its face distorted into a hideous, evil mask of pain. She recalled the terrible, soul-wrenching disappointment she had felt that night, when she had entered the cellars in the hope of freeing Andreas from the crystal. The pain and horror as she realised the terrible deception. How could she force herself to look again into those cruel, dark eyes?

*Don't you trust me, Mara? Should I not have brought you here?*

The desperation in Andreas's voice jolted her out of her paralysis.

'I . . . trust you, Andreas.'

*Then look down into the crystal. Reach out and touch me. Be with me now.*

She forced herself to look down. And, for an instant, her worst fears were realised as she looked down at the twisted features, the eyes that seemed to glitter like black diamonds within the crystal.

And then the picture began to blur, change, distort . . . It was as though the Master's useless body was dissolving, turning to a glass as transparent as the crystal. And within, she saw the face of Andreas Hunt as he had been. He was smiling and reaching out to her.

*I want you, Mara. I've wanted you for so long. Hurry – we don't have much time. Soon, you must return to the clifftop. I cannot hold you here for long . . .*

In a sudden spirit leap, she entered the crystal, melted into it, her soul blending seamlessly with the soul of Andreas Hunt.

It was the most intense sexual experience she had ever had – mind-fucking that transcended the body and brought with it a climax of the soul, an orgasm of the entire being.

As they fucked within the crystal, Mara at last understood how Heimdal and the Master had deluded her. Understood the pain of Andreas's captivity – and began to understand how she might free him.

Liz Exley stretched out her long, tanned limbs and smiled into the camera. Across the table from her sat the Master, sober and respectable in a well-cut grey suit.

He took a sip from the glass of iced water and answered all her questions with consummate ease, making sure the cameras got the full benefit of his strong profile and so-sexy blue eyes. An interview like this was no challenge at all and he had plenty of time to relax and take in his interviewer's undeniable charms.

This Exley slut had spirit but there was a danger in her. She was hot for him and he would undoubtedly enjoy fucking her, but something was holding him back. He could sense that she did not trust him, perhaps she wanted to get close to him just so that she could get access to information that would damage him – and give her the news story of her life.

Well . . . maybe he would fuck her anyway. If she started

causing trouble, she could be swiftly eliminated. Miss Liz Exley might think she could get the better of Anthony LeMaître but she was no match for the Master . . .

Liz turned towards him again, almost imperceptibly easing up the hem of her tight miniskirt as she crossed her legs and leant across to ask him another question.

'Mr LeMaître . . . you are certainly a popular figure here in India.'

The Master smiled modestly.

'I seek only to serve.'

'That's a very honourable ambition.' Exley was leaning over so far that the Master could see the twin globes of her breasts, firm and pert within the cream satin blouse. He wondered idly how it would feel to shove his dick between those two firm globes, have her kneel before him and squeeze them together around his shaft while he pumped his spunk all over her naked tits.

'I aspire to be a man of honour, it's true.'

'I see.' Exley was squaring up for the big one. 'And do you think you could carry on those ideals as a politician?'

'I'm not sure I quite understand what you're getting at, Miss Exley.'

'Oh, come now, Mr LeMaître. You must have heard the rumours.'

'And what would they be?' He was enjoying playing with her. Much as he would enjoy playing with those smooth rounded buttocks as he thrust again and again into her gloriously tight arsehole.

'It's rumoured that you are about to resign your Ambassadorship and return to England to stand in the Caxton-on-Thames by-election. Is there any truth in these rumours?'

The Master paused for a moment, just to give the right degree of modest reticence.

'I have given it a great deal of thought,' he replied, his face a mask of intelligent concern. 'And, while I am greatly attached to the people of India, I feel that I owe a duty to the people of Great Britain, also. In recent months, a series of grave scandals has afflicted a number of Republican Members of Parliament, bringing into question the integrity of the entire British Government, and even the Mother of Parliaments herself.

'This must not continue. It is time for all men – and women – of courage and moral fibre to stand up and be counted. And therefore – after much sober reflection – I have decided to accept an invitation to stand as a candidate in the forthcoming by-election. I shall be leaving for England next week to begin fighting my election campaign.'

Liz Exley's eyes were sparking with excitement now. The Master could have thrown back his head and laughed at her, she looked so comical. She was almost wetting her knickers in her eagerness to squeeze every last drop of this 'exclusive' story out of her celebrity interviewee. Hadn't she been the first journalist allowed into the inner sanctum of the Embassy? Hadn't she revealed to the world how Anthony LeMaître had calmed the epidemic of violence across India? And now here she was again, this time bringing the world the news of LeMaître's new venture into politics.

'And which party do you intend standing for, Mr LeMaître?'

The Master treated the camera to a winning smile.

'Why, the Nationalists of course,' he replied. 'After all, I do stand for clean, honest government.'

A continual procession of long black limousines drew up outside the front steps of Winterbourne Hall, decanting an assortment of MPs, media personalities and industrialists – in short, anyone who might be of use to the Master in his forthcoming bid to enter Parliament.

Mara ushered the guests to the terrace at the back of the Hall, where Heimdal welcomed each in turn with champagne – drugged with some of Madame LeCoeur's most potent aphrodisiac essences – and pretty whores in leather masks and diaphanous dresses. This was to be Heimdal's tour-de-force: a great outdoor masked ball which – with a cruel sense of humour – he had entitled 'The Immortals'.

Each guest had been instructed to arrive in fancy dress and

106

Mara could see a sprinkling of gods, goddesses, werewolves and even a few white-faced vampires strolling across the lawns, arm in arm with Heimdal's 'hosts' and 'hostesses'. The irony was not lost on Mara. She could not help feeling sorry for them, knowing what terrible fate lay in store for them. However unpleasant, arrogant and lecherous men like Hackman and Chesterton might be, even they did not deserve to feel the cold power of the Master's deathly kiss . . .

The thought of immortality drove her thoughts back to Andreas and to the few stolen moments they had spent together within the crystal. It all seemed like a dream now. She had to free him – had to free herself, too – from the Master's evil yoke. And yet, how could this possibly be accomplished? All around her were the dread symbols of the Master's unstoppable march towards power. She shivered as she looked at the laughing faces of the men and women who would soon be no more than empty shells: puppets dancing to the Master's seductive tune.

'More wine, girl. Do stop dozing!'

She turned to see Gonzales standing with hands on hips, gesturing angrily for her to fetch another bottle of champagne.

When she returned, she was greeted by Sir Robert Hackman and one of his friends, the Right-Wing Nationalist MP Jonas Ffoukes. Heimdal's whores were entertaining them with a display of exotic dancing on the lawns but their eyes strayed instantly to Mara as she approached, her body clearly visible through her semi-transparent dress.

'Ah,' sighed Hackman, rubbing the front of his trousers. 'If I'm not much mistaken, Heimdal, that's the delicious Miss Dubois behind that mask. You were right, my dear girl – this fund-rasing evening isn't quite like anything I've ever been to in my life! With your company, it will be even better . . .'

Heimdal quickly sized up the situation.

'Entertain our guests,' he instructed Mara. 'The main part of the evening's entertainment will be beginning soon.' As he turned to walk away, he whispered in her ear: 'You have done well. The Master will be pleased. And tonight, in my bed, you shall have your reward . . .'

Mara shuddered as Hackman and Ffoukes began pawing her, their hands hot and sweaty with excitement. Even if they had not been lecherous and debauched men, Madame LeCoeur's aphrodisiacs would have worked their dark magic by now. They never failed. In fact Heimdal, with his rough humour, liked to joke that they would even raise the dead . . .

The garden party was coming to life all around them. The grounds of the Hall were filling up with laughing, unsuspecting guests and their masked escorts – the finest whores and handsome young boys that Winterbourne could provide. Under the trees on the other side of the lake Heimdal had arranged for a stage to be built and a band was playing there – slow sensual rhythms cleverly designed to awaken other, secret rhythms within the bodies of the guests. Already the dark magic was working. Mara could see couples dancing together – complete strangers, pillars of the moral establishment, now pawing and kissing and stroking each other's bodies as they swayed in time to the music, desire swelling each cock and clitoris.

On the stage, semi-naked men and girls danced for the pleasure of the guests. These were the Master's servants, perfect bodies forever young, forever hungry. Mara could see their lust-filled eyes selecting victims, anticipating the ultimate pleasure which their Master himself had promised to them. Their gaze roved over the guests – MPs, media stars, all the great and powerful and ambitious who would shortly be using their talents in the service of a new master. Mara looked on and shivered, seeing not a laughing group of revellers but a macabre dance of the undead.

Standing a little way apart from the crowd Mara glimpsed the Nationalist MP for Guiseborough – a tall, thin woman with a hard, muscular body, the legacy of a career in professional sport. She was standing beside the lake, her eyes sparkling with a lust that only Madame LeCoeur's alchemy could have awakened within her. On his knees before her on the soft green grass was the Master's Ethiopian slave, Ibrahim; his perfect body well-oiled and gleaming in the soft moonlight. The woman was dressed in a short Greek tunic, which Ibrahim had pulled up to expose the dark triangle between her thighs, barely covered by a pair of white lace panties.

As Mara watched, Ibrahim pulled the panties down and Mara saw her begin to laugh uncontrollably as Ibrahim's tongue sought out the heart of her womanhood. Mara knew how good Ibrahim was with that strong, muscular tongue and how pleasurable it felt to have his fingers mercilessly probing the soft wet heart of her cunt. She let her spirit fly free and entered the mind of the woman MP for a fleeting moment, shuddering with pleasure as she felt the woman's excitement.

Mara's sudden shiver communicated itself instantly to her two suitors, and she was dragged back into the body of the vampire woman. Ffoukes pulled her to him, forcing his mouth against hers and wriggling his tongue between her lips. He stank of garlic and alcohol and she wanted to push him away and wipe her mouth clean of him; but she was as much a captive as he was. More so, in fact, for all those gathered here would be the most willing of sacrifices. If they had known what was to befall them, chances were that they would probably still have chosen it – what ambitious man could resist the lure of immortality and of unending, untiring sex?

'Come here, you gorgeous little tart,' grunted Ffoukes. 'God, I haven't felt this randy in years. Must be the champagne, eh?' He ground his pelvis against her and she felt the hard throbbing limb of his cock pressing up against her belly.

'I've had her and she's a good fuck,' commented Hackman, faintly menacing in his demon's costume, the grinning mask looking up at her out of the dusk. 'Most obliging, aren't you, my little wood-nymph?' He parted the dark folds of his cloak and Mara saw his hardening penis, ethereal white against the dark fabric. He put his hand on her breast, squeezing it hard through the thin muslin dress as Ffoukes ground the side of his hand between her thighs, bruising the delicate flesh of her cunt lips. 'The randy little bitch'll do anything you want. She's so hot for it, mind she doesn't burn your fingers!'

Their brutality hurt and angered her but it also excited, arousing her to a fever-pitch of sexual hunger which terrified her in its intensity. Nor for the first time, Mara understood the frenzy which overtook the Master's disciples, driving them to acts of lustful violence so extreme that they could only end in death. But death could not touch the night-creatures of Winterbourne Hall. They would live on forever, feeding on the sexual energies of those they sacrificed to the lusts which gave them life. Or at any rate, a sort of life . . .

Wrestling with the desperate passion within her, Mara forced herself to submit to the desires of the two men who sought to possess her. To resist them, to impose upon them the ferocity of her own needs, would be to court Lord Heimdal's displeasure. And that was a luxury she simply could not afford.

Ffoukes dragged her across the lawns towards a stand of beech trees near to the lake. As she followed him across the grass, hands reached out and plucked at her body, sleek and tempting beneath the filmy muslin robe. The music ebbed and flowed and bodies swayed in time to the seductive rhythms, already drunk with the lust they must soon slake.

'Here, I think,' muttered Ffoukes, pushing Mara up against a tree so that her soft flesh ground against the rough bark. She tried to turn round to face him, but his strong arms pinned her against the tree trunk.

'What . . .?'

'So eager to escape, my dear? I hope you're not going to disappoint me.'

'No . . . of course not. But . . .'

He gave a low growl of laughter as he forced her once again against the bark.

'Never mind, eh? I like a bit of spirit in my women. Makes it that much more fun to break them . . .'

For a moment she did not realise what he was doing as he kept her pressed to the tree-trunk whilst he fumbled with something behind her. Then the first stinging blow hit her and she winced with pain as she clung to the harsh, unforgiving bark. Ffoukes had taken off his leather belt and was beating her with it, thrashing her with hard rhythmic strokes that made her cry out as they tore away the thin fabric of her robe and stung her bare, white flesh.

Tomorrow, she knew, all traces of the beating would be gone – her torn and martyred flesh miraculously healed as it had been so many times since her transformation. But in these moments – these helpless, tortured moments – the pain was very real. Mara found herself biting the flesh of her hand but her cries would not be stifled; and she knew that with each new cry for mercy, Ffoukes's prick would grow stiffer and more sincerely grateful to his willing little victim.

The pain was intense, yet also extremely erotic. Mara could feel her cunt beginning to ooze moisture as Ffoukes increased the harshness of the beating. She realised that her cries of pain were swiftly becoming cries of desire . . .

'Take me, give it to me, give it to me harder . . .'

And Ffoukes was laughing, his voice like a mad scream in her head as he dropped the belt and pushed the tip of his prick between her bruised and bleeding arse cheeks.

He entered her like a hot knife, his prick distending the soft flesh of her cunt as he thrust one, two, three fingers into her anus and began tormenting her with this exquisite double violation.

Helpless to resist, Mara clutched the bark of the tree, excited beyond belief as the double penetration of cunt and arse joined with the sweet sensation of rough bark rubbing hard against her naked pubis.

She came twice before Ffoukes reached his climax and shot jets of boiling spunk into her cunt. Then at last he withdrew from her, leaving her to sink to the ground, exhausted, as he put his cock away.

'You were right – she is a good fuck,' Ffoukes noted to his companion, Hackman. 'Why don't you have her now, while I watch? Or she could suck me off while you take her up the arse. That bum is wonderfully tight. Maybe I'll have her again when you've finished with her. Or maybe even that pretty boy over there, with the silver ring through his cock . . .'

At that moment, the band stopped playing and all eyes turned towards the stage. Something was happening. Something important.

Something evil.

Mara felt the Master's presence even before the limousine glided into view along the driveway and parked at the rear of the Hall. The blackness of his soul seemed to spread out like a cold cloud, enveloping everything and everyone in its evil spell.

The car door opened and Cheviot got out, respectfully holding open the door for the Master.

'My God, it's LeMaître,' hissed Ffoukes to Hackman. 'I didn't realise he was expected back so soon from India.'

'I did hear he was planning to be here tonight,' replied Hackman, a smile spreading over his face. 'Now there's going to be some *real* fun, I'll be bound.'

Mara remained on her knees on the ground, watching with horror and fear in her eyes as the Master slowly ascended the steps to the stage, followed by Sedet, breathtakingly beautiful in scarlet silk cut low in the neck and slashed to the thigh. With each step her thighs flashed golden and sleek through the split skirt and her unfettered breasts moved like an ocean swell within the tight bodice. All eyes were on this golden couple, admiration and lust mingling in equal measure as the Master turned to the throng and spoke.

'Welcome to Winterbourne, my friends,' he began. 'I have waited a long time for this moment. And, since you have all been kind enough to accept my invitation, I must ensure that this is a night that none of you will ever forget.'

He snapped his fingers and Heimdal stepped onto the stage, dragging behind him a naked Indian girl with pierced nipples, a silver slave-chain linking her pert creamy-beige breasts. The Master nodded and Heimdal forced the girl to her knees. A gasp of pleasure and disbelief ran through the

112

onlookers as, with slow mechanical fingers, she unzipped the Master's flies and took out his prick.

'Suck me off, slave.' instructed the Master, revelling in the warm glow of pleasure as the Indian girl took his penis into the hot cavern of her mouth. Heimdal had schooled her well since the girl had been sent to him from India.

He looked down at his loyal subjects and those who were soon to join them and he felt he could allow himself an indulgent smile.

'Let the entertainment begin,' he decreed.

And there, in the dark blue twilight, Sir Robert Hackman felt the playful embraces of the youth in his arms turn to the passionate kiss of death.

Max Trevidian felt further from the truth than ever. When Liz Exley had hired him to investigate LeMaître, he'd never imagined it would be as difficult as this.

Five years ago, when his Aunt Aurelia – one of the country's leading mediums – had died, Max had sworn never to get involved in that psychic crap ever again. His aunt might have left him her house but she sure as heck wasn't going to bequeath her interest in the supernatural to him. He was convinced it was a load of nonsense and he'd always told her so. She'd just smiled at him and shaken her head – and told him that one day he'd know better.

And now he was beginning to wonder if that day wasn't upon him. Beginning to wonder if there really were more things in heaven and earth . . .

Funny things had been happening. Things that didn't quite fit. And there was the question of LeMaître's past. Oh yes, everyone knew he'd been to Eton and Cambridge and had a spell in the Guards – so how come Trevidian couldn't find one single person who'd known him for longer than eighteen months? And if he was right about him being Andreas Hunt, why the hell would a hack journalist want to pose as a man called Anthony LeMaître?

He watched the figures on the television screen, looking

for some clue that would lead him to the heart of the massive deception that he was sure was being perpetrated by LeMaître and his supporters.

The news reader was talking about the forthcoming by-election in Caxton-upon-Thames. Eight candidates – six no-hopers and the big two: Kenton Rowley for the Republicans and the Nationalist challenger for the seat – Anthony LeMaître.

As Max sat back in his chair and watched Nationalist leader Hugo Winchester officially endorsing LeMaître's candidacy, one thing puzzled him. Everyone was smiling, back-slapping, exchanging congratulations. Everyone except the Dubois girl. There she was, standing behind the Master, immaculate and beautiful as ever. She was one of LeMaître's most loyal supporters – she must be delighted that he'd been adopted by the Nationalists to stand for Caxton-upon-Thames. With all the scandals that had been besetting the governing Republican party in the last couple of months, LeMaître must be in with a chance of winning.

But if she was so pleased, why did she look bloody miserable? And why could he see a tear glistening on her cheek?

# 7: The Candidate

'I don't understand you, Caít, I just don't bloody understand you.'

'But, Donal . . . I . . .'

'Over these last few weeks, you've changed. Don't you realise that? You're a crazy woman, Caít O'Keefe.'

Caít sat on the edge of the bed and stared at him in utter misery, suddenly realising the awful truth – that Donal was going to leave her. She knew she'd been different lately but at first he'd liked it. He'd always complained that she was too prudish to satisfy him – frigid even. The sudden, inexplicable awakening of her sexuality had been a revelation to her. What more did he want?

'I only wanted to please you, Donal.'

He sneered at her, picking up the handful of leather and flinging it in her face.

'Leather and chains, Caít? You really thought that kind of stuff would turn me on? What kind of pervert do you think I am?'

'I'm sorry, really I am.'

'It's a bit late for that, Caít. I'm outa here. You're sick, do you know that? I mean – whips, handcuffs . . . You should see somebody. A shrink.'

He carried on stuffing socks and shirts into an old holdall, refusing to look at her. Anger rose in Caít as she thought what a hypocrite Donal was. What a poor deluded hypocrite. Oh, it was fine for him to sow his wild oats – bed any big-breasted little bitch he fancied and then come crawling home to his nice safe comfortable woman. And it would have been OK too if he'd wanted to tie Caít up and take his pleasure. But for Caít to express her own desires . . . well, that was a very different matter.

Surreptitiously, she unfastened the belt of her silky robe and eased it open a little at the neck, exposing the white swell of the naked breasts within. Still he refused to look at her.

She wondered why she was even bothering with him. Donal was so boring and predictable, so desperately inadequate to satisfy the needs she now felt welling up inside her like some secret spring. And yet, her desire was here and now and Donal was here with her . . .

Her hatred was here and now, too. The hatred that had bubbled and raged within her ever since she had seen LeMaître's smiling face that night on the television screen. And now the object of her hatred was back in England, running for Parliament, moving on to even greater success and adulation.

Why did she hate him so much? She did not know. She no longer even bothered to trouble herself with the thought. Her hatred was as unquestioning as the desire that drove her on, demanding more and ever more extreme sex.

The dreams came to her nightly now, tormenting and exciting her. Suggesting to her new and forbidden pleasure she had never before imagined existed. A voice spoke to her in her dreams, a voice that urged her on to ever greater sexual excesses – and ever greater hatred against the man it called The Master.

Her eyes were downcast but she was looking up at Donal from underneath sweeping brown eyelashes. The voice was speaking to her even now. Telling her how she could win him back, win back the sex she needed so badly.

Getting to her feet, she let the silky robe fall to the ground and spoke softly.

'I won't ever do anything you don't like, Donal. I promise. All I want is to give you pleasure.'

Donal's head jerked round to look at her, and his eyes

widened at the sight of her, naked and ready for him, her long dark locks tumbling over the snow-white curves of her shoulders and breasts.

He opened his mouth to speak but in the next second she was beside him, silencing him with a kiss that tore a great hole in his resolve to leave. He groaned as she slid down his body and began tugging at the button on his jeans.

It yielded, and in a moment she had pulled down his jeans and boxer shorts. His mouth was dry and his heart was thumping as her butterfly-soft fingers fluttered over his cock, teasing and arousing it as no other woman had ever done. Where had Caít learned to do these things? What's more, did he really care? His resolve was crumbling with each new touch of those sensitive fingers.

She sucked him and he moaned and sighed with pleasure, the sheer, unadulterated physical pleasure of sex. He no longer thought about leaving – why the hell had he thought of it in the first place? Maybe it was he who was crazy, not Caít.

Dizzy with pleasure, he allowed himself to be led across to the bed. He lay down and Caít bestrode him with her strong white thighs, her cunt engulfing his prick in a single delicious movement that had him shuddering and gasping for more. His bollocks were so heavy with spunk that he believed he couldn't last more than a few seconds, but Caít had a demonic skill in that tight wet cunt and seemed to hold him on the brink for an eternity.

As she rode Donal's prick, Caít felt a wild elation overtaking her, warming her throbbing clitoris into vibrant life and making her laugh with an insane pleasure.

*I wonder,* she thought as she bent to kiss Donal's throat. *I wonder* what it would be like to taste blood . . .

Winterbourne was strangely silent on this warm autumn afternoon, as the car pulled away down the drive. Over the last few weeks, as the Master orchestrated his election campaign, the faithful had been commanded to exercise restraint. To Mara's secret relief there had been no grand set-piece orgies, no initiations of influential people which – if they went wrong – might bring down a devastating scandal upon the house and its master. These weeks had brought a welcome respite for Mara from her role as the vampire-creature Anastasia Dubois.

There had been fucking, of course. Without fucking, the Master and his servants could scarcely survive, their energies plunging to dangerously low levels. And of course, the Princess Sedet had her special appetites which must be satisfied. On more than one occasion, Mara had been commanded to serve Sedet's cruel desire; playing the unwilling virgin to perfection as the Queen fucked her with an immense strap-on dildo that humiliated as it pleasured.

But activity at Winterbourne had been restrained. Even the Master had chosen for the time being to restrict himself to Winterbourne's whores and the homeless young girls Heimdal arranged to have kidnapped from the street to satisfy his hunger for living, virgin flesh. Yes, there had been fucking and Mara had been a part of it – serving Heimdal, the Master, Gonzales, the guards . . . anyone who wanted to enjoy the fruits of her sexy young body.

There would be fucking today, as well. Mara was driving up to Notting Hill with Takimoto, the irritating Geoffrey and Ibrahim. Apparently, the Master had commanded Takimoto to 'do a deal' – an important business arrangement which might have a bearing on the success of his political ambitions. They must be discreet but they must also be successful. Publicly, Mara worked for the Master's greater glory but, in her heart of hearts, she longed for apocalyptic destruction to destroy him and set free all the souls and bodies that he had enslaved. Already he had sowed the seeds of his cherished empire of lust. Soon, it might be too late . . .

Geoffrey swung the car into Twomey Street and parked outside a shabby building with a crumbling facade.

'This is it. Hillstar Videos. Shall I come in with you?'

Takimoto shook his head – probably doubting Geoffrey's ability to be discreet.

'You shall remain in the car. Ibrahim and the slut will accompany me. Come. It is time.'

Reluctantly Mara followed Takimoto and Ibrahim towards the tatty blue door with the tarnished brass plate: 'Hillstar Videos Ltd, Registered Office'. It didn't look much different from the offices of a thousand other down-at-heel video-rental companies. Maybe that was why the Master was so interested in it.

Takimoto rang the bell and after a few moments a chain rattled and the door opened slowly inwards. A brassy blonde appeared in the doorway, all eyeliner and jangling earrings. She had bright red lipstick smeared all over her teeth and her tight yellow mini-dress left nothing at all to the imagination.

'Yes?'

Takimoto gave a little bow and presented his card.

'I am from the Itsukita Corporation of Japan,' he explained. 'I have a meeting with your Mr Bates . . .'

'Oh yeah? Well I'spose you'd better come in then. He's a bit busy at the moment, though – I've been takin' one or two things down for him.' She leered suggestively at Takimoto, sizing him up as a possible sugar daddy. OK, so he was foreign, and she didn't normally go for short weedy blokes, but he looked rich and money was a real aphrodisiac to Cindy Jagger. Anyhow, Sid Bates wasn't keeping her in the style to which she'd like to become accustomed.

She led them up the stairs, past a series of faded promotional posters for films Mara had never heard of. No wonder Hillstar was doing so badly at the moment. But with over 200 high-street outlets nationwide, she could see why Hillstar presented a tempting proposition to the Master. And of course, if Mr Bates was short of cash, he might be willing to sell out at a low price without the need for . . . other methods of persuasion. Mara felt empty and lost inside. Why couldn't they have used one of the other whores? God knows, Winterbourne had plenty. Charlotte and Olivia, for example; they were classy – and keen. Or the ice-cool Joanna Königsberg with the cold blue eyes that had men grovelling at her feet, tearfully begging her to suck off their swollen, throbbing pricks.

Why Mara? She knew it was because Heimdal was so pleased with her recent 'successes'. She'd brought Chesterton, Hackman, Manley, Ffoukes and arch-masochist Stig Halvessohn to Winterbourne; and luring in the consummately stupid Nick Weatherall would surely be only a matter of time. She also suspected that the Master was trying to prove a point to Sedet: why should she be so irrationally suspicious of the Dubois slut who had always served them so loyally – and with such obvious enthusiasm?

At the top of the stairs, Cindy knocked at a door marked 'Private' but there was no reply so she pushed it open.

Bates moved quickly but not quickly enough to prevent Mara and her companions seeing what he had been up to. He was sitting in front of a TV set with his flies undone and he had obviously been wanking to the rhythm of the German porn stars silently fucking on the screen before him. Mara felt an unmistakable thrill as she glanced at the screen, watching a girl being fucked and buggered so stylishly by two big German boys. They were big in all senses of the word . . . The girl was lying on her side and one of the boys was filling up her cunt while the other thrust energetically in and out of her arse. She seemed to be enjoying the experience, too, her mouth open and closing in silent ecstasy.

As he realised he was not alone, the red-faced video tycoon shoved his prick back into his trousers and pointed the remote control at the screen, meaning to switch off the TV. But Takimoto stopped him with a respectful inclination of the head.

'Please, Mr Bates, do not inconvenience yourself. Our business here is simple and will not take long.'

Bates put down the remote control and swivelled round in his chair to face the three visitors. Mara felt his eyes travelling over her body, drinking in the perfect symmetry of her firm figure, perhaps comparing her to the big-breasted brunette on the screen behind him who was still taking her punishment with valiant enthusiasm.

Bates was not what you'd call an impressive man and his shabby surroundings served only to reinforce the image of a once-successful businessman down on his luck. But his cock was a different matter: Mara had seen it clearly, the massive shaft sliding smoothly between his fingers, and could not help wondering how it would feel in her cunt, in her mouth, in her arse . . .

Cindy was still standing in the doorway, leaning up against the doorframe as she inspected the chipped varnish on one of her nails. Evidently she was sufficiently interested to want to hang around.

'So – you be wantin' anyfing else then, Sid . . . Mr Bates?'

Bates pushed a hank of greasy hair off his forehead and shrugged his shoulders.

'You can stay, if you like. Take the minutes – make it all nice and official, eh?' He turned to his visitors and gestured to them to sit down. 'Take a seat. Sorry about the mess – we're just about to undertake major refurbishments, you know.'

'Really?' Takimoto eased himself disdainfully onto one of the rickety chairs, but Mara and Ibrahim remained standing behind him. Mara saw out of the corner of her eye that Ibrahim was moving gradually closer and closer to Cindy and she wasn't doing anything to discourage him. In fact, she was smiling and thrusting out her tits at him, as brazen as a bitch on heat.

'I have come to talk business, Mr Bates,' continued Takimoto, declining the tumblerful of whisky Bates pushed over the desk at him. 'So I shall not take up more of your time than is absolutely necessary. The Itsukita Corporation wishes to purchase your entire chain of video outlets, together with the distribution company. I think you will find this a fair price.'

Bates watched with raised eyebrows as Takimoto reached into the inside pocket of his jacket and took out a cheque. A cheque with more noughts on it than Bates had had hot showgirls. He stared at it blankly and for a moment Mara hoped he would just pocket the cash and let Takimoto get on with it.

To her left, Ibrahim and Cindy were certainly coming to a mutually acceptable deal. The Ethiopian had her sitting on his knee now and his hand was up her skirt, playing so skilfully between her cunt lips that the look of sullen inattention had completely left her face. Her breath was coming in little gasps and she was obviously more than ready for the fat black prick Ibrahim was unzipping just for her . . .

But Bates wasn't paying any attention to the little playlet being acted out in the corner of his office. He was too busy staring at the cheque. All of a sudden, a complete transformation came over him and a wild light seemed to flicker in his eyes. Picking up the cheque, he glared defiantly at Takimoto and then tore it, very deliberately, into four pieces and threw them onto the desk.

'Think you're so bloody clever, don't you?' he snarled and even Cindy paused for a moment, Ibrahim's dick firmly embedded in her cunt and her thighs wrapped round his hips. 'You foreign bastards think you can just walk in here and buy up anything you damn well like. Well, you can forget it, Mr Takimoto. Hillstar Video is not for sale.'

Takimoto sighed. He had hoped to avoid any unnecessary effort. After all, the man was a failure, patently unsuitable for initiation. But he might provide transient sexual sustenance and the girl Cindy was born to be a whore. She had the kind of low-born sluttishness which seemed to appeal to so many foolish Englishmen.

He returned Bates's glare with a conciliatory smile.

'Forgive me, Mr Bates. I did not mean to insult you. Perhaps you will allow me to make amends?'

Bates looked at him suspiciously. He'd seen what Cindy was up to in the corner with that black stud and – while he didn't approve of her fraternising with the enemy – the sight of Ibrahim's dick in her cunt had made him hot again. The throbbing of his unsatisfied prick, still stiff from his abortive wank, was sending treacherous messages to his lust-dulled brain.

'Come, slut.' Takimoto beckoned to Mara and she stepped forward, reluctant yet curiously excited. Bates's sleaziness intrigued her; made her want to know how it would feel to be fucked by him, to have his massive dick spurting into her mouth. 'On your knees. Show Mr Bates how sincerely we are sorry for the insult to his good name.'

Obediently, Mara knelt before Bates, head bowed and trembling with anticipation.

Bates stared incredulously, first at Mara and then at Takimoto.

'I . . . can have her? Do anything I like with her?'

Takimoto gave a nod of assent.

'Anything you choose. The girl is my gift of atonement to you, as is our way in Japan. She is an obedient slave – almost as skilled as a true geisha. She will give you all the pleasure you desire.'

Bates licked his lips, his mouth suddenly dry with excitement. Could this be true? Could he be dreaming or had a Japanese businessman just offered him the gorgeous nubile body of his personal assistant?

Mara wondered if his indecision would save him. If he refused Takimoto's offer, Bates might yet escape the fate that had been prepared for him. But Bates was a weak-minded fool, she knew he had not the will to refuse – any more than she had the will to resist the burning need to fuck. They were victims together now, victims of the Master's dominion of sex.

'Take off your knickers and get down on your hands and knees,' he whispered hoarsely to Mara. 'I want to see you naked.'

She slipped off her panties and flung them to the floor, an incongruous knot of scarlet silk and lace on the cracked and grimy tiles. Pulling up her skirt to expose her rounded arse cheeks, she knelt before him and at once felt the cool wetness of his saliva as he licked her, greedily seeking out and probing her most secret places.

She could not suppress a groan of delight as his tongue wriggled into her arsehole, a lewd living creature burrowing deep into her and awakening the very heart of her lust. Sexual hunger was in her belly, her gently pulsing cunt, the tingling tips of her hardened nipples. She must have sex, sex, sex . . .

As he slid his fine fat prick into her, Mara gave a sigh of satisfaction. At last she had the pleasure of a dick in her cunt and probing fingers up her arse. At last came the surge of sexual energy that eased her pain and liberated her mind, setting her soul free to soar for a moment in the realms of the spirit, where Andreas Hunt was calling to her.

Bates was far too engrossed in his own pleasure to notice Takimoto standing behind him, his glittering sharp teeth, poised to pierce the flesh of his unsuspecting throat. And as Bates shot off into Mara's molten flesh, the pleasure of orgasm far outweighed the pain of Ibrahim's deadly kiss.

The crowd were enraptured, just the way Heimdal had known they would be. Even without the aid of Takimoto's subliminal propaganda, the Master could manipulate an audience with expert ease. Accepting the invitation to take part in a debate at Caxton College had proved to be an inspired decision. The young and the beautiful seemed instinctively drawn to the Master, as though they somehow understood that only through him could youth and beauty continue forever.

The Master stood in the spotlight, centre stage, and acknowledged the applause of his adoring public. Which was, of course, exactly as it should be. He expected no less reward for his efforts. Sedet was looking on from the wings, the perfect political partner: loyal, beautiful – and silent. Still half-locked in a world four thousand years dead, Sedet understood little of the machinations of modern politics. She had wanted to speak in support of him but he had silenced that plan instantly. Too much meddling and she could become a liability. What he needed from her was the psychic sexual power that ignited from the spark of their two spirits.

The election campaign was going well. The good folk of Caxton-upon-Thames had been badly shaken by the sudden – and very unfortunate – demise of their Republican MP. The recent colourful profusion of political sex scandals had been another bombshell to them, and as for the Jerry Singleton exposé . . . when would it end? Not until the Master was good and ready. And, even then, the nightmare would just be beginning.

The Republicans would get over it this time – repair the holes in the dyke and keep on in government – for a while. But the Master smiled to himself with the certainty of ultimate success. In six months, a year, eighteen months maybe, the Government would be dealt a death blow from which it would never recover. And then . . . Then his time would come.

What did it matter how long it took? He and his followers had all the time in the world.

He would be patient – he could afford to be. For now, he would content himself with the pathetically easy task of winning this marginal seat in the heart of Merrie England. Already his public loved him. He scanned the audience, mentally selecting those who would have the honour of joining him in his victorious empire; those who would fulfil the simple function of sexual sustenance and pleasure.

The audience of youthful intelligentsia here at Caxton College offered many intriguing possibilities: the girl down there with the dark hair and the almond eyes; the blond boy in the white T-shirt, his muscles rippling underneath the thin tight fabric. Energies were flowing out of his audience and into his soul, refreshing and enlivening it: the energies of their adulation, their excitement, their desire. He could feel how much they wanted him – wanted to touch him, feel him, be possessed by him. It was well that he should enjoy such success with these young people: the cream of the intellectual elite who aspired to be the future leaders of their country. Doubtless some of them would in time become the intimate servants of the Master and his Queen.

As the debate ended and he left the stage, the Master was mobbed by adoring women and smiled obligingly for the benefit of the press. No-one seemed to be taking much interest in his opponents and they were spitting fury, pathologically envious of his effortless success. Undoubtedly wheels were turning within wheels – undercover agents from all the major parties would be working night and day to uncover dirt on him which would scupper his chances of getting into Parliament. The Master resolved to be careful – he would be ready for them.

As he and Sedet walked out of the ancient college hall into the cool of the evening, the Master spotted Liz Exley, standing alone by the gate. He'd noticed her early on in the debate, of course, sitting near the front of the hall and looking up at him, eyes constantly fixed on him. Was she trying to unsettle him or was that the look of sexual obsession? She was dressed in a figure-hugging dress of deep blue velvet, slit up one side to give tantalising glimpses of her slender thigh as she walked. She was an intelligent woman. Doubtless she knew that he wanted her as much as she wanted him. But did she also realise that Sedet desired her? Wanted to taste her desire, drink it down and then torment her until she cried for mercy?

He'd had his doubts about Exley from the start, suspecting she was out to cause trouble for him. Well, after tonight he wouldn't have to worry about her any more. His cock was throbbing for her and he could feel the heat of Sedet's need, burning like some great inferno in her cunt. Together, they would enjoy Liz Exley and teach her a few tricks that even a streetwise news reporter had never encountered before. They would find out if the woman's sexual versatility matched her skill as a journalist.

He beckoned to Liz to come over and the three of them got into the back of the Master's car. Ibrahim turned the key in the ignition.

'Drive on,' instructed the Master. 'Miss Exley is coming back with us to Winterbourne.'

Tonight, the Master and Sedet would enjoy her together, feeding on her energies, testing her to see if she was worthy of the Master's service. Tonight, they would decide whether Liz Exley would live or die.

'Well, well! I haven't seen you since . . . wasn't it at Chester Races? I never forget a pretty face, you know. Or a nice firm pair of tits.'

Mara turned round and found herself looking into the face of Nick Weatherall, the Nationalist MP she'd so very nearly seduced at the racecourse, that day back in May. His father had been an entertaining fuck . . .

'Fancy having a quiet drink with me, girlie? These fund-raising dos really piss me off.'

Sandwiched between an elderly stockbroker and his wife – a knitting enthusiast – Mara welcomed any interruption which might give her a chance to escape from the deadly tedium. She glanced across the dinner table and saw that Heimdal's eyes were on her. He was smiling and nodding, encouraging her to go. Hardly surprising, really – Nick Weatherall still featured strongly in the Master's future strategy.

Mara made her apologies and left the huddle of campaign managers and PR consultants. Tonight's banquet, at one of the old guildhalls in the City, had been financed by Chesterton and a group of merchant bankers who had been initiated at the Immortals Ball. The aim was to wine and dine some of the most influential members of the Caxton-upon-Thames business community – very discreetly and very respectably – and the occasion was every bit as dull as Mara had feared it would be.

Meeting up with Nick Weatherall wasn't likely to bring much in the way of intellectual stimulation, but as for physical stimulation . . . She couldn't help noticing that he was even more handsome than she'd remembered – his dark, wavy hair falling in an unmanageable fringe over his forehead, beneath which glittered a pair of striking blue eyes. His grip was hot and firm on her arm as he led her out of the main function room and down a corridor which led to the private gardens at the back of the medieval hall. She felt desire coursing through her and yet the inane babble of his voice in her ear irritated her beyond belief. How could someone so handsome, so sexual, be so . . . thick?

At the end of the corridor, Weatherall unbolted the double doors and they stepped out into the cool night air.

'Bit of fresh air – clear the old bonce, what?'

'It's a bit cold. Maybe I should go back in and get my coat.'

'Don't worry about that, Miss D. I know some splendid ways of keeping warm.'

He grinned and winked, giving Mara what was evidently intended as a subtle come-one but which came across like an embarrassing facial tic. She wanted to laugh out loud at this ridiculous man, this creature animated only by its appetites: greed and hunger and the constant need for sex. He would fit in well with the Master's followers and Mara told herself that she needn't feel too bad about luring him to his doom – there was nothing about him worth salvaging.

And yet, as he turned to kiss her, she did think there might be one thing worth saving. That glorious, desirable, fuckable body. Not for the first time she imagined Andreas's indomitable spirit in that irresistible frame and desire crackled and bubbled within her, making her cunt dripping wet.

Weatherall led her through the Elizabethan knot garden to the old summer-house, deserted on this chilly autumn evening. Distant sounds of music floated on the air from the hall as the band struck up and the dancing got underway. It was all so different from the night of the Immortals Ball at Winterbourne and the frenzied dance of the doomed, fucking for their lives in the shadows of perdition.

They sat down together on the stone seat beneath the wooden canopy. Weatherall's hand strayed to her breast, kneading and stroking the flesh with practised skill.

'My God, you're lovely,' he whispered. 'You've got the most gorgeous tits I've ever seen.'

She closed her eyes as he unzipped her dress and pulled

down the shoulder straps, exposing the bare flesh of her breasts to the cold night air.

'Bloody gorgeous,' he murmured again, cupping a globe in either hand and squeezing the nipples – at first gently, then with a cruel precision that took Mara to the sweet, unbearable edge of pain. She gasped and, with eyes still closed, began to imagine that it was Andreas touching her, Andreas's hands pinching and teasing and tormenting her nipples. Soon it would be Andreas's cock in her cunt, driving in and out of her, setting the rhythm of their mutual need.

Her thoughts went back to that day on the clifftop when Andreas had called her to him. To the memory of that glorious mind-fuck as they melted together, body and soul, within the crystal. With Weatherall, there could be no conjunction of the mind and she shunned his soul as she would shun all darkness and selfish greed. But, physically, they were perfect together. She cried out as he bent to kiss her breast, taking her nipple into his mouth and tormenting it slowly between lips and tongue and teeth. She wanted him so much . . .

'Fuck me,' she murmured. 'Fuck me now.'

He slid up her skirt and in a second tugged down her panties, discarding them on the cold ground. And then she was lying on her back on the stone seat and he was kneeling between her thighs, lapping at her wetness like a greedy kitten.

'More, more!' she gasped, clutching at his shoulders as his face pressed close to the heady sweetness of her sex, stimulating the throbbing bud of her clitoris to paroxysms of ecstasy.

As he thrust his cock into her and began fucking her, a familiar voice spoke in her head.

*Come to me, Mara. Come to me now.*

Andreas was calling to her. And this time, his voice was clear, strong, unmistakeable. He was not calling to her from far away, from within the crystal, but from within the body of Nick Weatherall. Opening her eyes, she saw Andreas Hunt smiling at her from the eyes of her transient lover.

She sent her spirit out to him on wave upon wave of pleasure, and his spirit answered her call.

*I can feel it, Mara. I can feel your cunt around my dick. It's so good. Am I dreaming . . .?*

*No, it's not a dream. It's real. The pleasure is so, so real. But how . . .?*

*His mind is weak. He couldn't fight me.*

As they moved together, it was Andreas's cock that was fucking her. Andreas's hands that squeezed and stimulated her nipples. Andreas's thick white semen that flooded into her as her cunt muscles tensed and she shuddered with the long spasms of orgasm.

When she opened her eyes, he was gone and in his place was Nick Weatherall, panting and groaning on top of her naked breasts. But the memory of Andreas was still vividly alive and, as she looked at Nick's beautiful empty body, a new hope stirred within her.

'Morning Mr Trevidian, sir. The usual, is it?'

'Morning, Fred.'

Max scanned the newsagent's shelves. All the papers were full of it, of course – 'Landslide Victory in Caxton-upon-Thames By-election'. Reluctantly he selected a copy of the *Daily Comet*. He didn't usually bother with such scandal rags but, ever since his suspicions about Andreas Hunt, he'd been buying the *Comet* occasionally in the hope of coming up with some clue as to what was going on. In a mad moment he'd even had a word with Hunt's old editor, who poured scorn on all his conspiracy theories and put forward the theory that Hunt was simply an idle tosser who'd pissed off to the Greek Islands with some bimbo he'd met up in Whitby. A girl called Mara Fleming . . .

Max handed over his money and was about to leave but Fred was in the mood for a chat.

'Seen the story about that vampire woman, then?'

'What?' Max wondered why the word 'vampire' struck such a chord in his mind.

'Page four, bottom left-hand corner – "Caxton-upon-Thames Police Seek Vampire Woman". Seems some crazy woman's gone and bitten a chunk out of her husband's neck whilst they were on the job, see. And now she's wandered off and nobody knows where the hell she is. Irishwoman, I think. Course, they're all nuts, you know.'

Max scanned the story. Caít O'Keefe. Had he heard that name before? He didn't think so. But could there be any connection between this brief story and the series of deaths, disappearances and apparent personality changes that had afflicted a whole host of influential people over the last few months? Did he dare to make that connection?

'Don't know what the world's coming to. Sex, violence – they've got no respect these days. Of course, now that LeMaître chap's got in, he'll put a stop to all this nonsense. Clean honest government, that's what he stands for.'

Trevidian said nothing. But there was a cold, dark feeling in his heart and he had a hunch it wasn't going to go away . . .

# 8: Hall of Darkness

Sex was in the air. Standing above the entrance hall at Winterbourne, Mara could breathe it in, as potent and as heady as pure oxygen.

Since the Master's remarkable victory in the recent by-election, the new Member for Caxton-upon-Thames had been celebrating – in style. For the benefit of a curious press, he and Sedet had given many society parties at the master's town-house in Blackheath, keeping up the all-important illusion that Anthony LeMaître was an aristocratic ex-soldier of independent means – one who hadn't lost the common touch.

Meanwhile, at the discreet pleasure-palace of Winterbourne Hall, the Master held court for the faithful: summoning them to the odd country house hidden in the depths of the English countryside miles from anywhere. This was the true heart of the Master's power, the Master's unchallenged realm of dark, unending pleasure.

Mara walked quickly down the main staircase, deliberately paying little attention to the two whores laughing over the prone body of a businessman who had spent an eventful night at the Hall. The conjunction of sex and death had become an everyday occurrence at Winterbourne. Mara must not draw attention to herself by betraying her revulsion.

'Slut!'

Mara looked down and saw Geoffrey standing in the entrance hall. He made her flesh creep but, since he was Heimdal's most devoted servant, she must be civil to him.

She walked slowly down the rest of the carpeted staircase, painfully aware of his eyes travelling down across her breasts to the swell of her hips and thighs. She hoped he would enjoy looking up her skirt and leave it at that.

'Yes, Geoffrey?'

'The Master wants you.'

'Where?'

He grabbed her wrist and pulled her to him.

'Steady on, Anastasia. I want you first.'

Suddenly his hands were all over her, unfastening her buttons, exploring the bare flesh beneath, slaking his lust with the blind power of touch. Mara did not struggle but looked him straight in the eye and spoke calmly. She couldn't afford to anger him.

'Are you seriously suggesting I should delay obeying a command from the Master? Do you want us both to feel the force of his anger?'

'OK, OK,' protested Geoffrey feebly. 'I was only joking. He wants you to go to the meeting in the Library. I think he's got some of the MPs in there with him.'

Mara turned to go. Geoffrey hesitated for a moment, then added: 'Be careful. Mistress Sedet is in a capricious mood today. She whipped one of the kidnapped girls to within an inch of her life, then had her thrown to the guards. It wasn't a pretty sight.'

Mara stared back at him with contempt, knowing that it was malice and not concern which made him tell her these things. There was a cruel streak in Geoffrey which had not existed when she first met him. That night long ago, he had been a fresh-faced innocent who wouldn't have hurt a fly. Ever since his initiation he had grown steadily more unpleasant. There was a danger within him now and Mara could not help blaming herself for the changes in him. If she had not blundered into the caravan park that cold November night, naked and desperate for comfort, Geoffrey Potter would probably still be an innocent boy today.

She walked down the corridor to the Library and stopped

134

outside, pausing for a moment before she knocked. Despite the Master's obvious approbation, Mara feared a confrontation with Mistress Sedet. Sedet's powers might not be a match for hers but even in that fact danger might lie. Would she not wonder why her mind could not subdue that of the vampire-slut Dubois, unveiling the simple pattern of her thoughts? And surely a loyal servant of the Master would have nothing to hide from Mistress Sedet?

Mara knocked on the door.

'Enter.'

The Master sat at the head of the polished conference table, feeling the strength of victory flooding into him. The body of Andreas Hunt had served him well, earning itself a far greater immortality than Hunt could ever have aspired to. And now he was about to enter Parliament and make his maiden speech – just as he had planned. It was so, so good to feel his plans taking shape and his empire gradually taking shape around him.

'Sit down, slut,' he said to Mara. 'We shall have need of your services later.' He turned to the men and women assembled round the table: MPs from both major parties, a sprinkling of media figures and businessmen . . . and of course the journalist Liz Exley, who had given such pleasure to Sedet over the last few nights.

Liz had furnished both pleasure and a fund of useful information. The Master understood why he had suspected the woman's motives – all along, she had been trying to investigate him, hunting for scandals that could make her name and ruin his. Still, that should present no future cause for concern. Exley had been defeated by her own sexual hunger. She was now his devoted – and lustful – slave and, as for her accomplices, they were of little account and would be dealt with as necessary.

Casting his thoughts out into the chill autumn skies, he saw a man sitting amid a jumble of pictures and press cuttings. A man afraid, suspicious . . . but not dangerous. A man called Max Trevidian.

Ironically enough, the man had latent psychic powers and as the Master's spirit entered him he seemed to shiver, a sudden inexplicable coldness rippling across his flesh. But, throughout his entire life, this man had fiercely denied his powers and as long as he continued to deny their existence he could pose no threat to the Master. Perhaps, thought the Master – he passed the thought to Sedet and her dark spirit shook with silent laughter – perhaps it would be amusing to torment him a little, play with his mind and then, when they had tired of him, destroy his body.

The Master relaxed in his chair as a pretty youth masturbated his cock, rubbing sweet oils into the flesh to soothe and stimulate and prolong his pleasure. After his years of captivity and bitter disappointment, such pleasure was his rightful due.

He snapped his fingers and Hackman flicked open his briefcase.

'The speech.'

'I have prepared it as you instructed, Master. As planned, our supporters on both sides of the House will heckle at predetermined points during your speech on law and order . . .'

'. . . And I, of course, shall parry their attacks brilliantly.' The Master threw back his head and laughed. The boy's hand was silky smooth on his tool, wanking the shaft back and forth with an automatic skill. Yes, young Malik had been a useful acquisition – another pretty little souvenir of a profitable sojourn in India. Malicious glee bubbled up inside the Master as he thought of the fakir Gurandjit's tortured face, ivory-white with terror and pain as his old body sank inexorably down onto the razor-sharp points of his bed of nails.

That had been another old score settled. Through those long years of pain and darkness in the crystal, he had never forgotten the sweet taste of vengeance and the unparalleled pleasure of a cruel victory. And that pleasure was not over yet. Some had escaped him through death but there were others who must also pay for their part in the treacherous Allied plot to destroy him. He was going to enjoy exacting his vengeance from them as well. He would let Sedet play with their minds a little and feed on the sweet succulence of their fear, then he would watch them die.

As the youth licked his balls, running his lewd tongue over the velvety purse of his scrotum, the Master set out his plans for the future. With loyal servants on both sides of the House, he would be in an ideal position to consolidate and then strengthen his power. He would proceed carefully, though. His rise must not be too meteoric, too suspiciously effortless. For the time being, he would be content to play the humble – but obviously able – Opposition backbencher.

Already the Home Secretary was in his pocket, and once the Prime Minister had been persuaded to pay a little visit to Winterbourne . . . Feeling the spunk boiling in his shaft, the Master cast a sidelong glance at the Dubois slut, contemplating the pleasure of fucking or buggering her here and now, on the polished tabletop. She was a loyal slave, hot as a bitch in heat, and hungry for all the dick she could get. And skilful, too, for all that Sedet decried her. Already she'd brought him Chesterton, Ffoukes, Manley and Hackman. And he had every faith in her ability to bring Republican Party boss Hugo Winchester to heel as well.

'Slut.'

Mara's heart pounded. Eyes downcast, she tried not to look up into LeMaître's piercing blue-grey eyes. She knew she would never get used to the sight of the Master wearing Andreas's body like some designer suit.

'Master?'

'Come here, slut. And look at me. I want to see that pretty little mouth.'

She obeyed, trembling with a guilty excitement as he forced his will upon her, dreading that at any moment he might choose to search the depths of her soul and discover the forbidden truth within.

But the Master – secure in the warm glow of his own self-importance – was intent only on pleasure. He pushed away the Indian boy and he fell to the floor, gazing up at his beloved Master with pleading eyes.

'Go from me, Malik, I tire of you. There are others here whom you may pleasure.' He turned back to Mara, now standing before him, tall and slender in her ice-blue silk dress. There was lust in her eyes.

Pushing back his chair a little way from the table, he enquired: 'How many cocks have you sucked today, slut?'

Mara blushed, the sudden truth surprising and somehow exciting her.

'Ten, Master.'

'Good, good. I hope you still have the taste of their spunk in your mouth. Do you like the taste of spunk? Does it make you feel strong?'

'Yes, Master.'

'Those who serve me must be strong. Strong and beautiful. And you, my dear, are indeed a beautiful little slut.'

'You honour me, Master.'

He laughed, well pleased with this obedient sex slave. He ought to have this one more often – she was definitely one of his favourites, especially since she'd grown more adventurous, so much more . . . knowing. Sometimes, she even reminded him of the white witch Mara who had led him such a diverting dance before he had at last trapped and destroyed her in the Valley of the Tombs of Kings. Just occasionally, though he hardly wished to admit it to himself, he regretted the death of the Fleming girl. She had been almost a match for him. An irritation, assuredly, yet without her to stretch his powers he was in danger of becoming bored.

'Kneel, slut. Since you so enjoy the taste of semen, you shall lick it from me. Every droplet, do you hear? Every droplet, or you shall pay dearly for it.'

'Yes, Master.'

Mara knelt between the Master's thighs, remembering how she had once performed the same delicious duty for Andreas Hunt. She wanted to make some act of defiance against this servitude but what good would defiance do?

What could one poor servant do against the might of the Master's evil empire?

And she could not fight the power of her own lust – the lust that was now her lifeblood, forcing her to the darkest, guiltiest pleasures. The salty taste of the Master's spunk excited her and she knew he was excited too. She could smell his desire for her, taste it in the droplets of spunk that the youth Malik had milked from his cock. The semen lay in big opalescent droplets on the dark grey woollen fabric of the Master's trousers and she lapped them up, one by one, each salty mouthful as rich and sensual as whipped cream.

To her surprise, Mara saw that Mistress Sedet was taking not the slightest notice of her. She was far too busy enjoying the lavish caresses of the new whore, the newswoman Liz Exley. Mara felt a pang of regret as she saw the blond reporter kneeling between Sedet's thighs, running her eager tongue over the Queen's love lips. At great risk to herself, Mara had once tried to warn Liz, but her oblique references and desperate, formless warnings had been completely misinterpreted. Liz had of course assumed that Mara was just one of LeMaître's jealous mistresses, eager to keep all her lover's favours for herself.

And so it was that, a few nights ago, Liz Exley had come to Winterbourne with the Master and Mistress. She had seemed so excited, so triumphant; certain that in winning LeMaître's favours, she had ensured herself a glittering media career.

Well, she had certainly earned herself a certain immortality. Now Mara's master was Liz Exley's, too.

As Mara lapped up the last of the semen, she felt an unbearable wave of desire washing over her. She needed sex. Needed it so badly. Andreas was the only man she truly desired but sex was a desperate need within her. So great a need that she would fuck any man or woman who wanted her.

She looked up into the Master's face and saw that he was smiling.

'You have done well, slut. Shall I reward you for your efforts?'

'If . . . if it pleases you, Master.'

Mara's heart was pounding, her mouth dry and her palms sweating with excitement. This was the evil monster who had robbed Andreas Hunt of life – the sex-vampire who had stolen her body for his beloved queen. And here she was, desperately hoping that he would fuck her. Hoping and yearning, for there was a ravening in her belly that only sex could satisfy.

'I shall reward you with my cock, slut. My sacred cock in your cunt. Get onto the table – on your belly. Quickly now! I hunger for your flesh.'

Mara obeyed. All eyes were on her. Takimoto in particular looked as though he would die of frustration. He had craved her body for so long . . .

She lay face down on the table, hitching her skirt up so that the ice-blue silk ruched up under her belly, exposing the generous swell of her bare buttocks. As the Master preferred, she was wearing no underwear. There must be no impediment to the satisfaction of his sacred pleasure.

'Spread your thighs.'

She obeyed, and winced with pain as the Master twisted a lock of her thick, auburn pubic curls about his finger.

'You have a pretty enough cunt, slut. I shall honour you with my cock.'

Standing by the edge of the table, her Master lifted her legs and held them around his waist as he entered her in a single brutal thrust. The pleasure was exquisite as his fat cock distended the soft flesh of her vagina, stretching it to the delicious point between pleasure and pain.

Half-dazed with pleasure, Mara heard herself moaning as the Master's prick toiled in and out of her cunt. As he fucked her, he ran through the preparations for the forthcoming week's events.

'The videotapes. They are ready?'

Takimoto bowed, desperately trying to control his lust as

140

he watched the Master's dick sliding in and out of Mara's well-greased crack. Oh, how he had longed to shaft that auburn-haired tart with the aristocratic English looks. How he had longed to beat and humiliate and subdue her, exciting her lust as he subjugated her to his will. But the Dubois girl was his Master's possession. He might covet but he could not possess her unless the Master permitted it. Perhaps, if the Master was very pleased with him, he might lend the whore to him for one night . . .

'All is as we planned, Master. The subliminals have been carefully selected. Only the most subtle messages have been chosen. The videotapes will be rented out through our Hillstar Video outlets.'

'And the video presentation for the Cabinet Office?' He thrust further into the girl's pussy and she cried out for him to be harder, more brutal. Well, he saw no reason to disappoint her.

'The videotape is being . . . modified . . . even as we speak, Master.'

The Master was enjoying himself. The Dubois slut really was a remarkably good fuck. These days, she spent most of her time screwing his enemies, seducing them into a false sense of security so that, after a little of Winterbourne's hospitality, they might become his friends. His oh-so-devoted friends. But he liked to fuck her himself from time to time, just to remind himself what a wonderful arse she had; what a skilful mouth and plump juicy tits just ripe for the tribute of his spunk.

'Feel my energy flowing into you,' he breathed as he felt the spunk bubbling and surging in his shaft. 'You are honoured indeed. Feel my sacred essence spurting into your belly, my darling little slut.'

'Master, Master!' cried Mara, no longer able to control the passion within her. Already she was surrendering to the first agonising, delicious spasms of her rebellious cunt. The Master's seed boiled and foamed within her, searing and caressing as it spurted against the neck of her womb.

He withdrew from her, leaving her gasping and panting on the glossy table-top, their mingled juices flooding out of her in an opalescent pool.

'Success is at last in sight,' announced the Master, addressing his faithful disciples. 'And we must all strengthen our powers for the tasks which await us. Tonight, the Mistress has arranged an entertainment for you in the Hall of Darkness. I think you will find it . . . piquant and refreshing.'

Takimoto's resolve broke. He could not keep silent. Desire was like the ache of hunger to a starving man.

'Master . . .'

'Ah yes.' The Master gave a dismissive wave of the hand. 'I have finished with the slut. You may all enjoy her now. Do whatever you will with her. Her flesh will whet your appetites for tonight's ceremonies.'

As Mara followed Mistress Sedet down the steps into the darkness, she wondered if Andreas could feel her there, feel the dark sensual energy flooding out of this grim procession. Here, in the cellars at Winterbourne, they were close, so very close, to the bricked-up chamber where Andreas Hunt lay trapped within his crystal prison.

The rough stone steps down to the cellars were lined with burning torches that cast weird, cadaverous shadows on the faces on ten cloaked figures wending their way down towards the Hall of Darkness: Sedet's very special kingdom, where pain and pleasure mingled in an exquisite harmony and the Mistress's will was the only rule.

Mistress Sedet was in a good mood tonight. They were descending with her into her own dark underworld where she was to be the mistress of ceremonies, all-powerful, all-unforgiving. Magnificent in a catsuit of studded leather, she felt invincible, all-powerful again for the first time in four thousand years. With the delectable Exley whore to attend to her pleasure, she was going to enjoy this evening.

At the bottom of the stairs was an elaborate wrought-ironwork gateway, decorated with the grotesque grinning faces of demons, their bodies locked in an unholy orgy of copulation. Mara tried to avert her eyes but she could not banish the fleeting impression from her mind: all the demons seemed to wear a single face – the evil face of the Master.

As they passed through the gateway into the cold bare dungeon, Mara saw the girl: very young, very blonde and almost naked, sitting on a gilded chair in the centre of the bare concrete floor. She was staring blankly into space, lost in the silent ecstasy of a drug-induced trance. No doubt Madame LeCoeur had worked hard on the girl, plying her with the sweet syrupy wine that banished all fears and left behind only the intoxicating undercurrents of sensual desire.

Mara looked at the girl, knowing exactly what was to befall her. She too had experienced the cruel pleasure of Mistress Sedet, submitted to the bite of the whip as she hung, helpless and afraid, from iron hooks in the bare stone walls. But this girl would be a willing victim. Lost in a seductive dream of Madame LeCoeur's making, this child-woman would have no desire to resist until it was too, too late.

The Master and his disciples gathered in a circle about the girl, their dark cloaks open at the front, revealing their eager naked pricks.

Sedet smiled, stroking the blonde captive's hair with a leather-gloved hand.

'She pleases you, my Lord?'

'She has potential.'

The Master ran an exploratory finger over the gauzy robe that barely covered the girl's budding breasts. Why, the girl could only be sixteen years old – ripe, juicy and full of promise. Perfect for the renewal of his disciples' strength. Perfect for sating their insatiable appetites. He nodded appreciatively as the girl gave a little moan of pleasure, her nipples hardening instantly at his touch.

'So you succeeded in persuading Manley to give up his beloved Annabel to the sacred cause?'

Sedet laughed.

'The Shadow Home Secretary's loyalty is unquestioning.

How could it be otherwise, since it is only through the good offices of our powerful friends that his Shadow Cabinet position has been saved? He soon saw reason. A pretty virgin daughter is a small price to pay for safeguarding one's reputation . . .'

'She is schooled to pain?'

'My Lord, I myself have taken the whip to her back a dozen times these last few days. And I swear the little whore cried out in ecstasy when Ibrahim passed the slave-ring through her clitty.'

The Master licked his lips in anticipation of this delicious morsel. It had been too long since he last enjoyed a pretty little virgin like this one.

'Part your thighs, girl.'

Annabel obeyed slowly and silently, like a ghostly automaton in her gauzy white robe. The Master pulled up the filmy skirt and thrust a finger into the tightness of her cunt. A virgin. A juicy, plump, tender virgin. How sweet her blood would taste . . .

Clapping her hands, Sedet brought forward two masked boys, armed with whips and chains.

'Chain the girl to the X-frame. The Master and his companions wish to take their pleasure of her.'

The boys pulled the girl to her feet. She seemed quite happy to follow where they led as they took her across to the wooden X-frame and fastened her to it securely with heavy iron shackles at wrist and ankle.

She looked so tempting that Sedet could not resist enjoying the first, satisfying blows. Weighing the bullwhip in her hand, she swung it viciously against the girl's back, cutting through the snow-white flesh at the first stroke.

The girl moaned but it was the cry of a girl well-schooled in the sweet pleasures of pain. She writhed in her bonds but served only to present her flesh more advantageously still to the lash.

'You have taught her well,' observed the Master, seizing the whip and using it with gusto. 'The girl has the makings of a useful whore. But first,' he turned to Heimdal. 'First let her serve the pleasure of the faithful.'

Heimdal nodded to the assembled disciples, who picked up birch canes and whips, and began striking the girl in a frenzy of violent lust. The girl's back reddened into a fierce criss-cross of stripes and welts, and her breath quickened as the fire of pain joined with the eternal flame of lust which burned within her.

In her mind, she was dancing – dancing with a dark and handsome man whose kisses burned like fire. As he danced, his cloak parted and she glimpsed the thick white shaft of his erect cock. Wetness was dripping from her virgin cunt, unknown longings boiling and surging within her. At last she could keep silent no longer.

'Master!' she cried, as the lash fell once again upon her back.

They cut her down, laying her martyred body on the cold hard floor. But she did not feel the discomfort. Her only feeling was lust, boiling burning lust that tormented her and would not let her go.

The Master towered over her and she looked up at him, uncomprehending and unafraid.

'What is it that you want of me, my child?'

'I . . . I do not know, Master. But there is such a burning within me, a longing . . . I can hardly bear it.'

'Do you want me to fuck you, child?'

'Yes, Master. Fuck me – fuck me now!'

The Master let his black cloak slip to the floor. His naked body gleamed in the flickering candlelight, his cock strong and merciless and hungry for the sustenance of virgin flesh.

A murmur of desire rippled through the watching disciples. One word, repeated again and again:

*Fuck, fuck, fuck . . .*

He took her there, on the stone floor, entering her without mercy, and she cried out as he tore through her tough hymen, spilling her virgin blood on the cold stone floor. But her cries were the cries of a bitch on heat, the cries of a she-cat to her mate. *Come fuck me. Come do what you will with me. I am yours for ever. Yours to do with as you will . . .*

A buzz of energy was filling the Hall of Darkness, an electricity which excited and elated even Mara, disgusted as she was by the spectacle. She could hardly bear to watch and yet the hunger within her made her a part of the spectacle. But she would not give in. Would never give in to the barbarism of the Master's depravity.

His teeth met so neatly in the flesh of Annabel's throat that she hardly seemed to notice the life-blood spurting from her – the energies of her youthful virginity passing from her body and into those of the vampire-creatures around her.

'Fuck!' cried Sedet, as the Master got to his feet, Annabel's blood a red stain around his mouth and hands. 'Open the gates and admit the faithful to the Hall of Darkness!'

The gates opened and in flooded the faithful of Winterbourne Hall: the whores and servants and devoted disciples of the Master, all eager to share in the unholy rite. Beautiful young men and women, naked and eager for sex. Suddenly a whip was in Mara's hand and she was wielding it like a madwoman, knowing that if she flinched the Mistress Sedet would be watching, waiting, hoping to catch her off her guard.

*Mara, no!*

The young man in front of her: the strong young man with the dark eyes and the stiff prick . . . he was looking into her eyes and silently beseeching her . . .

*No! Don't hit me. Can't you see? It's me, Andreas . . .*

He was beautiful. His muscular, naked body glistening with aphrodisiac oils whose spicy aroma made Mara's head spin. Andreas. Andreas had felt the dark power of this moment and had come to her, entering the body of this naked boy. His eyes were full of lust for her and his arms were stretching out, pleading for the sensual heat of her embrace.

*Come and fuck me, Mara. I want you so much . . .*

She turned and saw Mistress Sedet, her violet eyes narrow

with excitement, urging her on. *Go on, slut, do it. Beat him and prove you are the Master's loyal slave.*

She raised her arm and, as his mouth opened in pained surprise, she brought the whip down on the glistening, naked back . . .

Andreas was drifting, floating, travelling. Travelling towards the distant energy-pulse of frenzied sex.

Nearer now. Drawn like a magnet into the heart of a dark sun. There was evil all around him. He could feel it enveloping him like the cold, creeping, suffocating blanket of a glacier. Ice-energy that burned and seared as it touched his soul, sparking it into agonising life.

Light, now. Flickering light in a deep and terrifying blackness. And in the blackness, shadows within shadows, the dancing forms of white-fleshed creatures hungry for sex. A glimpse of sleek oiled thigh; a man's face twisted like a satyr, glistening with a thin film of sweat; the swirl of a long black cloak as it opened, revealing the hardening shaft of an eager cock . . .

In the darkness of this man-made hell there were faces that he recognised, though they swirled and blurred around him. The bitch-queen Sedet, a vision of triumphant evil in Mara's beautiful, lost body; the blond bear Heimdal, roaring out his pleasure as he drank the virgin blood dripping from the still, silent girl's cunt.

And the Master. Anthony fucking LeMaître.

Rage swelled and burned within him and, with a sudden rush that left him breathless, Andreas found himself sucked into the body of a naked boy: a pretty, empty-headed creature whose only function in life was to give pleasure.

He took faltering steps towards Mara, holding out his arms to her; wanting her so much that he could barely articulate the words in his head. He prayed that she would catch his thoughts, hear the need within him and answer it with the warmth between her legs.

There was fear in Mara's eyes. Fear that Andreas could not

understand until he felt the bite of the whip upon the bare, unprotected flesh of his back.

As he screamed in pain, his soul spun back into the dark oblivion whence it came. And the body within the sarcophagus flinched, the long-dead muscles tensing in one great spasm that sent shock-waves reverberating through the crystal.

The Master lifted his head for a moment from the virgin's ravaged, throat. He had felt something – a surge of energy, a fleeting mind-picture that left his mind as quickly as it had entered. A life-force, somewhere near: a life-force that, for some curious reason, reminded him of that gullible fool, Andreas Hunt.

But it couldn't be anything to do with Hunt, because Hunt was satisfyingly, definitively, dead. Buried under several tons of granite and securely embedded in a block of crystal from which – even if by some fluke he was still alive – Hunt would be far too stupid ever to escape. Any thoughts of Hunt must be down to the energy-traces still embedded in the stone of these ancient cellars: snapshots in stone – memories of that agreeable night when Hunt's body had acquired a far more worthwhile owner.

With a laugh he returned to the virgin's body, stirring already from the sleep of death, awakening to a new and much more sinister life.

If the Master had chosen to look beneath the lid of the sarcophagus, he might have been interested to see the crack – a finger's-breadth wide in places – which scored a jagged path across the surface of the crystal.

Caít gasped in pain. The crystal ring was burning hot again, searing her flesh like red-hot metal. She had tried to take it off but somehow it seemed to have grown tighter. She could have sworn it had slipped on and off easily when Donal first gave it to her. Now it was as though it refused to leave her hand.

Donal. It was three days now since she'd left him unconscious and bleeding on the bed they'd shared in the flat

148

in Caxton-upon-Thames. Why had she done it? She still didn't understand. But she knew it had something to do with the ring. Ever since she'd worn it, the oddest things had happened to her. On one or two occasions, she'd been looking at it – just admiring the intricate carving – and suddenly she'd felt drawn to look more closely at it. There was a cloudiness deep within it, like a swirling mist of white fire, ever-changing, ever-fascinating.

Had she really seen something moving, swirling . . . living, within the depths of the ring? Had she really seen the face of a man – dark-haired, bearded, cruel-mouthed – smiling at her from within those depths?

And what did the name 'Delgado' mean to her? Why did it keep flashing in and out of her head?

She walked wearily down the city streets, no longer knowing or caring where she was going. She was running from the police – but where was she running to? Ragged, lost, hungry . . . and on heat. She was a she-cat on the prowl. Would she find a mate to satisfy the burning lust within her? Each time she stopped to rest, the ring burned and blistered her flesh, refusing to allow her to end this quest she did not even understand.

Weariness racked her body but an instinct drove her on now. She hardly realised that she was walking down dark, dangerous streets where the unwary might falter . . . and never be seen again.

She was walking towards a featureless door in a featureless wall in a nameless street. Her hand was knocking on the black-painted wood: once, twice, three times. Waiting now. Waiting for the door to open and eager arms to usher her into the welcoming darkness.

# 9: Corridors of Power

In his new office at the House of Commons, the Master was enjoying the fruits of his success. The Manley girl made a passable secretary and she was a delicious fuck . . . It felt good to be enjoying her body here on his Government-issue desk, mocking the Establishment of which Anthony LeMaître MP was so ostentatiously a part.

Annabel Manley bent forward over the burgundy leather desk-top and opened her thighs for the Master. The crystal collar sparkled about her throat, discreetly veiling the still-fresh scars of a night she would never forget.

A few days ago, she had been nothing – a sixteen-year-old virgin, a gauche, insignificant sixth-former in an all-girls' public school. And now: now, she was the Master's slave. How she worshipped him for what he had done for her – ushering her into a new world of velvet darkness, teaching her how to use her sexuality in the service of glorious, magnificent, triumphant evil.

'Wider,' grunted the Master, driving hard into her. The girl was still virgin-tight and it had been a hard choice between her cunt and her arse. No doubt he would enjoy both before the day was out. Outside the window, a couple of prim and proper lady MPs walked past and nodded to the Master – completely unaware that the law-abiding, ultra-respectable Mr LeMaître was shafting his pretty young secretary right before their eyes.

Cheviot busied himself with the pile of papers on Annabel's desk.

'Plenty of letters from your constituency,' he observed. 'All praising you to the skies, of course. That maiden speech of yours has really got you into the public eye . . .'

'As I knew it would,' replied the Master, amusing himself by twisting Annabel's silver clitty-ring. He so enjoyed watching the little slut's pain turn to pleasure before his eyes.

'Of course, they're all begging you to get out there and do something about law and order. There's one here from a newsagent – says you ought to get hold of this crazy who's been going round biting people, and have her put away. "Such depravity has got to stop, and as the champion of clean government, you are the man to do it" – that's what he says.'

The Master roared with laughter. But there was a slight unease at the back of his mind. Why should this woman want to go round biting her lovers? Could she somehow have understood what he was doing and be trying to emulate him? More to the point, could her foolishness result in any danger for him?

He pulled apart Annabel's arse cheeks, and teased the sensitive membrane of her puckered arsehole, delighting in the way she squirmed and gasped.

'Silence, slut,' he commanded her; knowing that silence would be a torment for her. 'Your indiscipline will have us overheard.'

The girl gave a stifled sob as the Master explored her arsehole with the point of his nail, before plunging in his finger, right up to the knuckle. She was young, hot, deliciously naive. He could do anything he chose to her and she would still worship him. That was how he liked his women.

Unlike Sedet, of course. She was proud and strong – almost a match for him in psychic power and perhaps even more assiduous in her pursuit of ingenious cruelties. He so admired the way she coaxed submission from the slaves, punishing them with such skill that they existed solely for the sweet release of her subtle pain.

One thing did worry him about Sedet, though, and that was her obsession with the Exley whore. At times, her jealous lust verged on the inconvenient. He, too, enjoyed the pleasure-palace of the Exley woman's cunt but, to him, she was a mere toy to be enjoyed and then discarded. He was beginning to fear that for Sedet, fucking with Liz Exley was fast becoming a need.

And yet . . . the Exley slut had potential, there was no doubt of that. Most of the whores at Winterbourne were painted dolls: empty-headed beauties whose souls and bodies offered him little sustenance. All except for the Dubois slut . . . and Liz Exley. His cock still tingled with the memory of her sharp little teeth, teasing his shaft.

So many sluts to be fucked, so many games to play and minds to corrupt and enslave. He thought of the investigator that Exley had told him about, a pathetic man too scared even to admit to the psychic powers within him. Such an inflexible psyche was unlikely to pose much of a challenge but the Master was in need of a diversion. Trevidian would have to suffice . . .

But he would not spoil his enjoyment of the Manley girl. Her backside was as smooth and velvety as a peach; a young girl's backside, taut and firm and so, so juicy. Pulling out of her cunt, he shoved into her arse with a sudden urgency that made her moan and writhe again beneath him.

'I said silence, slut!'

He fucked the girl silently and luxuriously, taking the time to enjoy the warmth of the energy flowing into him. Later, perhaps, he would call Liz Exley into his office. It was time for her lessons to begin . . .

Max Trevidian sat at the table, staring at the pictures plastered all over the living-room wall as he took a pull at his beer. Just the one – got to keep a cool head. All around him were images of Anthony LeMaître – or was it really Andreas Hunt? Oh God, it was hopeless. Maybe he'd got in too deep – or maybe it was just that there wasn't anything worth investigating. Maybe he'd been wrong all along and Anthony LeMaître was just a regular guy. But then, so was Norman Bates . . .

No, something funny was definitely going on. You didn't get to be a Parliamentary Private Secretary and junior environmental spokesman *that* quickly unless you were up to something. Or unless you had something on somebody. Certainly Derek Manley was rapidly becoming LeMaître's number-one fan and Hugo Winchester, leader of Her Majesty's Opposition, hadn't wasted any time in proclaiming his support for the new boy. Now he'd even given him a cushy little Opposition job – one in which LeMaître could make the maximum impact. These days, the bloody man was never out of the papers or off the radio. Max had given up watching the TV – he was getting sick of Anthony LeMaître's smirking face.

So why did he keep on surrounding himself with pictures of the man? Why didn't he just ring up Liz Exley and explain to her that he was going nowhere fast, so could she just stump up his expenses and he'd bow out of the case? Maybe it was just stubbornness. Or maybe . . . Maybe he really was onto something but hadn't yet realised what it was. Of course there was another possibility. Maybe he just wasn't a very good investigator.

Suddenly he looked down and noticed something odd about the picture on the table: a half-face portrait of LeMaître, cut from the *Evening Standard*. Nothing very remarkable about that, only . . . the eyes seemed to be glowing, burning. He tried to look away, but those eyes just wouldn't let him go.

And something else was happening, too. Something impossible. Trevidian rubbed his forehead and wondered if three mouthfuls of dodgy brown ale could really do this to you.

There was no denying it. LeMaître was turning towards him, looking him straight in the eyes. There was such a depth of malice in that look. And now he was opening his mouth to speak.

'Bow to your master.'

The words chilled and terrified Trevidian and the glass fell to the ground, shattering into dozens of glittering fragments.

He clutched at the edge of the table, dizzy and sick with fear. Tearing his gaze away from the picture, he thought he had escaped the cruel hallucination.

But suddenly all the pictures on the walls were alive, too. Alive and chorusing their impossible mantra:

'Bow to your master, bow to your master. Bow, bow, bow . . .'

As the words chased round and round in his head, Trevidian felt his sanity slipping away from him and he took refuge in the merciful blackness that overwhelmed his consciousness.

Caít had come home.

She knew she had come home the moment the caressing hands undressed her and led her into the warm dark room – to safety and comfort and sex. She made no effort to resist for she was dazed and unafraid, and a strange excitement burned within her. As her clothes were peeled away, she felt as though she was leaving her old life behind, exposing new layers of her being. Becoming her true sexual self.

The women's voices wove a net above her, whispering as they pulled off her clothes and explored every intimate secret of her body.

'Beautiful . . .'

Hands weighed the fullness of her breasts; lips tasted the firm swell of her buttocks and the dewdrops of love-juice glistening on her glossy pubic curls.

'A born whore. See how she trembled at my touch. She's so excited . . .'

'Her body is slender, yet so voluptuous.'

Fingers probed and Caít gave a little shiver of pleasure as hands forced apart her thighs. A fingertip wriggled between her plump cunt lips, exploring the moist heart of her womanhood.

'Good and tight. She'll fetch an excellent price.'

'We haven't had such a promising girl sent to us since our dear Señor Delgado was so cruelly taken away. Why, she's almost worthy of Winterbourne . . .'

Delgado. The name found an echo in Caít's mind and she felt instinctively safe, secure. She had never met Delgado, knew nothing of him, and yet she knew he was to be her destiny. But Winterbourne? The name did not mean anything to her so why did the very sound of it fill her with anger and pain?

A week later, Caít was lying on her bed, in the afterglow of an afternoon's energetic coupling. These past days had been a revelation to her, opening up a sexual potential she had never dreamed existed within her. She had sucked so many cocks, taken so many in cunt and arse, swallowed so much semen that she felt drunk and giddy with excitement. What did it matter that many of her clients were old and disgusting? The more repellent they were, the more they filled her with a perverse excitement.

Here in the Maison Delgado, London's most secret, most exclusive house of pleasure, there were no taboos and no restrictions on enjoyment. Here, a young woman might explore the very depths of depravity and feel no shame as pleasure overwhelmed her. Here, the most piquant of pleasures could be enjoyed without fear of discovery.

The door opened and in came Madame Olenska: a hard-faced Russian woman whose skill with the cat-o'-nine-tails was legendary. Caít had never seen her naked but it was said she wore nine golden rings, piercing the flesh of her breasts and navel and cunt: the symbols of her art.

'A client for you, Caít. He is waiting for you downstairs.'

'Yes, Madame.' Caít slid off the bed and tidied herself up, smoothing the pink silk robe around her.

Madame Olenska smiled.

'Such an eager worker. It is a delight to see you work. Dress carefully tonight – the black basque and fishnet stockings, I think. Oh, and a fresh birch cane. The gentleman is very particular about his pleasure.'

'Yes, Madame.' Caít began undressing, letting the silk robe slide from her shoulders and casting it onto the bed. Madame Olenska looked at her hungrily, desiring the sweet fragrance of the girl's cunt. But such pleasure must wait until later. Caít's client must not be kept from his whore. He was a very important man.

'Come downstairs when you are ready,' instructed Madame Olenska. 'Sir Robert is waiting for you in the punishment room.'

'Sir Robert?'

'Sir Robert Hackman, my dear. He is one of our most important regular clients. This is a very great honour for you.'

Sir Robert Hackman looked up as the girl walked into the room: a strong, lithe young woman with a tumbling mass of dark hair and nice plump breasts, squeezed into a wasp-waisted black basque. The large, reddish circles of her nipples were clearly visible through the black lace cups and he wanted her instantly. Her rounded backside was set off to mouthwatering effect by the tight-laced waist of the basque, so tiny that you might almost encircle it with two hands. Those creamy, naked globes looked so inviting, so juicy, so tempting. Ah yes! Madame Olenska had such good taste. She never let him down.

As he looked up, the girl flicked his naked back with the tip of her birch cane, making the flesh sting most agreeably. So, the girl had skill as well as looks.

'Do you dare to look at me, slave?' demanded Caít, playing her role to perfection. 'You shall be punished for such insolence!'

Sir Robert lay spreadeagled over the saw-horse, his naked back and buttocks an easy target for Caít's enthusiastic ministrations. How he enjoyed a beating from a pretty girl! The only thing that was missing was a battery of television cameras, recording his humiliation for his own special delight.

'Harder, harder,' he gasped. 'Make me bleed. Make me bleed for you, Mistress . . .'

She wielded the supple birch-rod with a demonic skill. Where had she learned to whip a man so skilfully, with such exquisite cruelty? How could it be that these hands, once so prim and plain, now sported blood-red talons that thirsted to rake across their victim's helpless flesh? Caít did not seek to understand the changes that had come over her. All she cared about was the desperate need to slake her thirst for sex.

Hackman groaned and writhed in his bonds but the rough hempen cords held his wrists fast to the saw-horse. There could be no escape from this avenging angel and his resistance was only a token one, a device to make his punishment seem more convincing, more arousing.

His cock was leaping to attention now, hungry for cunt. Hungry for the tight wet haven that this black-clad mistress refused to offer him. She was so beautiful, so cruel. She was punishing him just as skilfully as he had punished two generations of hapless interviewees and he was loving every minute of it. Just the touch of her lips on his cock, the merest flick of her cane across the glistening purple glans . . . that would be enough to make him come, in a great white fountain of pearly spunk.

'Fuck . . . I need to fuck . . .'

'Silence!' commanded Caít. 'You are not yet worthy of your pleasure, slave.' And she brought the cane down smartly on his backside, insinuating the flexible tip between his arse cheeks so that it stung the delicate flesh and made him sob with mingled pleasure and distress. 'First, you shall pleasure me . . .'

She was standing in front of him now, releasing the collar about his neck so that he could look up at her. His eyes were full of fear, full of a guilty longing, and that made her more excited than ever. She squeezed her thighs together, intensifying the dull throb, throb, throb of her lonely clitoris. There was moisture there too, oozing and dripping from the secret folds of her cunt.

Hackman gave a little sob as she took hold of his head and pressed his face into the moist fragrant triangle between her thighs.

'Lick me out, slave,' she ordered him. 'And if you do not

158

perform your task sufficiently well, I shall be forced to punish you again.'

As an incentive, she flicked the cane across his shoulders and he arched his back in humble reverence to his mistress's skill.

Parting her cunt lips, she pressed her womanhood close against his face and closed her eyes with a little sigh as she felt the muscular tip of his tongue forcing itself into the heart of her.

He licked her hungrily but without skill; so clumsy in his eagerness for her that she was forced to give him several strokes of the birch-cane to remind him of his duties.

But she could not give her full attention to punishing this unruly slave. As the sensations intensified, strange pictures entered her head; silent and dreamlike, like a slow-motion film shot through a soft-focus lens. A great house, set among trees . . . the heart of some ancient forest. She was walking . . . no, drifting, gliding . . . up a flight of stone steps towards the elegant portico. She had never been here before and yet a voice inside her whispered 'Home, home, home . . .'

Up the steps, and now the door was opening, very slowly. Into a massive entrance hall and past a broad central staircase to a pillared hall where naked men and women were fucking for their lives.

Their deaths . . .

Excitement was rising in her, taking her over; making it hard to see the images that unfolded beneath her closed eyelids. The men and women fucking on the floor of the hall . . . they had seen her. She did not recognise him and yet they were smiling and stretching out their arms to her. Their lips were moving, silently framing the same word over and over again.

*Delgado, Delgado, Delgado . . .*

At last she felt pleasure overtaking her, carrying her away on the wild waves of an orgasm that challenged reason, destroyed all doubts and speculation. All that mattered now was the carnival of sensations in her belly, the tyranny of the heat searing her cunt as pleasure burned and danced in the sweet bud of her clitoris.

'Put your tongue into my hole,' she commanded, scarcely able to speak for the sensations that were flooding through her. 'Faster, now! I am hungry for my pleasure. Deeper . . . I want you to drink all my honey-dew.'

He obeyed and, as she came, he tasted the sweet nectar of her pleasure, drinking it down as though it were some costly wine. His enjoyment was unfeigned, few women had proved themselves such effective mistresses of his perverse desires. She seemed to have an instinctive understanding of the game and if it were not for the fear of her anger, he would have yielded to the delicious impulse to let his spunk jet out all over her creamy thighs.

Afterwards, satisfied with her slave's obedience, Caít let him fuck her and he knew that it had been worth the wait. He scarcely noticed the pain from his bruised back as she straddled him with her cunt and seemed to suck the spunk out of his aching balls. And she revived him so effectively, too, satisfying his hunger with a single, powerful orgasm.

The sexual energies seemed to radiate from her like heat from a mighty furnace. She was a good subject, highly receptive to sexual suggestion. Good-looking too, with a cunt like warm velvet. He so longed to taste her blood, to take from her that priceless life-energy which would increase his own power and bestow upon her the gift of immortality.

But the Master had ordained that there must be no risk-taking, no scandals. And the Master's word was law. Still, she would make an entertaining companion whenever he felt in need of a little . . . sexual novelty.

Adjusting his tie in the mirror, Hackman took out his wallet and counted out the price of his pleasure: five crisp twenty-pound notes. As an afterthought, he added an extra one. She was well worth her fee. Besides, it was best to keep her sweet for the next time he wanted to screw her. Some of the girls at the Club Venus had refused to cater for his unusual tastes and he'd thought it wise to avoid the place since Jerry Singleton's little 'accident'. Once bitten, twice shy . . . He grinned to himself at his little joke and turned to go.

Caít was lying on her belly on the bed, propped up on her arms so that her plump and tender breasts hung like juicy fruits, daring him to pluck them. She was so tempting, so . . . interesting. And she was smiling at him, as if she was pleading with him to do it to her again. He really wanted to . . . But no, he must resist.

'Thank you, my dear,' he said. 'A most enjoyable interlude.' He paused. She was quite presentable, as well as eminently fuckable. 'Tell me, are you interested in current affairs?'

'Why, yes . . . but . . .?'

Hackman took a small business card out of his pocket and flipped it onto the bed.

'Ring that number and my secretary will get you a complimentary ticket for one of my forthcoming television shows.' He smiled. 'I look forward to seeing you again, Caít, after the show . . .'

Max gave up scraping the burnt toast, and chucked it into the pedal bin. It wasn't his day. Wasn't his week either, if truth be told, nothing was going right. Max Trevidian was a pathological worrier. His Aunt Aurelia had always joked that if her nephew didn't have anything to worry about, he'd worry about that instead.

He needed help – but it didn't look as though Liz was about to give him any. He hadn't seen anything of her since just before LeMaître's maiden speech and it was beginning to look more than a little suspicious. No matter how many messages he left on her answering machine, she refused to respond. Was she avoiding him – and if so, why? Or had something more sinister happened to her? Some pretty weird things had been happening to him: maybe some even weirder ones had been happening to Liz. Whatever it was, he'd bet the entire contents of his piggybank that Anthony LeMaître had something to do with it.

Was he imagining it all? Maybe Liz had just gone away on holiday and forgotten to tell him. Over the past few years, Max had built himself up quite a reputation as a 'psychic investigator' – a confirmed sceptic who'd used his encyclopaedic knowledge of the paranormal to debunk a hundred different types of weirdness. For all that he'd respected Aunt Aurelia, he'd never been able to swallow all her crazy stories about raising demons for the British Government in World War Two. Too many pink gins, that was her problem. And when she'd tried to tell him that he, too, had 'the sight' – well, he'd just laughed in her face.

Sometimes he felt a teensy-weensy bit guilty about using the knowledge his aunt had given him to discredit everything she'd stood for. But a fraud was a fraud; and there were some right prats out there who needed protecting from their own gullibility.

But this latest weirdness – this was something different. Talking pictures – geez, that was weird. 'If I had a talking picture of you' . . . no thanks.

As he washed up the breakfast plates, it occurred to him that what he really ought to be doing was behaving more like a proper investigator. And what would a proper investigator do? Simple! He'd break into Liz Exley's flat and find out what the bloody hell was going on.

Of course, it was easier said than done. He'd never actually broken into anywhere before but, since he knew where Liz kept her spare front-door key, that shouldn't be a problem. What worried him was what he might find there.

Feeling inexpressibly silly, Max unlocked the wooden cupboard in his Aunt Aurelia's bedroom. This was where she'd kept the tools of her trade – grimoires, crystals, bits of dead lizard . . . all sorts of magical paraphernalia. Slowly and deliberately, Max picked up the German pistol his aunt had had ever since the War. He knew the old girl had kept it cleaned and loaded 'just in case'. In case of what? He'd never found out. Maybe he was going to find out now. As an afterthought, he picked up an assortment of bits and bobs: a crucifix, a small vial of holy water . . . This was stupid. Still, better safe than sorry. Better get going and get this thing sorted out, once and for all.

Maybe he'd find out whether Liz had talking pictures of Anthony LeMaître, too . . .

Mara moved across the cellar towards the sarcophagus. She wanted Andreas, needed to feel his forgiveness for what she had so unwillingly done to him that night in the Hall of Darkness.

Hands held over the sarcophagus, she let her energy flood into the unyielding stone, making it vibrate and sing in time to the rhythm of her thumping heart. Little by little, the stone began to grow transparent, the outline becoming more and more indistinct until it had melted away, leaving the dark mass of the crystal exposed to the chill, damp air.

Mara lifted the lantern and forced herself to look down into the crystal, into the evil twisted face which she no longer feared because she now understood. The cast-off body of the Master was nothing but a mask, hiding and imprisoning the spirit of her lover. She ran her fingers over the smooth surface, picking out the crack which now ran diagonally across the crystal from top to bottom, exposing the dead white flesh beneath.

'Andreas – I am here. Come to me.'

Andreas's spirit stirred but it was sluggish, unresponsive. Had her own cruelty drained him of his strength? She must do something to make amends . . .

Climbing onto the crystal, she felt instantly closer to him, felt a stirring within him as he strove to reach and to touch her.

'Mara . . .?'

'Hush, Andreas. Be still and let me love you.'

Kneeling above the twisted face, Mara began touching herself, giving herself the pleasure that only she could give, for only she knew the intimate touches that would spark this borrowed body into vibrant, sensual life.

'Watch me pleasure myself, Andreas. Let my sex give you back your strength.'

With her left hand she pinched her nipple, while the fingers of her right hand slid between her thighs, opening up the flower of her sex and exploring the delights within.

'I'm all wet for you, Andreas. Do you remember how I used to get wet for you when we fucked? Do you remember . . .?'

Mara remembered. She remembered one insane night, all those many months ago, when they had driven to the coast and made love at the end of the pier with nothing but sea and cold air and night sky all around. She still recalled how it had felt to have the cold hard wooden boards under her bare arse as Andreas – always in a hurry for pleasure – unzipped his pants and flung himself on top of her on the walkway.

She'd had her revenge, of course; rolling him onto his back and straddling him with her strong brown thighs. And taking his wonderful hard dick up inside her. He was her captive that night. She remembered looking down, seeing the dark sea glittering through the slats of the boardwalk and the distant reflection of stars in a clear black velvet sky.

Mara rubbed her clitty harder, thighs spread wide over the surface of the flawed crystal. She was impervious to pain as her flesh pressed against the sharp edges of the crack.

*Do you remember, do you remember . . .?*

She remembered. Remembered a sunlit afternoon in a wheatfield. Remembered Andreas towering over her, naked and aroused. His prick danced with desire upon her belly as they embraced and she felt the rush of honey-dew to her yearning cunt.

*Fuck me, Andreas. Fuck me now.*

Memory brought back the sensation of Andreas's lips on her nipples, his teeth teasing the flesh into erect crests. The unforgettable feeling as he drew her up onto hands and knees on the hard earth and thrust smoothly into her cunt.

The sun was warm on her back, her backside, her naked breasts, as Andreas spurted into her then rolled her onto her back and began licking her out. The very first touch of his tongue in her vagina almost made her come and she cried out with the exquisite thrill of it.

He put his fingers inside her: one, two, three; and then the whole hand. Was this how it felt to be torn apart? It was wonderful, new, extreme. As he fisted her, she began moaning an inarticulate song of purest sex.

Pleasure then. Pleasure now . . .

*Yes, Mara. Yes. I remember. Don't stop . . .*

She could feel Andreas now. Really feel him, hard and strong beneath her, his spirit gaining in strength with each second that she rubbed her clit. Gradually she sank down, her cunt closer and closer to the surface of the crystal, oblivious to everything except the warmth of the pleasure spreading through her like a forest fire.

And then: pain.

A sudden sharpness that made Mara gasp as she pressed her cunt close against the crystal and a jagged splinter from the cracked surface pierced the tender flesh of her thigh. A little blood, a tiny cut in her thigh . . . nothing to worry about, nothing to divert her from the overriding need to come.

And yet, as she masturbated and a few slow drips of blood dropped from her thigh onto the crystal, mingling with the sweet ooze of her cunt juice, something very strange began to happen. As the blood fell into the crack, it began first to glow, and then to shine with a brilliant light that seemed to come from within.

Was she imagining it, or did the dead flesh within the crystal really seem less greyish-white, more . . . alive?

There must be some truth in this, must be some hope for them both. Blood, tears and cunt juice mingled as she wanked with a new urgency; the precious fluids mingling as they dripped together through the crack and into the heart of the crystal.

'Yes, Mara! Yes; don't stop!'

For the first time, Mara heard Andreas clearly and knew that his strength was growing with her pleasure. Beneath her, the crystal shone blood red and seemed to vibrate with a volcanic inner life.

'Life, Mara – I can feel life. I can feel *you*!'

The crystal grew darker and darker, until crimson turned to deep red and then boiling black. The surface of the crystal was scalding hot beneath her as she fought back the need to come. *No, no – got to make it last longer* . . .

'Not yet, Mara. Not yet. Too soon . . .'

But it was too late. Already her orgasm was upon her, shaking her body with irresistible spasms of pleasure, tensing her cunt in a multi-coloured waterfall of sensations. She could give no more.

Then all was as before: the crystal cold and dead beneath her, Andreas silent and still.

Exhausted and defeated, Mara wept. The Master would pay dearly for this. He would pay for it as she had paid for her own folly: in pain.

Getting into Liz Exley's flat proved to be more of a problem than Max had envisaged. The spare key wasn't in the flower-pot and in the end he'd had to break a window at the back. Good job it was a ground-floor flat and Liz's neighbours were out all day.

He stood in the living room and looked round. It certainly didn't look very lived-in. There was a furry-looking cup of coffee on the floor and a three-week-old newspaper sprawled across the settee. Where should he start?

Crossing to the answering machine, he could see it was overflowing with messages. He played a few:

'Liz, this is Nigel. Where the hell are you?'

'Ms Exley? Hanbury Optical Centre here. Your contact lenses are ready for collection.'

'Look Liz, this is Nigel. It's about the vox pop interviews for the *World in Focus* programme. Ring me back will you?'

'For God's sake, Liz, will you stop messing about and pick up the phone? I know you're there.'

So – it was plain that Liz hadn't been home for quite some

time. Max shivered, feeling a sudden creepiness. It was a bit like going through a dead friend's possessions. But Liz wasn't dead. Was she?

A small sound behind him made him wheel round, alarmed. He couldn't afford to be caught in here – he'd be done for breaking and entering.

But it was only a shadow: his shadow. Funny, though – it didn't look normal, somehow. As he looked down at it, it started to change – getting darker and more distinct. On impulse, he took a step to the right. It remained exactly where it was. A coldness gripped at his heart. Oh God, no – not more weirdness.

This wasn't happening to him. It wasn't.

Hang on a minute – this wasn't even a man's shadow. It was the outline of a woman's body; very dark, very sinuous and very very shapely. As he watched it, suddenly entranced, it began to move. It was dancing! Dancing for him and him alone. He could clearly make out the hard tips of its nipples, the womanly smell of the breasts, the slender waist and the smooth curve of the hips.

All at once, Max no longer gave a toss about weirdness. He'd stopped being afraid. The shadow was a happy, laughing creature that wanted to draw him in, play with him, give him pleasure. All he had to do was to enter the darkness and lose himself in it.

And he suddenly realised what the woman's shadow was doing. It was seducing him.

More by instinct than design, Max reached into his pocket and pulled out Aunt Aurelia's gun. Pointing it at the dark heart of the shadow, he squeezed the trigger.

# 10: The Maze

Sedet nibbled Liz's neck, teasing the firm white flesh with her little pointed teeth. After long years of agonising captivity it was good to play, good to enjoy the Master's playthings. And how she enjoyed this one . . .

The Exley slut unlocked her sexual energies as no other woman had ever done. As no man had ever done, save the Master himself. With Liz, Sedet was hot, vibrant, powerful. Her wild cruel heart pounded and her juices flowed as she lost herself in the fragrant pleasure of Liz's warm wet cunt.

They writhed together on the hearthrug; naked, sweating bodies locked in an indissoluble embrace. With teeth and nails they tore and clawed at each other's flesh like two tigresses, magnificent in the ferocity of their lust.

Wearying of this game, Sedet sank back onto the ground. The flames from the open fireplace were dancing on her smooth tanned body as she ran scarlet talons down Liz's lithe and supple flank. She was a creature of pure lust, a creature of flames.

'Lick me out,' she commanded, her voice a seductive purr as she spread her thighs for her willing slave. Such a joy it was, to have this strong woman so utterly subjugated to her will; to have her knowing tongue lapping between the fragrant flower-petals of her sex, seeking out the silver clitty ring and teasing it between tongue and teeth.

Liz obeyed instantly, eager to please.

'Your pleasure is my pleasure, Mistress.'

'That is how it should be,' assented Sedet, toying with her

own nipples as Liz knelt between her thighs. 'It is a supreme honour for you to be allowed to pleasure my body.'

'Yes, Mistress.'

Liz was so wonderfully changed since the night when she had accompanied the Master and his Queen back from the triumphant election meeting at Caxton College. That night she had been elated, jubilant even – certain that at last she had captured Anthony LeMaître in her web of intrigue. Certain that, as LeMaître's mistress, she could look forward to a glittering media career.

That night had changed everything and awakened Liz Exley to a new world in which sex was life and food and power. Over the last few months, Liz had become a most agreeable slave, one whom Sedet was anxious to keep for herself, guarding her as jealously as if she had been some prize Arab mare.

Liz was licking and fingering her cunt now; one finger up her mistress's pussy and one up her arse, whilst with her tongue she lapped at Sedet's burning clitoris, teasing the silver ring which passed so neatly through the little rosebud of flesh. Sedet stretched and sighed with delight, feeling the energy sparking and cracking between them, the strength flooding into her.

Sedet came with a shudder of approbation, her juices flooding Liz's mouth with the nectar of passion.

'Again, slave,' commanded Sedet. 'This time, you may lick out my arse.'

Liz was about to obey when the door of the library opened. The Master entered, flanked by Cheviot and Ffoukes. His spirits were flagging after a difficult day in the House and he had intended to fuck Sedet, but Liz had other ideas . . .

'Master!' she exclaimed, leaping to her feet and rushing to welcome the Master, falling at his feet and kissing his hands. 'Tell me how I may serve your pleasure.'

'My energies are low,' replied the Master, putting his briefcase on the table. 'You may suck me off.'

Liz was already tugging at LeMaître's flies, tearing down

the zip and taking out his stiffening prick. As she took the throbbing shaft into her mouth, Sedet looked on, a jealous passion burning deep within her. She longed to have Liz's fingers on her cunt, her strong muscular tongue wriggling in and out of her arse. The pain of rejection felt like a dagger twisting in her heart. How could her favoured slave betray her like this? How could she disobey her commands and run to the Master, without a thought for the mistress who had treated her so well and taught her so much? Someone must answer for this act of treason.

'All things considered, Mr Trevidian, I'd say we're being very understanding. Very understanding indeed.'

Max Trevidian sat in the interview room at Caxton Hill Police Station, and wished he had never been born. The Detective Sergeant was right of course. It did look suspicious. When they'd got to Liz's flat, they'd found the walls peppered with bullet holes and Max lying half-naked on the carpet, his cock still erect from the sensual hell he'd just experienced. To make matters worse, of course, he'd got a pocketful of crucifixes and holy water. So now they didn't just think he was an amateur burglar – they thought he was some sort of pervert as well.

'Now, let's get this straight,' continued DS Pinkerton, who was enjoying Trevidian's ritual humiliation. He didn't like weirdos and in his book anyone who described himself as a 'psychic investigator' was a weirdo. Not to mention the deeply unusual circumstances in which this one had been arrested. 'You say you went to Miss Exley's flat to investigate her alleged disappearance?'

'That's right, yes. I hadn't spoken to her for several weeks and, as she had hired me to undertake the investigation, I felt it was odd that she just seemed to have . . . well . . . disappeared.'

'Ah yes, your investigation. Exactly what were you investigating, sir?'

Max paused. Should he be revealing this sort of information?

Would they believe him if he did?

'Anthony LeMaître, the Nationalist MP. Miss Exley hired me to look into certain suspicious aspects of his election campaign.'

'Really?' Detective Sergeant Pinkerton looked him straight in the eye, making him squirm. 'And what would you say, Mr Trevidian, if I told you that Miss Exley is alive and well and working as a personal assistant to Mr LeMaître?'

Max sat and stared at the Sergeant, mouth opening and closing like a stranded goldfish.

'You . . . I . . . she can't be!'

'I'm sorry to disagree with you, Mr Trevidian, but I'm afraid it's absolutely true. So you see, your claim that you were investigating Miss Exley's "disappearance" doesn't really hold water, does it? Perhaps you'd better start all over again, only this time I suggest you tell us the truth.'

Max swallowed hard. Shit creek had never looked so deep. With difficulty he found his voice.

'I . . . I want to see a lawyer.'

Sergeant Pinkerton folded his arms and shook his head, very slowly and calmly. He was smiling.

'No, I don't think so, Mr Trevidian. I don't think you're going to be seeing anyone for quite some time . . .'

The Master was exploring Sedet's body; exploring his own mind, too, and trying to understand what the images had meant.

At the orgy last night, in the Great Hall at Winterbourne, the Master had entertained many of the elect. Together they had celebrated and consummated the growth of their power; and shared the incomparable delights of the fresh new whores whom Heimdal and Madame LeCoeur had obtained for their entertainment.

Pretty young boys from the streets of Athens and Istanbul; shameless young Scandinavian whores with pert breasts and mouths so skilled that they could make a man spurt out his come with just a single kiss; dancing girls from a Bedouin tribe, to delight the eye and thrill the prick.

Heimdal's entertainments had not disappointed. But there, at the very heart of the orgy, the Master had felt a presence among them. Not a strong presence, not yet, but one which he recognised instantly. He turned and almost expected to see the man standing beside him as he had so often done: a swarthy-skinned man with a dark beard and a limp, leaning on a silver-topped cane.

But that was impossible. Delgado was dead.

Almost before he had recognised the presence among them, it was gone and the pleasure continued as if nothing had happened. Since then the Master had been unable to puzzle out the mystery. Like the energy-trace of Andreas Hunt, could it simply be some memory of the man indelibly imprinted on the fabric of the house of pleasure which he had been so instrumental in creating? Delgado had died through his own envy, greed and disobedience; and yet, if Winterbourne was the finest whorehouse in England, it was so because Delgado had created it.

'Fuck me again, Master,' purred Sedet, on hands and knees on the silken bedspread. 'Blend your spirit with mine. I want to feel your semen burning in my belly.'

Dismissing the puzzle from his mind, the Master knelt behind her, pinching and kneading the firm, tanned flesh of her perfect backside. Yes, the Fleming woman's body had been an excellent choice for the Queen's immortal spirit; a pleasure-palace worthy even of the Master.

Pulling apart Sedet's plump arse cheeks, he amused himself by teasing the delicate membrane of her arsehole with an inquisitive finger. Sedet moaned and wriggled at the tormenting caress, but he offered her no mercy. She expected and wanted more. All she wanted was for her Master to glut her senses with pleasure.

The Master's finger was in her arsehole now, buried up to the knuckled in her willing flesh whilst with his other hand he teased the erect bud of her clitoris.

'You are as hot as a furnace, my Queen,' he growled with

pleasure as her juices trickled over his fingers. 'Are you ready for me?'

'Yes, yes, my Master. I am ready for you as I was that first night, on the banks of the Nile. That first night, when you saw the power within me and you chose me as your Queen.'

'Only you,' murmured the Master, licking and biting the juicy flesh of her buttocks. 'You alone are worthy to stand beside me. Your cunt alone is worthy to accept the sacred phallus of Osiris . . .'

Wanking himself energetically to iron hardness, he eased apart Sedet's buttocks and slid into the warm wet depths of her cunt. Images passed through his mind once again but now they were images which he shared with Sedet: images of the sun-baked land where he had once reigned as the High Priest of Amun-Ra, images of their delicious fucking on the banks of the Nile. He shivered with pleasure as he recalled the cool Nile waters flowing over their naked flesh as they stood together in the shallows, Sedet's thighs wrapped round his waist as he eased her up and down on his cock.

Sedet was moaning and writhing now, bracing herself against the carved wooden bedhead as she took the full force of the Master's cock in her cunt. She too was recalling that day in Egypt, four thousand years ago, when their immortal spirits had entwined as their lithe young bodies fucked joyously in the furnace of the noonday sun.

He felt Sedet's cunt tense and allowed himself to reach orgasm, withdrawing at the last moment to enjoy the spectacle of his semen spurting all over her firm tanned flesh. Annabel Manley and the Exley slut were good; Mara Fleming had been even better; but there was none to compare with his beautiful regal whore, Sedet.

At that moment, there was a knock on the door. It opened to admit an apologetic Heimdal.

'Your forgiveness, Master. There is a messenger downstairs.'

The Master glared at Heimdal. If there was one thing he

hated more than being interrupted at his work, it was being interrupted at his pleasure.

'Tell him to go away. Can you not see that I am busy?'

'Master, it is the Chief Constable. He says it is a matter of importance . . . about the man Trevidian.'

'I see.' With a sigh of regret, the Master wiped his cock and left Sedet with a parting kiss. 'I shall return soon. I am sure the Lord Heimdal will amuse you adequately in my absence.'

'No, my Master. I shall accompany you. I wish to understand all that is done in the name of our empire.'

The Chief Constable was awaiting the Master in his office. A normally confident man, well-used to wielding authority, he felt more than usually nervous as the Master entered the room. Perhaps today . . . perhaps today the Master would think him worthy of the ultimate prize.

He rose to his feet but the Master motioned to him to sit down.

'You have brought it, I see.' He nodded towards a small, squarish brown-paper parcel which the Chief Constable had placed carefully on the Master's desk.

'It is exactly as you instructed.'

'Good.' The Master sat down in his favourite armchair and smoothed the flat of his hand over the package. The game was proving too simple to be a challenge, and yet there was a certain amusement in it. 'Tell me what has been happening since we last spoke.'

'Last night, the man Trevidian visited an apartment owned by Elizabeth Exley.'

The Master nodded impatiently. This, he already knew.

'And then?'

'And then . . . we had him arrested, sir. When my men got there, they found him half-naked with a gun in his hand and a bottle of holy water in his pocket.'

The Master could not suppress a guffaw of mocking laughter. These amateurs were so, so naive. Did Trevidian really think that sort of mumbo-jumbo would be any use to him now? He might as well get himself a four-leaf clover and a lucky rabbit's foot. And a silver bullet to shoot himself with . . .

'It took us a while to calm down the neighbours but I think we've managed to hush the whole thing up, sir.'

'And what have you done with our Mr Trevidian?'

'He's safely locked up, sir – just as you suggested. He won't be bothering anyone where he is, don't you worry.'

'Good, good, you have done well.' The Master picked up a pencil from the desk and began idly playing with it, testing its strength between his fingers. So far, the game was progressing rather well, but he would have to do something about Trevidian. He knew for certain now that his suspicions had been correct. Why else would he have felt such anger at the mere scent of the man's paltry little soul?

There was no other explanation for it. Trevidian had *her* blood in his veins; her psychic powers, too, though the fool was fighting a constant battle to keep them beneath the surface of his consciousness. The sins of the fathers . . . She had escaped but her nephew would not be so lucky. Trevidian carried her blood, he must also bear her guilt.

He would enjoy vanquishing the cursed blood in Trevidian's veins but he would not give him the satisfaction of an easy death. No, he would do it his way. Through despair.

Fifty years of rank corrosive hatred bubbled up within him, and the Master's fingers tensed convulsively, snapping the pencil into two jagged halves.

'Sir . . .? Have I displeased you in some way . . .?'

The Master turned back to the Chief Constable, suddenly irritated by this yapping lapdog, so eager for praise and reward. Unquestioning obedience he demanded as his due but he despised servility. Well, perhaps this lapdog could be taught to perform new tricks.

He turned to Sedet; she understood instantly. As his thought entered her mind, her blood-red lips parted in a smile, revealing the gleaming points of her perfect teeth.

'Kneel for your reward.'

'Oh thank you, thank you, sir!'

The Chief Constable fell to his knees before the Master, head bowed and throat bared for his mistress's kiss. Pathetic fool, thought the Master, settling back into his chair. He loved to watch Sedet feeding on her victims and, afterwards, they would screw.

Mara sat down on the rickety wooden chair, the swell of her bare breasts clearly visible through the plunging neckline of her wrapover silk dress. Sitting on the other side of the Formica-topped table, Max looked tired, haggard, worried.

'I don't understand all this,' he kept repeating as he stared down into his empty coffee cup. 'I just don't understand . . .'

When he looked up and saw Mara, he hardly knew whether to be impressed, aroused or deeply worried. After all, wasn't this Anastasia Dubois, the woman he'd so often seen at Anthony LeMaître's side? All his investigative instincts told him that she could be big trouble, but his instincts as a red-blooded male told him that her cunt would be like silk round his dick . . .

'Why have you come here? Who sent you? What do you want from me?'

'It's all right,' smiled Mara, crossing her legs so that the silk dress fell open, exposing the long slender line of her thighs. 'You asked for a lawyer, remember? Well, I'm your lawyer. I've come to prepare your defence.'

Max stared back at her with dead eyes.

'Three days I've been in this hell-hole of a cell and I've seen no-one. They push my food in through the grille at the bottom of the door, you know. I don't even get to see their faces . . .'

Mara reached across the table-top and took hold of his hand. He looked at her questioningly.

'What are you doing? What . . . ouch!'

'Quiet!' Mara pushed the tiny, needle-sharp sliver of shattered crystal into the soft flesh of Max's wrist and he gasped with pain as it disappeared under the skin, leaving behind a tiny crimson droplet of blood. 'This is necessary for your safety. With the crystal within you, he will find it more difficult to probe your mind, more difficult to hear what we are saying.'

Max stared at her, doubt turning to bafflement. But Mara got to her feet and leant over the table, silencing his protests with a kiss. As her tongue probed the warm soft interior of his mouth, Max felt a strange energy pass through him, a power that seemed to come from the woman's flesh and enter the very soul of him. He did not understand; did not even know the woman except as one of LeMaître's voluptuous 'assistants' – and she was certainly nothing like any lawyer he'd ever come across. But for some reason he could feel a goodness within her, an honest passion that made him relax instinctively and return her caresses.

Drawing away from him for an instant, Mara stroked his face with gentle fingers.

'So it is true . . . you have the power.'

Max didn't want to understand now. This woman's words echoed what his Aunt Aurelia had so often said, and he had so often denied, especially to himself: 'You have the power, Max. And nobody can take it from you.'

He wanted to push the woman away, tell her he wasn't having any of her trickery. But her hands were so soft and gentle on his skin, stroking his cheek, the nape of his neck, undoing the buttons of his shirt.

'This way now. You must try to trust me . . .'

Powerless to protest, Max allowed himself to be led across the room to the wooden bench-bed in the corner of the dismal bare cell. A single fly-specked light bulb swung slowly from the ceiling, casting sinister writhing shadows on the whitewashed walls.

Mara sank backwards onto the harsh grey blankets, rough against the bare flesh of her thighs.

'Come to me. I want you now . . .'

Slowly, infinitely slowly, Mara unfastened the belt which held together the blue silk dress. As the sides of the wrapover dress parted, Max gasped with amazement. The shameless hussy was completely naked underneath! He could see everything – her gorgeous firm tits, the taut belly, the glossy tangle of auburn curls at the top of those strong slender thighs . . .

Max's emotions were in turmoil. Here it was: his dream come true. A beautiful, irresistible young woman was lying practically naked on his bed, spreading her legs and begging him to give her the fucking of her life – and where was he? In some grotty police cell, with a woman he knew he ought not to trust as far as he could throw her.

He ought not . . . So why did he feel so tremendously drawn to her? Why did he look into those bright emerald eyes and see only the honesty of passion?

'Take me,' breathed Mara, pulling him down on top of her. She smelt of spring meadows, acres of wild flowers tossing their heads in the April breeze. The warm, sweet scent of sun-warmed gorse was in her hair, her lips, the compelling fragrance of her cunt. He just had to have her.

Her fingers worked skilfully at his belt, unfastening the buckle. Then the trouser buckle . . . and the zip slid swiftly, efficiently downwards. He wanted to help her undress him and yet it was so seductive, so wonderful to feel helpless in her hands. Just like when he was a child and his nanny undressed him in the nursery before she read him a story and kissed him goodnight.

She caressed his prick with butterfly-soft hands and he could have come there and then, spurting his come all over her naked belly. But he wanted to hold back. He was afraid since they'd brought him here, really in fear of his life. Well, if he was going to die, or something equally horrible, he didn't want to die knowing that all he'd ever done with this woman was wank over her belly. No, he wanted to have the memory of his cock inside that wonderful silken cunt.

Strange that. Strange how, without even touching her, he felt he had known this woman forever. Some long-buried instinct whispered to him of the secrets of her glorious body, whispered to him that it was not only a wondrous plaything but an exquisite prison. Pity and fear and desire washed over him in equal measure and he just didn't understand.

As she guided his cock between her thighs, he did indeed hear her whispering to her. Not words of love or even lust. Words he couldn't – or didn't want to understand.

'We must be careful. The crystal offers us some protection from his powers, but he may see us, even here. Fuck me slowly, slowly. There is so much I have to tell you. About the Master, about the crystal. About Andreas Hunt. You see, my name is not Anastasia Dubois. I am the white witch Mara Fleming . . .'

In the library at Winterbourne, the Master was relaxing in his favourite armchair, his soul feeding on the sexual energy from the Dubois whore's latest little performancé.

She was good, very good. She'd got that poor fool Trevidian so hot for her, he didn't even know who he was any more. And now they were fucking on Trevidian's bed, the slut sucking the spunk out of his balls with that wonderfully tight cunt of hers. Randy little whore that she was, her sexual energies had reached such a fever-pitch that they were clouding the images, impeding the Master's view of this pretty little entertainment.

The Master stroked his shaft slowly, luxuriously, in no hurry to come. He was enjoying the show too much just to jerk himself off quickly. No, he'd relax and enjoy himself and, afterwards, he would watch Takimoto and Heimdal fucking the two young boys the guards had caught the other night fishing in the trout stream by the southern perimeter fence. More delicious, expendable pleasure . . .

How many women had Trevidian had in his life? Not many like Anastasia Dubois, that was for sure. His face was a picture of ecstatic agony and the Master laughed heartily for the sheer pleasure of his little mind-game. When the Dubois slut returned to Winterbourne, he would reward her well. Perhaps reward her with the gift of his body . . .

The pictures were cloudy, indistinct, and he couldn't hear what the slut was saying to him. No matter, it was a minor inconvenience. She was a loyal whore and he hardly needed to hear their conversation. When the Dubois slut had taken her pleasure of Trevidian, he would have a little more fun with him.

A most agreeable warmth was spreading through his loins, the velvety sac of his balls tensing with the anticipation of pleasure. A little longer and his spunk would flood the palm of his eager hand. Yes, for now the Master would simply sit back and enjoy the spectacle.

On the narrow wooden bed, Max and Mara were fucking; fucking slowly, luxuriously.

Max was lost in a world of riotous sensations, his prick the centre of his universe now. He was living only for the sweet torment of feeling his balls shoot their spunk up his shaft, into the warm welcoming embrace of Mara's delicious cunt.

How could he be expected to understand the words she was whispering to him as her silken thighs embraced his hips, drawing him again and again into the depths of her? A body and a spirit, entombed within a block of crystal; rituals and magical rings; a man who called himself Anthony LeMaître but was really the Master, his soul a malevolent parasite within the body of Andreas Hunt . . .

No, no. He could not understand, would not accept. His only care now was for the pleasure that was coursing through him. He was going to come; his prick was swelling, hardening, almost ready now to explode.

Could this man – this man she called the Master – really see into his head, read his thoughts, feed on his energies?

Pleasure. Burning, searing pleasure. The spunk was rising up his cock and she was whispering in his ear:

'Come, come, come . . .'

As he spurted into her, he felt her cunt tense around his cock. His head spun as she clutched him in the throes of her own secret pleasure. As the spasms of pleasure died away, she was whispering to him again:

'Run, Max. Run! I'll say you overpowered me. It's your only chance . . .'

At first he didn't understand what she was saying but, as he glanced around him, he saw that the cell door was standing ajar with no sign of anyone in the corridor outside.

'Run, Max! Hurry now. I don't have the power to save you, not yet.'

On a sudden impulse, he pushed her away from him and fled; ran for his life, flinging open the door and pounding down the corridor towards what he hoped would be freedom.

The Master was roaring with laughter. It was all going so perfectly. At this rate, Trevidian's sanity wouldn't last out much longer, and that was exactly the way he wanted it.

On the table at his elbow lay a torn sheet of brown paper and, beside it, a square object made of crystal-clear glass. The Master picked it up and scrutinised it closely.

It was a glass model of a maze; a network of tiny glass corridors, intricately interconnected. A miracle of craftsmanship.

And in the heart of it, there was the tiny running figure of a man.

With a smile of pure malice, the Master lifted up the maze and began to shake it.

Max was lost, and desperate. Every corridor he ran down looked exactly the same – whitewashed and empty. Every corner he turned led into more identical corridors. Where the hell was he, and more to the point: how was he going to get out?

Suddenly, the whole place began to shake. What the hell was happening? It was like an earthquake . . . no, it was as if the whole damn building was being tilted repeatedly from side to side. He tried to get his footing on the smooth floor but just kept being thrown from one side of the corridor to the other. This was *seriously* weird.

In a blind panic, arms flailing, he struck his wrist against the wall and cried out with pain as the crystal splinter worked its way further under his skin. Big, dark droplets of blood were dripping out of his wrist and, my God!, when he looked down at the ground, he could see a trail of footprints, glowing blood-red on the floor. The prints of a pair of high-heeled shoes.

Mara's footsteps?

Stumbling, he half-walked, half-crawled along the floor, scarcely conscious of what he was doing and knowing only that he must follow the trail. Was this yet another trick, another deception, more and ever more unpleasant weirdness?

'I'll never doubt you again, Aurelia,' he found himself muttering as he staggered round the next corner, slipping and sliding and clinging to the wall.

With a sigh of relief, he saw a door in front of him. Whatever was behind it, it couldn't be any worse than this. With a mad lunge he pushed it open and found himself in the twilight world of an abandoned police station: empty desks, files scattered all over the floor, and a roaring wind whipping up the papers into a snowstorm about his head.

Got to get out of here. Got to get out. Now.

Running through the room, he came to a dead end. Nothing but two blank walls and a plate-glass window, opening onto empty darkness.

He turned to go back the way he had come but the wind was pursuing him, laughing, whirling about him. As he gazed into the heart of the whirlwind, it seemed to take on form and substance. Was he imagining it, or was it really turning into a gigantic, baleful, bloodshot eye?

In horror, Max backed away, not knowing what to do, where to go. The eye was pursuing him. The nightmare was becoming a horrible, inescapable reality . . .

In desperation, no longer caring what happened to him, Trevidian ran forward, head down, and flung himself through the plate-glass window, tumbling into the empty darkness in a shower of broken glass.

In Trevidian's cell, the single light bulb swayed crazily from its frayed flex, casting long, sinister shadows on Mara's naked, unconscious body, sprawled across the narrow bed.

The glass maze lay on the floor of the library, shattered into a thousand glittering fragments. The Master stirred the fragments with the toe of his shoe, well pleased with the game.

The Dubois slut had served him well. Tonight, her body would afford him additional enjoyment.

# 11: Mind Games

'You're an agreeable little slattern, my dear; but you must run along now and let me get ready for tonight's show.'

With the utmost reluctance, Caít got up off her knees and wiped away the last traces of Hackman's semen from the corners of her mouth. He had tasted good, salty and strong, and she yearned for more of her lover's come on her tongue. The taste of him was still in her throat, the hunger for him still in her belly.

Hackman slipped his cock back inside his designer pants and zipped them up; then turned back to the make-up mirror, admiring the aristocratic lines of his profile as he plastered on the pan-stick. Sir Robert Hackman was, after all, the uncrowned king of chat-show hosts. He had to look his best. And tonight he would be about the Master's business: his task to interview – and humiliate – Health Minister Joanna Bamborough. If his incisive cross-examination didn't do the trick, he felt sure that the photographs would . . .

Feeling disgruntled and more than a little frustrated, Caít slipped away and wandered off down the corridors of Television House. What was a girl to do when she was hot and wet and ready for love?

She'd meant to make her way to the canteen, but something drew her to the door of one of the dressing-rooms. Standing outside, she hesitated to open the door, not knowing who might be inside. At that moment, the door opened, and a heavily made-up showgirl looked out. Caít gave a little shiver of appreciation as she caught sight of the girl's enormous breasts, completely naked inside the flimsy wrap. She felt so hot, she just needed to fuck: it really didn't matter whether it was a man or a woman. And this woman was really something – a real tart, brassy and oh-so-sexy with it.

'Hello! You haven't seen Marco, have you?'

'Sorry, no – who's Marco?'

The showgirl laughed.

'Don't worry, darling – he's just my no-good dresser. Tell you what – you busy at the moment?'

'No, but . . .'

'Look, you wouldn't mind just helping us out for a few minutes, would you? These costumes are hell to get into – all buttons and hooks.'

'Well, I suppose I could. You'll show me what to do?'

'Nothing to it, love. My name's Tania, by the way.'

Caít followed Tania into the dressing room, where three equally well-endowed showgirls were sitting around, doing their hair and plastering on their make-up.

'This is Sam and Tricia and Caz,' explained Tania, slipping off her robe and making Caít gasp with delight at the sight of the huge firm globes of her breasts.

'I'm Caít. What would you like me to do?'

Tania laughed and, to Caít's surprise, she took her chin in her hand and crushed her lips against Caít's mouth. The kiss was intense, passionate yet playful, and it left Caít gasping for more.

'That's what I'd like to do, sweetheart, but you look like a straight girl to me – I don't suppose you'd find me very interesting. Ever been had by a woman . . .?'

Caít was dry-mouthed with lust, her crotch burning now with the need that Hackman had so callously failed to satisfy.

'Here, Caít. Help me into this, would you?'

The showgirl took down a hanger, loaded with sequinned fabric, and handed it to Caít.

Tania stepped into the skin-tight costume – a short, figure-hugging dress covered in scarlet sequins that caressed and moulded her heavy breasts as Caít longed to caress them: to cup them in her palms and feel the delicious weight.

'Do me up, darling, would you?' Tania's hand brushed lightly, almost imperceptibly, across Caít's breast and she felt the juices flooding to her sex-hungry cunt.

On a sudden impulse, instead of doing up the hooks at the back, Caít slipped down the bodice of the dress and watched Tania's breasts tumble out, great pillows of soft flesh that begged to be kissed. Reaching out to the dressing-table, Caít picked up a lipstick and drew it slowly over the flesh of Tania's breasts, reddening the outline of each nipple in a crimson circle.

In a moment, Tania was holding her close, kissing her, pressing her face to the crimson-tipped crests of her bosom and Caít opened her mouth to suck like a greedy baby. She had forgotten the other girls in the room, forgotten their hungry eyes as they watched Tania with her new playmate. But Sam and Tricia and Caz wanted to play, too. All of a sudden, Caít felt their hands on her, unfastening the buttons of her blouse and skirt, easing them off her as she lay helpless in Tania's strong arms.

Skilful fingers unhooked her bra and tugged down her panties. But Caít didn't care, she felt no shame. She was crazy with lust, crazy with the need to have cunt and arse and mouth filled, to taste the sweet elixir of desire.

A fist rammed into her cunt, stretching the delicate flesh to the delicious crisis-point between pleasure and pain. Tongues lapped at her breasts, her clitty, the amber rose of her arsehole.

'Come, sweetheart, feel how much I want you to come.'

Caít stretched out her hand and felt wetness: the warm, unmistakable wetness of Tania's cunt.

'Wank me off, Caít. I want you to feel me come.'

Caít was a creature of pure sex now, a wonderful, ethereal combination of sensations. Tania's nipple pulled away from her breast and was replaced by another woman's cunt. The woman was straddling her face, wanking herself so that her juices dripped onto Caít's face, trickling onto her thirsty tongue.

*Fuck, fuck, fuck . . .*

Caít came in an explosion of coloured lights, as Tania's cunt spasmed in her hand, spreading sticky cunt juice all over her fingers.

Afterwards, their lusts satisfied, they drank gin and talked and laughed together for a while.

'What are you doing in Television House anyway, Caít?' enquired Sam. 'I mean, I can see you're not in showbiz. Not that you haven't got the talent, mind you,' she giggled.

'I'm a guest of Sir Robert Hackman,' replied Caít rather cagily, not sure that she should divulge any more about their burgeoning relationship. Madame Olenska had been very clear about that. As Sir Robert's favourite whore, Caít was responsible for the good name of Madame Olenska's pleasure-house. She must be discreet at all times. No-one should even suspect the existence of the Maison Delgado.

The girls laughed and exchanged knowing glances.

'So you're the latest to share Sir Robert's bed,' observed Tricia. 'I've heard he's got some pretty kinky tastes.'

'Yeah, but he's one hell of an interviewer,' chipped in Tania. 'Really crucified that Martello guy when he had him on his show. I wouldn't want to be on the wrong side of Robert Hackman, I can tell you.'

'You reckon he's good, then?' Caít was suddenly interested. Very interested.

'Good!' Tania raised her eyes heavenwards. 'Listen, sweetheart, that guy's destroyed more interviewees than I've had hot fannies. There's not a politician in the land as could get the better of Sir Robert Hackman.'

She thought of Anthony LeMaître's smiling face and there was hatred in her heart. But a thought was growing in her head, the seed of a plan.

Surely if anyone could destroy LeMaître, it was Sir Robert Hackman.

* * *

Andreas was looking for Mara. A great surge of sexual energy had jolted him out of his dark slumber and now his spirit was floating free in the Great Hall of Winterbourne.

She was not here. He could not feel her presence in this place, though he knew she was not far away. He had heard her calling to him: *Come to me, Andreas. Fuck me, fuck me now.* Since the night when she had knelt on the crystal, and her juices had flooded into its heart, Andreas had felt inexplicably stronger, more alive, more receptive to Mara's thoughts and feelings. Captivity was weighing heavily on him more heavily than ever now. He didn't yet know how, but he felt convinced that the time of his liberation was near.

One day soon, he would fuck Mara Fleming and make her flesh sing with pleasure.

No, Mara was not here. But he found himself in the middle of a great seething maelstrom of sexual energy, a riot of naked bodies locked in an orgy of perverse pleasure.

This was the Master's doing. His servant, the magician Heimdal, was standing in the middle of the room, arms raised above his head as he summoned all the powers of darkness to officiate at this ceremony of unfettered lust.

Energy fizzed and crackled about Andreas, strengthening and clarifying the images that filtered into his free-floating consciousness. The great hall was not as he remembered it. It had been transformed into a dark place of shadows and flickering candlelight. Lanterns hung from a low timbered ceiling and the smoke from a central brazier filled the room with a sweet-smelling, narcotic haze. The floor was strewn with rushes and aphrodisiac herbs, and a troupe of naked acrobats was performing a lewd entertainment for the benefit of the Master's guests.

The guests were happily entering into the spirit of the entertainment, as yet blissfully unaware of the fate which awaited them. Their invitations to Heimdal's Nordic orgy had come as a pleasant surprise. After all, they had heard such tantalising rumours about the fabled Winterbourne Hall. Did this legendary palace of pleasure really exist? And if so, could the stories they had heard really be true? Tales of such unique pleasures, such mysterious delights. It was said that no-one who had accepted an invitation to Winterbourne Hall was ever quite the same again.

Along one wall of the great hall ran an immense table, carved from coarse oaken planks and groaning beneath the weight of great cauldrons of steaming mulled wine. Madame LeCoeur had been busy tonight. Lord Heimdal had given the strictest instructions that the Master's guests were not to be disappointed.

Andreas scanned the scene, looking for clues that would help him find Mara. A group of blonde girls, naked but for their fur wraps, huddled together on a platform at the far end of the hall. They were beautiful, desirable . . . and afraid. Andreas saw their shackled hands and feet and knew what Heimdal had in mind. Another of those slave auctions which had proved so popular with a succession of sex-hungry guests whose lusts had overcome their good judgement.

Hatred boiled and bubbled within him as he looked at the smiling figure of LeMaître, pouring more drugged wine into a guest's cup as the grinning idiot let a naked slave-girl rub sweet oils into the throbbing shaft of his dick. He might be enjoying himself now but Winterbourne's whores were the most expensive in the world: a night with them could cost you your life.

In spite of his revulsion, Andreas surrendered to the power of the desire within him. One day, he was going to destroy the Master, as the Master had tried to destroy him. And if he was going to succeed, he would need all the strength he could get. He could still hear Mara's voice, echoing in his head:

*Sex will make you strong. Sex will bring us together.*

Industrialist Sir Barriemore Blake was having the time of his life. The idiot who'd warned him against going to Winterbourne would laugh out of the other side of his face when Blake told him what he'd missed. Gorgeous girls in furs and leather; the prettiest boys imaginable, all dressed up in

Viking slave-gear. Yes, this Heimdal guy certainly knew how to throw a party.

What's more, he served a bloody good wine, too; as soon as he tasted the first sip of warm mead, honey-sweet and cinnamon-spiced, he'd felt his flagging spirits subtly revived. His cock was so hard it felt as if it was going to burst; and he'd been assured by the charming Madame LeCoeur that the whores here were so skilful that, no matter how often he fucked, he would still be able to rise to the occasion. He could fuck all night if he wanted and, by God, that's exactly what he intended to do. Why, he hadn't done that since his student days, at King's. Yes, whatever his host had slipped into the wine, he wanted the recipe.

'May I pleasure you, sir?'

Blake looked up to see the smiling figure of the most exquisite youth, angelic in his golden curls and short white slave-robes.

'As you can see, sir, I am entirely at your mercy. You may take your pleasure with me in any way you choose.'

He lifted his wrists to display the heavy iron manacles, and Blake felt instantly randier than ever. However had Heimdal discovered his intimate preference for boys – the younger and the more helpless the better?

He put down the goblet of mead and cast a drunken glance at the golden-haired slave boy. Unzipping his trousers, he beckoned to the boy to approach.

'Come here, boy,' he leered. 'Come and suck my prick.'

At the other end of the table, Countess Anne-Marie Waslawska was discovering the delights of Heimdal's hospitality. At her feet knelt two flaxen-haired Rhinemaidens, their wicked hands and tongues exploring their mistress's flesh as, little by little, they lifted the hem of her flimsy muslin gown.

The Countess's head was thrown back, her eyes closed in mute ecstasy as now a fingertip, now a tongue, pushed between her love lips and flicked across the hypersensitive rosebud of her clitoris. How right dear Madame LeCoeur had been to suggest rubbing the warm, sweet oils into her cunt. The aphrodisiac herbs and spices had kindled such a flame within her that she could not imagine her lust ever being satisfied. And now these big-bosomed wenches were toying with her, playing her until she began to sing like some musical instrument. The pleasure was so exquisite – almost too intense to bear. Would her dream come true? Would those pretty fingers clench into fists and force their way into the hot, wet pleasure-palace of her cunt? She groaned in anticipation of delights she had scarcely dared dream of.

Andreas looked on, lust and despair at war within him. These fools, these poor fools – just like him, they had believed they had the strength to face whatever Winterbourne could offer them. Exploited by their own lust, their own greed, their own ambition, by every vice that the Master had seen deep within their hearts, they had come to Winterbourne Hall in the hope of finding the answer to all their hopes and dreams. And they had not been disappointed. Here, they would meet the embodiment of their darkest fantasies. Here, they could enact those fantasies and take them to their darkest, uttermost limits.

Oh yes. Winterbourne was everything they could ever have dared hope for. Winterbourne was the fulfilment of all their dreams.

Heimdal, ever the smiling host, was graciously buggering a snake-hipped beauty whom Andreas recognised instantly, with a start. Good God! Megan Rowe, News Editor of the *Comet*! How many times had he tried it on with her at the office party? How many times had she told him to piss off and go screw himself? Heck, it was almost a tradition.

Well, well, well. And here she was now, all her talk of phallocentric male oppression apparently forgotten as she trust out that taut backside to receive Heimdal's prick. And a very impressive prick it was, too – long and thick and pierced at the end, with a big jade ring that stretched and tormented Megan's sensitive flesh as Heimdal's dick rammed in and out of her tight little arse.

Why couldn't he get inside one of these bodies? Why was his spirit still floating free, refusing to be anchored inside some fitting host? Why, oh why, couldn't he have a stiff, fat cock to rub as he watched this blond bear of a man getting it on with Megan Rowe?

All around him, the Norse banquet was turning into a true orgy as Madame LeCoeur's secret elixir took a hold on the guests. They had drunk freely and deeply of the sweet essence of lust. There was a desperate hunger in their eyes, a willingness to forget all inhibitions and think only of the desire to fuck and be fucked. Bodies were locked, their flesh sticky with sweat as cock met cunt and arse opened like a flower to admit the point of an eager tongue.

Andreas was very close behind Heimdal now and he could feel the desire radiating from his body, hot and strong. If he thought very hard, he could experience some of the sensations, too, as he had done when he mind-fucked with Mara in the crystal. How satin-smooth Megan's arsehole was. How Heimdal was enjoying the slick tightness as his dick slipped in and out of her. How angry she would be if she knew that Andreas Hunt had enjoyed it, too . . .

He needed Mara. Needed Mara for the strength of her soul, the shared ecstasy of their coupling. But Mara was not here and he couldn't understand why.

Ah well . . . seeing as he was here, maybe he'd better take advantage of all this sexual energy. As he relaxed and let the energy flow into him, Andreas let his thoughts run riot. Let himself fantasize a little.

An Arabian Nights orgy, that's what he'd really like to see. Lots of sexy bell-dancers with see-through chiffon pants, so you could see their nipples and the glossy curls of their pubic hair through the gauzy fabric. The dance of the seven veils, slow and sensual – not vulgar, like this Nordic nonsense. Really tasteful and . . . yeah, artistic.

Ah yes, Andreas Hunt might not know much about art, but he bloody well knew what he liked.

* * *

Mara sunk back into the soft leather seats of Nick Weatherall's sleek black Porsche and eased up her tight skirt high onto her thighs. She wasn't normally in the habit of pursuing men, but in Nick Weatherall's case she was prepared to make an exception.

The Master wanted Weatherall. Heimdal was most insistent that she should spend as much time with him as possible. Charm him, seduce him – and then lure him back to Winterbourne. Well, that suited Mara down to the ground because she wanted him even more than the Master did.

Yes, he was thick. A complete dickhead, in fact. If brains were gunpowder, Weatherall wouldn't have enough to blow his hat off. But he was beautiful, so beautiful, with a long thick pipe of a cock that hardened instantly at Mara's touch. Beautiful: with a slender yet strong body with a hint of muscle that rippled beneath the surface of his smooth tanned skin with the promise of a stallion's potency. Oh yes, Weatherall's body was beautiful enough even to house the soul of Andreas Hunt . . .

It was so easy, too. On several occasions already, Andreas's soul had slipped into Weatherall's body whilst he had been fucking Mara, and she had again felt her lover's unmistakable, unforgettable touch; the ecstasy of his strong arms about her as he pulled her towards him and that long stiff cock smoothly onto the moist haven of her cunt.

Would he come to her again today?

She laid her hand gently on Weatherall's knee and he cast her a lecherous glance, torn between keeping his eyes on the road and drinking in the long sinuous curves of Mara's body. He just couldn't get enough of the Dubois girl. She was the most exciting woman he'd ever had – and he'd had hundreds. Sometimes, when she took his prick between those full red lips or let him take her from behind, scything into the hot pleasure-ground between her arse cheeks, sometimes . . . he almost felt as if his soul was floating out of his body, looking down on himself fucking as though he were a detached observer. Funny, that. But he didn't dwell on it. Nick

Weatherall wasn't into deep thinking.

Slowing down to take a sharp bend, he slid his hand across and squeezed Mara's bare knee. He loved the way she went naked under her clothes – no underwear, no stockings. He absolutely adored the certainty that, beneath her smart designer suit, this shameless hussy would be wearing precisely nothing but her bare, creamy-white skin.

'Why don't you wank me off, darling?' purred Mara, easing her skirt still high on her thighs. 'I'm really hot for you.'

'What – here?' Weatherall shot her an incredulous look. 'Well, OK then. Shall I pull in to a layby?'

'No need for that,' laughed Mara, guiding his fingers to the moist triangle between her thighs. 'See – I told you I was hot for you.'

With regret, Weatherall pulled his hand away and changed up to fourth. God, she was irresistible. He could smell her on his skin, the heady fragrance wafting up from his hand and filling the whole car with its exotic incense.

'Tell you what,' breathed Mara, 'if you can't pleasure me, why don't I pleasure you?'

Without waiting for his reply, she reached across and unzipped him. He groaned and gripped the steering wheel more tightly as she slipped her hand in through his flies and cradled his balls. They were heavy, golden, succulent: filled with spunk that Mara yearned to taste, to feel . . .

'Oh no, you can't . . . I mean, it's not . . .' moaned Weatherall, pleasure making him lapse into incoherence.

Mara wasn't listening to him. She was busy working his shaft up and down, wanking him with such instinctive skill that she knew he couldn't last long. Not that that mattered: when they'd finished, she'd reawaken his desire and they'd do it all over again.

With all her psychic strength, she called out to Andreas, sending out her thoughts across the astral plane.

*Come to me, Andreas. Feed on the energy. Come to me and fuck me now.*

He did not answer. And yet Mara knew that he was there,

somewhere not very far away. But he was preoccupied. There
was a sense of great sexual energy about him, enfolding his
spirit and making it difficult for her to communicate with him.

She sighed. Andreas would not come to her today, though
she yearned for him. But Weatherall was here and he was
beautiful, and she was holding his cock in her hand. She
might as well make the most of the opportunity.

His cock felt smooth and hard as stone between her
fingers, and Weatherall was sitting rigid beside her, hands
tense around the steering wheel and staring blankly ahead of
him. His breathing was laboured and hoarse, and he had
given up trying to speak. It was all that he could do to keep the
car on the road.

'Relax, relax,' soothed Mara, rubbing his shaft a little
harder. She too was enjoying their encounter, her own hand
between her thighs and pressing on her throbbing love-
button as the car sped on down the dual carriageway and
Weatherall gasped and moaned towards the peak of his
orgasm.

As a familiar warmth gathered in Mara's belly, power
seemed to surge into her.

'Mara!'

Andreas's voice was suddenly loud and clear in her head
and, as Weatherall's spunk jetted out and her cunt tensed in
the delicious agonies of her climax, amazing things began to
happen.

A brilliant yellow lightning seemed to arc and crackle
around them and, for a moment, Mara, Weatherall and
Andreas were all suspended in time, frozen at the moment of
unbearable ecstasy.

And then it was over. Blinded and disorientated, Weatherall
let his hands slip momentarily from the steering wheel and
the car veered off sideways, careering across the central
reservation, straight across the path of several huge lorries,
heading towards the insubstantial retaining fence . . .

The Porsche hit the grass verge, broke through the fence
and bumped over the edge into empty space, somersaulting

once before coming to rest halfway down the steep grassy slope. Only yards further down, at the bottom of the railway embankment, an Inter-City 125 was speeding past on its way to Glasgow.

Unhooking himself painfully from his seat-belt, Nick Weatherall put his head in his hands and groaned.

'What the hell happened there?'

'I don't know,' replied Mara, dazed yet strangely elated. 'I really don't know.'

Max didn't enjoy drinking in wine bars, but in the circumstances he felt he didn't have much choice. He had to do something to steady his shattered nerves and tonight he didn't feel like drinking alone.

Just exactly what had happened? One minute he'd been fucking the Dubois woman in his police cell; the next, he'd been scrambling and stumbling along a corridor from Hell. He should have known he couldn't trust any woman who associated with Anthony LeMaître. And then – had he really done that? Had he really jumped through a plate-glass window? Was he really that crazy?

By some miracle, it had turned out to be a ground-floor window, and he'd escaped with a few bruises and a couple of minor cuts. It was almost as if he'd dreamed the whole damn thing. Only that silver of crystal was still there, embedded in his hand, and for all his suspicions of Anastasia Dubois – or was it Mara Fleming? – an instinct told him to leave it well alone. Maybe, just maybe, it really would offer him some protection. He really did need all the help he could get.

He finished his second whisky and slid off the bar stool. A couple of high-class tarts were giving him the eye but the last thing he was interested in just now was sex.

He left the bar and walked the three or four blocks to his office: a single room in an old building behind Waterloo Station. He wasn't sure if it was safe but he didn't dare return to the Manor and he badly needed a shave and a few hours' kip.

The minute he stepped out of the lift he knew there was someone there, waiting for him. The door of his office was ajar and he could see the vague shape of a figure through the opaque glass. His heart pounded in his chest. Was there still time to turn tail and run?

No. He wasn't going to run. He hadn't done anything wrong, and sooner or later he was going to have to face up to whoever it was that was persecuting him. And if that someone turned out to be Anthony LeMaître, well, he was as ready to face him as he'd ever be.

Hand trembling, he pushed open the door. Inside sat a young man in a leather jacket and jeans. His face was haggard and there was a pad of cotton wool taped to the side of his neck.

The young man got to his feet as Max came into the office.

'Mr Trevidian? Thank God you're here – I thought you'd never come!'

'Steady on, man, sit down. You look as bad as I feel!'

'I have to talk to you,' insisted the young man. 'My name's Donal O'Keefe . . . I don't know if you've seen the papers recently . . .'

'Ah. I see.'

Max might have been in jail for three days but he'd certainly heard of Donal O'Keefe. So this was the poor bastard whose wife had taken a lump out of his neck whilst they were bonking. He could guess why the guy had come here even before he spoke.

'Will you help me find my wife, Mr Trevidian, before she does something terrible to herself – or someone else? They're saying she's a vampire woman, isn't that crazy?'

'I'd have thought you'd be pretty pissed off with her, considering what she did to you.'

Donal shrugged.

'Oh, sure, I was mad at her at first – mad as hell. But all this vampire nonsense . . . She's just a sick woman, Mr Trevidian, a sick woman who needs help. Will you help me?'

Max paused for a moment but his mind was made up. The

crystal in his hand had already told him he'd be wise not to refuse.

Mistress Sedet relaxed on the slatted wooden bench, enjoying the steamy heat from the sauna. The Exley slut was behaving herself again and Sedet was in the best of moods. Ah yes, the feel of the birch twigs on her naked back was most stimulating. She rolled over and parted her thighs.

'You may stimulate my cunt, slave. I have a fondness today for the spice of pain.'

Liz brought the bundle of birch twigs down on Sedet's cunt lips, and the Queen gave a low growl of pleasure. She so enjoyed pain – the pain of others, more often than not, but from time to time she liked to savour the bite of leather or birch on her own naked flesh. The experience of pain taught her how to inflict discomfort more scientifically upon the flesh of her victims.

The Master was enjoying watching Takimoto being buggered by Lord Heimdal. He knew very well how much Takimoto loathed the humiliation of the act and yet craved the guilty pleasure of having Heimdal's massive prick ramming into his arse. The subjugation would do him good. The Master could not allow even his most trusted servants to become too full of self-importance.

He turned to Sedet.

'Your researchers have met with success?'

'Indeed, my Lord,' replied Sedet with a wicked smile, savouring not only the pleasure of the birch twigs on her clitoris but also the delightful memories of her researchers in the House. 'Rhys Llewellyn is one MP who is ours for the taking – a lecherous man through and through.'

The Master nodded.

'I have it in mind to enslave him,' he assented, 'but the Shadow Health portfolio does not greatly appeal to my . . . talents. Tell me of the other Shadow Cabinet members you have investigated.'

'Edwin Chambers may pose problems. He seems a

genuinely puritanical man, with little interest in the joys of the flesh.'

'That is a fault which may yet be remedied,' observed the Master, pinching Sedet's nipple between his thumb and forefinger.

'Piers Rankin, at Education, and the Shadow Chancellor...'

'Rillington?'

'Indeed. These are powerful men with dark fantasies. They would not lend themselves willingly to our cause but, with persuasion, they could be most useful to us.'

'I have a fancy to take over the Environment portfolio,' yawned the Master.

Sedet looked up at him, momentarily surprised.

'From Fenton Harcourt, my Lord? But did you not deem him incorruptible?'

The Master laughed.

'Just because a man is a member of the General Synod and an incorrigible bore does not mean he is incorruptible, my sweet. He would make an amusing new toy.' He stroked Sedet's cheek thoughtfully. 'Have you not seduced priests and bishops, my Queen? Why, your cruel beauty could raise the dead . . .'

A thin smile spread across Sedet's face.

'So you wish me to take charge of the matter, my Lord?'

'Certainly. You may have a free hand to use your talents in whatever way you see fit.' He kissed her full on the lips. 'Bring him to me, my Queen. Bring him into our fold.'

He gave a murmur of satisfaction and lay back on the bench.

'And now to pleasure. My Lord Heimdal.'

'Yes, Master.'

'What entertainments have you planned to satisfy our appetites?'

Heimdal smiled. He had had an idea. A rather good idea.

'Master, with your permission I thought we could stage another orgy for the elect. An Arabian Nights orgy, with beautiful slave girls and the dance of the seven veils . . .'

\* \* \*

Andreas was pleased with himself. Although he might be a prisoner, at best a floating vapour, forced to watch others having riotous sex as if he were strapped down in front of a television screen – well, now it seemed that he could choose the channel . . .

# 12: Temptation

Fenton Harcourt turned over happily in his bed. His wife was waking him up in a very special way . . .

Why was she being so good to him today? She wasn't normally like this. Usually it was a quickie under the covers on a Saturday night – with the lights off. She was a deeply religious, moral woman, was Jacqueline Harcourt. But today . . . Today, she was wriggling down his body under the duvet, teasing him with the wickedest caresses and covering his body with kisses as she slid down past his chest, his belly . . .

And fastened her lips on his cock.

He could hardly believe it. She was awakening passions in him that he'd never dreamed he had. What on earth had come over her?

Never mind that. He wasn't about to complain. This was wonderful. Her fingers were fluttering over his balls. It was so good they felt as if they were about to explode. Her mouth was closing round his shaft, her tongue flicking over the glans, making him ooze the clear, salty evidence of his desire.

Where on earth did Jacqueline learn to give blow-jobs like this? Whenever he'd asked her – humbly, tentatively – to pleasure him with her mouth, she'd always told him his desires were evil and that he must pray for forgiveness. Well, whatever the cause, he thoroughly approved of this sudden change of heart.

'Suck me, suck me,' he moaned quietly as Jacqueline's tongue lapped at his cock. It was just too much. He couldn't hold back any longer. He had to come.

The spunk shuddered out of him in powerful jets that must have splashed against the back of Jacqueline's throat, but, to his amazement, she did not gag or draw away from him in disgust. On the contrary, he could feel her swallowing, sucking him dry.

A sense of regret flooded him as the last waves of pleasure ebbed slowly away. He supposed that that was it. She'd done it once, on some crazy whim, and now she'd see the error of her ways and he'd never have it ever again.

Just how wrong can a man be? A few moments later, by some miracle, she was teasing him back into hardness. Never – not even on their honeymoon – had Fenton Harcourt been woken up quite like this.

She was scratching and gouging at him now, her fingernails digging great furrows down his chest and belly, but Harcourt didn't mind. Eyes closed, he was loving every minute of it. He *wanted* her to hurt him, wanted her to draw blood with her delectable claws.

Wanking him to a straining throbbing erection, Jacqueline turned round and slid back up his body, her back to him and her buttocks nestling in the hollow of his belly. He didn't remember Jacqueline's body feeling this good, but then again it was years since he'd even seen her naked.

When she offered her arse to him, he couldn't believe his luck. She reached behind her and grabbed hold of his cock, guiding it between her buttocks to the secret spot he had never, in twenty years of marriage, even dared to touch.

Not since Eton had he fucked anyone in the arse, and then it hadn't been a woman. As he entered her, the pleasure was extreme, brutal, and he gasped with excitement as her tightness closed around his yearning prick.

They fucked slowly, luxuriously, and Fenton began to fantasize. If Jacqueline was letting him do this, did it mean she had had a complete change of heart about sex? Did it mean that sometimes, just sometimes, she would let him do this to her again?

He spurted into her in a burning frenzy of passion, sinking

back onto his pillow panting and exhausted.

Suddenly there was a click as the bedroom door opened and, at the same moment, Harcourt's lover turned around and looked him in the face.

She was a complete stranger.

As he stared at her, open-mouthed, she just . . . melted away and vanished, sweeping over him in a mist and a breath of faraway laughter.

Jacqueline Harcourt padded into the bedroom, every inch the respectable matron in her housecoat and furry slippers. She put his cup of weak tea down on the bedside table and raised a quizzical eyebrow as she spotted the red welts on her husband's chest.

'You all right, love?' she demanded.

And Fenton Harcourt knew that he wasn't.

Max gave up on the Rubik cube. He was getting nowhere with it and it certainly wasn't making him feel any more relaxed. The noisy, sweaty atmosphere of the transport café wasn't making him feel any better, either. He needed time and space to think.

No matter how hard he tried, he just couldn't fathom out what had been going on over the last few days. Deeply shitty things had been happening to him. Fear had made him so crazy he'd even thrown himself through a plate-glass window. And now his whole hand glowed red, for God's sake! He didn't like that. He didn't like that at all.

On the other hand, he mused, Donal O'Keefe had come to him and that was a big break.

The Caxton-upon-Thames 'vampire' case had been all over the tabloids and so far it seemed that the police had got precisely nowhere in their investigations. Not that he trusted the police – not after what had happened to him the other day. He could only hope they'd lost interest in him and wouldn't bother coming after him.

Maybe if he concentrated on the O'Keefe case he could put it all behind him. Yes, that was it: track down Donal's nutty wife and disprove all this vampire nonsense and he'd be a big success yet. The Dubois girl – fascinating though she was – would have to wait for the time being. Anthony LeMaître, too. Caít O'Keefe was his quarry now and he had a hunch where, sooner or later, she'd end up: Soho.

Max got up and put on his coat, leaving a fifty-pence tip in his saucer because he felt sorry for the hollow-eyed sixteen-year-old clearing the tables.

He completely forgot about the Rubik cube. But it hadn't forgotten him. On the table in the tea-bar, the coloured squares continued to click round until finally it was done: the pattern was complete.

Only it was different, somehow. The uppermost surface of the cube, instead of being one plain colour, displayed something much more interesting: a blood-red eye, set in a sea of midnight black.

Harcourt drove slowly, nervously even. He hadn't quite got over the shock of the other morning and he couldn't afford anything to go wrong today. Today he was delivering his big speech to the House.

The Nationalist opposition had had its back up against the wall for too long. Now, in the wake of a series of damaging scandals, the Republican government was starting to look just a little shaky. Harcourt's keynote speech on the wholesale pollution of the English countryside was going to put a few cats among the pigeons and it had to go completely according to plan.

He tried to think about what he was going to say but his thoughts kept going back to Jacqueline and what had happened the other morning. Come to that, what *had* happened? None of it made sense. One minute, he'd been dozing in bed; then, all of a sudden, some naked young woman – and he'd sincerely believed it was Jacqueline – was rubbing her tits against him and teasing his cock with the tip of her wicked little tongue.

He shivered with a mixture of fear and pleasure at the

memory of those unbelievable, incomparable sensations. God-fearing Synod member that he was, Fenton Harcourt had never experienced anything like it. So had he dreamed it? Imagined it? Could this have been nothing more than the dazed ramblings of a disordered brain too long starved of red-blooded female companionship?

But Fenton Harcourt wasn't an imaginative man. He was the sort who bought his wife the same brand of perfume every year – not because either of them particularly liked it but because he couldn't think of anything else to get her. He suspected that Party supremo Hugo Winchester had chosen him for the Environment job precisely *because* he had no imagination. A man as moralistic, boring and predictable as Fenton Harcourt was easily controlled and unlikely to do anything to harm the Party's renascent fortunes. Surely his mind-set wasn't up to creating such vivid – and pleasurable – hallucinations . . .

Besides . . . he still had the welts on his chest to remember her by. The girl. The girl with the long dark hair so like Jacqueline's and those amazing violet eyes. Oh, you could lose your soul in those eyes. He could still picture her as she turned to face him, a look of triumphant malice on her face. Her mouth was like a scarlet peony, flecked with opalescent dew-drops of semen that glistened and sparkled on her moist succulent lips.

It had been a fleeting glimpse, no more, yet he could still picture her as clearly as if he had known her all his life. He had an uncomfortable feeling that his destiny, and this girl's, were somehow inextricably linked. And he wanted her so much. She had awakened a hunger within him that must have been there, lying dormant, for years, suppressed under massive layers of guilt and prudishness.

Turning down the slip-road onto the motorway, Harcourt tried to banish thoughts of the girl, but she was a tenacious presence in his mind. Her scarlet lips seemed to be pouting at him, teasing him to chase and catch her; and her laughter still echoed in his head. That body, too: slender and yet so, so voluptuous. A tight waist, flaring to the soft curve of womanly hips, and the smoothest, roundest arse cheeks that begged him to part them and thrust right into her, in a single delicious knife-thrust of passion. Those breasts . . . large, firm globes just made for cupping in his hands as his dick worked in and out of that glorious tight arse. A body to die for . . .

He sensed that, if they ever met again, he'd surely be unable to control himself. He'd never met anyone like this girl and he just knew he couldn't ever get enough of her. His cock was getting stiff just thinking about her . . .

He really must try and concentrate on his driving. The road was wet and greasy from last night's rain and you couldn't be too careful. Why, only a couple of days ago, that prize idiot Nick Weatherall had lost control of his brand-new Porsche and ended up halfway down a railway embankment near Stevenage. Probably had his eyes on some tart's cleavage, instead of on the road.

A pang of anxiety broke into his wet dream. What if the girl was some sort of 'honey-trap', set by the Republicans to discredit him? Fenton Harcourt wasn't just a politician: he was a moral phenomenon. Everyone knew he stood for strict Anglican precepts, the sanctity of the family, the dull grey values of a more restrained age. His image was so squeaky-clean that half the population probably thought he was celibate.

The Republicans could have got wind of his speech. Could have decided to try and discredit him, to minimise the impact of the Nationalist propaganda campaign. Well, if the girl was some sort of agent, she was a damned attractive one. He'd have to be more careful in future.

But how could she just disappear like that? Sort of . . . vapourise, as if she'd never been there?

He sped on down the motorway, rehearsing the key sections of his speech:

'I put it to the House that the Honourable Member for Felsham West does not have, and never has had, any intention of bringing in legislation to regulate the disgraceful dumping of contaminated waste in Britain's historic waterways. Furthermore, according to the document before me – a confidential memorandum typed on House of Commons paper and dated last May – the Secretary of State for the Environment states that funding to environmental protection authorities is to be cut by a reprehensible forty-five per cent . . .'

That would fix them, he smiled to himself. Hugo getting his hands on that secret memo had been a spot of luck – though they never did discover who the 'mole' was in the Republican ranks. Now let's see, the thundering conclusion . . .

'Hello, darling.'

Startled, Harcourt glanced to the side of him and almost swerved off the motorway.

There she was, sitting in the seat beside him, her violet eyes sparkling with malicious glee as her scarlet lips parted in a welcoming smile. Dressed all in black and straight from Hell to torment him.

'Who . . . what the . . .?'

But the girl just shook her head and placed a scarlet-tipped finger to her lips.

'Hush. I've missed you.'

His heart was thumping so hard in his chest that he thought he was going to have a heart attack. The driver behind him was hooting his horn hysterically as Fenton struggled to keep control of the Rover, unable to look away from those violet eyes, those golden breasts, rounded and juicy within the inadequate covering of the girl's low-cut black dress. The black dress was stretched taut across her chest and her rock-hard nipples were standing out clearly under the thin fabric.

In a turmoil of lust and confusion, Harcourt swung the Rover across the lane and – ignoring the hoots and catcalls of other drivers as they sped by – he managed to coast safely to a halt on the hard shoulder.

Wiping the sweat from his brow, he turned back to the girl,

meaning to ask her what the hell she was up to, and what trickery she'd used to get into his car. Why, she must have been hiding on the back seat all the time . . .

She was gone. Only the scent of wild violets remained to remind him that she had ever been there – that, and the throbbing of his unsatisfied cock.

On the seat beside him lay a little card – black with silver writing. With trembling fingers, he picked it up and read it.

'I want you. S.'

A knocking on the window made him turn round abruptly, half-hoping, half-fearing that she would be standing there, beckoning to him to come after her.

But the face that peered in at him was not that of the mystery woman. It was the ruddy face of a motorcycle cop, his notebook and pencil at the ready to take down details of this 'traffic incident'.

The cop beckoned to him to wind down the window and he complied, completely numb with shock.

'Good morning, sir,' began the police officer, his pen poised for action. 'I think you've got a little explaining to do, don't you?'

Hugo Winchester was seeing a whole new side of Anthony LeMaître and he liked what he saw. The man might be a bit of an unknown quantity but he was a real crowd-pleaser and he certainly knew how to throw a private dinner party.

In a private function room at the exclusive Mayfair Club, the Master was hosting a little public relations exercise in aid of a very worthy cause: himself. Lunch with the 1922 Committee had gone even better than he had expected, with several of the most influential back-benchers openly voicing their support of him. And now here he was, in a secluded back-room at his favourite club, having a nice cosy chat with Winchester and his parliamentary private secretary, Giles Fortescue.

The only fly in the ointment was Winchester's continued reluctance to promote him to the Opposition front benches.

Oh, Winchester would give him what he wanted sooner or later, but he was getting bored with waiting. He would perhaps have to take steps to break down that reluctance a little more quickly.

'I realise that high office must be earned.' The Master was getting better and better at playing the humble supplicant, the loyal backbencher who sought only to please his Party leader. 'But if there were some opportunity for me to do more for the Party . . .'

'You have ability,' conceded Winchester, downing his glass of port. 'And I have certainly been impressed by your handling of potentially difficult situations, both in domestic politics and in your overseas diplomatic postings.'

'You are too kind, sir.' The Master took the opportunity to top up Winchester's glass from the decanter.

'However,' continued the Nationalist leader, 'I must bear in mind the loyalties and abilities of those who have served the party over a period of many years. Edwin Chambers, for example, is an excellent spokesman on foreign affairs, and a loyal and valued personal friend. Piers Rankin and Rhys Llewellyn have performed their duties to my complete satisfaction. Fenton Harcourt is the cornerstone of our environmental policies and Ray Rillington . . . well, I could not possibly dispense with his services. Admittedly, he is not perhaps from the social background which I would have chosen for a potential Chancellor of the Exchequer but no-one can deny that he has an unrivalled expertise in financial matters. Besides, he gives our party the common touch which our opponents so often accuse us of lacking.

'These are all men whose support I cannot afford to lose; men who have established solid reputations in the public eye. So you see, Mr LeMaître – able though you undoubtedly are, there is no scope for promotion to the Shadow Cabinet at the present time.'

The Master's eyes narrowed. He wasn't letting go that easily.

'Harriet Southcote . . . I heard she was thinking of standing down soon. Something about family commitments . . .'

'Ah yes,' broke in Fortescue. 'But Harriet is one of our few token women. Got to pander to the feminists these days, old boy. If and when she goes, we shall have to replace her with another woman. Tiresome, I know – but there you go.'

'Quite – no can do, I'm afraid.' Winchester settled back into his chair and took another sip from his rather good glass of vintage port. 'You mentioned some further entertainment, LeMaître?'

He was endeavouring to sound indifferent but he was burning with curiosity. There were some intriguing stories about LeMaître – not least, about his private parties. Winchester had never yet attended one but rumour had it that Anthony LeMaître's intimate acquaintances included some stunning – and more importantly, very discreet – young ladies.

Winchester valued discretion, almost more highly than any other gentlemanly virtue. He wasn't going to let himself get caught in some squalid tart's boudoir, like one or two of his unwary Republican adversaries. On the other hand, Winchester also valued his own pleasure. So the prospect of a little discreet enjoyment made his stout Nationalist heart pound a little faster.

'Ah yes,' smiled the Master, nodding to Cheviot who was standing quietly by the door, waiting for the signal. 'Perhaps you would like to meet one of my research assistants?'

The door opened and in walked a breathtakingly beautiful Indian girl, tall and slender, her delicious body tantalisingly wrapped in a filmy sari of midnight blue, spangled with silver stars.

'Sunita, dance for our guests. Pleasure them. Refuse no request that they make of you.'

The Master looked on with intense satisfaction, closely observing Winchester's reactions to the girl as she bowed respectfully to him and then began performing a long, slow, sensual strip. Heimdal had done a good job in training Sunita, noted the Master. She had that natural talent for seduction that he found so valuable in his slaves. And she was certainly doing a good job on Fortescue – his eyes were out on stalks.

She danced for her masters, gold jewellery glittering at her throat, masking the still-visible scars of her initiation. She moved like a snake, with a liquid grace that tantalised and enchanted, as a swaying cobra mesmerises its victim just before it strikes.

Slowly and seductively, Sunita began unwrapping the yards of sparkling chiffon, turning and whirling in a floating cloud of blue as, inch by inch, her sleek honey-beige skin was revealed to hungry eyes. The Master glanced at Winchester and saw that he was enjoying himself, sprawled back in his chair as his eyes followed each sinuous movement of Sunita's golden body. His cock was stiffening, too, pressing its eager head against the fabric of his trousers, demanding liberation – and satisfaction. Well, Sunita was not the girl to disappoint him.

Round and round she turned, her braided hair like a glossy black rope, interwoven with gold and silver threads. As the last folds of chiffon fell away, she stood before them clad only in a tight white sari-blouse and white cotton panties, the fabric so thin that the dark shadows of her nipples and pubic hair were clearly visible through the fine weave.

She paused a moment, tantalising her appreciative audience with this glimpse of delights to come; then she reached for the hem of her sari-blouse and tugged it up over her head, liberating the firm golden apples of her breasts.

Fortescue gave a groan of pleasure as he saw Sunita's pert little breasts bobbing on her chest and a sigh as she peeled down her tight cotton panties to display a tangle of jet-black curls, veiling her plump mound of Venus. Her golden flesh was prettily ornamented with traditional patterns of henna dye – intricate whorls and swirls of mahogany and deep chestnut, ringing her distended nipples.

Sunita was indeed an unusual and stimulating little slut, well able to cater for the most refined and discriminating of sexual tastes. Her nipples and cunt lips were pierced by silver rings, linked together by a network of the finest silver chains that jingled prettily as she swayed. Naked, she pressed her palms together and bowed her head, waiting for the next command.

'Very pretty and amusing,' observed Hugo Winchester, rubbing his cock discreetly through his pants. 'What else does she do?'

'She fucks,' replied the Master, casually removing an invisible speck of dust from his wine glass. 'Don't you, slut?'

Without replying, Sunita crossed the room to where Hugo Winchester was sitting, kissed him passionately on the lips, and calmly unzipped his trousers.

'Sahib, do you wish me to suck you off?'

Winchester laughed.

'I like a girl who knows her mind,' he replied. 'And you're a pretty little thing, aren't you?' He reached up and plucked at the silver chains, twisting the rings through her nipples and making her gasp with pain. 'No – sit on my lap. There's a mirror above the fireplace – I want to watch us fucking.'

Obediently Sunita turned her back on Winchester and lowered herself onto his lap, holding apart her cunt lips so that he slid easily into the very depths of her.

'Hmm . . . nice tight cunt,' remarked Winchester. 'I wonder how many dicks you've had up you, you little slut. I bet you love having three dicks in you at once – one up your cunt, one up your arse and one in your mouth. If you're a good girl, I'll let you have my dick up your arse. You'd love that, wouldn't you? You're a born whore. I can feel the pleasure rippling through you . . .'

He didn't expect an answer, nor did he get one. Both he and Sunita seemed completely mesmerised by the silent, moving image in the mirror before them: the image of a man in a business suit, with a naked girl on his lap, her backside rising and falling as she lowered herself repeatedly onto his turgid prick.

As he watched his own fingers playing with Sunita's jewelled cunt lips, he felt their mutual pleasure rising to a crescendo and, a moment later, his spunk jetted into her in a series of satisfying spurts.

'Very nice,' commented Winchester as Sunita got off his lap, her thighs dripping with the residue of their coupling. 'You have a connoisseur's taste in whores, LeMaître. Perhaps I shall enjoy her again in a little while. In the meantime, why don't you give her to Fortescue to play with? Poor boy looks like he could do with a good fucking – his cock's practically bursting out of his pants.'

It was true. Giles Fortescue had had quite a few women in his time but none of them remotely like the delectable Sunita. His cock ached for her as it hadn't ached for any woman since the day he'd lost his virginity, as a boy of fourteen, to a busty village girl on his father's estate.

Sunita walked over to him and his mouth went dry with excited anticipation. This was what he called a business lunch! What would he ask her to do for him? Let him fuck her? Bugger her? Make her take his cock between those eminently kissable lips . . .?

As Sunita knelt between his legs and closed her lips around the throbbing shaft of his cock, Fortescue felt LeMaître's hand on his shoulder.

'A word in your ear,' he whispered as Sunita began sucking Fortescue's cock. 'Remember me when the next Shadow Cabinet reshuffle comes around.'

'But there aren't any vacancies,' gasped Fortescue, rapidly losing control of his libido and rushing headlong towards a massive orgasm.

'Oh, things change quickly in politics. You'd be surprised at what can come up,' replied the Master with a knowing smile. 'Very surprised indeed.'

Harcourt offered up a brief prayer for success, then walked into the chamber and took his seat on the Opposition front bench.

That had been a lucky escape. It was a good job the traffic cop had recognised him as the incorruptible Fenton Harcourt and been persuaded to accept his implausible story of a sudden attack of dizziness. The one thing the cop had found hard to swallow – and let's face it, Harcourt was having trouble coming to terms with it, too – was the fact that one minute there'd been a girl in the car and the next minute she was gone.

The chamber was packed this afternoon for the environment debate. Harcourt felt excited, nervous, and just a little sick. After all, some pretty crazy things had been happening to him lately and he was beginning to wonder if the strain wasn't starting to get to him.

'Good to see you, Harcourt.' Winchester greeted him with a nod. 'I was beginning to think you weren't going to make it.'

'Bit of a hold-up on the motorway,' apologised Harcourt. 'Got stopped by the motorway police, but it all worked out OK in the end.'

'Well, I hope your speech is up to scratch,' observed Winchester. 'Those Republican bastards are baying for blood after we defeated them in the Irish vote last night.'

The debate began with a series of boring speeches that belied the mounting sense of tension in the chamber. The Nationalists already knew about Fenton Harcourt's speech; the Republicans didn't, but they were beginning to suspect that the Nationalists had something on them and they didn't like that one bit.

Harcourt felt as if he was going to faint with nerves but as soon as he got up to speak the old skill came back to him. This was just like it had been in the old days on the hustings, when he was a struggling Nationalist candidate contesting a rock-solid Republican seat. Well, he'd turned a fifteen-thousand Republican majority into a four-thousand Nationalist one then, and he didn't see why he couldn't win the day now, either.

Fine words and phrases rolled off his tongue as if he was Lloyd bloody George. This was great. All eyes were on him. He was on a roll. You could see the horror in the Prime

Minister's face as he picked up the leaked memo and started to read.

'Hello, darling. You're not trying to ignore me, are you?'

He stopped in mid-sentence, trying desperately to concentrate on the speech but fighting a losing battle against the fear and desire and guilty excitement overwhelming him.

It was her. The girl who'd been pursuing him since that morning when he had awoken to the feeling of her tongue on his hardening penis. The scarlet-lipped hussy in black, her plump breasts stretching the flimsy fabric of her skin-tight dress. Lying on the table where the mace ought to be, her dress pulled up onto her thighs and her fingers toying with the moist pink flesh of her cunt.

'Oh my God, oh my God . . .'

'What the hell's the matter, Harcourt? Pull yourself together, man. Are you ill?'

He tried to tear his eyes away from the young woman writhing on the table in front of the Speaker's chair, but he couldn't. Why was everyone staring at him and not at her? Couldn't everyone else see her, too? He could feel Hugo Winchester tugging at his sleeve, hear his voice urging him to go on with the speech, and he opened his mouth but the same words kept coming out, repeating themselves again and again like a broken record.

'Demon! Harlot from Hell, harlot from Hell . . .'

Nothing else existed now. Just Fenton Harcourt and the girl with the long golden thighs, masturbating herself so shamelessly on the table in front of him.

'Come and fuck me, darling. I'm waiting for you . . .'

He tried – how he tried – but he just couldn't control himself. With a cry of agony he felt himself come, the spunk spurting out of him violently, staining the front of his trousers.

The whole chamber was in an uproar but Fenton Harcourt didn't notice. He didn't hear the laughter, the catcalls, the roars of indignation as he collapsed on the ground, his cock still oozing semen.

As his two colleagues dragged him from the chamber, all

he could remember was the mocking sound of her laughter and the lingering fragrance of wild violets.

'A telephone call for you, Master. From Hugo Winchester.'

Annabel Manley handed him the receiver and he accepted it with a satisfied smirk. This was exactly as he had expected.

'LeMaître here. Can I help you, sir?'

The voice on the other end of the telephone held a note of extreme irritation, which the Master sensed was not directed at him.

'I certainly hope so, LeMaître. Harcourt's disgraceful display in the House yesterday has made us a laughing stock.' He paused. 'Look, LeMaître, I'll be completely frank with you. Cards on the table. I wasn't intending to promote you for some time, but . . . hell, we need a safe pair of hands. Harcourt's clearly cracked up – he's just not up to the strain of high office. Are you still interested in serving on the front bench?'

'Most assuredly, sir.'

'Then can I ask you to move on from your junior post and take on the Environment portfolio?'

The Master smiled.

'I'd be honoured, sir.'

'Come to my office – nine o'clock, Monday morning. And don't be late.'

A click on the other end of the line indicated that the conversation was terminated. The Master sat down at his desk, gazing out of his office window into the gathering gloom.

Night was falling. Lights were going out in the windows of the offices opposite and the tower of Big Ben was silhouetted like a mighty phallus against the deepening blue of the evening sky.

He replaced the receiver and picked up something from the desk – something colourful and meaningless.

A Rubik cube.

# 13: Lords of Winterbourne

'Bring in the next girl.'

Heimdal was enjoying himself even more than usual. Since the Master had so graciously appointed him Lord of Winterbourne, he had had plenty of scope to indulge his every sexual fantasy and whim – more scope even than when he had been sexual magician to the jet set and occult gigolo to the rich and famous.

Immortality suited him, too. It had heightened his occult powers, though that scarcely mattered now that he was a disciple of the sacred Master. Under the Master's guidance and command, his slaves could satisfy any whim, enjoy any experience, slake any hunger, no matter how depraved. He had travelled the astral plane with the Master, overseen the corruption of some of the most powerful men and women in the country, and fucked the most beautiful whores in the world. What more could Joachim Heimdal ask?

Today, he was choosing pretty girls and boys for the Arabian Nights orgy; not the highly skilled whores who had made Winterbourne the greatest pleasure-house in England but sweet, disposable flesh to be enjoyed and then cast aside without a thought of remorse.

To help him in this onerous task he had Anastasia Dubois, the gifted slut who had grown considerably in his esteem since their return from Egypt. Before they went, he had never really lusted after the Dubois girl. Oh, she had always been a desirable enough body to fuck, but to him she had seemed rather shallow and uninteresting – little different from scores of other beautiful society women he'd had in his days at the mews house in Notting Hill. Why, on occasion he'd even questioned the Master's judgement in initiating her.

But ever since they'd been back at Winterbourne, Anastasia seemed to have blossomed in ways he could never have imagined. It was as though, there in that tomb in the Valley of the Kings, the Dubois slut's puny soul had drunk in some of the sacred energy from the Mistress's reincarnation, enjoying a sensual and spiritual renaissance of its own.

Yes, since Dubois had been back here, under his close supervision and guidance, she had developed the sexual skills of a very fine whore; and intellectually, she was almost — though obviously not quite — a match for him. Why, he derived almost the same type of pleasure from fucking with her as he had done from fucking Mara Fleming.

Pity the Fleming girl was dead — she'd been fun to play with, while it lasted. Too much trouble, though. And he had grown to hate her in the end for the way she had sought to belittle his psychic powers. How dare she think she could threaten him with her second-rate occult powers? Yes, her death had been timely and necessary.

Anyway, the Dubois slut was much more fun.

The next girl came into the conservatory, restored and rebuilt now since that terrible night when lightning had struck, shattering the glass and putting an end to the exquisite evil that had been Delgado.

It was hot in here, in the steamy tropical atmosphere, among the lush green foliage where brightly coloured birds and butterflies perched like living flowers. So hot that the Dubois slut had had to take off almost all her clothes. Heimdal looked at her covetously, mentally enjoying her as he scanned the smooth curves of shoulder and breast, backside and strong slender thigh. Her skin was glistening with beads of sweat and he longed to lick them off, running his tongue lower and lower down breast and belly until at least he reached the succulent pleasure-garden between her thighs, so inadequately veiled by the thin bikini pants.

That pleasure, alas, would have to wait. For now, he must turn his attentions to the candidates.

The latest girl looked promising. Nothing special to look at, granted – just another pretty girl – but he could sense a sexual energy within her and the surprising power of that sexuality stimulated his hunger. And she was dark and sultry, the very picture of a slave-girl in a Baghdad market. Yes, she promised well.

'Your name, my dear?'

'Karina, Mr Heimdal.'

'Well, Karina, do you know why you are here?'

She blushed. An appealing trait, mused Heimdal, as long as she didn't overdo it. A modest whore is a novelty, a prudish one an inconvenience.

'You want . . . girls . . . for a private party.'

'That is correct, Karina. And you have experience of this type of work?'

He knew that she did, of course, even before she started telling him the hard luck story of her life. How she had had to leave her northern home because there was no work and her father used to beat her. How she had got a part-time job washing dishes in a big hotel and lived in some squalid squat off the Old Kent Road. How she had met this nice boy at Kings Cross station and he had shown her a much easier way of earning money . . .

'Take off your clothes, Karina. I want to see if you have a good body.'

She peeled off her blouse and skirt and let them fall to the floor.

'The rest, too, Karina. If you want this job, there can be no secrets from us.'

The girl was shapely, with well-formed breasts and a smooth backside with a tiny rose tattoo. Her back still bore the faint traces of a recent beating, perhaps with a cat-o'-nine-tails or a bunch of birch twigs – a pretty criss-cross pattern of reddish welts and scratches that made Heimdal lick his lips in delicious anticipation. So, the girl was already schooled to pain. Well, well, Mistress Sedet was sure to be pleased with her.

'Tie her up, slut,' Heimdal commanded Mara. 'I want to see how she takes to the lash.'

Concealing her reluctance, Mara bound the girl's wrists to two of the iron pillars. With a sudden flash of grim humour, she thought how much she looked like Fay Wray in the original King Kong movie. Well, she reflected, they didn't come much more monstrous than Heimdal.

'Beat her,' instructed Heimdal.

'Which instrument of pain do you wish me to use, my Lord?'

He pondered for a moment.

'The cat. The one with the soft leather thongs, tipped with lead shot. She looks like a girl of spirit. Let us see how she stands up to my favourite little toy.'

It was a cruel instrument and the lead shot bit into Karina's back with the wicked precision of a jagged row of sharpened teeth. To Mara's surprise, the girl did not cry out, though her back arched in pain and she writhed in a silent dance of agony. Evidently Karina had already been taken to the very limits of pain. Mara felt a surge of rage as the girl's back reddened beneath the blows.

In a sudden paroxysm of insane fury, she turned the lash on Heimdal, bringing it down again and again upon the throbbing shaft of his cock. Somewhere in the distance, she thought she heard Andreas's voice shouting, 'Yes, yes, yes!'

What madness was this? Horror flashed through her: Heimdal would punish her dearly for this . . .

But Heimdal was roaring – with pleasure, not pain. Seizing Mara by the wrist, he pulled her towards him and prised the handle of the lash from between her fingers. Laughing, he brought her to her knees before him. His cock was straining, its purple tip glistening with an abundance of clear, slippery juice. Heimdal loved to fuck with all the amiable violence of a wild beast.

'Darling slut,' he growled. 'So the excitement of being a

mere spectator was just too much for you. Oh, Anastasia, you have the most delicious, the most stimulating ideas. And now . . .' He smiled as he raised the lash above his head. 'It is time for you too to experience the pleasures of pain.'

Mara was walking down the corridor leading from the conservatory to the main part of the house. Pulling her silk robe around her, she winced. Her heart was still thumping from the encounter with Heimdal and her back stung with the memory of the enthusiastic beating he had given her. She wondered how Karina would fare tonight. The last time she had seen her, she was still hanging from the wrist-ropes, a helpless victim of Heimdal's lust as he thrust his merciless cock into her defenceless cunt.

She had had a lucky escape – next time she might not be so lucky. How had she dared to turn Heimdal's violence upon himself? She had been very fortunate in encountering Heimdal in one of his stupider and most lustful moods. It hadn't occurred to him that his obedient little Dubois slut was doing anything other than introducing a little variety into their sex-play.

Turning the corner, she spotted the guard Gonzales, leaning against the door-frame outside one of the bedrooms. He was looking at her, and the moment she returned his gaze she understood . . .

'Andreas!'

'Hush, Mara. It can't last . . . the strength is already slipping away from me. Forgive me . . .'

He led her inside the room and pushed the door shut behind them. Mara noticed how sluggishly he moved, as though unaccustomed to the weight of this unfamiliar body, constricting and yet liberating his captive spirit.

'Forgive you, Andreas? I don't understand.' She was embracing him, covering him in kisses, feeling his hardness pressing up against her belly.

'It was me . . . I made you do that to Heimdal. I don't know how I did it, I just saw what he was doing and I hated him so much . . . The power just seemed to flash and crackle out of me, like lightning. Forgive me, Mara . . . he hurt you . . .'

'There's nothing to forgive.' She crushed her mouth against his, thrusting her tongue between his lips, letting his spirit enter hers, and slowly they sank back onto the bed.

Liberating his prick, Mara slipped off her silk robe and straddled him with her strong white thighs. He felt so good as he slipped into her, hard as iron, smooth as silk.

'Let me fuck you, Andreas. Let me fuck you and give you back your strength.'

She rode him desperately, urgently, slipping a finger between their bodies and rubbing hard on the throbbing button of her clitoris. Maybe her own passion, her own juices, would revive him just as they had electrified the crystal.

'Feels so good,' sighed Andreas, returning her passion with upwards thrusts of his hips. He could feel his bollocks slapping against her backside and he grabbed hold of her arse cheeks, desperate to hold on to her and never let her go. Already he could feel himself slipping away.

Mara felt it too. Even as their essence met and mingled, and she felt his spunk filling her like the warm gushing of a tropical fountain, she knew that she was losing him again.

As he slipped back into darkness, Andreas gasped out the words he needed to say. No time to explain properly, only time for these few words and to hope that Mara would understand.

'Max,' he gasped. 'Max Trevidian. Tell him . . . tell him, Eastbourne . . .'

'Congratulations, Mr LeMaître.'

'Thank you, Your Majesty. It is indeed a great honour.'

If the Master had been a humble man, he would hardly have believed that things were going so well. A few weeks on the Opposition front bench, sorting out the world's environmental problems with his own inimitable style, and here he was at Buckingham Palace, being invested as a Privy Councillor. Not bad going.

But the Master was nothing if not realistic and consequently none of this came as a surprise to him. What was success, if it was not his right and his due?

If cultivated, the King might prove to be a useful ally. Not that he was worthy of initiation, of course. The Master had no desire to introduce any competing power-base into his circle of initiates. Besides, the King was nothing more than a jumped-up German bourgeois, and a pretty unintelligent one at that.

He remembered the days, back in the Thirties, when Edward had acceded to the throne. He was a promising enough disciple on the face of it, but things had all gone horribly wrong. Before the Master had been able to initiate him, the damn fool had gone and got himself mixed up with some vulgar American woman. That folly had cost him the throne – and set back the Master's plans so badly that instead he had offered his powers to Germany's Chancellor Hitler. A few short years – and many Hitlerian follies – later, the Master had found himself tricked into a cruel captivity which had only ended when another prize idiot had come along: the hack journalist, Andreas Hunt.

The King led him through the ante-room into the small drawing-room where he liked to sit and talk to his most intimate acquaintances.

'Do sit down, Mr LeMaître.'

'Thank you, Your Majesty.'

'I heard that you have enjoyed . . . a long and intimate acquaintance with my family.'

'That is true.'

The King looked puzzled.

'But how can this be, Mr LeMaître? You are a young man – you cannot be above thirty-five years old and I have never met you before. And yet it is true that there is something very familiar about you . . .'

The Master smiled. The poor fool. How could he be expected to recognise his master, so changed in appearance since his great-uncle's day? How could such an empty-headed puppet even begin to grasp the ways of the undead?

He reached into his pocket, took something out and handed it to the King.

'Perhaps this will act as an aide-mémoire, Your Majesty. Do you recognise it?'

The King stared down at the gold signet ring in his hand, the blood draining from his face.

'But . . . this is the ring which my great-uncle gave to . . . a very great and powerful friend. His mentor . . .'

'His master?'

Their eyes met for an instant, and the Master saw disbelief warring with a dark hope in the King's dull brain. And now he was gazing at the ring again, turning it over and over in the palm of his hand.

'It was lost. Just after my great-uncle had his . . . misfortune, his friend and teacher was taken from him. One night, during a . . . ceremony . . . something went horribly wrong. There was a terrible fire . . . the west wing of the castle was gutted. At first, my great-uncle believed that everyone had escaped. And then he saw that his teacher was still inside. He was desperate, maddened with grief. He tried with all his strength to get back into the building, but the flames beat him back.'

'And his teacher, Your Majesty?'

'His teacher . . . died. All they found were the charred remains of his body, his ceremonial robes. The ring was melted and distorted beyond repair . . .'

He looked up and stared into the Master's eyes, as though sudden understanding had dawned.

'And now you have brought it back to me. That is impossible. But surely it cannot be a replica – none knew of its existence, save my great-uncle and his teacher.'

'It is no replica, Your Majesty,' replied the Master with a smile. 'And I, too, am the same as ever I was. Your great-uncle was a fool, I could have made him the lord of all the world. With me to guide him, the British Empire could have stretched over the face of the whole earth. But after his foolishness over the American woman I had to leave him. You see, he had become an embarrassment, a hindrance. Herr Hitler was far readier to listen to my advice, to accept the occult assistance which only I could give him. Until the weaklings and the degenerates fed their vile poison into his brain.'

'You . . . you knew Hitler . . .?'

'It is of no account now, Your Majesty. That poor fool is as dead as your great-uncle but, as you see, I have endured. There have been certain minor difficulties – mere trifles that hindered the progress of my power for a little while – but now I have overcome my enemies and power cannot but be mine. Four thousand years of waiting have taught me the art of patience. With the youth and vigour of this borrowed body, my spirit is stronger than ever it was and soon, very soon, I shall come into my inheritance. If you display a fitting humility, perhaps I shall permit you to enjoy it with me.'

He took the ring from the monarch's trembling hand and turned its blood-red stone towards the light. Deep in the heart of the jewel glittered a searching, all-seeing eye.

'And now, Your Majesty, I think it is time that we mixed business with pleasure. Your great-uncle so enjoyed the taste of the whip. I used to have him flagellated by two adorably sluttish little boys – he had such an insatiable appetite for their tight little arses that my agents had to scour the streets of Soho nightly to find new flesh to satisfy him.'

The mirrored doors of the drawing-room swung open silently and the King turned round to see two masked and naked boys walking slowly into the room, bullwhips winding like sleeping serpents around their arms. Such beautiful boys – such beautiful cocks, smooth as blush-pink marble above delightful shaven balls, he simply longed to take them into his mouth and suck.

The Master amused himself by toying with his helpless victim's mind, filling it with vivid pictures of the delights in store for him, if he would only submit to this greater, all-knowing power. Here were pictures of a violent pleasure that the King longed for, yet feared with all his soul; desires he had never dared admit to, even in the seclusion of his darkest, most secret fantasies.

Excitement and fear mingled within him as he thought of the pain of those cruel whips biting into his back, the pleasure of the insidious warmth of the blood trickling from his wounds. And the sudden fire as a marble-smooth cock forced its way between his arse cheeks, possessing him with a skilful brutality that pleasured as it martyred.

Transfixed by the sudden understanding of his own insignificance, the King sank to the ground, head bowed and trembling with awe.

'Master,' he breathed. And a chill hand clasped at his heart.

'Lookin' fer a good time, luv?'

'Why don't you come inside, darling? Have a nice, relaxing massage. Go on, let me spoil you . . .'

Max walked on faster, trying hard to ignore the raucous cries and whispered entreaties from the doorways of what seemed like a million sex-clubs, bars and brothels. He was no sexual sophisticate and this type of brazen sexuality made him nervous.

Red, green, blue. Red, green, blue.

The flashing neon illuminated painted faces, scarlet lips moistened by the tip of a lascivious tongue. It was like walking through a jungle surrounded by ravenous beasts.

Pausing for a moment to get his breath back, he stopped at a phone booth to make a call to Liz. He had to contact her somehow, tell her what had happened and find out what the hell was going on.

He still couldn't believe what DS Pinkerton had told him, that Liz was working as Anthony LeMaître's assistant. She'd been so suspicious of LeMaître, had even told him she wouldn't trust him further than she could throw him. Why had Max been hired if she was just going to throw in the towel and sell out to the man?

He picked up the receiver and dialled Liz's number. All

around the booth were little coloured cards, advertising sexual services: 'Nicole – wet and willing', 'Fifi – French maid', 'Sandra – pre-op transsexual. Greek specialist . . .'

Liz's answering machine clicked in and he slammed down the receiver in disgust. He felt like going home and forgetting the whole thing.

But Liz was still paying his expenses. He was still getting regular cheques in the post and, frankly, he could use the money. Besides, there was still Caît O'Keefe – the main reason why he was here, in deepest darkest Soho; the *real* powerhouse of London's sex industry, where the most bizarre fetishists and afficionados of the extreme got their rocks off. You were no-one if you didn't get your kicks here.

He walked on down the street, not entirely sure what he was looking for. Passing a darkened doorway, he heard a groan and glanced sideways. A flash of multi-coloured neon lit up two writhing figures: a big-busted whore with her skirts up round her waist and a man in a business suit, his pants round his ankles as he struggled to get his semi-flaccid cock into her.

The girl was regarding at her watch, looking supremely bored.

'Come on, luv – you only paid for half an hour, remember. An' the pigs'll be round any time now. You don't want to get me picked up for soliciting now, do you?'

Further down the street, a girl was pressed up against a wall, face and breasts pushed hard against the brickwork as her unseen lover stuffed his cock between the soft flesh of her arse cheeks. Max looked on with a horrible, irresistible fascination. He wondered what it would be like to have a girl like that, as casually and brutally as he might eat a meal or drink a glass of wine. Despite his revulsion, he felt his prick stirring rebelliously in his pants.

The Dubois girl. He remembered how it had felt to have her on that narrow wooden bed in the police cell. He'd never known pleasure like it – the feel of that silken cunt around his cock, the power that seemed to flood out of her as

229

her thighs tightened around his hips.

Had she tricked him? Used him? Maybe he'd never know. But one thing was for sure – he'd never forget the pleasure of having fucked her. Even now she was there in his mind, smiling and talking to him as she moved beneath him, answering his passion with sinuous thrusts of her hips. He could even feel her gentle, knowing fingers on his flesh as she slipped her hand between his thighs and cupped the aching heaviness of his balls.

And then, turning the corner into Harbin Lane, he saw something very interesting indeed. Something that made him forget all about Anastasia Dubois and Caít O'Keefe.

That was Hackman, he was sure of it. Sir Robert Hackman, television presenter and thorn in the side of two-faced politicians everywhere. So what had brought the eminent Sir Robert to this dubious neck of the woods? Why, precisely, was he leaving the exclusive Maison Delgado?

Come to think of it, where was Delgado these days? That was something that had been bothering Max ever since he started investigating Anthony LeMaître and his unholy entourage. One minute Delgado had been master of ceremonies at Winterbourne and the owner of a string of high-class brothels from Cairo to Kowloon; the next, he'd disappeared off the face of the earth. Had he perhaps learned something he shouldn't about LeMaître's activities? Had LeMaître had him eliminated? How could he find out what was going on?

On a sudden whim, Max turned up the collar of his raincoat and hurriedly crossed the road to the door of the Maison Delgado.

Raising his hand, he rang the doorbell and waited.

'Mr LeMaître, your success to date in the field of politics has been quite remarkable.'

The Master sat in his office chair, amused by this eager delegation of self-important fools. He did not reply, preferring to listen to their childish prattle.

'We have consulted the Grand Master of the Kennington Lodge and he has confirmed our judgement of you. He too believes that you would be an asset to our cause.'

'Indeed.' The Master smiled inwardly. This really was too absurd. 'And might I expect to rise within the brotherhood?'

'Yes . . . in time, of course,' the balding chartered accountant hastened to add. 'The brotherhood is generous to those who serve it well but high office must be earned through diligent service.'

Now where had he heard that before? Ah yes, Hugo Winchester and his pathetic excuses, that day at the Mayfair Club. Well, Winchester's objections to his preferment had been swiftly overcome and Winchester was a man of greater substance than these creatures.

Already he had read their minds – a simple task, for they were weak and easily swayed. Edgerton, the Court physician with the taste for sixteen-year-old virgins. Purleigh-Bowes, head of a City firm of chartered accountants and afficionado of the whip and the rack. The banker Grantham, so slick and debonair in his Savile Row suit. How different he looked when he was lying naked on the floor of his mistress's apartment, enjoying the exquisite torture of her spike-heeled boots grinding into his helpless flesh.

'It is a great honour to be asked to join the Kennington Lodge,' observed Grantham, rather sniffily. 'Most of the eminent figures in the Nationalist Party are brothers. It surprises me to see you hesitate.'

'Oh, I was not hesitating,' replied the Master. 'I was simply enjoying watching you make fools of yourselves. You miserable, self-important wretches: I do not think I would join your pathetic brotherhood if you got down on your knees and begged me.'

'How dare you insult us!' growled Purleigh-Bowes. 'Eighteen months ago, you were nothing. We can ensure that you are nothing again.'

'I think not,' said the Master quietly. And raised his hands very slowly to shoulder level.

'My God – what's happening?'

The three men stood and stared as the figures began slowly to materialise out of the dark shadows at the corners of the room. Shadows that deepened and became flesh. The delectable flesh of three beautiful naked women.

'Let me pleasure you,' purred Sedet, cracking the whip so that its tip flicked across Purleigh-Bowes' shoulder, tearing the fabric of his shirt and cutting into the flesh, leaving a thin red trail of blood across his collar.

'Feel the delights of my fingertips,' sighed Sonja Kerensky, ripping open Grantham's shirt and raking razor-sharp fingertips down the flesh of his chest and belly. He gave a little cry as she drew his blood and licked it greedily, but when she unzipped his trousers and pulled out his cock it was treacherously stiff.

'Let me suck your dick, darling,' breathed Joanna Königsberg, unbuckling Edgerton's trouser belt and sliding his pants slowly down over his hips.

'No, no . . .'

His cry was as feeble as his resistance. Edgerton's resolve was no match for Joanna's delicious skill. He looked down into her ice-blue eyes and knew that he was utterly lost.

Still sitting calmly in his chair, the Master shook with silent laughter. It was all so, so easy. His three unwitting victims had walked straight into the night of their lives. He looked into their minds and saw fear and doubt give way to the most exquisite pleasure. So suggestible, so corruptible were they that already they had forgotten the unnatural birth of the sex-sirens, and had given themselves up completely to a world of perfect pleasure.

It was a pretty sight, watching Sedet flaying Grantham's back and belly with the thick leather bullwhip. He felt his cock stiffening as Purleigh-Bowes groaned and whimpered with pleasure, the velvet globes of his testicles cruelly martyred by Sonja's razor-sharp fingernails. Edgerton was on the point of orgasm, his entire body trembling as Joanna Königsberg sucked at his cock, the flaxen curtain of her hair caressing his bollocks as she moved backwards and forwards, attending to his pleasure.

Well, he must not let them become too secure in their delight . . .

Raising his hands once more to shoulder level, the Master commanded the forces of chaos to join with him in his celebration of power.

Edgerton looked up, suddenly terrified as blue lightning crackled from the Master's fingertips, and the Tiffany lamp standing on his desk exploded in a shower of brightly coloured glass. He tried to pull away from the girl sucking his cock but she would not let him go. She was clutching at his flesh, her eyes flashing with a cold fire that turned his blood to ice. He looked at his companions and realised that a terrible change was happening. These beautiful women . . . they were turning into hideous spectres, incorporeal demons with flashing eyes and glittering, pointed teeth.

*Got to get away, got to get away . . .*

Selecting a victim at random, the Master reached out and casually pushed his entire hand into the flesh of Grantham's chest. The vampire Sedet, looking on with eyes of all-consuming flame, was smiling as his fingers passed through the mortal flesh and found what they were looking for.

Clenching his fingers round the warm, beating flesh of Grantham's heart, the Master squeezed . . .

'Oh my God, no, no, please . . .'

Grantham's back was sticky-red with blood and his face was bluish-white with pain and fear. Purleigh-Bowes and Edgerton were staring at him, paralysed with the mortal terror that transcends all pleasure, all pain.

The room was spinning and the Master was changing – his body growing claws and sharp, sharp teeth as it seemed to swell and fill the room. His voice was a dry rasping hiss, and still he was squeezing at Grantham's heart as he wept and begged for his life.

'What is the penalty for betraying the brotherhood?'

Grantham could barely speak for the pain.

'Death. The penalty is death.'

He squeezed harder, and his burning gaze searched deep into the souls of his terrorised victims.

'Who is your master?'

'You are. You are our master.'

Outside, the evening air was still and calm. But inside the Master's office, a maniacal laughter filled the air. It was all so easy, pathetically easy.

It hadn't been difficult to track down Max's office. In fact, a quick glance through the Yellow Pages had done the trick. 'Max Trevidian, Psychic Investigator, 43a Surrey Cuttings.'

Well, here she was. She didn't like breaking in, but it wasn't really breaking in when you could just sort of float through the wall, was it?

He wasn't there, of course. She'd been trying to contact him for days now, but she hadn't got anywhere. She'd tried reading his mind, communicating with him telepathically, but to her surprise she'd come up against a block – the psychic equivalent of a brick wall. He was refusing to open up the channel that would allow her to communicate with him. Maybe he didn't even realise that it existed. What was he up to? She could tell he had the sight and he was a psychic investigator, for heaven's sake, but he was showing all the signs of denying his powers. She just couldn't understand it.

She could find him, of course; that wouldn't be difficult. But what was the point if he was going to close his mind to her? She needed information: facts about Max that would help her to understand, help her to get through to him the true horror of what was going on. Well, if the mountain wouldn't come to Mohammed . . .

She glanced round the office, reassured by the sheer ordinariness of it all. For a psychic investigator, Max Trevidian had a refreshingly matter-of-fact approach to magical paraphernalia. She looked into the small glass case on the wall and smiled at some of the labelled exhibits: 'Fake shrunken head, Brixton Market 1989', 'Yet another load of mumbo-jumbo, Wimbledon 1992'.

But she wasn't here to look at magical curiosities. No, she was here to find out exactly what was going on inside Max Trevidian's head.

She crossed to the desk and slid open the top drawer. A few unpaid bills, a half-finished chocolate bar. The second drawer was no more promising: a stack of invoices and – intriguingly – a pair of women's pink panties. Well, well – Mr Trevidian was turning out to be a dark horse.

In the third drawer she found what she was looking for: Trevidian's case-book, detailing all his investigations over the last five years. It made interesting reading. Alleged hauntings, some woman who claimed to have a psychic cat, poltergeist manifestations . . . Trevidian had investigated them all and succeeded in debunking the lot of them. No wonder he was a cynic.

But there was one psychic phenomenon that Max Trevidian just couldn't explain away, and that was Anthony LeMaître. As she read on through page after page, Mara saw how confidence had turned to confusion, cynicism to unease as, month by month, his scientific methodology had failed to come up with the truth about what was going on at Winterbourne Hall.

So it was as the Master had said – Liz Exley had hired Trevidian to dish some dirt on him, give her something that would discredit him and give her a media scoop. She'd certainly ended up with more than she bargained for. And Trevidian had carried out her instructions to the letter, investigating every one of the principal players in the Master's game.

Everyone – including Anastasia Dubois.

'The Dubois woman seduced me and I wanted her so much. I've never known sex like it. But it was a trick, I know that now. She's in the pay of LeMaître and it was just one of his little games to throw me off my guard. I won't let her win.

'Tomorrow, I resume my investigations into the O'Keefe

case. I'm convinced she's going to turn up in one of the Soho vice dens. Kept watch on the Maison Delgado – saw Hackman entering but was refused admittance. I must find a way . . .'

Mara sighed. How was she ever going to make him understand? She closed the diary and replaced it in the desk drawer. It was going to be an uphill struggle with Max Trevidian but at least she knew where to find him.

Honoria Jepson MP sat and gazed into the eyes of her lover, the handsome man sitting across the committee table, apparently so absorbed in the agenda.

But she knew that his attentions were really elsewhere, for she could feel his stockinged foot sliding up the inside of her thigh and she slid her knees a little further apart to let him in.

LeMaître was such an imaginative lover. She'd met him, of course, at meetings of the Broadcasting Committee and she'd always thought he was rather good-looking, but she hadn't realised that he fancied here until a couple of nights ago, when she'd been showering after a workout in the House of Commons gym. Yes, she'd been standing under the warm water, eyes closed and dreaming of a St Lucian beach, when she'd felt the touch of strong hands on her breasts.

A hand slipped over her mouth, silencing her cries, and a voice whispered:

'Don't be afraid, it's me, LeMaître. I've been watching you and I know you're a hot little slut. I want you, Honoria . . .'

He pressed his cool nakedness against her burning flesh and began massaging her breasts and belly with scented shower gel, his fingers skating smoothly over her trembling skin as he moved resolutely nearer to the flower of her sex.

Her clitoris burned for him, throbbed with passion as he slipped his fingers between her love lips and masturbated her to the very brink of ecstasy. And then, under the cascading water, he had done something she had never dared ask any man to do: he had thrust his cock into the yearning depths of her arse.

She shivered with the memory of the pleasure and smiled

at LeMaître as the tip of his toe massaged the smooth skin of her inner thigh. They hadn't always seen eye to eye but, since they'd been lovers, Honoria had begun to share more and more of LeMaître's views. In fact, talking things over with him had really helped to clarify her opinions and she now knew which way she would go in today's vote.

The Chairman called the meeting to order.

'Right, ladies and gentlemen. I think we are now ready to proceed to the main business of today's meeting.' He picked up a sheet of paper. 'And the first item on the agenda is an application for a broadcasting licence – on behalf of a Mr Igushi Takimoto.'

# 14: The Web

'You!'

Max turned round and found himself face to face with the woman he knew as Anastasia Dubois: the woman who called herself Mara Fleming.

'Look, just go away, will you? You're just about the last person in the world I want to see right now.' He strode on past the Groucho Club, hands in pockets and shoulders hunched, trying to blot out the image of this woman he so feared – so desired . . .

'We need to talk, Max,' pleaded Mara, touching his arm very gently. As he prised away her fingers, she saw that there was a faint reddish glow around his hand. Good. At least he hadn't been stupid enough to get rid of the crystal, then. As long as he had it embedded in his flesh, it would afford him some protection. 'I know what you're thinking.'

'Oh you do, do you?' Max snapped. 'And I bet you'd like to know a lot of other stuff about me, too. Then you could run back to Winterbourne and tell it to your precious Anthony LeMaître.'

'I tried to tell you . . .' Mara's voice tailed off. 'Look, it's not safe here, even with the crystal. He may still be able to see us, even if he can't hear what we're saying. We need to go somewhere safer.'

'Such as?' Max was doing his best to keep up the veneer of hostility, but it was hell trying to hate this woman when she made him feel this way – excited, aroused, just plain randy. Could she really be the evil seductress she seemed to be? He had felt that same honesty, that same warmth in her when she touched him. He turned back and looked at her and his cock twitched in sympathy with his instincts. This woman was pure sex.

'There's a church near here,' suggested Mara. 'He has a problem with churches, you know. The positive energy fields disrupt his astral vision.'

A month ago – a week, even – he'd have dismissed all this talk of astral vision as just so much pseudo-psychic mumbo-jumbo. He had to be careful, he couldn't trust anyone – and yet . . .

'Well, OK. But don't try anything.' Oh God, now he sounded like Clint Eastwood. Did he feel lucky? Not so lucky that he dared take his hands out of his pockets – they were thrust down so deep that she couldn't see they were trembling.

'Walk behind me – look as if you're following me. There is a chance he may be watching.'

She walked ahead of him down the street and he watched mesmerised as that drop-dead gorgeous body paraded in front of him, the tight backside undulating gently within the clinging green dress; the long auburn hair like a glossy curtain down her sleek back, and those endless legs. He wanted her. He didn't trust her but he wanted her. Maybe it was all a trick to lull him into a false sense of security but, whatever the reason, his cock was straining the zipper of his pants and he was clenching his hands inside his pockets, digging his nails into his palms in a vain attempt to distract himself from the torment of that perfect body.

They reached the ancient church of St Hild and St Dane, and Mara turned to him and nodded.

'Wait a few minutes and then follow me inside. He must not see us enter the church together.'

She disappeared inside and Max waited outside like an anxious schoolboy on his first date, shifting from one foot to the other and wishing he'd taken up smoking. There was still time to get the hell out of here if he wanted to, but the instinct to fuck was proving stronger than the instinct for self-preservation. In any case, what did he have to lose? If he ran away, she'd find him again sooner or later. His great-aunt Aurelia had been right after all: the only way to overcome his fears was to confront them.

He pushed open the door of the church and went inside. It was dark and his heart was in his mouth as the heavy oak door swung slowly shut behind him, shutting out the last of the sunlight.

As his eyes became accustomed to the gloom he saw Mara, kneeling in one of the front pews, head bowed apparently in prayer. He almost laughed out loud at the thought of one of LeMaître's disciples in a church. The multi-coloured light from the medieval rose-window was falling on the auburn curtain of her hair and he wondered how it would feel to have her go down on him: the long glossy tendrils teasing and caressing his thighs and belly and balls as those full red lips closed about the yearning shaft of his prick.

He thought about turning round and leaving. But his cock wanted her still, and his legs kept carrying him on down the aisle towards the woman in the front pew.

He reached the pew and slid in beside her, kneeling awkwardly on a lumpy embroidered hassock. She glanced at him briefly and he was lost for a moment in the sea-green oceans of her eyes. Moving splashes of colour played across the creamy swell of her breasts as a breeze stirred in the churchyard and the branches of an old oak tree moved gently across the rose-window.

'I think we are safe here – but we shouldn't take any chances,' she whispered.

'You've got precisely five minutes to tell me what the hell is going on,' hissed Max. 'And it had better be good.'

He resisted the urge to reach out and touch her. The neckline of that dress was so low-cut, he could almost – but not quite – see her nipples. He could make out their hardening crests beneath the stretchy fabric. She was obviously not wearing a bra. All he needed to do was reach out and pull down the neckline and those two plump white breasts would spring out into his hands, his mouth . . .

What on earth was he thinking of? Concentrate, man. Don't let her get inside your head – or your pants.

'There's a plot, Max, and somehow you've got yourself mixed up in it. Millions of innocent people are in danger . . .'

He snorted in disbelief.

'Oh, come on – conspiracy theories? They went out with the ark. Pull the other one. I mean, LeMaître's a pretty dodgy bloke, but I can hardly see him taking over the world, can you?'

There was desperation in Mara's eyes. She'd hoped that, after all the weird things that had been happening to him, Max Trevidian might at last be receptive to the unpalatable truth.

'He feeds on sex, Max. Yours, mine . . . all who do not have the strength to resist him. He wants to have power over the whole world, until everything is his and he has established his evil empire of lust. He is almost invincible, Max. He drains the sexual energy from his victims and possesses their souls as he tastes the sweetness of their blood. I have the sight and the power, and yet he overcame me, tricked and almost destroyed me. It could so easily be you next.'

He'd wanted to believe her, really he did, but this was just too much. Did she really think he would swallow all this guff about sex vampires?

'What is it you really want, Anastasia? What are you trying to do to me? Is this just another game LeMaître has told you to play with me? And whilst we're at it, what's LeMaître *really* up to? Tell me that, if you dare.'

'I've told you, I'm not Anastasia Dubois.'

'Well, I've got photos that say you are.'

Mara sighed.

'Yes, this is the body of Anastasia Dubois, but I am Mara Fleming. The Master – LeMaître – trapped me. It is my body that he has used for the soul of Mistress Sedet.'

'And you seriously expect me to believe that, do you? I mean, who are you to talk anyway? You're just one of the

242

many obliging little mistresses of Anthony LeMaître.'

She grasped his hand suddenly, convulsively, and a great surge of spiritual pain seemed to flow out of her into his body. His hand was glowing again, too: a bright, angry red. He looked at her, startled, and anger and pity mingled with his feelings of lust.

'He isn't Anthony LeMaître.'

'No,' agreed Max Trevidian. 'He's Andreas Hunt, isn't he? But what the hell is he playing at? Tell me that.'

'He tricked me,' pleaded Mara, 'and he tricked Andreas and stole his body. Andreas's spirit is trapped within the crystal at Winterbourne Hall.' There were tears in her eyes and for a second Max almost bent to kiss them away.

'You have to help us, Max. I've seen the power within you, though you still deny its existence. You're the only one who can help us – help to free Andreas and help to overcome LeMaître before it is too late.'

Suddenly Max's patience snapped. She'd played with him for too long, flaunting her body and trying to make him feel sorry for her with her stupid, unbelievable stories of stolen bodies and sex vampires. He stood up, pushing her away angrily.

'Forget it, Dubois. You're a cunning little bitch, but you don't con Max Trevidian that easily. I've spent my whole working life exposing frauds like you, remember, and I'm going to expose Anthony LeMaître for what he is, too.'

He stalked off down the aisle towards the west door, but the woman called after him and he couldn't resist turning back to look at her.

'I spoke to him . . . to Andreas. He told me to tell you—'

'Tell me what?'

'Eastbourne.'

With a start, he stared at her for a moment, wondering if just maybe Andreas . . . But no. He'd given her enough chances and she'd blown them all. Without a backward glance, he strode towards the door and flung it open, letting in the full, honest glare of the noonday sun.

Seconds later, the door banged shut and he was gone.

Mara sat in silence for a few minutes, drinking in the healing power of this ancient, holy place. The forces of goodness had been worshipped here for thousands of years. Here she prayed, where the Master could neither see her nor pursue her. She would rest here for a little while, recovering strength and hope for what she must do next.

She did not run after Max. There was no need. With the splinter of crystal still embedded in his flesh, she would always be able to find him.

The tall African writhed in his chains, but there was no escape from the avenging fury of Hackman's lust.

Caît looked on in delight as Hackman brought the cat down on the African's back, each deadly thong lead-tipped and flecked with the delicious crimson of fresh blood. She was enjoying herself tonight at the Maison Delgado. Chained down on her hands and knees in Madame Olenska's Salon des Fêtes, she was savouring the delicious sensation of having one thick black cock up her cunt and another in her mouth. These days, she simply couldn't get enough sex – the more perverse, the better.

The crystal ring was glowing with a secret fire but she paid it no attention. It always seemed to glow more intensely when she was enjoying a particularly fine fucking and an especially delicious cock. Her unseen lover's hands were stroking and kneading her willing flesh as he drove into her, his massive penis distending the flesh of her cunt. And his whispers echoed in her head:

'Little bitch, little bitch on heat. I'm going to fuck you till you cry out for mercy. And them I'm going to take you in the arse . . .'

Only she couldn't cry out for mercy, even if she had wanted to. For the lover lying beneath her was straining to ram his cock further and further down her throat. She gagged, afraid she could take no more, that she would choke on the delicious flesh on his iron-hard shaft. But she didn't want him to stop. Oh no, she wanted him to go on thrusting into her until at last she would feel him shudder beneath her and give a final mighty thrust as his spunk jetted out of her and into her waiting mouth.

They were so beautiful, these Africans that Madame Olenska had magicked as if from nowhere for Hackman's private party. Where had she found them? One girl had told Caít that they were poor refugees, rescued from the streets and trained to the peak of physical – and sexual – perfection by Madame Olenska herself. Other rumours suggested that they were young athletes and boxers, brought to the Maison Delgado by a young Ethiopian ex-boxer called Ibrahim.

Wherever they had come from, they were exquisite and knowing lovers; and Caít was delighted with the ways they used their fingers and mouths and cocks to pleasure her flesh. They seemed so much more exciting than the European clients she had served in her time at the Maison Delgado. So much more imaginative, with just a hint of wildness and hidden violence that made her shiver with the ultimate aphrodisiac: a hint of fear.

With their perfect bodies carefully prepared with sweet aphrodisiac oils, they seemed like exquisite statues, brought to life by the power of sex. Their skin glistened like burnished black marble under the myriad lights from the chandeliers. Madame Olenska believed in creating an opulent setting for the pleasure of her most favoured (and lucrative) clients.

There were five or six whores in the Salon des Fêtes tonight and each girl had two magnificent lovers to pleasure her. The girls were chained to beds or strapped across the backs of chairs, so that their lovers could more easily take their pleasure with them.

One girl – the pretty French blonde Simone – was crying out with delighted pain as two muscular black twins tormented her with huge dildos that stretched and abused her flesh as they rammed into cunt and arse. The little Chinese girl, Qiu-

Xi, was being obliged to suck two men off at once, her rosebud lips stretching to accommodate the twin glistening heads of their pricks.

The Romanian girl, Celestina, was tied hand and foot to a brass bedstead, spreadeagled like a starfish across the white satin sheets as her lovers licked and nibbled at her helpless flesh, their tongues and teeth awakening passions that she could only express through the delicious wetness of her cunt, since her mouth was stopped by a heavy leather gag that reduced her voice to a far-away moaning.

It was indeed a pretty scene – and one which would be captured in all its glory. A battery of video cameras were whirring at various strategic points in the room, carefully set up by Hackman to ensure his continued pleasure when he replayed these lascivious scenes again in the privacy of his own Blackheath mansion. There were sure to be plenty of close-up shots of cocks entering cunts and mouths and arses – and plenty of sweet flesh, reddened and broken by the bite of the lash and the supple cane.

Of course, Hackman had saved the most magnificent of the boys for his own pleasure. Since Caít had served his pleasure on that first night in the Maison Delgado, he had become more and more adventurous and voracious in his pursuit of sex. Even now, as he brought the lead-tipped thongs stinging down on his victim's back, his brother African was kneeling behind Hackman, prising apart his arse cheeks and inserting the tip of his tongue into the pleasure palace of his arse.

Hackman's eyes were sparkling with demonic lust and, with a cry of hunger, he dropped the lash and began lapping the blood from his victim's back, with such sensual effect that the wounded victim began moaning again – this time with pleasure. In a second Hackman's cock was inside him and they were moving together like rutting beasts.

It was a scene which, a few short months ago, Caít O'Keefe would have been disgusted by. But this was not the old days, this was now. And now she had two wonderful cocks to play with and she understood the meaning of sexual hunger.

Drinking down one lover's semen, Caít thrust out her backside to take in the other lover's cock. Sensing that her own crisis was near, she tensed her cunt muscles, exerting more delicious pressure on the thick shaft within her.

In seconds, she felt him harden still further and, a moment later, he was spurting into her, his need for her hot and strong and bubbling like molten lava in her belly. With a shuddering cry, she let go, abandoning herself to the tyranny of complete ecstasy.

When consciousness returned to her she was lying on the floor, her wrists still chained to the foot of a bedstead and two different lovers stimulating her body with lascivious caresses. Lazily, she opened her eyes and looked across at Hackman, who had found his own Nirvana between the thighs of a beautiful Indian girl. He was sitting in a Louis XV *fauteuil* and she was on his lap, his hands cupped around her pert young breasts as she levered herself up on the arms of the chair, her cunt rising and falling on his prick.

Hackman returned Caít's gaze with a smile, little gasps escaping from his lips with each new thrust of his hips. This Indian girl was good but Caít was better still. He'd never had a woman so hot for him and, once he'd finished with this one, he'd get Caít to suck him off.

Caít seemed to read his thoughts.

'Will you require my services later, Sir Robert?' she enquired, parting her thighs to allow a probing tongue between her love lips.

'Yes, my sweet slut,' he replied. 'I think there is time before I have to be at Television House. But I shall be working hard over the next few weeks – I'm preparing a special edition, you know.'

Excited by the prospect, he squeezed the Indian girl's tits so hard that she squealed with pain. But that was good, he liked it when his women had a proper respect for him.

Caít listened with growing interest.

'A special edition – what about?'

Hackman glowed with pride. At last he was able to do something that would be of real service to his Master.

'Anthony LeMaître,' he replied. 'But don't tell a soul – it's still under wraps.'

Caít felt a sudden surge of rage burning through her. That name, that hated name . . . The ring was scorching her finger but her hands were chained and she could do nothing to still the pain.

But wait a moment . . . a plan was forming in her head, just as if someone was whispering in her ear. A dark-haired, bearded man with a Satanic smile. What was the voice saying?

She looked up at Hackman and smiled, a warm smile that promised sweet seduction.

'Really?' she said, feigning pleasure. 'What a good idea. Could I come to the studios and watch?'

'Of course,' replied Hackman. 'I'll get you a ticket for the studio audience. I didn't realise you took such a keen interest in our Mr LeMaître.'

Oh, but I do, thought Caít. A keener interest than you'll ever know.


Max glanced at his watch uneasily. Five past eight and Liz still wasn't here. However, this was the address her assistant had given him and when he'd arrived at the exclusive block of Mayfair apartments, sure enough, there'd been a key waiting for him at the desk. All the same, he couldn't help wondering if it was a set-up. After all those weeks spent fruitlessly trying to track her down and then suddenly her assistant had called him up out of the blue.

He struggled to get comfortable on the deep soft settee. He'd developed a dislike of soft chairs, soft settees, soft beds. You couldn't stay alert on a soft chair and he very much wanted to stay alert.

His thoughts wandered and he cast unseeing eyes over the decor: the little Deco statuette of a girl with a beachball; a fox-fur coat hanging on a hook on the back of the door; a bronze model of a sleeping tiger. The whole place reeked of material success – had Liz really come into *that* much money since he'd first met her?

He'd almost forgotten Liz when the front door of the flat opened and closed again with a couple of quiet clicks, and he heard footsteps coming along the corridor towards the living room.

'Max! It's been so long! Will you ever forgive me?'

He hardly recognised her. Oh, superficially she *looked* the same – same cropped blonde hair, same subtle eye make-up, same smart yet sexy clothes. It was the expression in her eyes that looked so different – all the warmth seemed to have gone out of them, leaving only a burning wildness that could be ambition, hunger, lust . . .

She smiled and settled down on the settee beside him. He swallowed hard.

'You don't mind, do you, Max darling?'

'Darling'? She'd never called him anything but 'Max' or 'Mr Trevidian' or 'you idiotic waste of space' before. 'Darling' didn't sound right at all. There was something vaguely threatening about this new, vibrant, sexual Liz Exley – and now her hand was on his thigh.

'We need to talk, Liz. Where have you been all this time? And what the hell are you doing working for that cunt, LeMaître? Don't you realise how dangerous he is?'

'Don't let's talk about that now.'

'But Liz – listen to me. This is important!'

'I've always fancied you, Max, did you know that?'

He opened his mouth to protest, to tell her that really, definitely, positively, they ought to get down to talking business. But Liz, it seemed, had other plans in mind. Without waiting for him to reply, she ran her smooth, well-manicured hand up to the top of his thigh and began lightly massaging his prick and balls through the fabric of his trousers.

'I want you, Max. Don't say no.'

He didn't say anything. He couldn't. He opened his mouth but no sound came out. Her touch on his groin electrified him into a paroxysm of sudden lust. It wasn't something he could fight even if he'd tried – and he just didn't have the will to try. What man in his right mind would resist a come-on from the delicious Liz Exley, with her firm body and her soft, soft touch?

It was madness. His instincts all screamed at him to get away before it was too late but, if something bad was going to happen, it was probably too late already. If he was going to cash in his chips, he might as well enjoy himself first.

She was unzipping him now and his cock was already fluttering into life just at the anticipation of her cool, cool hand on his most intimate flesh. He wanted that touch; wanted, too, to know how it felt to have the warm heart of her sex cupped in his hand.

'It's hot in here. Why don't you undress me, Max?'

She was right. It *was* hot. So hot, he could feel the sweat trickling down his face. How could he resist? With trembling fingers he reached out and began unfastening the buttons of Liz's blouse. They were impossibly fiddly buttons – there seemed to be hundreds of them, all defying the urgency of his lust.

But eventually he succeeded in undoing the recaltricant blouse and the sight of her breasts inspired him. Remembering the skills of his schooldays, he unfastened her bra one-handed.

All this time Liz was playing with his cock, awakening such desperate lusts within him that he began panting for breath. His balls were so, so heavy with spunk for her. And now she was naked and so was he, struggling out of the last vestiges of his clothing and lying back on the sofa, waiting for her to make her move.

He did not have to wait long. In seconds, she was on him like a bitch in heat, and her tight wet cunt was sliding up and down his shaft with an irresistible, ecstatic rhythm. He clutched at her buttocks as she rode him, laughing and smiling as her pert breasts bobbed up and down, just tantalisingly out of reach.

It was like a fantasy; and when Max came, it was with a violent pleasure he had only ever experienced in dreams. Exhausted, he fell back on the settee, eyes closed and breathing heavily. He could feel the cooling spunk draining out of Liz and onto his belly, the delicious memory of their coupling.

He opened his eyes suddenly, he wasn't sure why. Some sixth sense screamed inside him: for God's sake, save yourself!

She was smiling at him, but it wasn't the gentle, sweetly seductive smile of a lover. It was the predatory smile of a carnivore just before it sinks its teeth into the flesh of its helpless prey.

All too quickly, Max realised that he was the prey. Her teeth seemed sharper, more prominent than he remembered them and she was preparing to lunge at his throat!

As Max struggled beneath her, Liz hungered for his blood. Just a little taste of his sweet essence. She knew he had hidden psychic power within him and perhaps that power would enter her and make her strong. Stronger than her Mistress Sedet . . .

At the moment of crisis, a voice roared its rage inside her head.

'No! You shall not! I forbid it! I told you that the man Trevidian is not to be harmed. He is for my pleasure alone.'

The Master was angry. Liz trembled with the sudden realisation of her transgression. And yet . . . there he lay beneath her, afraid and helpless and so, so tempting. It would be over in a moment and perhaps with Trevidian's strength inside her, even the Master's rage could not harm her.

She lunged for Trevidian's throat but at that moment a terrible pain seared through her and she screamed, screamed for mercy.

Max could not believe his luck. One minute, Liz was trying to rip out his throat; the next, she was screaming and writhing, her body crumpling up as she fell to the floor, weeping and begging mercy from some unseen and unknown force.

'Master, Master, I beg of you – do not punish me so!' she cried.

But the Master had had enough of insubordination and pride. The Exley slut must learn obedience.

Max eased along the sofa, further away from Liz, not daring to get up and run for fear that she would pursue him. Besides, some very odd things were happening . . .

His eyes were drawn by a movement on the mantelpiece, and to Max's shock he saw something quite impossible: the bronze tiger was stirring, turning and looking at him, opening its mouth and roaring. Its teeth were wickedly sharp and stained red with blood. Next to it, the statuette of the girl was throwing back its head and laughing, laughing.

Turning away, he thought maybe he really ought to take the chance and run – naked or not. Better to be arrested for indecent exposure than eaten alive by a carnivorous statuette. Then he caught sight of the fox-fur coat. It was straining to get at him, its sightless glass eyes glittering and flashing with a malign lust.

Got to save himself.

He got unsteadily to his feet, weighing up his chances if he jumped out of the window. When he turned back to look at Liz, she was paying no heed to him. It was as though she was wrestling with an unseen force, an evil power that was crushing and tormenting her as she knelt on the floor, begging for mercy.

'No . . .!' she screamed.

And as Max watched, unable to believe his eyes, a bolt of lightning struck her, turning her into a writhing pillar of flame, a white figure within the raging inferno. For a second she turned her face to Max and then – she was gone.

Nothing remained. Not even a hint of the flames that seemed to have engulfed and consumed her.

But the room was shaking and there were voices all around him, screaming and laughing and mocking him.

'There's no escape, Max. No escape from the Master.'

It wasn't that Mara liked singles bars, On the contrary, she felt degraded and humiliated by the prospect of displaying herself there, like some commodity to be purchased and enjoyed and discarded. But there was a need within her – a need for sex which she must satisfy. Here, in the Pelican Club, she could satisfy her burning hunger innocently and anonymously, without fear of discovery.

She needed sex tonight, needed as much of it as she could get it if she was going to have the strength to help Andreas.

That man sitting near her at the bar – he looked promising enough. He was young and strong and had been giving her the eye all night. If she couldn't find anyone she preferred, maybe she'd go home with him tonight and let him screw her. The hunger was so bad . . .

'Anastasia . . . I mean, Mara . . .?'

She wheeled round, startled to hear the name that had been stolen from her.

'Max!'

'Look, Mara – I'm probably the last person you want to see. You've every right to be sick to death of me. But I had to find you. I had to tell you that I'm sorry.'

He looked tired; scared, too. Mara laid a protective hand on his arm and this time he didn't flinch.

'Does this mean you believe me now?'

'I guess it does – or at least, I'm ready to listen.' He sat down on the bar stool beside her and ordered a double whisky. After the night's events, he needed it. He'd been such a damn fool.

'We have to rescue Andreas, Max. And you're the only one I know with the power to help. Will you do it?'

Max nodded glumly. It looked as if he was going to have to.

Takimoto was pleased with himself. Better still, the Master was pleased with him and that meant that he would be regularly rewarded for his efforts.

The new cable station – Empire TV – was due to be launched soon, thanks to hard work on his part and the efforts of the Master and his allies on the House of Commons

Broadcasting Committee. With this new channel of media manipulation, there would be no stopping the Master's rise to power. And, of course, his most intimate servants would enjoy the fruits of power with him.

Sex – Takimoto loved it. Never in his former life had he enjoyed such unremitting pleasure, not even with the most skilful geishas that Kyoto could afford. Now he had slaves to pleasure him, and one was particularly pleasing.

The English slut Charlotte Madingley had such a refined touch with her fingers and tongue. He loved her peaches-and-cream skin, her natural blonde hair, her rounded body that invited every violation, every delicious abuse.

He bent her over his desk and pulled up her skirt. Good. As he had instructed, she was wearing plain white cotton panties and looked more like a schoolgirl than ever. He liked schoolgirls. For his latest reward, the Master had given him a nubile sixteen-year-old virgin from a Swiss finishing school and her flesh had been sweeter than sake.

But none of them pleased him quite like Charlotte. Pulling aside the gusset of her panties, he thrust a sharp fingernail into her arsehole and was rewarded with a little cry and a wriggle of her rounded backside.

Good, very good. The girl was hot for him and he didn't keep her waiting. With a swift, efficient thrust he was inside her and she felt wonderfully tight around his cock. His balls slapped against her backside as he buggered her and he thought of what he would do next, when he had enjoyed her. Perhaps he would get a couple of pretty boy slaves to fuck and beat her, so he could jerk himself off as he watched.

A knock on the door disturbed his concentration momentarily but when he turned and saw that the new-comer was Hackman, he did not even bother to interrupt his pleasure.

'It is confirmed,' announced Hackman, running inquisitive fingers over Charlotte's breasts and pinching her nipples. 'My special programme on the Master will be ready for transmission in two weeks' time.'

'Excellent,' replied Takimoto, thrusting a little deeper into the girl's tender young backside. 'In that case, we shall be able to broadcast it on the opening night of Empire TV.'

# 15: Aurelia

Max had his foot on the floor, but the old Morris Traveller couldn't do more than fifty without shuddering itself to bits.

'We must hurry,' urged Mara. 'If we don't get back from Felsham Manor before nightfall, the Master may start wondering where I've gone. I'm supposed to be at a political lunch with Nick Weatherall.'

'I'm going as fast as I can,' protested Max. 'The old crate can't take it like she used to and the wheel bearings are shot to bits.'

The car continued its progress through the fenland lanes. Normally Max would have stopped to admire the view but today there wasn't time. He was only too aware of the urgency, now that he understood what Mara had told him; and grateful, too, for the shard of crystal which still glowed in the flesh of his hand, protecting him perhaps from far worse than had already happened.

He glanced down at his hand. Funny, it didn't seem to be glowing as strongly as it had been. Mara must have noticed it too. She was gazing at his hand with a worried expression.

'What's the matter?'

'It's the power of the crystal,' explained Mara. 'It's fading fast. The power of all talismans has a limited lifespan. If we don't renew it soon, we'll lose its protection.'

Max glanced at her, suddenly more anxious than ever.

'And?'

'And then the Master will be able to see and hear us together. If that happens, Max, we're lost.'

'So what do we do?'

'Pull in here. There's no time to lose.'

Puzzled, Max pulled in beside the grass verge.

'What now?'

Mara smiled and slid out of the car. Above, the winter sun shone, feeble but reassuring.

'This is a good place. An ancient place. Come with me.'

She took Max by the hand and led him through the gate into the field. The bare earth was iron hard and frozen underneath.

'Undress,' Mara instructed him, and began pulling her jumper off over her head.

'What? You're joking!'

'The ritual must be performed sky-clad, as all high rituals of white magic. You have the sight and the knowledge, Max, you must know how important these things are. Only the unashamed conjunction of naked flesh will empower the talisman.'

Shivering already, Max slipped off his jacket and began unbuttoning his shirt. The wind came straight from Siberia, searing across the flat fenlands, whipping at his flesh and making his teeth chatter. He hadn't noticed it before but there were little flakes of snow in the air, too: powder-fine ice crystals, whirling about him like an icing-sugar mist. He was so cold that they didn't even melt when they touched his skin.

But Mara seemed not to notice the cold. She had taken off her sweater and was now calmly unbuttoning the camisole blouse she wore underneath. Even Max, frozen to the marrow, fingers blue with cold, could not fail to be excited by the gradual unveiling of her sumptuous body. Mara was every bit as desirable as he remembered her and, despite the bitter cold, he wanted her.

Naked and barefoot on the frozen earth, Mara looked like a beautiful statue of creamy-white marble blushed with pink. There seemed to be an inner energy within her, as though desire burned with its own secret heat.

She picked up the little velvet bag she had brought and

took out a small green glass vial, which she handed to Max.

'An oil of bergamot and patchouli, wolfsbane and myrrh,' she explained. 'And there are other ingredients, less appealing, more arcane. The oil is very powerful and you must use it to anoint my body in preparation for the ritual.'

Max stood there, dumbfounded and shivering. She had to take hold of his hand and pour a few drops of the clear golden oil into his palm.

The touch of the oil on his skin was like an electric shock arcing through his body and he looked up, startled and suddenly very aware, more aware than he had ever been of this woman's body, inviting his caresses. There was indeed a secret power in this oil.

'Touch me, Max,' urged Mara. 'Let the power of the magical oil unite our flesh.'

Her skin was satin-smooth and flawless, with not a hint of gooseflesh even in this bitter chill. The tiny snowflakes dusted her flesh but he smoothed them away, letting the flat of his hand skate gently over the surface of her body. He closed his eyes and explored her by touch alone.

Shoulders and breasts, belly and buttocks and thighs: these were the staging-posts in his sensual journey. He let his fingers slide over the ample curve of her breasts, lingering awhile on the hardening crests that begged him to kiss and play with them. Then he ventured down over the smooth firmness of back and buttocks, easing apart her arse cheeks so that he could massage a little of the oil into the secret furrow of her backside. He could hear her breath quickening, growing harsher as she abandoned herself to the alchemy of lust.

Moving down her belly, Max smoothed oil into the strong, slender thighs; working his way inexorably inwards, towards the pleasure-centre that he knew throbbed with the need of his touch. He did not need his eyes to tell him that Mara was aroused, passionate with lust for him. He could smell her desire, taste it in the clear sweet juices that ran from her fanny and into his hand as he slipped his fingers between her thighs and began working the oil into her love lips.

She began chanting – some sort of mantra, but Max didn't recognise it. He was beginning to wish he'd paid more attention to his Great-Aunt Aurelia when she had tried to teach him to recognise and use his powers. She had had such a treasure-house of magical knowledge, and he had brushed it all aside as so much mumbo-jumbo.

'Mene, mene, teherim. Mene, mene, teherim . . .'

The hypnotic sound of Mara's chanting combined with the subtle warmth that spread through Max's body as the oil was absorbed through the flesh of his hand. He was a creature of fire and of sex.

He had forgotten completely about the cold wind, still howling across the fens and raking at his bare flesh with jagged claws. The warmth in the belly overcame all mortal sensations. Now he lived only for the pleasure of the moment, desperate to have his cock inside Mara's cunt, desperate to feel her shudder beneath him as the orgasm wracked her body.

But Mara was mistress of this ritual and she had very definite ideas of how it must proceed.

Opening her eyes, she held him close and kissed him, her tongue probing his mouth with an eager insistence. Then she took another bottle from her velvet bag: a bottle of dark red liquid, with a strong and rather unpleasant smell. Max recoiled as she dipped her finger in the liquid and began painting the sign of the serpent about his cock.

'It is a simple extract of berries,' she reassured him. 'Mixed with wine and a little of the juices from a virgin's first fucking. It is a powerful sexual essence, vital for the ritual.'

She finished painting his belly and drew a star on her belly, its longest point directed towards her cunt. Then she held out the vial to him.

'Drink.'

He hesitated, but knew he must do as she told him. Raising the vial to his lips, he took a tentative sip and swallowed it as quickly as he could. It tasted bitter, nauseating, but he could feel a fire entering his body as the liquid seared his throat.

Mara drank from the bottle and then drew him to her, kissing him again. The taste of the red liquid was on her lips, but now he found that he welcomed the taste. He felt envigorated, hungry as a wild beast. He could feel her heart racing, desire pumping through her body. His stiff cock was pressing up against her belly. If she would just part her thighs for him, he could slip inside her and fuck her here, standing on the frozen earth in this barren winter field.

'First, I must absorb the energy of your spirit,' announced Mara.

'What must I do?' Desire was making his voice tremble and his hands grow damp with perspiration.

'You need do nothing,' replied Mara, with a smile. 'Leave everything to me.'

She slid to her knees on the hard ground and Max groaned as her lips parted and she took his cock into her mouth. A day ago, he would not have trusted her anywhere near him but now he was abandoning himself utterly to the care of his pleasure.

She was good, so good. As she sucked and licked at him, he stroked the long wavy mane of her hair, moaning and sighing with each new trick she devised to pleasure him. Her fingers were gentle and cool and soft on his scrotum and his balls felt as though they were about to explode. Now she was wriggling the tip of her tongue into the little weeping eye at the tip of his glans and slippery pre-cum was oozing out of him and he was crying out for the ecstasy of the sacred moment before pleasure turned into orgasm.

He pumped hard into her and she sucked diligently at his shaft, drinking down every drop of the precious fluid. Then she got to her feet and kissed him. He felt weak and unsteady, as though she really had taken part of the spiritual essence from him.

'Now kneel,' instructed Mara.

He knelt with difficulty on the furrowed earth and she took hold of his head and pressed his face close against the glossy auburn curls of her mount of Venus. The fragrance of her sex mingled irresistibly with the mingled aromas of bergamot and patchouli and myrrh. His head was spinning, his mouth parched with the need to drink her dry.

'Kiss me between my love lips,' breathed Mara.

He was only too ready to obey, for he thirsted desperately for her sex. Pushing his tongue through the forest of pubic curls, he entered the eternal spring of her desire. She tasted so good, so exciting, that he felt as though all he would ever want would be to drink at this fountain of everlasting pleasure.

Her clitoris was a hot, throbbing stalk of engorged flesh, so hard and long that he was able to take it between his teeth and tease it gently with tongue and teeth. Mara was chanting still, her voice struggling to achieve a calm serenity, but he could hear her breathing, hoarse and urgent, as he brought her to the brink of orgasm.

His fingers slipped around her hips and smoothed down the curve of her backside, gently prising apart her arse cheeks and sliding inside. She sighed as his fingertips sought out the secret amber rose and toyed with it, stretching and teasing the sensitive membrane as he licked and nibbled at the stalk of her clitoris.

With one finger buried to the knuckle in her arse, he excited her until she could take no more.

'So close, so close,' gasped Mara. 'The time . . . it must be now.' Taking his hand from her arse, she thrust it between her thighs. 'Quickly – the hand with the crystal. Put it inside me. It must be your whole hand . . .'

He thrust his fingers into her – one, two, three, then the entire hand – and she opened like a flower to take him in. With a cry of triumph she came, and he felt a sharp stabbing pain as her juices cascaded over his hand, inundating the splinter of crystal.

'Show me your hand, Max.'

He withdrew it from her cunt and lifted it to the wintry yellow sun. It was glowing with a blood-red inner fire.

'Well, this is it.'

The Morris Traveller turned up a bumpy lane and rattled to a halt outside Felsham Manor, a tumbledown house of indeterminate age and indefinable charm. It was one of those English country houses which have grown organically over the centuries and which defy all attempts at classification. It needed about forty thousand a year to keep it from falling down, but then again so did Max – and he didn't hold out much hope of either happening.

'I'm almost scared to go in,' admitted Max as he turned the key in the lock. 'I haven't been back here for days, not since . . .'

'I know.' Mara squeezed his arm reassuringly. 'But we have to. We have to find that grimoire.'

The house was in darkness. Even after Max had switched on all the lights, there was still an uncomfortable gloom. The pinboard, still festooned with pictures of Anthony LeMaître, exuded an aura of pure evil; and they avoided the study altogether.

'I keep most of Great-Aunt Aurelia's stuff in here,' explained Max, unlocking the door to the old parlour where Aurelia had spent long days and nights researching the high rituals of the ancient magicians. He'd always avoided going in here; it reminded him uncomfortably of the powers he'd always denied. But now, as they walked through the door into the parlour, it felt comfortable and welcoming, like going home.

'Her spirit is still here,' observed Mara, running her fingers lightly over the dusty surfaces of glass cabinets and jars of dried herbs. 'She is still protecting you and her will is strong. Whilst we remain in this room, and with the protection of the crystal, I do not believe that the Master has the power to harm you. She was a very great magician, a mistress of her art.'

'I suppose she must have been,' conceded Max. 'She told me she worked for British Intelligence in the War. But she never said much about it. To tell the truth, I didn't want to listen. I was too busy trying to prove all this magic stuff was a load of nonsense.'

Mara turned to Max and looked him straight in the eye. 'You have her power, if you will only learn to use it.'

Max turned away, suddenly afraid. It wasn't as if Mara was telling him anything new. But he wasn't ready for the truth yet; not strong enough to face the legacy his aunt had left him. Why did it have to be him?

He transferred his attentions to a bunch of rusty keys, trying to find the one that would unlock the old wall cupboard where Great-Aunt Aurelia had kept her grimoires.

'The answer is here,' whispered Mara, excitedly. 'I can feel it, very close now. Hurry . . .'

The fourth key he tried worked and the old padlock clicked open. He opened the massive doors of the cupboard to reveal an interior packed from floor to ceiling with musty books and papers. Mara gasped with awe and delight but Max groaned.

'I'd forgotten just how much stuff the old girl had. Looks like we've got our work cut out sorting through it all.'

Mara did not reply. She was standing in front of the cupboard, arms outstretched and eyes closed, concentrating every ounce of her psychic energy on the vast array of magical papers.

Outside, it was growing dark; low clouds were swirling and scudding across the murky sky, pushing away the light. A flash of lightning lit up the sky momentarily and in that instant something very strange indeed happened. The body of Mara Fleming seemed to melt away and in her place stood an impossibly familiar figure. It couldn't be! But she turned and Max saw her: Aunt Aurelia as she was in the photographs of her as a young girl, tall and slender with a bright curtain of golden hair.

She was holding a book in her hand and pointing to the open page.

'Aunt Aurelia!' gasped Max, reaching out to her. But she shook her head and remained tantalisingly out of reach.

'Seek and you shall find, Max. Do not be afraid to walk alone into the unknown.'

And then she was gone and Mara was lying unconscious

on the floor, an open grimoire beside her and her hand lying across the golden letters of a magical incantation.

'I have failed, Master. I have failed utterly to entrap our victim and I crave the blessing of your wrath.'

The Turkish boy knelt before the Master, his glistening brown nakedness surely a temptation for any man of refined tastes. And yet the youth had failed him. The Master clenched his teeth in rage, dealing the boy a savage blow which knocked him sideways onto the study floor. Sedet was looking on hungrily, the tip of her tongue moistening her lips in delicious anticipation. Sedet had a taste for punishment and would no doubt enjoy inflicting exquisite agonies on the foolish youth. The Master's face twisted into a cruel mask of malicious determination.

'I will have power. This mere mortal must not encumber my progress to my rightful inheritance.'

The Master was extremely displeased. Hugo Winchester was proving to be a more difficult prey to ensnare than he had anticipated. The man's sexual appetite was indisputable – had he not been only too willing to enjoy the favours of the slave-girl Sunita, that day at the club? But Winchester was a skilful politician. How else had he survived so long as leader of the Nationalists during their long years in the wilderness? Yes, Hugo Winchester was a wily character and thus far he had avoided every subtle honey-trap that the Master had set for him, in his quest to discredit his party leader in the public eye. Now there seemed little hope that he would be lured to tomorrow night's Arabian Nights orgy at Winterbourne.

Well, his luck could not last for ever, and the man would soon realise that he had met his match in Anthony LeMaître.

He looked down. The boy was licking his thighs, stroking the flesh and moving slowly towards his master's ever-lively prick. The Master deliberated for a moment: should he enjoy the trifling pleasure of being sucked off by this weakling, or should he move swiftly on to the far more piquant enjoyment of watching Sedet punish him?

The Master kicked the cringing boy away from him.

'You may have him now, my Queen. I tire of his pathetic broken spirit. Devise some fitting punishment for the snivelling wretch.'

Sedet looked hungrily at the boy. His cock was already hardening from the harshness of the Master's treatment. Well, in the hours to come she would have it iron-hard from the beating she would give him. She thought of the red-hot branding iron waiting for his sweet flesh and almost came to orgasm at the very thought. Yes, the boy would serve her pleasure most delightfully. And it pleased her, also, that the Master had chosen to entrust his punishment to her. Sluts might serve his appetites but she alone was worthy to be consort to the Master.

The Master turned to Liz, sitting obediently at her mistress's feet, still wearing the jewelled dog-collar which Sedet had imposed upon her for her disobedience. The girl was turning into a most pleasing whore, mused the Master. Breaking her spirit had been an enjoyable exercise and he now felt the need of a sustenance which only she could give. He snapped his fingers.

'Come to me, slut, and suck my cock.'

Eagerly, Liz scrambled across the room and flung herself at the Master's feet, tearing open his zip and covering the tip of his burgeoning cock with kisses.

Sedet looked on in fury, her mood suddenly changed from smug self-satisfaction to jealous rage. How could her own harlot, the slut she had trained with her own cruel hand, be so treacherous?

The disobedient little slut would have to pay.

'I am here, Andreas.'

Mara lay face-down on the crystal, its smooth surface now crazed and a broad crack running from top to bottom. There was such power here now, such energy within Andreas that she could almost reach out and pull his spirit from the imprisoning crystal.

*You've come to me at last, Mara. Where have you been? It's been so long . . .*

'I've been working – working for us both, Andreas. I think I've found a way at last. It will be very soon now, I promise.'

*It had better be. I'm hot for you, you little tease. If I had a cock, it would be between those thighs. I can smell your sex, do you know that, Mara? I can smell your sex and it's making me strong.*

She stretched out on her back on the crystal's surface. It was dark and forbidding here in the cellars at Winterbourne but she wasn't afraid any more. The old demons had fled, exorcised by the power of hope: the first real hope they'd had since that night. That night when she'd killed Andreas Hunt.

'There's something I must do now, Andreas. Join with my spirit and feel the power of pleasure.'

Slipping the dildo between her thighs, she let it slide slowly and pleasurably into her cunt. And, in the crystal prison, Andreas felt the silken grip of her cunt and gave a silent groan of ecstasy.

Max pushed open the door of his office, half-expecting to find something horrible with two heads waiting for him. He breathed a sigh of relief as the only things that met his eyes were a council tax bill and the mouldering remains of a bacon sandwich.

He thought about putting the kettle on, plugging the phone in, getting back into a routine; but no – there was other work to do. If he was ever going to get himself out of this bloody awful mess he'd got himself into, he was going to have to fight the Master on his own terms.

The Master was playing with him, he knew that. As long as he got the desired result, he wouldn't get suspicious. If anything impeded his perfect sound and vision, maybe the Master would start wondering what was going on. That would be dangerous for Max but a hell of a lot more dangerous for Mara. He'd probably give her to that sadistic bitch Sedet to destroy whilst he sat back and watched. Well, ordinary cowardly Englishman that he was, Max couldn't let that happen to her. He was getting fond of Mara.

Sitting down at his desk, he opened the top drawer and rummaged around. A scalpel, a pair of pliers and a box of Elastoplast. That would do.

Screwing up his face, he jabbed the scalpel into the soft flesh of his hand and drew blood. No point in whingeing, though. He prodded around with the pliers and managed to pull out the shard of crystal, still blood-red and glowing. It had served him well but now he had to meet the Master without its protection.

He slapped iodine and a plaster on his hand. It smarted. He poured himself a comforting glass of brandy and sat back in the chair.

It started again, more quickly than he had anticipated. And this time, the weirdness was really something. Dumbstruck, he watched all the pieces on his chess set turn red, playing their own silent game on a blood-red board. He went to pick up the brandy glass, but it had turned into a snake and was hissing at him. Paperclips were fighting on his desk and, when he tried to turn away and look out of the window, all he could see were Brazilian TV programmes projected on the glass. The phone was ringing and it wasn't even plugged in.

And there were eyes everywhere: eyes staring at him from the light-fitting, eyes in the walls, eyes glaring at him out of the open desk drawer. All equally malevolent and unblinking.

He was going to ignore it all. Well, he was going to try. It was all a trick the Master was playing on him and he didn't want to play any more. Closing his eyes, Max focused on the psychedelic world around him and tried to make it go away.

At first, nothing happened. And then, to his immense surprise, things began to calm down. He opened his eyes and the room had stopped whirling around him. Inanimate objects gave up misbehaving and went back to being their normal selves.

With a sigh of relief, Max stood up to leave. The sooner he got out of this place the better. On a whim, he turned back to the crystal, still glowing on the desk, and he seemed to hear his aunt's voice calling to him again across years:

*Don't be afraid to walk alone into the unknown.*

Well, he might be alone but he wouldn't look a gift horse in the mouth. He never knew when he might need the crystal again. He picked it up for a moment and turned it over in the palm of his hand, then made a snap decision. It was a simple act to unbutton the left breast-pocket of his shirt and drop in the crystal shard.

You couldn't be too careful, could you?

Heimdal stood in the shadows, resplendent in his Arab slaver's costume of turban, sleeveless jerkin and wide pants. The orgy was exactly as he had envisaged it. Even though Hugo Winchester had resisted the lure of a trip to the fabled Winterbourne, the Master was certain to be well pleased. They were all here: Hackman, Chesterton, the Da Silva woman and Dursley-Peterson, the media tycoon who'd been persuaded to put up so much useful cash for Empire TV.

The Great Hall at Winterbourne was a riot of colour, decorated by Heimdal's minions in a faithful representation of an Eastern harem. In the central sunken pool four naked Arab girls were cavorting with the Da Silva woman, whom they had pulled into the scented water fully clothed and were now undressing with playful, hungry fingers.

Half-dazed, her inhibitions broken down by the aphrodisiac wine Ibrahim had given her to drink, Miriam Da Silva giggled and writhed as the girls peeled off her clothes, exposing the not-inconsiderable charms of her buxom body. Heimdal watched with interest and amusement as one of the girls dived beneath the surface of the pink scented water and pressed her face between Miriam's thighs before returning to the surface with laughter and caresses.

The girls were making love to her as she had never been made love to in the whole of her life. Hiram Da Silva did not understand his wife's carnal needs. Birthdays and Passover were quite sufficient to satisfy any little desires he might have and for years Miriam had suffered in silence, with nothing but a few porn magazines and a three-speed dildo for company.

But tonight Miriam was having the time of her life. There were fingers in her cunt and arse, and lips and tongues on her ample breasts. She was singing and laughing – it was wonderful. She wouldn't care when the caresses stopped and the sharp teeth nuzzled into the crook of her neck. She'd never want for sex again.

Madame LeCoeur had done well this evening. Vast iron cauldrons boiled and bubbled on open braziers dotted around the hall. The precious liquid they contained was a sweet and deadly confection of her own invention: an aphrodisiac elixir so powerful that even old Hartmann, the octogenarian billionaire, was enjoying the hardest and most sensitive of erections. Tonight there would be play and pleasure – and worship. For the price of initiation was total obedience, the total abandonment of self.

Not that Heimdal felt hard done by. Since his initiation, he had risen swiftly to a position of supreme power and trust within the Master's empire. Best of all, he knew that the Master would never command him to do anything that he would not be more than delighted to do: for the Master had shown him the sweet liberation of pure evil. Nothing was forbidden: the darkest desires, the most perverse pleasures, were the food and drink of the Master and his servants. Heimdal was proud to serve such a generous and benign lord.

Harem girls – suitably attired in diaphanous pants and tight sequinned tops – passed between the male guests with trays of sweetmeats, each morsel imbued with the essences of sexual desire. Veiled houris with heavy tasselled breasts were kneeling between their masters' thighs, licking and sucking at their balls and running cool smooth hands over their aching, hardening shafts.

On a pile of rich embroidered rugs beneath a brocade awning, lay Liz Exley, irresistible in her role as Scheherazade; her skilful tongue her salvation as she sucked off a succession of guests for the Master's pleasure. The Mistress's, too; for Sedet seemed to be enjoying the deadly crack of the whip as she brought it down again and again on Liz's naked back.

As for the Master, he was setting his guests a worthy example, enjoying the sweet flesh of Sonja Kerensky and her sister whore, Joanna Königsberg. Sonja was in chains, her body strung starfish-like from the ceiling, and he was fucking her from behind whilst Joanna licked out his arse with all the eagerness of a little pet dog. Later, mused the Master, he would enjoy that sweet little doe-eyed virgin that Gonzales had caught for him. Silly little fool! Hadn't her mother ever told her that it was dangerous to hitch-hike? And more dangerous still for pretty little sixteen-year-old virgins with tits like ripe melons and cunts that begged to be violated . . .

On second thoughts, perhaps he would give the girl to his guests and laugh while he watched them fight over who was to have her first. Dursley-Peterson had a legendary appetite for virgins. The Master glanced at the girl, lying all in white on a golden cushion, her wrists chained to iron rings set into the wall. She was dazed with Madame LeCoeur's wine, her nipples already stiff with a pleasure she did not yet understand. The Master laughed as he thought that this would be the night of her life. If Gonzales had not found her, she would have been nothing. She ought to be grateful for her chance of immortality.

Heimdal brought his whip down hard on the back of the Indian whore who was sucking her guest's cock too slowly. It did no harm to give them a taste of the lash – it made them all the hotter and all the more grateful when at last you were gracious enough to give them your cock.

It would soon be time. The great gilded doors of the hall were swinging slowly shut upon silent hinges, and Mara knew what that must mean. The Master was caging his prey, ready for the pleasure.

And the cull.

Some would be worthy of initiation; others would die, here in the Great hall, their necks sticky with the red tribute of their soul's sacrifice. The Master was hungry. It would take a great deal of flesh to quench such a mighty hunger.

Valentina Cilescu

Beside Mara sat Nick Weatherall, mildly inebriated and very randy. He'd drunk too much wine but it hadn't put him off the idea of sex. On the contrary, he was hotter for it than he'd ever been. His hand was on Mara's fanny and his eyes were almost out on stalks. If she didn't get him away from here now, it would be too late. He would be initiated and Mara would have lost her chance for ever.

She ran her fingers playfully down his shaft and he growled with pleasure, tipsy fingers fumbling with the wetness of her crack.

'Lovely snatch you've got, Anastasia. Gonna give me some?'

She kissed him passionately.

'Oh yes, Nick. I'm going to give you the fucking of your life.'

He made a lunge for her, but she shook her head.

'No, not here.'

The music was hypnotic, the beat quickening as the orgy rose to its climax. Already couples were naked and fucking on the floor, on the gilded couches, on the opulent carpets.

'Where then?'

'Somewhere quieter. Come with me, I'll show you.'

She took him by the hand and led him towards a side door, unnoticed in the hubbub. No-one cared about one faithful slut taking her victim to a quiet place to enjoy the sweetness of his blood and the energy of his soul.

The corridors of Winterbourne Hall were deserted, every slave and whore had been summoned to the Great Hall to take part in Heimdal's latest entertainment – a spectacle worthy of Delgado himself.

The guard took no notice of the slut and her drunken companion as they laughed and swayed along the passageway. After all, wasn't the Dubois girl one of the Master's most trusted minions? And here she was, taking her victim to the seclusion of her rooms, there to enjoy his body and steal away his soul.

But they did not go to Anastasia's room. At the end of the corridor, they turned right and Mara guided Weatherall

272

down the flight of stairs which led to the cellars. They passed through the wrought-iron gate and into the Hall of Darkness, the wooden bench still damp with the blood of a Turkish boy Sedet had enjoyed here the previous evening.

Now there was only a single brick wall between them and the cellar where Andreas lay, watching and waiting.

'Gimme your snatch, you little prick-tease. I could make trouble for you with your boss if you don't give me what I want. And you wouldn't want that, would you?' Nick made a grab for her naked cunt and instead of pushing him away, she drew him more closely to her.

'Soon,' she breathed. 'I'll let you have me very soon.'

As she clasped him tightly to her, she focused her psychic energies on Andreas and slowly, very slowly, the wall began to glow and dissolve away.

*Come to me, Mara. I can feel you very near.*

*Patience, Andreas. I have brought him to you.*

It was a good job Nick Weatherall was half-drunk, mused Mara as she drew him across the dimly lit cellar towards the sarcophagus and the lid began to melt away, revealing the flawed surface of the crystal beneath. In his present state, Weatherall wouldn't notice a thing. In fact, the only thing he cared about right now was sex.

She drew him towards the crystal and laid him down on its surface. He was laughing at her as she peeled of her flimsy satin robe and knelt astride him.

'Hurry up and fuck me, you little slut.'

Mara was chanting. The words of the ritual were engraved upon her mind:

'Astaroth, Behemoth, Belzethroth; taniel mehe alzorel; taniel tehe alzorel . . .'

She sat astride him and took the firmness of his dick up into the waiting haven of her cunt. She was hot for him, too, and she felt no pain as she punctured her cunt lip with a sliver of crystal and let the blood drip onto his prick and balls.

There was a mad energy in the air and the pleasure of dick

in cunt was magnified a thousand times by the psychic excitement all around her. Her clitoris was throbbing madly and her cunt was dripping rivulets of warm sex juice as she rode him to the summit of pleasure.

At the moment of orgasm, she felt the change begin and, looking down, she found herself gazing not into Nick Weatherall's eyes but into the eyes of Andreas Hunt.

She knew from the old grimoire what she must do now and she feared for her life, her soul, her sanity. Feared that this vampire-body would gain the upper hand and pleasure would take over from necessity.

'Forgive me, Andreas,' murmured Mara as she bent to kiss his throat. 'But I must bind the charm . . .'

As she bit gently into his throat, Andreas felt a great change come over him. Strength that would never fade away; sight that would not blur or distort. Andreas Hunt was back. And this time he wasn't going away.

# 16: Andreas

Caít scanned the racks of clothes and felt a thrill of anticipation. PVC was such fun and here at Second Skin they had so much imagination.

She picked up a hanger and examined what appeared to be no more than a tangle of shiny black straps.

'That's a love-harness,' explained the assistant in matter-of-fact tones. She was used to the trade, nothing shocked her any more. Besides, ever since Caít had brought him to the shop, the distinguished guy in the blue suit had become one of the shop's best customers. She was pretty sure she recognised him from the telly, but even if she did guess who he was, you didn't go grassing up your best customers. Here at Second Skin, the byword was discretion. 'Want to try it on, luv?'

Caít turned to Sir Robert and gave him the eye, holding up the hanger so he could get a good view of it.

'What do you think, sweetie?'

He responded with an impish grin.

'Only if I can help you put it on – and take it off.'

The assistant turned back from her window display with a shrug.

'Sure, no problem. But careful with the merchandise. Mr Blakemore's very particular about soiling.'

Caít giggled and flounced off to the changing rooms with Sir Robert in hot pursuit. She was excited, full of life. In a few days' time, Hackman would be broadcasting his live interview with Anthony LeMaître and Caít would be there. Better still,

Caít had a plan that would put Mr Anthony LeMaître well and truly on the spot.

They went down a short corridor into a curtained-off cubicle.

'Nice and discreet,' murmured Hackman, checking the cubicle for any hidden security cameras – you couldn't be too careful. Satisfied with the degree of privacy, he pulled Caít towards him and began unbuttoning her blouse. 'Come here, you gorgeous little slattern. Madame Olenska did well in taking you on – you're such a hot little piece of ass. Now, hurry up and get your clothes off – I want to see you in this ridiculously sexy garment.'

Giggling, Caít wriggled out of blouse and skintight jeans. Hackman saved her the trouble of undoing her bra by slashing through the straps with his pocket knife. He so enjoyed doing that, it was like unwrapping some delicious gift-wrapped present.

Stepping out of her panties, Caít pressed the moist gusset against Hackman's face and he breathed in the heady fragrance with a growl of lust.

The PVC harness was an ingenious confection of straps and buckles which criss-crossed the body, exposing and emphasising the swell of breasts and pubis. Two straps crossed the breasts with a buckle which, when tightened, squeezed the flesh and made the nipples bulge most appealingly. Two straps passed between the thighs, holding apart the cunt lips and separating the arse cheeks so that they seemed ripe and ready for action.

Hackman chuckled with delight to see his favourite whore so prettily displayed for his delectation.

'I shall buy it for you,' he announced. 'But first, I want to fuck you in it – to make sure it turns me on as much as I think it does. Bend over – I'm going to take you from behind.'

Caít bent over the back of the chair, sticking out her backside so that her arse cheeks seemed more tempting than ever. Hackman couldn't remember being so aroused. His cock was a throbbing limb of flesh and he couldn't get it out of his pants quickly enough. Normally he'd get Caít to tease him a little before they fucked – whip him, perhaps, or lick his prick and balls. But today, he was just too exhilarated to wait. The hunger was like a live creature within him, demanding release.

Swiftly unzipping his pants, he pulled out his cock and paid thorough attention to Caít's pretty backside, so perfectly displayed in its harness, the creamy-white firmness of her buttocks a delightful contrast to the shiny black PVC. She was his filly and he was going to ride her.

'Give it to me,' groaned Caít, arching her back as he pulled apart her buttocks.

'Quiet! Do you want the whole street to hear?'

Caít giggled. She quite liked the prospect of entertaining the whole street with her body – maybe even fucking them all, too. It would be fun to do it outside, in broad daylight. She'd be bracing herself against the wall and their hands and tongues would be all over her. Their cocks, too. She shivered with delight as she thought of all those pearly droplets of semen, spattering her naked flesh as they wanked over her.

'Keep still and let me fuck you,' hissed Hackman, jabbing the head of his prick against Caít's rounded arse. With a sigh she gave herself to him, and his prick slid on a tide of slippery sex-fluid, down the deep furrow towards the glistening heart of her sex.

He soon discovered that the shiny PVC straps were fun to play with. If he pulled and twisted on the criss-cross straps about Caít's breasts, she gasped and moaned, and her tits bulged out like ripe melons, seemingly separate from the rest of her body. A tug on the straps between her thighs and she writhed like an eel, the hard rubber spikes on the inside of the crotch-straps abrading her erect clitoris quite ingeniously.

She really was a shameless hussy. Look at her – clutching at the back of the chair so hard that her knuckles were white with the excitement she dared not express. And she was thrusting out her backside to him like the hot little mare she was, loving every minute of it as his prick jerked in and out of her well-greased fanny.

He liked Caít. She wasn't like those annoying girls who demanded foreplay and fripperies. She got all her pleasure from a good firm shafting, or a nice fat cock to suck. Why, she could come to orgasm just by having her nipples sucked. That was just as it should be. Any woman ought to cream her pants at the mere thought of having Sir Robert Hackman's dick inside her. Yes, he liked a woman who didn't make demands on him – that way, he could concentrate on enjoying himself.

The assistant's voice floated up the corridor to the cubicle.

'You two all right in there?'

'Answer her,' ordered Hackman, enjoying the sight of Caít sweating and moaning beneath him, almost beyond the point of speech.

'We're . . . fine,' gasped Caít.

'D'you want to try anything else?'

Hackman smiled.

'Maybe later,' he replied. 'For the moment, this suits Caít very well indeed, doesn't it, my dear?'

But Caít didn't answer. Her eyes were closed and she was a mute slave to ecstasy, gripping the back of the chair more tightly than ever as she fought to control the surge of sensations washing over her, the spasms of pleasure in her belly. A little sigh escaped from her lips as she slumped forward on the chair.

Hackman ejaculated into her with silent satisfaction. He'd made up his mind – he was definitely going to buy the harness for her. If it made her this horny, it was well worth the money.

He pinched her nipples and she groaned as her helpless body awakened once again to despotic desire. Once wasn't enough – she ought to know that by now.

Withdrawing his cock, he wiped off the excess of semen on Caít's buttocks, then aimed at the tight brown epicentre of her arse. She shuddered as he entered her, his dry shaft no doubt causing her an agreeable amount of discomfort, but she was an obedient little whore, and she kept her silence.

Hackman buggered her with violent enthusiasm, like a man who hadn't had a woman for months. These days he was insatiable and the more sex he got, the more invulnerable, even godlike, he felt. He could have anything he wanted. The Master was pleased with him, and when the Master was pleased he would grant his servants any extravagance, any delicious depravity they craved. Perhaps even Mistress Sedet would smile upon him, granting him the sweet satisfaction of exquisite pain. After this week's LeMaître interview on Empire TV, Sir Robert Hackman would be able to ask for anything – anything in the whole wide world.

Andreas leant on Mara's arm as she led him into her room and closed the door behind them. Weak, head spinning, he still couldn't quite believe what had happened to him. One minute darkness and fear; the next, bright lights and Mara and a body that moved and talked and felt desire.

He put his hand to his head. Unbelievably, he had a hangover. Surely he couldn't have been drinking?

Together in the quiet of the bedroom, they stood and stared at each other. Andreas wanted to say something witty but for once his repartee had deserted him. All he could do was look into Mara's glittering emerald eyes and drink in the curves of her succulent body. She took a damp cloth from the bathroom and wiped away the last sticky traces of blood from his neck.

'I'm sorry, Andreas. I had to do it, or else the Master would have suspected something. He has to believe you've been initiated.'

Andreas managed a wry grin, remembering the night when he'd first met a flame-haired vampire-woman in a downtown singles bar. That had been the beginning of it all. The memories were clearing and refining now.

'You've changed, Mara Fleming. The last time I fucked you, you were Anastasia Dubois.'

She laughed.

'You've changed too, Andreas. Look at yourself in the mirror.'

He turned towards the full-length mirror on the wall and blinked. The man in the mirror blinked, too; only his eyes weren't blue-grey, they were brilliant cobalt blue. And those film-star looks, that sweep of unruly dark hair, that firm jaw . . .! This couldn't be him. It looked nothing like him. Was this just another cruel joke, generated by his maddened brain as he lay trapped within the crystal? He pinched himself. It hurt.

'Who the hell am I, Mara? Since when did I have blue eyes and a hunky square jaw? I look like a bloody matinee idol.'

Mara pulled him towards her and kissed him hard on the lips. God, she felt good. Her new body suited her. He slipped his arms round her waist and let his hands stray to the amplitude of her buttocks. They were exactly as he liked them: firm, with just a hint of softness. It felt so good, just to be able to feel.

'Your soul is in the body of a Nationalist MP called Nick Weatherall. A real airhead and not a very nice person either.'

'Gee thanks,' retorted Andreas, fiddling with the thousand hooks and eyes that lay between him and the conquest of Mara's delectable bosom.

'Listen to me!' protested Mara, giggling as Andreas freed her from the clinging gauzy top and started kissing her nipples. 'It's very important. You have to act the part, or the Master will know something is wrong. You're Nick Weatherall, Nationalist MP for Chester, you're extremely rich and sexually irresistible – and, from this night on, you're a devoted follower of Anthony LeMaître.'

Andreas's blood boiled.

'Oh, come on – surely you don't expect . . .? That bastard's stolen my body, for fuck's sake!'

She silenced him with kisses.

'You always were an idiot, Andreas Hunt. If it wasn't for Max Trevidian, you wouldn't have a body at all.'

'Max Trevidian, eh? So is he my deadly rival for your sexual favours?' He finished undressing Mara and picked her up in his arms. 'Because if he is, he might as well give up now. I'm keeping you all to myself.'

He dropped her onto the soft bedcovers and flung himself on top of her, suddenly strong and suddenly ravenous for her sex. To know that he could fuck her and know that it would not end in a return to that terrifying blackness, where the only sound was the sound of distant mocking laughter.

'Fuck me, Andreas,' breathed Mara. 'I've been waiting for you for so long.'

She stretched out on the covers, her whole body vibrating to the secret rhythm of sex. Andreas bent to kiss her lips, her throat, her breasts, her belly; leaving a moist trail of desire as he ran his tongue over her thighs and toyed with the glossy tangle of her pubic curls.

'You smell so good,' groaned Andreas, pushing apart her thighs and pressing his face into the moist triangle of her sex. 'Good enough to eat.'

He gently parted Mara's love lips and let his tongue enter her, its tip darting into the slippery depths of her cunt, his fingertips skating over the hard throbbing nubbin of her clitoris. He could feel her trembling beneath his touch and she was flooding his tongue with the sweetest abundance of honeydew.

'Harder, harder,' gasped Mara as he thrust three fingers into her cunny-hole and began lapping eagerly at her clitoris. 'I'm going to come!'

He felt her cunt tense and then relax about his fingers, again and again, as she abandoned herself to the irresistible need for pleasure. And then he could take no more. His cock was desperate for her. With one swift movement he was between her thighs, thrusting into her cunt as his lips pressed against hers and she tasted her own pleasure on his tongue, hot and strong and so sweet.

This new body responded more readily than he could ever have dreamed possible. Already Andreas had almost forgotten that he had not always been in this body; that his cock, sliding so easily in and out of Mara's cunt, had not always belonged to him. The body of Nick Weatherall, so long enslaved to a feeble petty mind, seemed to have welcomed in the spirit of Andreas Hunt and he could feel the strength and vigour and passion of youth pulsing through his veins, making his cock throb with eager lust.

They moved together almost silently now, rediscovering each other's bodies like new lovers on their first night of lust. They wanted to take it slowly, to savour each thread in the multi-coloured web of sensation, but pleasure came too quickly, welling up and overwhelming them.

In the wake of passion, they lay together on the bed, toying with each other's bodies. After a while, Andreas fell asleep, his dreams vivid but untroubled by the twisted smile of the man who called himself the Master.

When he awoke, Mara was standing in the doorway to the bathroom, a silky robe hanging open over her naked body. He gazed at the hard pink crests of her nipples and suddenly remembered. His face broke into a broad grin.

'Tell you what,' smiled Mara, letting the robe slip from her shoulders. 'There's plenty of hot water. Why don't I run a bath?'

'Why not indeed,' replied Andreas, sliding off the bed. 'Is there room for two?'

Max drained his coffee cup and looked Donal straight in the eye.

'I have to tell you, Mr O'Keefe, I think your wife is in grave danger. But I don't see how we can get her back unless she is willing to come of her own free will. And from what I've see . . .' He pushed the photographs across the table. Even taken through a window with a long-range lens, they weren't a pretty sight. Naked limbs entwined and lips pouted as they closed about a man's stiff cock.

Donal clenched his fist and punched the table angrily. One or two customers glanced round to see what the commotion was but he just glared at them and they turned away, embarrassed.

'She's a sick woman, Trevidian – anyone can see that. I can't just leave her the way she is. We've got to do something. And if you can't help me, I'll do something on my own.'

Max tried to calm him down.

'You don't know what you're letting yourself in for, Donal. It's not just Hackman – though God knows, he's a powerful man himself – it's Anthony LeMaître.'

Donal looked up, puzzled.

'What's he got to do with this?'

'I can't tell you the full story – I daren't – and if I did, you wouldn't believe me. But you can take my word for it that LeMaître's mixed up in this somehow.'

Donal was staring down at his knife, running his fingers over the blade most lovingly.

'I'll get him,' he whispered. 'I'll get the bastard.'

'No, Donal.' The firmness in Max's voice made Donal look up in surprise. 'You'll do this my way, or not at all. Listen: tomorrow night Hackman is interviewing LeMaître on live TV. Caít's bound to be there – she follows Hackman around like a pet dog. What do you say we go along to the recording? Maybe when she sees you she'll have a change of heart.'

Takimoto laid his hand on the Master's arm.

'Master, the screening is about to begin.'

The acquisition of a small chain of sleazy cinemas was the latest jewel in Takimoto's crown. And tonight he was taking the opportunity to screen the latest production by Hillstar Video – a red-hot sex film with some interesting subliminals.

'Slut.'

'Yes, Master?'

'Masturbate me.'

'Your pleasure is my only wish, Master.'

The dusky beauty knelt at his feet and began slowly wanking the Master's shaft, cradling his balls in her eager little hand. The Master relaxed and looked down from the projectionist's booth into the cinema audience.

'These are members of our very discreet mail-order video club,' explained Takimoto. 'Already their minds have been influenced by the subliminal messages on Hillstar video films. Tonight, the corruption of their minds will be completed.'

The film began: the typical high gothic of a cult SM film. A tall masked blonde slut in a skintight leather catsuit and spike-heeled boots was walking along a dark passageway between two lines of naked men, held fast to the rough stone walls by manacles and the jewelled collars about their necks.

As she strode past them, they strained to reach her, the chains taut about their necks and wrists. Their pricks were striving to reach their mistress, too, hard and glistening with the juices of their desire. But she showed them no mercy, her only kisses for them the occasional flick of her cruel whip upon their naked flesh.

It had been a good idea of Takimoto's to cast Liz Exley in the role of the leather-clad mistress, mused the Master. She was a strong woman, with an appealing streak of malice that made her a natural for the role of cruel dominatrix. Mind you, Sedet had not approved of his decision. Her inexplicable jealousy blinded her to Liz's merits and the girl had suffered in the Hall of Darkness for the insolence of daring to usurp her Mistress's role.

The Master was enjoying feeling the Indian girl's gentle touch on his cock. Her fingers had the devil in them – so soft, so unassuming in their touch, and yet they could spark fire in a man's belly. Sunita was rapidly becoming one of Winterbourne's most accomplished whores.

LEMAITRE IS YOUR MASTER.

The dominatrix was winding a leather thong about the base of a victim's balls, pulling it so tight that the flesh bulged and he writhed in an agony of lust.

OBEY THE COMMANDS OF YOUR MASTER

A picture of the Master flashed onto the screen. The Master surrounded by naked men and women, begging to suck his prick.

## WHEN THE MASTER SUMMONS YOU . . .

Images of the Master fucking a willing slave, tears of ecstasy coursing down her face.

## OBEY!

Suddenly the punters were falling over each other in their desire for sex. Naked girls had appeared as if from nowhere and the scent of crazy, chaotic sex was in the air. On the screen, the snake-hipped dominatrix was still wielding her cruel lash but no-one was watching any more. The Master had summoned his disciples and they were hungry to worship him with their bodies, their souls.

The success of Takimoto's experiment was pleasing to the Master but he was finding it hard to concentrate on the film. A powerful psychic presence was filling the ether and his mind was reaching out to meet and explore it.

He knew its identity, of course, even before he welcomed it into his mind. Trevidian's thoughts were so clear now that it seemed a sin not to read and enjoy them. He liked probing Trevidian's mind, the man was a complete innocent and yet his mind was such an excellent psychic channel that drinking in his mind-patterns was as easy and amusing as watching TV.

He took hold of Sunita's hand and made her wank him more brutally. He wanted to come and come and keep on coming until the whole world was filled with the taste and scent of his spunk.

Soon it would be time for fun. He hoped Trevidian was ready to play the game.

'It's been a long time.'

Andreas stood outside the cathedral and fought to exorcise the demon within him. He could still remember that night so vividly. He had come to Chester to find Mara and all he had found was terror and the Master's malevolent trickery. And just in case he thought it had all been a dream, the lightning-blackened oak remained in the cathedral close, another helpless victim of the Master's evil games.

'Hell, Mr Weatherall. It's ages since you've been back to Chester.'

Andreas spun round, suddenly realising that the schoolgirl was talking to him. She was wearing the shortest school skirt he'd ever seen and her uniform blouse was stretched taut across a pair of very generous breasts. Not a bad looker – if you were into cradle-snatching. Mara nudged him and hissed in his ear:

'It's one of your constituents. You're an MP, remember?'

He smiled and shook hands. The girl turned to go, then turned back with a coy grin.

'Can I ask you something?'

'Ask away.'

'Can I have a kiss? My mate really fancies you – well, we all do – and she'll be dead jealous.'

It was no great hardship to oblige. He could get used to this. Besides, he was supposed to be here on constituency business and it would do wonders for his image.

As the girl wiggled away, Mara burst out laughing.

'I told you you were irresistible.'

She pulled him to her in the seclusion of a deserted part of the old cloister and he felt her nipples digging into his chest. His cock stirred into instant rigidity and he thanked a thoughtful Providence that Nick Weatherall had been a randy sod.

'Ah yes, but the question is – can you resist me?'

'Never,' giggled Mara, grinding her pelvis against his cock. 'How do you fancy a fuck?'

'What – here?'

'Why not? No-one ever comes this way.'

She eased up her skirt and he slid his hands over the

smooth outline of her backside.

'No knickers! You little tease . . . What would the good burghers of Chester say if they knew their MP's girlfriend wasn't wearing any knickers?'

'Why change the habits of a lifetime? You always did say you liked me bare-arsed and ready for anything.'

That was true, mused Andreas. That first time they'd fucked, on the cold polished floor in Whitby library, he'd found her shameless nakedness miraculous. Almost as miraculous as the desire now rushing through his veins, stiffening this borrowed cock which was proving so willing to play all the games he most enjoyed.

'Well, I'm game if you are, sweetheart.' His eyes sparkled with excitement as he unzipped himself and took Mara's hand, placing it on the shaft of his cock. 'Go on – do your worst.'

She wanked him so beautifully that he could hardly keep himself from coming all over her hand. These might not be the fingers that had masturbated his shaft those many months ago, but the touch was unmistakeably Mara's. He reciprocated, pulling her skirt up higher at the front and insinuating exploratory fingers between her swollen labia. Her honeypot was overflowing for him, her clitoris a long hard stalk that felt inexplicably familiar to his fingertips.

She shuffled her feet a little further apart so that he could thrust his fingers further into her. He liked that, liked to feel as though he was really inside her; liked to toy with the elastic walls of her vagina, pressing the hypersensitive G-spot that always made Mara cry out with irrepressible pleasure.

He felt for the spot, high on the springy cunt wall, and was rewarded with a flood of sex juice as Mara's whole body tensed in a shuddering climax. It felt so good to be a man again, a man giving his woman the pleasure that only he could give.

When Mara opened her eyes, she was smiling.

'Shall I suck you off now?' she whispered, feeling him growing stiffer in her hand.

'N-no,' he gasped. 'It's your cunt I want. Let's see if we can fuck here . . .'

Bracing his back against the ancient stone wall, he took hold of Mara's hips and lifted her up, so that her knees were firmly round his waist and her cunt slid easily onto his upraised cock. Somewhere in the distance he could hear the sounds of chattering tourists, but he didn't care. This was all he cared about: Mara's silken thighs around his waist and his dick plunging ever deeper into her hairy slit.

Her eyes were closed as she moved up and down on Andreas's prick, feeling its tip nudging against the neck of her womb, filling her up, making her clitoris ache with need for him. Her love lips were swollen and oh-so-sensitive. With each new thrust of Andreas's prick she was sure she could take no more, and yet they kept on fucking, the strength of sex flooding into them as they reached the peak of ecstasy and climaxed together.

They might well have started all over again but at that moment Andreas heard voices and footsteps approaching from the other end of the cloister.

'I thought you said this place was safe!' Andreas hurriedly set Mara back on her feet and thrust his aching prick back into his pants. Mara, always the cooler-headed of the two, tidied herself up with a leisurely coquettishness which drove Andreas into a blind panic.

'Hurry!'

She just smiled back at him as she wriggled her skirt back down over her hips, then kissed him on the end of the nose.

'You worry too much.'

As they turned to walk towards the cathedral, a middle-aged guide appeared – a tweed-clad schoolmarm leading a group of old-age pensioners through the cloisters.

'Ah, Mr Weatherall, what a pleasant surprise! And I see you have a lady friend with you. How very romantic.'

As they walked away from the group, arm in arm, Andreas looked down at Mara and grinned.

'Well, you were certainly wrong about one thing.'

'What's that?'

'You said nobody ever comes here . . .'

The Master watched on closed-circuit television as Hugo Winchester charmingly but firmly dismissed the two foreign bankers with their tempting offer of a ten-million-dollar backhander.

He couldn't understand it. So far, Winchester had resisted all his attempts at corruption. Beautiful women, delightful boys, and now all the money he could ever want – the irritating little cretin had refused them all. Just one tiny fall from grace – lovingly captured on film by Takimoto – and Winchester would be forced to stand down. Then the field would be open for the Master. Instead of which, Winchester was behaving like the soul of discretion – almost as if he sensed the knives were out for him.

Winchester had had his chance. If he had co-operated with the traps laid for him, he could have resigned and escaped the breath of scandal. Anthony LeMaître and his Shadow Cabinet colleagues would have been very discreet. But it was too late for subtleties now.

He twisted the whore's long dark hair around his fingers and she sank to the ground in painful submission.

That was it. No more chances for Hugo Winchester. No more Mr Nice Guy.

# 17: Empire TV

Shadow Trade Secretary Tom Latham had always craved the adrenaline rush of success. Naturally, at the end of his career as an Olympic pentathlete, he had looked for something else to give him a comparable buzz. There could only be one contender: it had to be politics.

He'd got into Parliament at the first attempt, eased into a safe seat by Nationalist Party agents who knew only too well the power of his media profile. A couple of Olympic golds were worth far more than an Oxbridge MA or an impressive command of economics but, happily, Tom Latham had all three.

Yes, getting into Parliament had been a breeze. Within two years he'd been a Junior Minister, heavily tipped for Cabinet office. And then the Nationalists had lost the General Election and for the last ten years he'd been relegated to the Opposition front bench, wondering from time to time if he hadn't backed the wrong horse.

He'd never really thought seriously about challenging for the leadership. Everybody knew Hugo Winchester was perfect for the job: well-respected, with experience of high Government office. Only lately . . . lately Tom Latham had been having some very interesting dreams.

More truthfully, it was the same dream over and over again. The Statue of Liberty had come to life and she was kneeling at his feet, sucking his cock. The whole world wanted him to screw it and he was powerful, potent, virile.

Every night it was the same. In his dream he was lord of the whole world; there was nothing he couldn't do and no pretty woman he couldn't screw. There were soft lips around his cock and a dark-haired woman with violet eyes smiling at him as she stripped off her leather basque and lay naked on the polished table in the Cabinet Room.

She was waiting for him. Could power be waiting for him, too?

He had agonised about it for days now. You couldn't just challenge for the leadership of the Nationalists on a whim, at the instigation of some crazy dream. On the other hand, perhaps the dream was his unconscious mind's way of telling him he wasn't exploiting his full potential. He'd waited too many long years for the success he knew he deserved. If it wouldn't come to him, perhaps he could do something to create his own success.

Derek Manley. He was pretty sure he could trust him. He picked up the bedside phone. He'd ring Derek for some advice.

Winter was nearing its end. You could feel the hint of spring in the air. Sun filtered through the bleak white sky, and Andreas and Mara were standing high above the Cheshire Plain, on Alderley Edge.

'Why here?' Andreas surveyed the patchwork quilt of the landscape laid out before them.

'This is an ancient holy place,' explained Mara. 'A place of powerful magic, where battles were fought between the powers of good and evil. Many white witches lived and died here. Such ancient places offer us protection from the Master's psychic vision. And here I may create other charms to protect and empower.'

She reached into her bag and took out a small box.

'Open it. It is for you.'

He did so, and found a gold identity bracelet, embossed with the name 'Nicholas DeQuincy Weatherall' and the family crest: a dragon baring its teeth at a cowering lion.

'A bit tacky, isn't it?'

'Oh, definitely – but it's Nick Weatherall to a T. And see the tiny stones – the dragon's eyes?'

'Yes – diamond chips, are they?'

She shook her head.

'I had the diamonds removed and the bracelet reset with fragments from the crystal. Though he is strong, the Master becomes weak and confused when confronted by the power of the crystal which imprisoned him. Its power has already given protection to Max Trevidian. Through magical ritual, we may empower these fragments of the crystal and perhaps trick the Master into accepting your fake identity.'

'A dangerous game,' observed Andreas. 'What if he doesn't buy it? What if he puts two and two together and works out who I am?'

'Then he will destroy you. But, Andreas, if we do nothing he may do that anyway. You have no psychic powers to cast a veil about you. He will sense the spirit within you and pursue you to the ends of the earth.

'Here, in this ancient place, we must summon up the spirits of the white witches who died here. Through our bodies' union, we may empower the crystal, if the spirits are with us.'

She took an unremarkable leather suitcase from the car and opened it. Inside lay the ritual trappings of her former life: the ceremonial jewellery which she and Andreas had worn at their joining, the vials of magical oils, pure water from the Celtic spring where Merlin had once drunk, the stave and coronet of high rank. She had taken a big risk going back to the flat to collect these but she had to have them for the protecting ritual.

It seemed a whole lifetime ago that Mara had performed the ritual of astral perfection and had been appointed High Priestess of her coven. But she had forgotten none of her skill. Though she was forced to hide them from the Master's sight, her powers were greater than they had ever been and she knew Mistress Sedet had sensed something remarkable about her. That was why she had treated her so cruelly – until Liz

Exley came along and provided a more amusing target for her obsessive passions.

Picking up an armful of magical items, Mara turned to Andreas.

'Come with me. There isn't much time. We mustn't give the Master any cause to wonder where we are or what we're up to.'

He followed her, knowing better than to question her judgement. He could argue till the cows came home, but Mara would be right – she always was. Besides, he was too busy appreciating the tantalising tremble of her firm buttocks, encased in the tightest jodhpurs he'd ever seen. As she led the way along the hillside, he wondered if she'd mind him pulling down her pants right here and now. He was certainly ready for her.

It wasn't that he didn't appreciate the seriousness of the shit they were in. He still carried the painfully vivid memory of long months' captivity in the crystal and he was determined to get his own back on the bastard who'd put him there. But he'd only just begun to enjoy the freedom of this new and very responsive body. There was a breath of spring in the air and Andreas Hunt's thoughts were turning – as ever – to fucking.

'Here we are,' announced Mara, looking back over her shoulder at him. Her breasts were soft and rounded and so, so fuckable in that tight skinnyrib jumper. 'Follow me.'

At first, he couldn't fathom what she was talking about. All he could see was a blank hillside and a load of bracken. But Mara was pushing and pulling at the vegetation, and suddenly he realised that there was some sort of hole. He didn't much fancy going inside but Mara dragged him into the darkness. There was a smell of wet earth and the sound of dripping water.

'Wait while I light the lantern.'

A few moments later, Andreas blinked as a feeble orange glow illuminated the inside of the cave. It was much larger than he had imagined, with a high vaulted roof and walls that dripped with green slime. Funnily enough, it wasn't cold – in fact, there was a hot stuffiness which made him feel thoroughly uncomfortable.

'This is the cave of the witch Brigante,' explained Mara. 'Goddess of hearth, home and sex. We must conjure up her spirit if she is to help us in our quest. Can you feel her power, burning and boiling in the stones?

'Take off your clothes and put on the bracelet and ceremonial robe.'

Andreas felt almost grateful to get out of his shirt and pants – it was so oppressively hot in here that the sweat was trickling down his back. Not that the heat stopped him feeling randy. He'd never felt hornier than when he was lying on a sun-kissed Greek beach, surrounded by gorgeous girls massaging their tits with coconut oil – and the effect was much the same. His cock was rigid and throbbing, pressing against the loose white cotton robe and leaving a hint of dampness on the flimsy material. The frustration was almost unbearable. If he didn't have her soon, he'd have to jerk himself off. Just the sight of Mara's perfect body, encased in the tight riding-gear, made him want to cream himself.

Mara wriggled out of her jumper and his cock leapt to worship her as her creamy-white skin came slowly into view. First the lean taut flesh of belly and ribcage, then the sudden miraculous moment when the jumper peeled upwards that critical extra inch and her gravity-defying breasts sprang into view, stiff-nippled and begging to be kissed.

Next the riding-boots, so tight about her calves that he had to help her pull them off. As he put her foot between his knees and heaved at the boot, his eyes couldn't help straying back to that wonderful quivering bosom, just tantalising inches away from his lips.

The zipper of her jodhpurs slid down with a little whispering sigh, and Mara eased the tight stretchy fabric down over her hips and thighs. A glimpse of glossy red curls made him shiver with appreciation. No panties, he thought – that's my Mara!

Casting aside the jodhpurs, Mara stretched out her arms to him.

'First, the ritual of preparation,' she announced, setting down the lantern in the very centre of the cave floor. Its orange light cast unnatural and alarming shadows on the rough-hewn walls and Andreas felt his soul shrink back from the premonition of evil.

Taking a vial of spring water, she described a circle about the floor of the cave, murmuring an incantation as her bare feet wove an inner circle of secret wishes. As Andreas watched, baffled, it seemed to him that the darkness beyond the circle was growing deeper, blacker, more intense.

'Do not let your feet stray beyond the margin of the outer circle,' Mara instructed him. 'There are malign spirits in the shadows intent on doing us harm. Observe the ritual and you will be safe. Now prepare yourself for the cleansing.'

At the sight of the silver-handled riding crop, Andreas flinched and took a step backwards. But there was nowhere to go and his back fetched up against the damp oozing wall of the cave with an unpleasant squelching noise. Suddenly he realised that he was perilously close to stepping outside the circle and he jumped forward in alarm.

'There will be pain but it will be followed by pleasure, I promise you,' Mara assured him. 'This part of the ritual is essential for the cleansing of our desires. Keep silence and respect the power of this place.'

Reluctantly he braced himself against the cave wall, feet firmly inside the circle and his hands clutching handfuls of slimy rock as he tensed his back in readiness for the pain.

The first stroke felt like a hornet-sting on his unwilling flesh and he could not suppress a groan of startled pain. But Mara was not listening to him. She was chanting a mantra to the rhythm of the riding crop.

'Pain bite.'

The riding crop swished through the air and bit again into his flesh.

'Pain burn.'

A third blow began the genesis of a strange warmth that spread through his belly and dulled the edges of his pain.

'Pain sear.'

The discomfort was intense but so – strangely enough – was the pleasure. His balls seemed to be filled with boiling spunk and his cock was so achingly hard that it felt as though it was the centre of his whole existence and the rest of his body a mere adjunct. He wriggled and writhed and when the fourth blow came he welcomed it as sister to his desire.

'Pain cleanse.'

With a little cry he felt the spunk gathering in his shaft and jetting out onto the cave wall. As it dripped to the ground beyond the edge of the circle, it seemed to sizzle and smoke, and a jet of flame erupted from the fractured stone.

He faltered, weak and dizzy with pleasure, and Mara gathered him up and dragged him back to the safety of the inner circle. She kissed him passionately and he felt the strength coming back into his limbs and his cock.

'Now you must cleanse me,' breathed Mara, handing him the riding-crop, its black-and-silver-plated lash dotted here and there with the red stickiness of his blood.

As she knelt before him, murmuring her own mantra of atonement, Andreas wondered if he would have the will – or the strength – to strike her.

'Do it, Andreas. We are fighting for your life.'

He brought the riding-crop down on Mara's proffered back and, to his surprise, the sensation of leather on flesh gave him a fleeting thrill of pleasure.

'Again, Andreas. Harder, now!'

Again and again he struck her and she did not flinch at his blows, though with each new kiss of the riding-crop her flesh grew redder with welts that he longed to kiss away.

Pleasure grew and as darkness gathered about the margin of the circle, Andreas felt his cock stiffen with the anticipation of other games, more adventurous still.

'Enough! The cleansing is complete.'

Mara slumped forward onto the cave floor and Andreas picked her up, supporting her body in his arms. Her nipples were hard and tempting, and he cupped one breast in his hand as he bent to kiss and bite the succulent flesh.

'The joining,' gasped Mara. 'We must prepare for the joining and the conjuration of Brigante. The bottle of scented oil I brought with me – you must rub it into your prick and my breasts, and then we must be joined.'

The oil was a dark emerald in colour and had a sweet, musky scent which made the head spin and the senses reel. As he massaged it into Mara's breasts, he grew hungrier than ever for her; and when the drops of oil touched his cock, and Mara's delicate hands began smoothing it over the surface of his shaft, he began trembling with the need for her. The oil both soothed and burned, and when she trickled the last few drops across the glistening tip of his swollen glans, he lost control.

'I've got to have you, got to have you.'

'Yes, now! Take me now, Andreas.'

He thrust into her and she felt the sensitive membrane of her arse grinding deliciously against the rough earth as his weight bore down on her, his oil-drenched cock toiling frenziedly within her oh-so-willing cunt. The potent oil soaked into her, stimulating the sensitive lining of her vagina, and she felt the power washing over her as she chanted the words of the ritual.

> 'Mother Brigante, hear our cry,
> Mother Brigante, answer our need.
> Mother Brigante, accept this act of worship.
> Mother Brigante, come to us!'

Andreas hardly knew what was happening to him. He was spinning in a vortex of pleasure, coloured lights flashing in his head with each thrust of his cock. He could hear Mara's voice but it seemed very far away as ecstasy came and he ejaculated into her cunt.

Suddenly he could feel a presence around him; a power that was neither good nor evil – a force of pure sexuality. The voice seemed to come out of the darkness. He looked around but he could see nothing, nothing but the shadows moving in the corners of the cave.

'Who dares to summon Brigante?'

Mara's voice was steady, almost elated.

'I, the High Priestess Mara.'

'What boon do you ask of me?'

'Your protection on this amulet.'

The goddess's laughter was deep and menacing.

'And you are willing to pay Brigante's price?'

Mara glanced at Andreas.

'We are willing.'

All at once the whole cave was filled with a thick white mist, swirling and dancing as though it had a life of its own; a hot, stifling mist that caught in Andreas's throat and half choked him. Mara's hand was on his wrist and she was telling him, over and over again:

'Have courage, Andreas. Have courage.'

He saw her eyes first: the burning red coals of a lustful demon. And then her dark hair, falling in a great black mass over brown shoulders and glistening breasts. She was there beside him in the circle, a carnivorous smile on her face, and he felt Mara's hand slipping from his. Was she abandoning him to this monster of sexual hunger? Her voice seemed further away than ever.

'She desires you, Andreas. You must do anything she asks of you.'

'The price, mortal,' hissed Brigante, and her sleek brown thighs parted as she pressed her cunt lips against his unwilling mouth. 'If you please me, perhaps I shall not destroy you. Perhaps I shall even deign to empower your puny amulet.'

The main hall at Woking University was packed tonight. According to Del, the oldest porter on the main gate, they hadn't seen such a crowd since the Beatles played the campus, back in '64. There had been a surprisingly enthusiastic response to the news that Sir Robert Hackman would be interviewing Anthony LeMaître live on Empire TV – in fact, tickets had sold out weeks in advance. Odd, really, who'd have guessed that today's eco-minded students would be so interested in the rantings of a Nationalist MP?

Max felt uneasy as he ushered Donal to a seat near the back of the auditorium. He hoped he wasn't going to do anything stupid – especially not on live TV. Mind you, even he wasn't sure what they were going to do. He'd given up trying to think up a cunning plan to prise Caít from Hackman's greasy grasp.

Nervous as he was, Max didn't notice Caít sitting in the front row, teeth clenched with anticipation and loathing as she waited for the moment of her hated enemy's humiliation. She was so hot with hate that she was wanking herself surreptitiously under cover of the evening jacket slung across her lap. Fingers under the hem of her short tarty skirt, she slipped them under the gusset of her panties and toyed with the fringed casket of her sex.

Later, if he behaved himself, perhaps she'd let Sir Robert play with her, too. Over the last weeks she'd done her best to poison his mind against LeMaître, slipping him subtle snippets of information which would enable him to do a swift and efficient demolition job. She no longer heeded the burning of the ring on her finger. She had learned to accept it as a sign, and tonight it would be the sign of her victory.

Hackman was on stage now, warming up the audience with some cosy fireside chat and a few well-judged one-liners. Max shrank back into his seat as Hackman moved into the big build-up:

'Now, ladies and gentlemen of the audience, what are the political issues which most interest us all today?'

Someone shouted 'Defence!' An elderly man with a dog grunted 'Old-age pensions!' But most were calling out 'The environment!' and that was exactly what Hackman had planned. Takimoto's slaves in the audience were doing their job well tonight.

'The environment – an issue which affects all our lives. And tonight, ladies and gentlemen, I have the pleasure of interviewing one of Britain's most sincere and committed environmental campaigners: Anthony LeMaître MP, Shadow Environment Secretary.'

Hackman stood up to welcome LeMaître as he strode confidently onto the platform and took his seat centre-stage, taking care to make sure the cameras got his best profile.

The interview began – only it wasn't so much an interview as a panegyric. Hackman sat smiling and nodding as LeMaître outlined his policies, agreeing with practically everything and not displaying even a hint of his usual aggression. In the front row of the audience, Caít O'Keefe was boiling with indignation, her hands clenched into such tight fists that her manicured fingernails were digging into her palms and there was a warm ooze of blood escaping from between her fingers.

Max and Donal exchanged incredulous glances. This wasn't what they had expected at all. Sir Robert Hackman was well known for his Genghis Khan approach to interviewing, and here he was oozing slimy charm all over Anthony LeMaître. Realisation dawned in Max's mind. Was Hackman in on the conspiracy, too?

It was all too much for Caít. How could her lover betray her like this? How could he do such a vile thing? The ring was scalding hot on her finger and that voice was inside her head again. Only this time it was screeching, spitting fury. 'Kill him, destroy him, humiliate him . . .'

She didn't know what she was doing any more – scarcely even knew who she was. Flinging back the chair with a clatter, she stood up. Eyes were on her but she wasn't aware of them. All she knew was that Anthony LeMaître was there, on that stage, and she hated him. This time the voice was her own, screaming loud above the astonished gasps of the audience and the syrupy-smooth voices of Hackman and LeMaître.

'You're a crook, LeMaître – a dirty, filthy crook. These people don't know who you are, but I do! I'm going to destroy you, LeMaître; going to destroy you . . .'

LeMaître was staring at her, open-mouthed. What the hell was this he was seeing? He rubbed his eyes but the stroboscopic effect didn't go away. Shifting, flickering images made his brain reel. One second he saw a pretty Irish girl, screaming abuse, the next a dark-haired, bearded man with a silver-topped cane, laughing at him silently as chaos erupted all around him.

*Delgado . . . ?* But Delgado was dead.

Everything seemed to happen at once. Takimoto, sensing impending disaster, signalled to the camera crew to shut down and put up the card: 'We apologise for the break in transmission but . . .'

Hackman was standing up, trying to calm down the woman in the front row, and hissing to Gonzales in the wings:

'For God's sake, get rid of the crazy woman.'

Uniformed guards appeared from the edges of the hall and began moving swiftly towards Caít. Seeing his woman standing there, Donal's self-control snapped, just as Max had feared it would. He tried to hold him back, but Donal shook him off, clambering over people and seats in an attempt to get to the front of the auditorium.

Donal's behaviour was sufficient to divert LeMaître's attention from the girl in the front row, and towards a familiar figure hunched up at the back, trying to look inconspicuous.

Max Trevidian. Why hadn't he noticed him there before? Was all of this his doing? Did he think he could play games with the Master? Rage spilled over and, as he stared into the eyes of Max Trevidian, objects started flying around the auditorium – microphones, books, chairs, all seemed to have a life of their own. Panic spread rapidly through the crowd as the audience trampled each other in their haste to get out of this place of fear.

'Block the exits,' the Master instructed his guards. But it was too late.

When the chaos had died down, three people were very noticeably absent from the auditorium: Caít, Donal and Max Trevidian.

\* \* \*

Andreas stumbled out into the gathering dusk and breathed in the cool night air. It felt unbelievably good to be out of that terrible place, that hot, foetid cave where passion became a penance and lust a torment.

He turned to Mara.

'You might have warned me I'd have to shag Mother Earth. For a while I didn't think I was going to get out of there alive.'

'If I'd told you, would you still have agreed to go through with the ritual?'

'No.'

'There you are, then.' She giggled and poked him in the ribs. 'At least you have the charm now to protect you.'

'Ah, but who's going to protect me from you?'

He grabbed hold of her and they rolled together on the damp grass. He was still trembling but the warmth of Mara's body was replacing one form of tension with another, much nicer, one. He slid his hand up underneath her sweater and cupped the comforting globe of her breast.

Suddenly she went very tense in his arms.

'What's the matter? Gone off me?'

He looked down into her eyes. Her face was grave in the dusky-blue twilight.

'It's Max, Andreas. He's in deep trouble.'

Max knew the Master's style by now and he wasn't going to hang around waiting for retribution to catch up with him. He knew what the Master wanted now, too: he wanted to feed on his passions, his lusts . . . and his submission. Well, he was going to wait a long time.

He just wished the train to Waterloo wasn't full of snakes and that the people around him weren't snakes too. He wished that everywhere he looked he didn't see snakes, writhing and hissing at him – all with the eyes of Anthony LeMaître.

These were illusions, just illusions. He took out his handkerchief and mopped the sweat from his brow, only it felt wrong. He looked down at his hand and saw that he had no fingers.

Only snakes.

Caít was alone now, very alone and afraid. She hardly noticed that she was barefoot as she stumbled along the old cobbled backstreets, face stained with tears. He had betrayed her. That was all she could think of – the pain and the betrayal.

It was dark here, in the winding backstreets of the old town. There were few streetlamps to break the thick black darkness that enfolded her. She wanted to go home, but she couldn't remember where home was.

Turning the corner, she came upon four ragged figures, huddled round a brazier. They were swigging from bottles of cheap sherry, rubbing their hands together in the warmth from the red coals. Caít looked longingly into the heart of the flames. Warmth. She needed warmth. And she needed something else, too. She needed sex. As she hesitated there, on the margin of the group, they turned to her and she saw an answering need in their drink-deadened eyes.

Their hands explored her clumsily, mechanically. Their breath was heavy with alcohol and the sweet scent of decay and their clothes stank of ammonia and the ingrained filth of years on the road. They repelled her, and yet she needed and wanted them. Their touch made her feel alive again, awakened the warm heart of her desire. Their whispering surrounded her, making her feel fleetingly secure.

'You hot little tart,' growled one toothless old man, feeling under her skirt with a grubby paw and wrenching down her panties. 'Begging for it, aren't you?'

'Have a drink, darlin'.' A bottle was thrust into her hand and she drank automatically, gratefully, welcoming the brief warmth that the cheap alcohol gave her.

''ave 'er up against the wall, like the little bitch she is.'

She didn't struggle. Why struggle, when this was what she wanted, what her body craved? Her cunt and arse were happy to welcome these transient guests, the grimy stinking cocks and fingers that brought with them the oblivion of pleasure. She found herself responding to the rhythm of their hunger, thrusting out her backside as they clutched and clawed at her clothes, baring her breasts.

'Save some for me, Charlie. I want her to suck me dick.'

'Get off her! Leave her alone!'

There was something about the voice that Caít recognised. The newcomer was laying about him with his fists now, pulling the old tramps off her, and she was moaning with distress, her cunt and arse bereft of the comfort she had craved.

'Steady on, guv, there's plenty for everyone. You can see she loves it . . .'

'Shut up, you bag of filth!'

The young man's fist slammed into the vagrant's chin, and he fell to the ground like a poleaxed ox. He'd have a bigger hangover than usual in the morning.

'For pity's sake come on, Caít.' He grabbed hold of her arm and she looked up into his eyes with a glimmer of recognition.

'Donal?'

'Yes, Caít. It's all right now, it's all right. Now just come with me, will you?'

He half-dragged her away from the back alley and towards the light from a row of shop windows. But she stopped, clinging onto the brickwork as they passed.

'Stop, Donal. Please stop.'

'What's the matter, Caít?'

She reached up and put her arms round his neck. Her body felt warm and responsive against his. Even the faint odour of her coupling seemed to excite him.

'I want you, Donal. Please fuck me. I want you now.'

She sank to her knees in the doorway and he sighed as he felt her fingers unzipping his pants, pulling out the hardening limb of his prick. It had been so long since he had felt those fingers on him, easing the pleasure from him. So long since he had felt her lips closing around his shaft.

And then she remembered. Donal. The flat in Caxton-on-Thames. The taste of his cock on her tongue. Everything was going to be all right now.

This was home.

As she sucked at Donal's cock, she did not notice the ring easing itself from her finger and falling softly to the ground. Crisp, white moonlight danced upon the pure circle of crystal as it rolled silently across the pavement and into the darkened doorway of a jeweller's shop.

Takimoto surveyed the line of golden boys and girls with a certain sense of pride. Under the Master's guidance, his personal empire had grown to include not only his computer corporation but ten cinemas and a thriving video business – all in the loyal service of the Master.

There were fifty branch managers, fifty branches of Golden Sun, Takimoto's new fast-food franchise. Over the last couple of years Japanese food had become so chic and accessible that these restaurants were sure to attract just the right sort of clientele.

He sprinkled a little of his 'special Kyoto seasoning' over a bowl of rice noodles. The psychotropic ingredient was entirely herbal, entirely legal and extremely palatable. The fools would never guess that, with each bite, they were opening their minds to the commands and desires of the Master.

# 18: Prey

The mall was clinical white with shiny marble floors and an endless loop of kitsch piano music, piped in through discreet speakers in the parlour palms.

Sitting outside the Café Bonjour, Liz toyed with her cappuccino, making patterns in the creamy froth as she kept a watchful eye on her potential victims. She was dressed in her favourite black suit: the really sexy one, with the side-slit skirt that bared her long slim leg to the thigh, giving a tantalising glimpse of a lacy black stocking-top. Dressed to kill.

She had friends nearby – fellow-sluts and slaves who would move in when the time was right. But it was Liz who must choose the time to strike, Liz whom the Master had honoured with the task of initiating his latest little game. Sedet had been most displeased; she hungered for new flesh and resented the Master's latest favoured slut being so pampered and indulged, particularly after the regrettable incident with Max Trevidian.

But the Master had swiftly forgiven her and, as he had pointed out, Sedet was now too familiar a face among the House of Commons' wives and mistresses. It would never do for her to be seen indulging her tastes so publicly. Liz smiled to herself. Another little victory to her. Why, these days she was almost becoming more powerful than her Mistress . . .

All around the central concourse of the mall were giant video screens, the gift of Takimoto's Japanese corporation. She glanced up at the nearest screen. A couple of wide-eyed bunny rabbits were gambolling across a cartoon field. On another, footballers were re-enacting the highlights from a European Cup fixture.

It was all so innocent. No-one would ever suspect the hidden power of the subliminal messages skilfully edited into the videotape, ticking away like a time bomb in the minds of the susceptible and the weak-willed. One day soon, all minds would be in the thrall of the Master, all bodies the willing servants of his dark desires. And when that day came, lust would rule over the whole earth.

Another sip of coffee. And then she saw them: the perfect young couple walking together across the concourse, away from the Golden Sun Japanese takeaway, and towards the ornamental fountain. Yes, they would be perfect. He was tall and blond and fuckable, with a tight arse and a good-sized prick bulging the front of his white Levis. And she . . . she was a succulent morsel of a girl, a fluffy little blonde with a floaty dress and such a prim and proper blouse, inadequately concealing the tantalising swell of her breasts.

Getting up swiftly from her chair, Liz smoothed down her skirt and sauntered across the concourse, neatly intercepting her two young victims just before they got to the fountain.

'Excuse me, but . . . could either of you tell me the time?' she enquired sweetly, making sure that the low neckline of her blouse hung open at just the right angle.

'Er . . . just on half-past,' replied the boy, reddening slightly at the sight of Liz's bare breasts. He made to move on but Liz had other plans for him.

'Fancy spending a little time with me?'

She ran playful fingers down his cheek, his belly and over the wonderful, plump swelling in his jeans.

'What the . . .?'

Liz pressed harder on the swelling prick, tracing its growing outline with her scarlet-tipped talon.

'Get off my boyfriend. I've heard about women like you. Bloody whore, that's what you are! Well go away, he's not interested.'

The girl was trying to push Liz off her boyfriend, but Liz

parried her easily, grabbing hold of her wrist and twisting it so that the girl squealed with discomfort.

'Your boyfriend may not be interested but you are, aren't you, my little convent girl? You're a dirty little slut at heart, do you know that? Oh, don't look at me with those innocent eyes – you know it's true. Do you remember that afternoon at school, when you went behind the cricket pavilion with your music master?'

The girl was ashen-faced with horror and embarrassment. Liz wanted to laugh. The Master had taught her a little of the art of reading minds, and it was so easy to get inside this silly child's head. It was plain to see that the episode was one the girl hadn't told her boyfriend about, either, because he was shaping up for a fight.

'Look, Miss whoever you are, just piss off, will you? Go away and leave us alone before I call the police.'

'No, I don't think so,' Liz smiled sweetly. And she gave him a push which sent him staggering back, with a loud splash, into the ornamental fountain. 'Now, my dear, I think we have some unfinished business to attend to.'

The video screens were showing a very different film now: film of a sexy black woman stripping to the sound of a hypnotic dance beat. It was the sort of film you couldn't help glancing at, even if the subject matter revolted you. And just a glance was all it took to activate the images lying dormant in minds nourished by a daily diet of Empire TV and cheap video films.

The subliminal messages were crude, but effective:


'FUCK.'


'THE TIME IS NIGH. THE MASTER COMMANDS YOU.'


She gazed into the girl's eyes and felt her resistance melt away. Really, it was all too easy – hardly a challenge at all. With a swift movement of her hand, she ripped down the front of the girl's modest little blouse, exposing the plain cotton bra beneath. Scared and aroused, the girl made no move to resist her.

'You ought to show your body off, Melissa,' chided Liz, 'not hide it like this.' She took a penknife out of her pocket and slashed through the fabric of the bra, letting the knife-blade slide downwards, slicing through the skirt and panties. Underneath, the girl was golden brown and as tasty as a fresh-baked cookie. Liz just had to have her.

'Kneel, slave. You're going to worship my cunt.'

Slowly, like an automaton, the girl sank to the marble floor, her clothes in tatters around her.

Liz pulled up her skirt and exposed the bare flesh underneath. She at least was not shy about displaying her charms, and the astonished gazes all around her bore witness to the allure of that firm backside, those endless, stocking-clad thighs and the knot of peroxide blond curls decorating her pubis.

There was an electricity in the air. Figures moved slowly towards the fountain as though drawn by a magnet. Liz felt strong, invincible. The smell of sex was all around her and she was the centre of attention. At a given signal, they would erupt into an orgy of unquestioning lust, after-wards remembering nothing of the strange urges which had driven them to seek out complete strangers for their sexual delight.

'Lick my cunt out – and make sure you do it well.'

The girl was inexperienced but willing. Liz reached down and pinched her nipples as a little added incentive. The girl groaned and pressed her face into Liz's blonde bush, her delicate fingers stroking Liz's inner thigh with a growing passion.

Liz felt the juices welling up, spilling onto Melissa's tongue as the acolyte worshipped her high priest.

'Put your fingers into me. All of them. Right inside.'

The girl was trembling as her fingers reached up inside Liz, marvelling at the touch of her first woman, the feeling of the tight vaginal flesh around her hand, the slippery juices inundating her flesh.

Liz turned briefly towards the video screens, and in that brief second the command flashed up:

### 'NOW, SLAVES. FUCK, FUCK, FUCK!'

Andreas yawned, stretched, rolled over and got out of bed, stumbling to the door of the hotel room to pick up the morning paper from the mat. Catching sight of his face in the mirrored wardrobe, he did a double-take and then grinned with realisation. He still hadn't got used to any of this but, boy, it felt good. He'd fucked Mara all night long and already he felt the need to do it all over again.

Heimdal was an arrogant sod, with far too active an interest in Mara, but at least he'd come up with the half-decent idea of sending the Master's new initiate, Nick Weatherall, on a 'fact-finding trip' to assess the depth of support for LeMaître across the shires. Of course, Weatherall was far too stupid to be sent anywhere on his own so the trusted slut Anastasia Dubois had to go with him.

Yes, these few days had given them a golden opportunity to get to know each other again; to explore each other's bodies away from the hell of Winterbourne. Andreas touched the bracelet on his wrist – it seemed so innocent and yet he could feel its reassuring power vibrating into his fingertips. He prayed that its power would be strong enough to protect them both from discovery. Generosity towards his enemies was not one of the Master's strong points.

Oddly enough, Andreas didn't fed guilty about pinching somebody else's body. Well, not very. When he'd found out just how much of a waste of space the little creep was – well, it had made hard-nosed newshound Andreas Hunt look like St Francis of Assisi. It was almost embarrassing having to become a bloke like Weatherall, who wasn't happy unless he'd evicted half-a-dozen widows before breakfast. Embarrassing – but what the hell? He could live with it.

He slid back into bed, beside Mara, her sleeping body exuding a tempting fragrance of sex. Not surprisingly, the bedclothes had slipped down during the night and her smooth perfect breasts were uncovered, peeping seductively through the amber curtain of her hair.

As he pulled up the duvet and snuggled down beside her, she woke up and wriggled closer to him, curling her arm around his waist and gently stroking him. He gave a murmur of pleasure as his cock twitched into appreciative life.

'Good God, there's been a riot in a shopping mall!' He scanned the front page of the *Comet*, ruefully remembering how he'd always coveted that front page byline, those two-inch banner headlines with their monosyllabic power. 'Violence broke out in the St Gregory Centre yesterday afternoon. Without warning, two hundred shoppers abandoned themselves to a two-hour sex-romp that turned into an orgy of blood-lust.'

Mara sat up and read the story with mounting alarm.

'Are you surprised?'

'I don't think I understand.' He hadn't been back in the real world five minutes, and already it was eluding all his attempts to make sense of it. Evidently he still had a lot of homework to do.

'It's just another stage in the Master's campaign for ultimate power', explained Mara. 'I told you about Igushi Takimoto, didn't I? Well, he can reach millions through computers, TV, cinemas, even fast food. Through subliminal messages, the Master can make those who are susceptible do anything he wants them to.'

Andreas looked puzzled.

'So how does an orgy in a shopping mall fit in?'

'Civil disorder. LeMaître isn't just interested in the environment, he was elected on a law-and-order platform – remember how he quelled those riots in India? Haven't you been wondering how he managed it?'

'Subliminals again?'

'Spot on, darling. You're learning.' Mara slipped her hand

underneath the newspaper and began massaging Andreas's cock into even more rampant life. He gave a sigh and settled back onto the pillow. 'The Master wants to set himself up as the saviour of a corrupt and lawless society. People look up to him.'

'Stupid gits,' grunted Andreas, uncomfortably aware that he too had been a stupid git. Only most of this lot wouldn't be getting a second chance.

We have to do something to stop him,' sighed Mara, gently wanking Andreas's shaft. 'I have sent astral messages to other white witches, but even if we unite against the Master we do not yet have the strength to oppose him and all his minions. We need Max. There's something special about him; a power, a stubbornness even. We need his help.'

Andreas turned the page of the newspaper. He wasn't really reading it, but it felt good to be masturbated whilst he pretended to read the morning paper. His balls were hot and hard, and he wondered if he could persuade Mara to take them into her mouth, to soothe their burning fever with the cooling touch of her slippery tongue.

That would be nice. But would it be nicer still to lick out her fanny whilst he straddled her face, his engorged shaft sliding easily in and out of her eager mouth?

She was pressed up close to him now and he had his hand under her buttocks, grabbing handfuls of the firm flesh. His eyes were half closed and he saw nothing, lost in a glorious daydream of his spunk fountaining across that magnificent backside.

Mara leant across to kiss him and suddenly he felt her hand tense on his cock. She stopped wanking him and he felt almost cheated. Struggling back to reality, he turned to look at her and saw that she was staring fixedly at a photograph in the middle of page seven.

'You stopped!' he protested, with characteristic perception.

'The picture, Andreas. Look at the picture – it's changing.'

He followed the direction of her gaze. It wasn't a very prepossessing picture. It showed an ancient Irishman who'd just fathered his hundredth child. He was grinning toothlessly at the camera and telling the world he owed it all to loose underpants and Guinness. Andreas was about to tell Mara to snap out of it when he saw that she was right. It *was* changing. The old man's face seemed to be blurring and in its place appeared the familiar features of Max Trevidian.

He looked scared – really scared – and his mouth was opening and closing as if he was trying to tell them something. But his terror was silent and, even as they looked on helplessly, his face began to distort and dissolve away, like melting plastic.

Until all that was left was a blackened scorch mark where once there had been a photograph.

Mara was out of bed and getting dressed even before Andreas had had time to put two and two together. She threw him his shirt and pants and he snapped out of his paralysis, understanding what they had to do before she spoke. He too had understood the look in Max Trevidian's eyes.

Max was in deep trouble: they had to find him fast.

Shadow Trade Minister Tom Latham had never realised just how incredibly sexy he really was. The blonde research assistant with the big IQ and the even bigger boobs just couldn't do enough for him.

Sonja had only started working for him that morning, but the minute their eyes met he'd known she wanted him to get inside her knickers. She'd been trying every trick in the book all day to get the message across. Leaning over him to get something off the desk, so that her massive tits brushed against his face. Telling him how much she admired strong men, as she took his jacket and let her hands stray downwards to the first stirrings of his desire. Pretending to straighten his tie, whilst smoothing her hand over his chest, still muscular after all these years driving a desk.

Tom Latham liked to keep himself in trim and it was obvious that Sonja was a fit lass too – big-breasted and firm-thighed with not a spare ounce of flesh on her juicy young body. So it was no great surprise when he finished working out at the House of Commons gym and found Sonja waiting for him in the showers.

His eyes nearly popped out of his head as he stared at her standing there, leotard pulled down to the waist, revealing the glorious expanse of her soft white breasts. She'd obviously been working out too, because she was glistening with sweat and he could smell the faint aroma of her cunt, heavy with the muskiness of sexual hunger.

'Mr Latham, I've been waiting for you for ages,' breathed Sonja, running playful fingers over her pink-crested boobs.

'I . . . didn't realise you were in here.' Latham swallowed hard. He really ought to get out of here at the double – mixed showers were strictly against the rules and he didn't want to wind up on the front page of the *News of the World* – but she was just so delectable. She brought out all the sexuality he had been suppressing for years.

'You're so strong, Mr Latham. I just love strong men.' Sonja was standing right in front of him now, pushing those massive, pillow-like breasts against his chest. 'You know, I'd do anything for you.'

'Anything?'

She looked him straight in the eye.

'Anything at all. I've never wanted a man like I want you. There's such an aura of power around you. Women love that – men, too. A man like you could be anything he wanted. Maybe even Prime Minister . . .'

She pulled the hem of his vest out of his shorts and tugged it up over his chest. He made no attempt to resist as she stripped him of vest, shorts and then underpants. He was throbbing with hunger for her and he had indeed felt strong – strong as a lion.

'I could suck your cock, Mr Latham. Would you like that? I only want to please you.'

He was going to just sit back and enjoy it, but a sudden impulse made him pull her to him and start tearing at her clothes, pulling the skintight Lycra leotard and tights down over her belly and hips, exposing the roundness of a backside just made for spanking.

Swiftly, he locked the door of the shower-room. You couldn't be too careful. Then he sat down on one of the wooden benches and beckoned to Sonja to come to him.

'Over my knee. You're a bad girl, do you know that? A bad girl who deserves a good hiding.'

Her eagerness to bend over his knee like a naughty schoolgirl was matched only by Latham's eagerness to feel her fleshy buttocks quivering under the shock of the first blow. At first nervously, then with growing confidence, he began spanking her. His hand began to sting, but he didn't care. Sonja was moaning and writhing and each blow seemed to drive her into a greater frenzy of lust for him. He walloped her really hard with the flat of his hand and her reddened backside leapt up in the air with the delicious shock of it.

'Oh sir, sir, give it to me! Harder, sir! Please, please . . .'

It was funny how much the knowledge of his own power increased the pleasure of the game. The girl was clearly besotted with him – and why shouldn't she be? He was an attractive man, fit and virile and strong, and if she was a good, obedient girl perhaps he'd let her have his dick. Every well-behaved little schoolgirl deserves a lolly to suck . . .

His cock was oozing pre-cum all over her belly as she danced up and down on him, responding eagerly to the pain of the spanking. Much more of this, and the frottage alone would make him come.

Sonja was right. Derek Manley was right. He had what it took and Hugo Winchester didn't. That pretty much decided the whole matter for him. It wasn't as if he was being disloyal – merely using his God-given potential for the good of his country.

He was going to come. Sonja's belly was jiggling around on top of his cock and it was all too much for him. With a little grunt of triumphal pleasure, he relaxed and gave her the gift of his spunk, spurting out all over her belly as she writhed in an agony of frustrated passion.

It wasn't fair to leave her like that, unsatisfied. Besides, his cock was still aching with need and there was plenty of semen left in his capacious balls. He pushed Sonja off his lap and stood up.

She looked the perfect harlot, standing there with his spunk dripping down her belly in great thick white gouts. He ran his fingertip through it and made her lick it off his finger. Her tongue curled greedily about his fingertip and he thought how agreeable it would be to let her service him with her mouth.

To his surprise, Sonja pulled away from him.

'I think we could both do with a shower, Mr Latham,' Sonja observed with a wicked grin and turned on the water full-blast. The sound of rushing water would drown his cries of pleasure as Sonja Kerensky's lips closed about his throbbing shaft.

'For God's sake, LeMaître, what happened? One minute you were being interviewed by Hackman, the next the screen went dead.'

Shadow Foreign Secretary Edwin Chambers was not pleased. There was only one topic of conversation at this morning's Shadow Cabinet meeting, and that was the peculiar events during the Empire TV live broadcast from Woking University.

'Yes, I think you owe us an explanation,' agreed Ray Rillington. The Shadow Chancellor recognised LeMaître's abilities as a personal threat rather than a Party asset. Here was an opportunity to take him down a peg or two. 'We've all heard some pretty weird rumours about what went on whilst the cameras were switched off – chairs and tables flying about the room, people so terrified they were falling over each other to get out.'

The Master nodded. His ingratiating smile concealed the fact that even he was still not entirely sure what had happened that night on the university campus. Somehow, that troublesome man Trevidian appeared to have conjured up the illusion of Delgado's spirit. But it mattered little: Trevidian was shortly to be dealt with permanently and the Master was thoroughly looking forward to it.

'It is certainly true that some strange things occurred the other night,' he agreed. 'But there were Republican *agents provocateurs* in the audience, hell-bent on causing trouble for the Party.'

Hugo Winchester agreed. Just recently, he too had been experiencing what appeared to be Republican attempts to discredit him – delicious young women sent to accost him and exploit his hunger for sex; a delegation of bogus foreign bankers desperate to bribe him and no doubt make public his corruption. Well, Hugo Winchester might have an avid appetite for money and sex, but he wasn't stupid. If he wanted to get into a girl's pants, he did it discreetly. If he wanted cash, he just called in some of the debts of gratitude he'd accumulated over the years. Anyone who wanted to expose Hugo Winchester in a corruption scandal would have their work cut out.

'Mr LeMaître is no more immune to the would-be scandal-mongers than the rest of us, pointed out Winchester. He flashed a knowing glance at Derek Manley, who had the good grace to squirm as he recollected that night when the nation's press had almost ended his political career.

The Master was looking at Tom Latham. Not that he needed to look at the man – he positively reeked of sex. So Sonja Kerensky had been doing her job like a good girl. Excellent. It would not be long now, and what with the riots . . .

'Derek – what are we going to do about these outbreaks of sexual violence? Can we exploit them in any way to discredit the Republicans?'

Manley glanced at LeMaître, getting his cue from his Master.

'It's clear that the Republican laissez-faire approach is having no success,' he began. 'This present government has destroyed the moral integrity of society – what is needed is a

318

party that stands for law, order and strict moral values.'

The Master smiled, reflecting on the moral integrity which had made Manley so eager to sacrifice his precious daughter's virginity to the never-sated hunger of his Master and Mistress. Manby was playing his part well today. Perhaps there would be a little reward for him tonight, in the shape of the delicious Joanna Königsberg or the equally delectable Sunita.

His eyes strayed again to Tom Latham. Seduced by megalomanic dreams and Sonja's pretty breasts, the man's mind was ready now, opening like a flower to the poison of treachery.

The Master reached out and entered Latham's spirit. It welcomed his evil with the delighted innocence of a child.

Sedet had made up her mind: pleasure was her right and she was not going to wait any longer to assert it. The Master's little favourites were not going to have all the fun – and that insolent slut Liz Exley was certainly not going to steal her thunder. The Master would be profoundly grateful to her once he realised how much she had done to advance their sacred cause.

If she was going to start an orgy she needed somewhere public and yet discreet enough to safeguard her identity. Wimbledon Library seemed a good place to begin. She'd dressed carefully – a chic black leather miniskirt and matching jacket, teamed with white stilettos and a tight white jersey top. No bra, of course – she wanted the hard outlines of her pierced nipples to show clearly through the tight white fabric. If the elderly male librarian's reaction was anything to go on, her experiment was going to be an unqualified success. His watery grey eyes had stared, transfixed at her cleavage for many long moments before he handed over a richly illustrated copy of the *Kama Sutra*.

She sat down at the sloping desk in the reference library and glanced about her: one or two young students, a few chic middle-class women, a businessman doing some market research – not perfect material, perhaps, but not bad. The boy in the tight white jeans was already making her mouth water with anticipatory pleasure. She thought of him tonguing her clitoris and a shiver ran right through her body. She couldn't wait any longer for the fun to begin.

Beside the enquiry desk, a teletext screen flashed up the day's share prices. Sedet knew Takimoto's organisation had infiltrated the network, that even now subtle subliminal messages were being beamed at anyone who cared to glance momentarily at the screen. But Sedet didn't need subliminals. She could summon up a festival of sex with the power of her mind alone.

Sliding her miniskirt higher up her thigh, Sedet pressed herself up against the student sitting beside her. He glanced up, startled, and she gave him a carnivorous smile. Slowly and automatically, he put down his pen and his hand moved to the bare tanned flesh of her thigh.

Concentrating all her mind's energies on the people around her, Sedet began to call her disciples to her side. Eager to serve their mistress, they rose slowly from their seats and began to move towards her across the polished parquet floor. Their eyes were sightless, filled only with the overwhelming need to fuck, and Sedet smiled as she welcomed them to her.

The Master would be well pleased with his Mistress's work today.


The 1957 Morris Traveller rattled through the Cambridgeshire lanes with a sound like a bread-bin falling down a manhole.

Max Trevidian wasn't listening to the engine misfiring, nor to the back bumper trailing intermittently on the road surface. He was trying to concentrate on the road ahead and ignore the dead creatures stuck to the windscreen. It didn't help much, knowing that the severed limbs and sightless eyes were just hallucinations. The blood still trickled down the glass, obscuring his view of the road, and the bits of matted hair and gristle still clogged up the windscreen wipers.

Peering determinedly ahead through a red fog, Max steered the car round the next bend and thanked his lucky stars that he knew these roads like the back of his hand. He closed his ears to the voice in his head, but it was too late because he had already glimpsed it, sitting there on the passenger seat beside him, and he knew it was still there – and what it was. It was the long-dead corpse of Maisie, the little girl he'd failed to save in his first-ever case as a psychic investigator. The poor deranged kid had thrown herself off the balcony of a high-rise block, and you don't look very pretty after you've fallen twenty floors. Still, she didn't seem to bear him any grudge – she was sitting there beside him, singing happily to him as she prattled on about her dolly.

He'd never lost the guilt he'd felt after that case. No doubt the Master knew that perfectly well and was now exploiting it to the full. The Master seemed to know all Trevidian's weaknesses, every dark secret his heart had ever held, but what did Trevidian know about the Master? Only the fragments that Mara had been able to give him. Fragments which didn't add up to much at all. And so the Master was able to play him like a fish on a line, gulping and writhing in its hopeless captivity.

The sliver of crystal was still in the breast pocket of his shirt but he resisted the temptation to push it back into the flesh of his hand. The days when it had offered him a useful protective veil were long gone. He had to use his own wits to handle this one.

If he could get back to the Manor, he could take refuge in Aunt Aurelia's study, the one room where he knew he would be safe – at least for a while. There, he could go through his great-aunt's papers and grimoires in the hope of finding something – anything – which would offer him a hope of outwitting the Master. It wasn't beyond the bounds of possibility and he knew it. After all, the Master had gained his evil powers through magic and magic could also take them away.

He changed gear and swung the car round a hairpin bend. He'd left it pretty late to have a change of heart about magic. He could only hope it wasn't too late. Had Mara received the desperate plea for help which he had tried to telepath to her? Would she think he was worth the trouble and danger of helping, now that she'd got her beloved Andreas back?

Suddenly he noticed that the cadaver and the bits of dead animal had gone but the weather was turning nasty – big black clouds were rolling across the dusky blue sky. It was getting dark, too dark for a spring evening. And there was a preternatural heaviness in the air, a suffocating heat that felt unnatural. Another of the Master's little games.

He heard it before he saw anything. Well before he turned the nose of the Morris into the long driveway, he heard the sounds of music and laughter floating up from the Manor. There was a strange yellow glow on the skyline too.

Music and laughter? At the old Manor? But there hadn't been a party or a dance at Felsham Manor since Great-Aunt Aurelia was a young girl. These days, it was just an empty shell of a house, neglected and lonely.

As the car turned up the driveway and approached the front of the old house, Max blinked in astonishment and fear. The house was lit up like a Christmas tree, lights blazing from every window and crystal chandeliers sparkling in every room. This was Felsham Manor as Max had never seen it: before poverty and decay set their unmistakeable stamp upon it, turning the ornamental gardens into a tangled mess and the ballroom into a storeroom for unwanted furniture.

He hardly recognised the place as he parked the car and hesitated for a moment, unsure as to whether he should get out or turn tail and run. Naked couples were fucking amid the neat shrubs and perfectly regimented flowerbeds, their bodies glistening with oils or sweat and their faces twisted into grotesque masks of desire. The air was heavy with the scents of lust.

He sat in the car, hand still on the key in the ignition, terrified to switch off the engine because it was as if he were offering himself up for his own destruction. Through the ballroom window, once half boarded-up because he couldn't afford a new pane of glass, Max saw naked men and women dancing, embracing, fucking. Masked flunkeys were passing between them, carrying trays of glasses filled with a ruby-red liquid that Max knew instinctively was not wine.

Some of the guests he recognised and his heart missed a beat: Mistress Sedet, magnificent and cruel, her eyes flashing as she raised a bullwhip and brought it down upon the back of a man he recognised as Sir Anthony Cheviot. Sonja Kerensky, Derek Manley, Chesterton, Detective Inspector Pinkerton... so many he knew, so many who had wrought these terrible changes in his life.

On the gravel in front of the house, an Indian girl was kneeling, naked save for a dog collar and leash which was being held by a tall blonde with cropped hair and a hard muscular body. The blonde turned and looked at him with a smile. His blood ran cold as he mouthed her name silently:

*Liz Exley.*

But it wasn't Liz who decided him to do what he had to do. Turning back to the house, Max watched as the front door swung open and a crowd of revellers tumbled down the front steps, eagerly pawing and sucking at each other's flesh. Behind them stood another figure, a tall handsome man in immaculate white dress shirt and black tuxedo. He was leaning on one of the stone lions on either side of the doorway and sipping casually from his glass. He was not looking at Max but Max knew that the Master had seen him.

A distant peal of thunder rolled across the heavy sky and a few slow drops of rain began to fall. Slamming the car door behind him, Max crunched determinedly across the gravel and towards the front steps of the house. He couldn't chicken out now, though his every instinct screamed at him to get the hell out of here. There was too much anger inside him to run away.

As he approached, the Master turned very slowly to face him and saluted him gravely with a lift of his glass.

'At last, Mr Trevidian. I'm so glad you could make it to my little celebration.'

The music was frenetic, naked dancers whirling and

tumbling around him, their bodies gyrating and pumping to the quickening rhythms, so that Max just wanted to close his eyes and ears to it all and sink into the deep blue quietness of the night.

'Silence, my children – no more!'

The Master snapped his fingers and suddenly there was all the silence and darkness Max could crave. The dancers, the glittering chandeliers, the naked couples cavorting in the ornamental gardens – all were gone, the illusion of their presence dispelled by the Master's command. Max looked up at the old manor house, caught between fear, relief and regret as he saw it returned to the way he had always known it – decrepit and empty.

The Master surveyed his victim with a silent satisfaction. There was time to amuse himself a little more before he dealt the final solution to Mr Max Trevidian, as a cat may torment a fly before it crushes it between its jaws.

'What do you want of me?' demanded Max, finding his voice.

'You have caused me a great deal of inconvenience, Mr Trevidian,' replied the Master, sipping from the glass of red liquid. 'I believe I have been extremely patient with you.'

Max exploded with righteous indignation.

'Patient? Oh come on – hallucinations, imprisonment, attempts to kill me . . . I don't call that patience.'

'Normally, I would have dealt with you more quickly, more . . . cleanly, the moment you caused me the least annoyance. But your lineage made you of some interest to me.'

'My . . . ?' Max tried hard not to look baffled. He needed the Master to believe he knew more than he did. He guessed. 'My Great-Aunt Aurelia.'

'Indeed.' The Master's eyes were narrow angry slits now as he recalled the act of treachery which had stolen him from his seat of power at the Führer's court and brought him to England to be imprisoned in a block of crystal in the cellars of Winterbourne Hall. He hardly noticed Max standing there in front of him as he relived the moment of his humiliation,

'Besides the Colonel and his men there were four of them, four sorcerers drawn from the farthest corners of the world. For one magician alone could never hope to vanquish me. Four magicians : the fakir, Gurdanjit; the American, Ryhope; the German, Essendorp . . . and the Englishwoman, Aurelia Trevidian.'

The truth clicked in Max's brain. So Aunt Aurelia really had been working for the British Secret Service and using her magical powers to defeat the massive evil of the Master. He felt a tremendous surge of regret for all his former cynicism.

'Their puny charm was sufficient to disable me for a while', continued the Master. 'But they were fools, believing that the magic of mere children could ever destroy me. And since my liberation from captivity, I have been putting a few records straight. The fakir Gurdanjit fell easily to my superior powers. But Aurelia Trevidian escaped me through death. And so it is upon you that I have chosen to direct my vengeance, Mr Trevidian.'

The rain was falling more heavily now; hot rain like sweat that coursed over Max's skin and soaked his trembling body.

'I suppose you think I'm just going to stand here and let you kill me?' Max's anger drove him to recklessness. 'I've waited a long time for a chance to get even with you, Mr Anthony LeMaître, and if this is some sort of ego-trip and you're expecting me to start calling you my 'Master' you can forget it, because that's something you'll never be.'

He took a step nearer the Master. He wasn't sure what he intended to do, but by God he was going to do something. If Aurelia was right, and he really did have 'the power', maybe all he had to do was just summon it up.

He'd taken precisely two steps towards his mortal enemy before the Master put a stop to his plan.

'A fool is bad enough, but an insolent fool I simply cannot tolerate,' observed the Master coolly, raising his left hand and clenching his fingers tightly.

Instantly Max found himself rooted to the spot, unable to move, unable to breathe, fighting a terrible tightness that encircled and threatened to crush him. Darkness nibbled at the edge of his vision and he knew that if it lasted much longer, he would lose consciousness.

The Master unclenched his fingers. As the tightness of the Master's grip relaxed and Max panted for breath, he understood what he was expected to do. The Master wanted him to run, scuttle like a rabbit across the overgrown garden and into the open fields. The Master wanted some fun.

Well, he wasn't going to play the game. He stood there, returning the Master's gaze, fighting his will with all his strength. But he could feel it ebbing away from him. The Master was trying to force him to his knees and he could feel his legs buckling underneath him.

'Kneel,' hissed LeMaître, his eyes glowing red with triumphal anger. 'Kneel before your Master.'

'Never,' gasped Max, but his strength was almost gone.

'Acknowledge me as your Master.'

'I'll go to Hell first.'

'Then die!'

The Master raised the wine glass and flung it at Max's feet. As the red liquid hit the earth, it fizzed and crackled for a moment then burst into an inferno that engulfed Max in a glowing red fireball.

A fraction of a second later came darkness. There was not a sign to show that Max had ever stood there, save a scattering of fine white ash blowing across the gravel path and the engine of the Morris Traveller, still purring lazily on the drive.

Head thrown back in a maniacal laugh, the Master turned and walked back up the steps into the house. As he stepped across the threshold into the darkened hallway, scarlet flames erupted from the cracks in the tiled floor, licking and caressing his incorruptible flesh like the tongues of his favourite mistresses.

The house was old and the wooden door and window frames dry as kindling. The fire took hold within minutes until the whole of Felsham Manor was a mass of leaping scarlet flames, an inferno that illuminated the entire night sky with a blood-red glow.

'You are pleased with me, my Lord?'

Sedet sat at the feet of the Master, her tight black leather basque setting off the golden swell of her plump, juicy breasts. The Master reached down into the bra cups and pulled out her right tit, squeezing the nipple hard between finger and thumbnail.

'There was danger in your actions, Sedet.'

For a moment she thought he was going to punish her; and there would have been some pleasure in the punishment, for Sedet had often enjoyed a taste of the tawse or the training-stick at her master's hands. None but the Master dared raise a hand to the all-beautiful, all-powerful Mistress of Winterbourne.

But the Master was not angry. His face broke into a smile as he twisted and tormented Sedet's hypersensitive nipple.

'Yesterday's events at the library have featured strongly in the newspapers today. There are calls in the House for strong government, for a leader who can bring law and order and moral discipline to this lawless land.' He laughed. 'Am I that leader, Sedet?'

Sedet crawled between his legs and unzipped the pants of his dark grey suit. She lapped the teardrop of clear sex-fluid from the tip of his cock.

'You and you alone.'

'And now that weak-minded fool Tom Latham has challenged Winchester for the leadership of the Nationalists. All is as we planned, my Queen.' He held her head between his thighs so that she took the full length of his prick into her eager throat. 'Soon you shall rule beside me in a realm of devoted slaves.'

Harcourt, Trevidian and, soon, Hugo Winchester. Things were indeed proceeding as he had hoped.

He smiled to himself as Sedet sucked eagerly at his prick.

His smile was the smile of a basking shark.

# 19: Master of the House

'Oh my God, no . . .'

Andreas and Mara stood outside what had once been Felsham Manor. The still-smoking shell of the building towered above them like the skeleton of some dead creature.

'The Master,' whispered Mara, clutching Andreas's hand. 'The Master has been here. I can smell his presence everywhere.' She stepped through the blackened doorway and led the way down the burned-out hallway into what had once been Max's drawing-room.

Andreas stood beside her, feeling awkward as hell. He'd never known Max Trevidian that well but he owed the guy his life. Looking at what the Master had done to the house suddenly made him feel sick.

'You think we're too late . . . that he's dead?'

Mara turned and shrugged her shoulders. There were tears in her emerald eyes.

'It looks that way. The signs – I can't read them. Max's spirit is still strong here but it's probably just a lingering memory in the fabric of the house. He'd lived here so long, he'd become a part of it.'

They wandered silently through the ruined house, avoiding blackened timbers that fell from shattered ceilings and stepping gingerly over unsafe joists.

One door seemed less damaged than the rest – blistered and cracked, but still intact. Wrapping his handkerchief around the metal handle, Andreas turned it and kicked open the door.

'Wasn't this his Aunt Aurelia's room . . . the one where you said he'd be safe?'

The room was almost as they remembered it, scarcely touched by the flames though the ceiling was scorched and sagging from the fire on the first floor.

And on the floor, marked out in a tiny trail of white, powdery ash, was a single word: EASTBOURNE.

Andreas dropped to his knees, tracing the word with his fingers.

'I don't understand,' said Mara, her turn to be puzzled.

Andreas looked up at her, the trace of a hope passing across his face.

'This is going to sound daft. But Eastbourne . . . we worked together there once, on a case. We were trying to track down this weird serial killer who got close to his victims by impersonating people they knew. When I got you to mention it to Max, it was my way of telling him that something wasn't right, that Anthony LeMaître wasn't who he said he was.'

'You mean . . .'

'That's right, Mara. I don't know what the fuck's going on but you can take it from me – something here isn't quite what it seems.'

As a sudden gust of wind scudded across the floor of the room, the word was wiped out for ever. Had Max Trevidian also been wiped out so easily?

Liz Exley was feeling randy – and angry. Mistress Sedet was the Master's firm favourite again, ever since she'd initiated the riot in the library, and Liz was pathologically jealous of her Master's favours.

Well, she would show the Master her true worth, prove to him that she and she alone was worthy to be his favoured consort . . . maybe even to be his queen? But in order to prove herself to the Master, she must stage a spectacle that would remain in his mind for ever.

Canterbury Cathedral – the heart of the English

Establishment. What better place to arouse forbidden lusts and the guilty passions of the faithful and the faithless?

The nave of the cathedral was deserted at this late hour. There were no prying eyes to see Liz Exley as she slipped off her blouse and dropped it casually onto the floor. No-one to lust after her as she eased the skirt down over her slim hips and let it fall about her ankles with a soft swish. She was naked now, save for her white silk basque and matching stockings framing the swell of backside and bosom, emphasising the rosebud tattoo on her right arse cheek that danced as she walked. There was no-one to see the pink lips of her cunt, freshly shaven for her victims' greater pleasure.

No matter. She had not come to this place merely to scandalise the ordinary townsfolk – the pathetic cringing worshippers as they knelt, whispering in the semi-darkness. There were others in this place. Others whose enslavement would gain her far more credit with the Master.

She kicked off her shoes and her bare feet padded silently along the central aisle of the nave. The cold tiles felt good, their coolness matching the delicious chill of her soul.

She was the avenging angel now and the bullwhip in her hand had become the serpent of Eden: the serpent which brought the gifts of knowledge, pleasure and pain . . . and the sweet secret joys of punishment.

Breath quickening, nipples hardening with the anticipation of stolen pleasure, she reached the door of the Chapter House and turned the handle very slowly – she wanted this moment to last.

At first they did not see her, the men with their long black cassocks and serious, lustless faces. Here were some of the most influential men in the English church, and every one of them now at her mercy. They were sitting around a central table, lost in deep discussion, a weak orange light casting the shadows of demons all around them. But as the door opened it gave a little creak and they turned as one towards the encroaching darkness, their eyes widening and the blood draining from their faces.

A tall stooped man with grey hair was the first to find his voice. He passed a bony hand over his forehead and a little gasp of astonishment escaped from his lips:

'Who . . . ?'

Liz stepped inside the Chapter House and closed the door behind her. She didn't want any annoying little disturbances to mar their pleasure.

'Aren't you going to welcome me?'

One, bolder than the rest, stood up slowly. He was a strong man, muscular and vigorous. Liz passed her tongue over her lips as she looked at him appreciatively, undaunted by the ferocity of his gaze.

'I don't know who you are, miss, but I'm afraid you'll have to leave.'

'Oh. Really?' Liz gave the whip a gentle flick and its tip snapped across his face, leaving a livid welt that would soon be red and angry. 'I think I call the shots around here, gentlemen. And I am hungry – hungry for your submission.'

A murmur of alarm ran round the assembly but Liz knew she was completely in control. The minds of these fools were unguarded and weak with innocence; she could manipulate them as easily as the mind of a child. How pleased the Master would be with her diligence. Already she could feel the heat and hunger flooding out of them, overwhelming all their inhibitions and releasing the flood-tide of their deepest darkest fears – and their secret, guilty desires.

She ignored the dark-haired man and turned towards a younger victim, a deacon with startled blue eyes that made him look like some wary forest creature, all wildness and instinct. She stroked his smooth face and he shivered. The gift of his flesh would be sweet.

'Kneel,' she commanded him.

Under the horrified gaze of his superiors, he obeyed like a pet dog, eyes bright with eagerness to please. Sliding to his knees before her, he looked up at her, terrified of her and yet powerless to challenge her will.

She brought the whip down on his shoulders and he cried out in distress.

'Learn to love the whip,' she intoned as the lash fell again and again upon his back, ripping away the black fabric of the cassock and exposing the white flesh beneath, so tender and so sweet. Perhaps when she had savoured his body she would taste his blood. She was certain the young man would make an agreeable addition to Winterbourne's establishment of pretty male whores.

'Please, please, please . . .' he was whimpering and Liz knew he wasn't begging her to stop whipping him. He was begging for a taste of her cunt. Well, perhaps she would let him have his heart's desire . . . but later. There were so many to choose from and her vagina was throbbing with the need for her first orgasm. Why this pretty boy's pain alone had almost made her come on the spot.

She scanned the room and her eyes lighted once more on the tall dark man. He was watching her, the hunger in him undisguisable as he fought the feelings he dared not confess. Well, he must learn obedience and honesty. The red mark across his cheek was the mark of his mistress's possession.

'You.' Liz flicked the tip of the whip at him but he did not flinch. 'Undress. I want to see your body.'

'Never.'

She advanced towards him but he stood his ground.

'Get away from me . . . bitch of Hell . . .'

She was right in front of him now, the scent of her hungry cunt wafting into his nostrils. Yes, he might try to look away but she was driving him mad with lust.

'That's not a very nice way to talk to your mistress.'

'Get away from me, devil-woman.'

She laughed. What a quaint mythology these ecclesiastics had. Well, she was happy to play the demon if it made him feel more at ease. She reached out her hand and touched his cock through the folds of his cassock. To her delight it was hard and ready for her. She laughed.

'You are mine already, slave. Now, kneel for your mistress.'

She cracked the whip again but he averted his eyes from her, trying desperately not to look at the source of his tormented lust.

'It is useless to struggle. See how your companions are already enslaved to me.'

Instinctively he looked around him and despair overtook him. His companions were silently undressing, eyes glittering with need, their naked pricks hard and throbbing for their new mistress's touch.

'Now you, slave. Undress for me and kneel for the kiss of my pleasure.'

'No . . .'

It was a feeble protest. His hands hung limply at his sides and he made no attempt to resist as Liz took matters into her own hands, ripping away at the fabric to expose the tanned muscle beneath. Slowly she slid her hands down his chest to the waistband of his underpants and pulled them down.

His cock-tip was glistening with the clear slippery fluid of irresistible need. Liz had a fancy to lick that juice away, to curl her tongue about those heavy golden bollocks, but no, not yet awhile. Her slave had yet to prove he was deserving of such favours.

'On your knees.'

The third stroke of the whip fell across his cock and he fell to his knees, sobbing with humiliation and with hunger. Victory at last. And so many more slaves to subdue, so many more sweet bodies to enslave to the supreme power of the Master.

She whipped him frenziedly, her arm rising and falling to the rhythm of her pounding heart, her pulsing cunt. Honeydew was oozing from her love lips, her sex hot and wet and hungry to be filled. There would be tongues and cocks aplenty to satisfy her cunt and arse and skilful lips to reward the absolute obedience she craved. In the sweet oblivion of their pathetic gratitude, the bite of her sharp white teeth in their flesh would be no more to them than the fulfilment of pleasure.

The dark-haired priest was moaning incoherently as she

whipped him, the lash biting into his flesh again and again, his back criss-crossed with moist red stripes.

Suddenly she felt a presence behind her. Too late, she paused and tried to turn round. Strong hands were on her, wresting the whip from her grasp.

Too late, she realised that her instrument of punishment was being turned upon herself.

The kiss of the lash was perfect delight. As pain stung her and aroused her to a new peak of sexual pleasure, she heard the echo of cruel laughter in her head.

'Submit to me,' hissed Sedet, determined to show her errant slut no hint of mercy.

'My only Mistress . . .' gasped Liz, sinking to the ground in an agony of bliss.

'How does he do it? How the hell does he do it?'

The second policeman shrugged his shoulders.

'Beats me, Trev. Five minutes ago we had a riot on our hands, and now . . . Look at them, like little lambs they are. He's got them eating out of his hand.'

Whether it was by design or simple coincidence that Anthony LeMaître happened to be visiting the football ground on the precise evening that violence erupted on the pitch, no-one ever quite worked out. Nobody had quite realised what an avid football fan LeMaître was – but then again, there were a lot of things about Anthony LeMaître that wouldn't have borne close inspection.

What mattered was that, just as events looked like turning really ugly, the man had just strolled onto the pitch, as bold as brass, and started sorting things out. The effect of his presence was almost magical. Within five minutes, the whole situation had been defused and the game had restarted.

And just in case anyone doubted LeMaître's role in quelling the violence, Empire TV cameras were there to record those incredible moments.

Up in the Directors' Box, Councillor Eric Wrigglesworth turned to his companion.

'I don't care how he does it, Stan. We need more men like Anthony LeMaître. He's the man the Nationalists ought to be looking to for leadership, not Tom bloody Latham.'

'Winchester is as good as dead and buried.'

The Master stroked Sedet's smooth backside as he buggered her over his desk. Life was good, success was certain, and Sedet's virgin-tight arse felt like heaven about his prick. He thrust a little deeper into her and continued to talk to the inner circle of disciples gathered in the library at Winterbourne: Takimoto, Cheviot, Ffoukes . . . and Nick Weatherall.

Andreas trembled silently in the corner, hoping to God that the Master hadn't noticed anything odd about his new disciple. He'd been doing his best to act as thick as pigshit and twice as unpleasant but, heck, it was difficult when you were the biggest smartarse ever to grace the inner pages of the *Daily Comet.*

'Feeling is running high against Winchester in the Party,' continued the Master, savouring the feeling of his balls slapping against Sedet's backside. 'My agents have been building up support for Tom Latham, as I instructed them and of course . . .' He gave an alligator smile that had too many teeth in it. 'Of course, I have remained steadfastly aloof from the contest.'

'When will our final move be made?' demanded Cheviot. 'The ballot is next week . . . we're leaving it awfully late.'

The Master quickened the pace of his fucking and felt Sedet tremble with delight at the brutality of his touch. A ripple of irritation passed across his face at Cheviot's lack of faith.

'When will you learn to have patience? Do you dare to question the judgement of the Master?'

Cheviot reddened with shame.

'No, Master.'

Mollified, the Master seized Sedet's hips and began working her like a doll up and down his shaft, delaying his climax for as long as possible so that the enjoyment would be greater for them both. He could feel her vibrating with pleasure as he ground her pubis against the hard edge of the old mahogany desk. Then he spoke the word Andreas had been dreading to hear.

'Weatherall.'

Andreas stepped forward, his heart in his mouth. Instinctively his fingers slipped to the tiger bracelet around his wrist. It felt cold and unresponsive and, in a moment of panic, he suddenly thought: this is ludicrous. How can a couple of tiny lumps of crystal protect me from this carnivorous monster? He's fucking well going to eat me alive . . . He swallowed hard.

'Yes, Master?'

The Master ejaculated into Sedet's arse and slid out his still-hard prick.

'To my surprise, you have been shaping up since your initiation, Weatherall.'

'I . . . thank you, Master.'

'Evidently the immortal condition has heightened and strengthened your intellectual powers. We are like-minded individuals, Weatherall.'

Damned if we are, thought Andreas. But he smiled and nodded.

'You honour me, Master.'

'You have influence in the House and I have plans for you. But, if you are to be useful to me, you must have a flawless public profile. Your incessant womanising has become legendary and it must cease . . . or, at least, you must carry it on discreetly, behind closed doors.'

'Yes, Master, but . . .'

The Master threw back his head and laughed.

'Have no fear, Weatherall. I am not condemning you to the famine of celibacy. On the contrary, I have chosen you a companion – someone we can trust.'

Andreas felt sick. Who the hell was the Master going to palm off on him – Sonja Kerensky, Joanna, Charlotte, the terrifying Liz Exley . . . ?

The Master snapped his fingers and the servant Gonzales rushed to open the library door. Outside stood a tall, slender woman with long auburn hair and emerald green eyes, her shapely breasts tightly encased in body-hugging black Lycra.

Mara's eyes met Andreas's, and there was a playful sparkle in their emerald depths.

'Enter, Dubois. There is work for you to do.'

The Master turned to Andreas with a wave of his hand.

'You may fuck her now, Weatherall. I feel in need of a little entertainment.'

Tom Latham's brain was reeling. The dreams had been getting more than he could bear, and the more he fucked Sonja Kerensky, the more his dick ached for the taste of her sweet cunt and arse.

Lately the dreams had been getting wilder, more uncontrollable. It was funny, really. He'd never been into all that kinky bondage stuff but just recently he'd been getting a real appetite for it. In his dreams, a leather-clad woman with violet eyes was standing astride his naked body, beating him with a silver-handled riding crop – and he was loving every minute of it.

He'd started getting a few issues of a leatherwear magazine and in due course curiosity had turned to temptation – and then obsession. He couldn't get the images out of his mind and, as the days and nights went on, he wanked to them and realised that if he didn't get the real thing pretty damn quick, he was going to go out of his brain with frustration.

And yet it was madness. He was challenging for the leadership of the Nationalist Party and here he was contemplating kinky sex with a woman in black leather and six-inch stilettos. The mere thought of what that could do to his image made him blanch with terror.

It was Sonja who'd suggested the Maison Delgado – good, compliant, loyal Sonja who worshipped him and wanted only to please him. Apparently, anyone who was anyone went there – even the eminently respectable Sir Robert Hackman.

And if Hackman could get away with it – why not Tom Latham?

Sweet, sweet Sonja. Such a blessing she was. He'd just spent an afternoon of utter bliss at the club, being strapped and sucked off by a Rhinemaiden in a shiny black PVC catsuit, and suddenly he had felt cleansed and released, his mind freed of the torment that had held it prisoner for so long. Now he had only to slip out of the back door, into his chauffeur-driven Mercedes, and back to the House to prepare for next week's ballot. Opinion was moving inexorably in his favour. The fates were with him. He couldn't lose.

As he stepped out of the back door of the Maison Delgado, into the glare of a dozen pressmen's flashbulbs, Tom Latham hardly took in the barrage of questions being fired at him from all sides. Only one thing stuck in his mind as he contemplated the humiliation of tomorrow's banner headlines.

'How do you feel, Mr Latham – now that Anthony LeMaître has announced his intention to stand against you and Hugo Winchester for leadership of the Nationalist Party?'

The Great Hall at Winterbourne was a riot of colour and lights. Brightly coloured streamers fluttered down from a central canopy, and in the sunken pool naked revellers fucked in glorious uninhibited abandon to the hypnotic beat of the music.

The massive video screens at the far end of the hall depicted the scene at the House of Commons: the dejected faces of Hugo Winchester and Tom Latham as the results of the first ballot were announced.

Even before the figures were flashed up, the Master's loyal servants knew the result was a foregone conclusion.

'One hundred and thirty-eight votes,' mouthed the presenter. 'A decisive overall majority on the first ballot which confirms Anthony LeMaître as the new leader of the Nationalist Party.'

'God help us now,' muttered Andreas, squeezing Mara's hand.

339

He sank down on top of Mara, despair making him hungrier than ever for her, and she pulled him close to her. His hardness sought the entrance to her eager cunt and she sighed as he slid into her, her fingers gripping his backside as though to let go would be to let go of life itself.

'Fuck me, Andreas, fuck with me and let us renew our strength,' she whispered. 'From now on, we're going to have to help ourselves.'

# 20: Beginnings

Harry Greenberg, of Greenberg's High Class Jewellers, was busy arranging his shop window. A nice tray of wedding rings – they were selling well, now the fine weather was here and everyone was getting married – and a good selection of silverware for the christenings that were bound to follow. The birds and the bees had been kind to Harry.

He gave a final polish to a Victorian gold locket and set it back on the black velvet that set it off so well. The second-hand stuff wasn't doing badly either, but that crystal ring he'd found in his shop doorway all those months ago just wouldn't shift, no matter how eye-catching the window display or how tempting the price tag. It seemed nobody'd touch the bloody thing with a bargepole. It wasn't really his type of merchandise anyway – a bit too New Age for his taste – maybe he should just cut his losses and chuck the damn thing in the bin for some other sucker to find.

Nah – give it one more chance. Harry Greenberg didn't like passing up the chance of a fast buck. He stuck the ring back in the window and went back to reading *Antiques Today*.

So engrossed was he in his magazine that the jingling of the doorbell didn't filter into his consciousness.

'Mr Greenberg?'

Startled, he looked up. He really ought to remember the security lock – anyone could walk through that door, club him over the head and make off with the stock. Still, the stranger looked OK, pretty ordinary really. He slid off his stool and gave his prospective customer a winning smile.

'Can I help you, sir?'

'That crystal ring in the window – how much do you want for it?'

Harry's mind went through a second's utter turmoil. Should he offer it at a knockdown price to get rid of it, or should he go for the fat profit he'd been hoping for all along? Old habits die hard. He went for the fat profit.

'Very unusual piece that, sir. Very old, too. See the ornate etching?' He handed it to the stranger as reverentially as if it were made of pure diamond.

The customer seemed unmoved.

'How much?'

'Forty quid.'

'Done.'

Harry watched in pure amazement as the gullible stranger produced a cheque book. As he pushed the cheque across the counter, Harry noticed the unusual name on the guarantee card.

Max Trevidian.

The Master stood at the window of his new Westminster office, looking down at the mere mortals scuttling past across the grass. He'd been Leader of Her Majesty's Opposition for just one week and already the job felt too puny for him. Success felt good: ultimate power would be even better.

He turned to Weatherall, silent and respectful at his side. For a complete fool, the Chester MP had made significant strides since his initiation into the empire of the undead. Besides which, Weatherall had money and influence – and his loyalty was unquestionable. There could be no better choice.

'Weatherall.'

Andreas's heart missed a beat. He still hadn't got used to this new and unfamiliar world, this identity which he was sure would slip any moment now and plunge him and Mara into utter disaster.

'Yes, Master?'

'Next year there will be a General Election.'

'If the Prime Minister decides to call one. He may prefer to hold out until the following year.'

The Master shook his head.

'There will be a General Election, I shall ensure that there is. And as for you, Weatherall . . . immortality has changed you for the better. I have decided to entrust you with the management of my election campaign. This time next year, I intend to be Prime Minister.'

For the first time in weeks, Andreas felt like laughing. Here was his deadly enemy, the master of lust and evil who had robbed him of his rightful identity, now unwittingly handing him the weapon of his own destruction.

A sly half-smile spread across Andreas's face.

'You may depend on me, Master,' he replied, welcoming this first glimmer of sweet vengeance. 'Leave it to me – I'll do *everything* that needs to be done.'

As he left the library to rejoin Mara in the red BMW, there was a spring in Andreas's step. The identity bracelet felt warm and reassuring on his wrist, and the dragon's crystal eyes glittered with a secret, savage joy.

# *Bonjour Amour*

## EROTIC DREAMS OF PARIS IN THE 1950s

### *Marie-Claire Villefranche*

Odette Charron is twenty-three years old with enchanting green eyes, few inhibitions and a determination to make it as a big-time fashion model. At present she is distinctly small-time. So a meeting with important fashion-illustrator Laurent Breville represents an opportunity not to be missed.

Unfortunately, Laurent has a fiancée to whom he is tediously faithful. But Odette has the kind of face and figure which can chase such mundane commitments from his mind. For her, Laurent is the first step on the ladder of success and she intends to walk all over him. What's more, he's going to love it . . .

**FICTION / EROTICA 0 7472 4803 6**